THE LIEUTENANT'S
BARGAIN

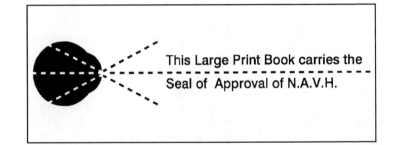

This Large Print Book carries the
Seal of Approval of N.A.V.H.

THE FORT RENO SERIES, BOOK 2

THE LIEUTENANT'S BARGAIN

REGINA JENNINGS

THORNDIKE PRESS
A part of Gale, a Cengage Company

Farmington Hills, Mich • San Francisco • New York • Waterville, Maine
Meriden, Conn • Mason, Ohio • Chicago

LIBRARY OF CONGRESS CIP DATA ON FILE.
CATALOGUING IN PUBLICATION FOR THIS BOOK
IS AVAILABLE FROM THE LIBRARY OF CONGRESS

ISBN-13: 978-1-4328-6168-1 (hardcover)

Published in 2019 by arrangement with Bethany House, a division of Baker Publishing Group

Printed in Mexico
1 2 3 4 5 6 7 23 22 21 20 19

THE LIEUTENANT'S
BARGAIN

CHAPTER ONE

December 1885
Indian Territory

If she'd known there were so few washrooms in Indian Territory, Hattie Walker wouldn't have drunk three cups of coffee at breakfast that morning. The stagecoach jolted over another rut as she pulled the lap robe higher on her chest. She didn't favor leaving the cozy coach and braving the sharp wind, but nature called.

Hattie lifted the heavy leather curtain on the window and blinked as a cold gust caught her right in the face.

"For crying aloud, what do you want now?" Mr. Samuel Sloane, a telegraph operator who'd been on the stage since Fort Smith, had complained every time she'd requested a stop. And she'd requested many stops.

"I'm sorry to trouble you," Hattie replied. "Go back to polishing that big pocket watch and pay me no mind."

The pocket watch had caught her eye, but his cutting remarks offset his fine duds, so Hattie wasn't impressed. Besides, she hadn't left behind all the agreeable beaux back home to fall for a churlish lout on the road.

"Next stage I catch, I'm requesting a gentleman's-only coach," replied the tired, dried-up Agent Gibson. "A woman traveling across Indian Territory unchaperoned is folly. Better to stay home in the kitchen than come out here in the nations, risking your life." Despite the apparent danger, he pulled his big-brimmed hat down over his face to nap against the heavy traveling bag he'd insisted on keeping in the seat next to him.

Hattie had yet to meet the man whose kitchen sounded more interesting than her plans. She steadied her box of Reeves watercolors and Devoe oils and prayed that she'd made the right decision. Frustrated by her refusal to accept any of the proposals that had come her way, her parents had given her an ultimatum — she could go to Denver and try to find success as an artist, but if she failed, she had to come home and settle down. They feared she was wasting the best years of her life pursuing an unlikely future. When she'd bemoaned the limited resources available to her in Van Buren,

Arkansas, they had called her bluff. Two months. That was all she had. Get a painting in an exhibit, sell a work, or come back home and plan for her future.

It had been a terrifying answer to prayer, and now Hattie was traveling with strangers across one of the most dangerous areas of the country, wondering if she had made the right choice. Wondering if the stories about the Cheyenne and Arapaho Indians were true.

She pushed aside the curtain again, leaned out into the frigid air, and called up to the driver. "Excuse me, please. I need to stop."

The wheels kept turning even though he barked back an answer. She squirmed in her seat as the coach hit another bump, knocking her paints against her. "It's an emergency. I wouldn't ask if it wasn't necessary."

Mr. Sloane's mouth turned down with impatience. "And I thought my boss was insufferable."

The agent sitting opposite her might be hiding his face, but he wasn't hiding his opinion. "Do you need to get some fresh air, or do you have to refresh your powder? Which emergency is it this time?"

Hattie's blush spread from ear to ear. They had no idea how uncomfortable it was to be

9

the lone woman traveling in a public coach. Had she known how difficult the journey would be, she would have given it more thought. But what were her choices? According to the directors at the art galleries she frequented, her paintings lacked depth, lacked an understanding of the world, and that was what she was after. If those critics thought she hadn't experienced enough tragedy to be taken seriously, they should see her now. She was on her way to the majestic Rocky Mountains, and in three weeks she would have a painting ready for consideration in the Denver Exhibition. It was too late to turn back.

Hattie took a deep breath of cold air and leaned out the window. "Stop this coach!" she hollered. "Please."

Agent Gibson snickered. Mr. Sloane checked his pocket watch and looked fretfully out the window.

The coach rolled to a stop, the brake sounding as it was pushed into place. Before Hattie had the door open, she had already spotted a gully that would give her some privacy.

She pushed the lap robe away, then hesitated. Her box of paints was her prized possession. Separating herself from it was never done without care. She glared a look of warning at the two men before arranging it on the seat next to her and stepping out of the coach.

Hattie's knees jarred when she landed on the frozen ground. The wind whipped her skirts, the cold air making her errand even more imperative. She paced the gorge, looking for an easy way down the embankment. Finally, sliding on loose dirt, she skidded down and out of sight of the stagecoach to take care of necessities.

Hattie was just about to return to the coach when she heard a loud cracking noise. What were they doing now? Trying to rush her? She arranged the hood of her coat snugly over her bonnet and planted her foot on a high shelf of red clay. Another loud pop — a couple, in fact. The top of the stagecoach came into view as she climbed up. The driver crouched in his seat.

"Stay down," he yelled, waving her away.

"What?" She caught the edge of her hood to keep the wind from snatching it.

The leather window covering flapped open, and a pistol emerged. Smoke puffed out of it, and a second later a sharp crack split the air. Agent Gibson was shooting at someone, and Mr. Sloane was right behind him. The door opened, and the agent used it to shield himself as he continued to return fire.

Hattie felt the blood drain from her face. It couldn't be. The hard dirt scraped her cheek as she ducked and hugged the ledge. The driver had turned and taken up the reins.

"Wait!" All her paints and canvases were on that stage. They couldn't leave her behind.

But then she saw the horseman racing toward them. The driver of the coach was hunched over the reins, urging the team forward, when suddenly he stiffened, then slumped to the side. The stage's horses jerked into motion even as he fell out of his seat.

Hattie ducked out of sight. No. Why? Suddenly the boorish men she'd been traveling with didn't seem so bad, and they needed help. But what could she do?

Another shot made her rise up just in time to see Agent Gibson topple out of the door as the stage careened away. She could only see the back of the outlaw, but she could feel his deadly intent as he walked his horse slowly toward the crumpled figure.

If Agent Gibson wasn't dead already, he would be in the time it took to twitch a trigger finger unless she intervened. She rested her chin against the ledge. Why was she considering such a reckless act? She didn't owe the agent anything.

Before she could think better of it, Hattie stood to her full height and waved her mittened hand over her head.

"Over here!" How small her voice sounded on the prairie. How frail. But it was enough. The killer led with his pistol as he turned his horse toward her. His nose twitched like a dog on the scent, and his mouth hung open like he was tasting the air.

Of all the dumb decisions Hattie had made in her life, this was the worst. She might have bought Agent Gibson a few minutes to make his peace, but at what price?

With a quick prayer for the men scattered on the plain, Hattie dropped to the dry creek bed and ran down the narrow corridor of the gully, following its twists and curves, looking for a way to save her life.

The hooves pounded behind her. The outlaw's voice echoed through the canyon, furious at her disappearance. Her stays pinched her ribs as she forged on, expecting to see his dark figure above her at any moment. As she ran, the ground rose beneath her feet, and the gully grew shallower.

Zing! She heard the high-pitched buzz

streak past her ear before she heard the report of the gun.

Hattie dropped to the ground. He was hunting her. The ditch wasn't deep enough here. She would be exposed. She had to go on, but the maze was running out. Who knew when she'd reach a dead end? But she couldn't stay here.

She remembered that the dry creek bed had split a few yards back. If he was looking for her up ahead, maybe she could get back to the turn and get away.

She felt tears on her face. Her side hurt. Knowing the consequences if she raised her head, she scrambled back the way she'd come and prayed that she could beat the killer to the fork and find a place of safety.

An hour later, Hattie was still alive and praying with every breath. She held her frayed mittens to her mouth and blew warm air onto her numb fingers. She'd burrowed into the deepest, darkest crevice she could find, her heart racing at every noise. The driverless stagecoach had raced away, the terrified horses dragging it and her paints along, but the killer had stayed, pacing the flatlands above her.

She was so cold and miserable that part of her wanted to stand up and get it over with, but he might decide not to kill her right away, and that uncertainty kept her huddled in the muddy ditch with icy water pooling around her feet.

Reins jangled and hooves could be heard retreating. Was he finally giving up? Straining her ears for any clue, Hattie shivered as the seconds ticked away.

She had to get out and find help, but what would she face when she left her sanctuary? What would she see when she climbed up?

As much as she'd hated the shooting, it had meant that her traveling companions were fighting back. But it had stopped long ago. She knew she was the only survivor, and she had a job to do.

It wasn't until the moon had risen that Hattie found the courage to creep out of her hiding place and toward the two motionless bodies that lay discarded on the cold ground. No one created in God's image should be left out there without a kindness shown. Teeth chattering and tears icy on her cheeks, Hattie scurried forward, bent double against the wind. She reached the driver first. He lay on his side, crumpled over with both hands holding his middle. She wouldn't look at his face — that she had already decided. Instead, she pushed against his shoulder. His whole body rocked.

Even the strange angle of his blood-covered fingers remained set. Forcing down the bile in her throat, she removed his hat and put it over his face the best she could without looking. Saying a quick prayer to God for the family he might have left behind, she scurried to the next man.

Agent Gibson lay on his back with arms outstretched. Still hunched over, she began a wide circle around him so she could approach away from the direction he was looking. Something about being caught in the sight of a dead man's eyes made Hattie supremely uneasy.

She'd almost reached the formerly apathetic agent when she heard the first yipping howl. Hattie spun around. Wolves? Coyotes, more likely. Another reason she shouldn't be out on the frontier alone. While coyotes weren't difficult to scare away, she didn't like being out in full view of anyone who happened to be watching. What if the murderer returned? She needed to be far from here.

In the melee, the agent had lost his hat. Hattie lowered the hood of her coat to untie her bonnet and carefully laid it over his face. The wind would blow it off, but it was the best she could do. The fact that he didn't flinch when the bonnet touched him told her that he was already beyond any help she could provide.

Mr. Sloane's body hadn't fallen out of the stagecoach. She'd seen him just briefly through the open door, pistol drawn, but he'd undoubtedly met the same fate. His body could be miles away, beyond her help. She uttered another quick, desperate prayer, more to remind herself that God was there and that she wasn't alone than to ask for anything specific, and then she had to go.

She shivered and held her hands over her ears to keep the wind out until she'd slid down the slope and into the gully again. The red clay felt like ice, but it was the warmest place she could find. This time, instead of hunkering down and hiding, she kept moving, putting distance between her and the scene of the massacre until she had no more strength. Then she huddled against the dirt wall and tried to stay warm.

How long before her parents learned of her fate? When she failed to show up at the boardinghouse in Denver, the proprietress would surely contact them. Hattie could imagine their anguish when they heard she was missing. Most of all, she didn't want them to blame themselves.

Hattie's parents had always encouraged her considerable artistic talent. They'd bought her the box of paints, paid for lessons, and taken her to every exhibition within fifty miles of Van Buren. But when she'd reached adulthood, they expected her ambitions to change.

It wasn't as if Hattie hadn't made an effort. She'd had more beaux than Ole Red had fleas, but one by one, they'd disappointed her. Inevitably, the more comely the man, the less he'd developed the finer qualities. With every rejected offer, her parents' desperation grew. Just as she was fine-tuning her talent, they expected her to set it aside, but she'd yet to meet the man who could tempt her to quit. She'd be better served finding beauty on a canvas than in a corduroy suit.

After what seemed an eternity of sleepless exhaustion, the eastern horizon began to glow even as the temperature continued to drop. Hattie's fingers were stiff, and she couldn't feel her toes at all. Her stomach growled. Her teeth clattered. But the worst part was the fear. She was lost, without a town or a house in sight. The only thing she knew for sure was that there was a very bad man about, and he had murdered the only decent people in the area.

Marginally decent people, anyway.

At least they were people.

How long before anyone realized she was missing? Would the stagecoach make it to Fort Supply? How long before someone came looking for her, and would they find her?

She licked her lips. They were dry, and her nose was so cold it was painful. She shook against the dirt hill she'd cuddled up on. She had to do something or she'd freeze and starve, and she wasn't sure which would be first. At least it was morning now. There were no more coyotes howling in the darkness, but she knew not to return to the bodies. Not if she wanted to keep her sanity.

She got to her feet, but her legs felt as thick and stiff as barrels. Bouncing up and down, she forced the blood to start pumping beneath her tattered wool coat. The tears started pumping, too. She had no plan besides running in terror from all threats.

When she climbed out of the ravine and took a look around, the helplessness of her situation assaulted her again. If she had her paints, she could have captured the remote, wind-scraped landscape with all the elements of tragedy the gallery directors could ever desire.

Which way should she walk? She hadn't paid any attention to where they were.

Landmarks were scarce on the prairie. She looked at the morning sun, but there was no going back. Her only hope lay ahead, although she could see many miles and nothing on the horizon could be deemed promising. With her hands in her pockets and her chin tucked beneath her dirty scarf, she started walking west.

Not a thought cheered her until she saw some horsemen in the distance. Frantically, she wrestled her scarf off with inept fingers. She waved the scarf over her head and yelled as its length caught the wind and the horsemen's attention. It wasn't until they got closer that she realized her mistake. What if they were more bad men? What if she'd attracted deadly attention to herself?

But they weren't outlaws coming toward her. It was even worse.

They were Indians.

CHAPTER TWO

Fort Reno
Cheyenne and Arapaho Reservation,
Indian Territory

Lieutenant Jack Hennessey buttoned the last of the shiny buttons on his dress uniform. Today was his commander's wedding, and they couldn't be late. Finally, Major Daniel Adams was marrying the woman he'd fallen in love with — who also happened to be the governess he'd hired to teach his daughters. Finally, all the sentimental arrangements would be complete, and the fort could return to its daily routines.

"I forgot my gloves," Daniel called from the spare room next to Jack's. "I'm going next door to get them."

Another excuse? Jack stepped into the hall to intercept the major. "For the hundredth time, you can't see the bride before the ceremony. Settle down."

21

"Easy for you to say. You're not the one getting married today."

No. He wasn't.

"I'll get your gloves for you once I'm ready. Until then, you stay put. And no peeking out the windows, either." It was fun bossing around his commander for a change. Not that he didn't frequently share his opinion with Major Adams, but today the major had to listen to him. Jack took his belt and gloves off the stack of books that balanced on his nightstand.

Major Adams was one lucky man to have found a wife. Women didn't just appear out on the prairie very often, and definitely not ones as fetching as Miss Bell. Who cared if she had faked being a governess? It showed she had imagination. And Major Adams had been able to overlook her lack of qualifications once he looked her over.

Jack smiled at himself in the mirror. He was happy for them. He was. How could he be jealous when the only girl he'd ever carried a torch for probably didn't remember that he existed?

He'd done his best back when they were in school. He'd looked for every opportunity to assist her, even spying in the teacher's gradebook to see what subjects she might need his help with. He'd complimented her on her drawings and showed her any illustrations he came across in his books. He'd nearly lost his head the day she'd asked to borrow his copy of *Peter Parley's Wonders of the Earth, Sea, and Sky* so she could try to replicate a drawing. Then she'd forgotten to return it, and he'd never had the nerve to remind her.

Jack buckled his belt. What a timid child he'd been, studious and awkward. Joining the cavalry had toughened him up, although it probably hadn't improved his skills with the ladies. What he'd found instead was an outlet for his academic pursuits. His studies with the local Arapaho tribe had earned him commendations, and his work to promote the Darlington school for Arapaho students was showing progress. But as much as the army had changed him, it hadn't been able to erase his sentimental streak. No one quite measured up to the memory of his charming childhood sweetheart.

So good for Major Adams, and good for Miss Bell. Today promised to be quite a celebration. Louisa Bell, former saloon singer, knew a thing or two about productions, and she'd planned this one down to the last detail. The fort's chapel had been stacked with evergreen branches, and if the musicians could breathe through all the

23

pine scent, there'd be music performed for hours. As Major Adams's best friend, as well as the one who introduced the happy couple, Jack was ready to celebrate along with them.

It was almost time. He went into the hall again and found Major Adams pacing. "I can't find the ring," he said. "I left it in my boot last night, but it wasn't there this morning."

"No ring, no wedding. Miss Bell is going to be heartbroken." Jack shrugged. Then, seeing the stricken look on his friend's face, he fished the ring out of his pocket. "You gave it to me for safekeeping."

"I did? I don't remember."

"You said something about my house being full of clutter and it going missing."

"I'm never this distracted before a campaign." Major Adams took the ring and slid it on his pinky finger. "I won't lose it again."

"Another half hour, and then Miss Louisa won't let it out of her sight for the rest of her life," Jack said. Or at least that was how he'd imagined his bride would behave, and in all his imaginations, the future Mrs. Hennessey looked an awful lot like the girl he'd left back at home.

Someone was pounding on his door.

"It's time?" Major Adams looked slightly

ill as they hurried down the stairs.

But it wasn't the parson at the door; it was Sergeant Byrd, his mustache waxed straight-out horizontal for the special occasion.

"Major Adams." He saluted. "I've got a message from Chief Right Hand. We've got trouble."

Jack stepped forward. "I'll handle it, Byrd. Major Adams is a mite busy today."

"I figured Major Adams would send you to do it anyway," Byrd said. "Just keeping the chain of command."

"What's the message?" Major Adams asked, his nerves settled by the thought of a military challenge.

"There's been a stagecoach robbery. The Arapaho found the tracks of the stagecoach and the bodies of two passengers, one of them Agent Gibson. Looks like he put up a fight, but he's dead, and there's no sign of the funds he was bringing in. That gold was due to the Cheyenne and Arapaho. If it's missing, we've got a humdinger of a problem on our hands."

Both Daniel and Jack digested the news in silence. Jack rubbed the back of his neck. Why today, of all days? A bridegroom shouldn't go to the altar with these worries on his mind.

"Does the chief know the money was on that stage?" Major Adams asked.

"No, sir. They told me the name of the victim, and I surmised the rest."

"Let's keep news of the payment confidential," the major said. "In the meantime —"

"I'll take care of it, sir," Jack said. "You don't think twice about it."

"It's my job."

"It's your wedding day. Leave it to me." Turning to Byrd, Jack said, "I'll get a small force together to retrieve the bodies. I suppose it can wait until after the ceremony, though. No hurry now."

"Actually, according to Chief Right Hand, there is an emergency. There was a survivor. A white woman from the coach."

Jack's throat tightened. "A survivor. Who has her?" His fingers clutched the handle of his saber. The Cheyenne had a dark history with captives. If they mistreated another, all the progress they'd made would be pointless. The army would show no mercy, and Jack dearly wanted there to be mercy.

"Don't worry. She's with the Arapaho, but they asked that we hurry."

"Chief Right Hand said to hurry? She must be anxious to be rescued."

"It's not her that's anxious. It's the Indians."

26

The flap of the tepee opened, exposing Hattie as she frantically dug against the side of the wall. She spun around and huddled over the pile of fresh dirt, trying to hide her progress from the gray-haired woman wrapped in blankets, but the old woman wasn't fooled. Although Hattie didn't understand her words, she knew that a guard would now be stationed at the back of the abode in addition to the one at the door. Her chances for escape were dwindling.

She should have fought longer, run faster, but the Indians had overpowered her and brought her back to their village. Now she was their captive, and the Lord only knew what they had planned for her.

The woman approached with a steaming bowl in her aged hands. Why were they doing this? Were they trying to poison Hattie? The first time the woman had entered, she'd acted sympathetic, but after Hattie had refused the bowl of clotted milk, the woman didn't hide her disdain any longer. This time she spoke sharply, motioning with the bowl and pointing at Hattie.

Hattie's chin quivered. The stew smelled so good. Seeing her resolve slip, the woman's eyes softened. Her voice grew more pleading, even though Hattie couldn't understand the words.

Her tears started again. How long could she hold out? Did anyone even know where she was?

The woman pushed the bowl of stew at her and covered Hattie's pale hands with her own dark, wrinkled ones. Hattie's stomach growled. She'd heard stories about captives. Knowing her propensity for nightmares, her big brother used to tell her terrifying tales of torture and cannibalism that would keep her sleepless for weeks. She knew it was only a matter of time before the Indians tied her to a stake and began filleting her. They were probably fattening her up.

She looked at the stew again, chunks of meat with some sort of grain floating in thick juice. She wasn't strong enough to resist. She was on the verge of giving in.

"No!" Hattie would not give in to weakness. She hurled the bowl of stew against the slanted wall of the tepee, splattering food everywhere. After surviving what she'd been through, she wasn't going to succumb to hunger, but she'd only been here two days and already she was growing weak. Time was running out.

Pushing past the woman, Hattie made a dash for freedom. She burst through the flap and into the bright sunshine. The men squatting next to the tepee looked surprised. A dog tucked its tail and scurried away. Hattie fled, but no matter how she pumped her arms, she couldn't run fast enough. Footsteps behind her. Shouts. Then something knocked her to the ground like a sack of grain. She tried to kick free, but the man had her legs pinned. She dropped her forehead to the ground as all hope drained away.

She was jerked to her feet as the Indian woman approached, then forced back to her prison. The woman had grabbed a smooth wooden staff along the way and shook it in Hattie's face, scolding and lecturing as they made their way through the village to the tepee. Hattie's stomach grumbled as the scent of the spilled stew greeted her inside. Angry voices continued around her as she huddled on a pile of buffalo hides and tried to block them all out.

If only she'd never taken this trip. But then she remembered what awaited her at home, and she dropped her head onto the shaggy pile of blankets. Once her parents heard what had happened, they'd never let

her out of their sight . . . if they ever saw
her again.

CHAPTER THREE

Jack had heard the vows in the chapel while Sergeant Major O'Hare prepared a unit to ride. Then, knowing that time was of the essence, Jack skipped the wedding cake and punch and took out on the prairie, following his silent guides to the Arapaho village.

It was hard to imagine that Agent Gibson was gone. Jack wouldn't have considered him a friend, but his life was worth more than the gold he was carrying. Had someone known about the shipment? Was the stagecoach targeted? If the Bureau of Indian Affairs had asked, Major Adams would have sent troopers to escort the coach, but perhaps they'd thought secrecy was a better defense. Unfortunately, their miscalculation had been tragic.

Other questions taunted Jack as his horse carried him across the frozen buffalo grass. Who was the woman? Agent Gibson's wife? How many other passengers were on board?

The stagecoach company had been wired, but they hadn't responded with their passenger list yet. There could be more victims who hadn't been recovered.

Hours later, the sharp tepees appeared on the riverbank. This time of year especially, they reminded Jack of a group of Christmas trees covered in snow. The paths between the tepees were empty with everyone staying snug inside, which was exactly what Jack should have been doing as soon as the wedding celebration had ended. But as much as a mug of coffee and a good book by the fire appealed to him, coming to the aid of a victim in his territory would always be more rewarding.

Coyote, his escort and interpreter, pointed to a boy coming out of a tepee. "This is the chief's nephew."

The boy looked surprised to hear Jack's greeting in his own tongue, and Jack was surprised to understand his answer. His study with Coyote and Ben Clark, the peerless scout, was paying off. Major Adams had recommended that Jack make this trip without the interpreter, but Jack wasn't ready. Soon he hoped to be able to converse without relying on help, but with such important matters to discuss, accuracy was too important to wager on his uncertain skill.

"This way to the council tent." The boy waved his hand in front of them. Jack followed before Coyote had a chance to translate. So far, so good. But when he ducked through the opening of the tepee, he knew he'd have to ask for help.

The woman looked to be in her seventies, her dark skin lined like a trail map, while her sinewy body remained unbent by the years. With her hands flapping and her eyes flashing, she was giving the stately chief what for. Her long gray braids showed that she remembered the days when Chief Right Hand was strapped to a cradleboard, and she wouldn't hesitate to speak her mind in his presence. Which was precisely what she was doing.

Chief Right Hand stood with arms crossed, only nodding occasionally as the woman's words came even more quickly. His smooth face remained motionless despite her antics. Suddenly she held her arms up and mimicked someone dumping something on the ground. Jack's Arapaho was coming along, but he couldn't catch much at this speed.

"What's going on?" he asked Coyote.

Coyote managed to get a question spoken

through the woman's tirade. When she turned to answer, she pointed at Jack, then raised her fists to the sky. He couldn't tell whether she was pleased or angry to see him.

"She's having trouble with the woman they brought in," Coyote explained. "She told the chief that they should've left her out to freeze to death, because that's what she wants. They have to watch her night and day to keep her from running away. And she refuses to eat."

That was odd. In all of Jack's dealings with the Arapaho, they'd always treated their guests well. "Is there something going on that I don't know about?" he asked Coyote.

"Nothing has changed since the last council. They are still listening to you about the school, although they are getting anxious for the payment that is due." Then, seeing the chief was ready to speak, Coyote motioned Jack closer.

Jack greeted the chief in his own language but was afraid to go any further, lest he make a mistake. Someday, he promised himself. Someday he'd be as fluent in Arapaho as Coyote was in English. Then the interpreter wouldn't be necessary.

"Earlier this week, I visited the Darlington

school," Jack said. "Your children are kept warm and are fed well. I only wish more of them were enrolled."

"It's hard to part with our children," Chief Right Hand said. "The village is sad without them."

"I understand —" Jack said.

"No, you don't." Coyote winced at interrupting Jack but had to continue to keep up with the chief. "You do not have children. You have no wife, yet you want to tell us how to be fathers. First, the lieutenant should learn something about being a man."

The chief knew how to cut a fellow to the marrow, but the military had taught Jack to curb his blunt tongue. "What you say is true," Jack said. "I don't have a family of my own, but I've seen how beneficial the school can be for your children. They will learn to read and write in English. They will learn how to farm or learn a trade. We believe that the Indian students are every bit as clever as the white students. They just need a chance to prove it. And Darlington is on the reservation. You can visit them whenever you like."

The chief gazed at his nephew, a handsome boy with proud shoulders and quick eyes. "You're my friend," Chief Right Hand said. "You want to help, but you don't understand the protection a man has for his family. Let our children live in a tall brick house without their tribe, with no one who understands their ways? It's a hard thing you're asking us to do."

Jack could appreciate that. The very reason Major Adams had hired a governess in the first place was that he didn't want his daughters shipped off to their grand-mother's to be educated. When Jack became a father — if he became a father — he could imagine himself feeling the same. And yet whatever was best for your kids, that was what you did, right?

"It is hard. And I have the highest respect for your ways. The courage and resilience of your people will make you successful. We just have to figure out how to fit you into the world without destroying what's impor-tant to you."

Coyote stood silent as the chief had a conversation with his men. Then he spoke to Jack again. "My men are ready to take your soldiers to where the stagecoach is. We left the bodies alone, but we studied the tracks that the bandit left. Only one rider. He headed east."

Only one? He must be an ambitious sort to take on a stagecoach driver and pas-sengers alone. And lucky to have picked a coach carrying so much gold. "What about the survivor?" Jack asked.

"She has caused much trouble. We've tried to help her — Spotted Hawk made her stew and brought her blankets — but she acts like a madwoman. Unreasonable."

Which wasn't unexpected in a woman, Jack figured. Especially after surviving a stagecoach robbery. An ambulance had been dispatched as he left the fort and would catch up later in the day. The last thing Jack needed was a hysterical female on horseback all the way home.

"Take me to her," he said.

O'Hare led the rest of the troopers out with the Arapaho men to investigate the site of the holdup and recover the bodies, while Jack followed the chief's nephew through the village.

The tepee was situated near the center of the village, a sign that a prominent family had been given the honor of caring for the woman. Jack would make sure to give them something for their trouble, especially if the lady had been unpleasant company.

At the door, Spotted Hawk stopped. "Ladies first," Jack offered. He didn't need an interpreter to understand the look she gave him. Spotted Hawk opted to wait outside, despite the cold.

With a quick salute for Spotted Hawk — Jack understood who was in charge at this tepee — he lifted the flap and ducked inside without an escort.

The dark room was cozy and warm, but the smoke took some getting used to. He heard scuffling before his eyes adjusted and he could see the woman rising from the pile of bedding. Her brown hair was matted, and her clothing was muddied and tattered. She was young to be traveling alone. Younger than he'd expected. And prettier, too. His heart twisted at the thought of her being abandoned and left to die on the prairie. Despite the wedding cake he'd missed at the reception, he wished he could have reached her sooner.

He tipped his hat, but before he could properly introduce himself, she said, "Quick, that woman will be back any second. We've got to go."

Her voice. It was different, more mature, but so familiar it gave him chills. She came closer, and he recognized her face, as well. It was impossible. How could she be here?

"I apologize for the delay," he said. His throat jogged painfully. He looked for a wedding ring on her finger and didn't see one. "We got the report only this morning.

We'll be ready to go as soon as the wagon —"

"You have to get me away from here." She clasped her hands, straining her red, scratched knuckles. "What do we have to do? Are we going to sneak out once it's dark?"

Jack felt like a dolt. This had to be a dream. Or a joke. Had Daniel arranged this? But one look at the rumpled Miss Hattie Walker, and he knew she had no thought of a lark. Yet here she was, and Jack's analytical mind was spinning with what it meant.

"Sneak out?" He looked over his shoulder. She didn't think this was a hostile situation, did she? After all, the tribe had rescued her. She had everything backward.

Before he proceeded, he should introduce himself, but his mouth felt full of marbles. Despite all he'd accomplished since seeing her last, he felt like the same tongue-tied boy. What if he said his name and she didn't remember him? Why couldn't he think straight when she was around?

"When she comes back," Hattie said, "she'll see you and raise the alarm. We don't have much time."

He'd sat by her at school, helped her with her homework, walked her home when he had the courage. He'd even invited her to

39

his send-off party when he'd joined the army. She hadn't attended, but had she completely forgotten that her old classmate was in the cavalry? And the letters. Jack had braved a few letters to her over the years — just friendly correspondence to keep in touch — but she'd never responded.

Gathering his wits, Jack puffed out his chest. "I don't sneak or hide, miss. Maybe if I'm off duty, I might draw the shades. It seems like the major never thinks of anything he wants to chat about until then. But I don't hide from danger, if that's what you're worried about." He had to forget who she was. Treat her just as he would any other problematic civilian on the reservation.

"They aren't going to give up a captive that easily," she said. "Walking out seems foolhardy, if you ask me."

"As far as danger goes, this is so diminutive I couldn't even measure it with my caliper." As soon as he'd spoken, Jack wanted the words back. He'd always tried to awe Hattie with his intellect, and she had never been impressed. He could do better. "What I mean is that I've been in more danger several times. A lot of times, actually."

"I knew what you meant." She kept an

40

uneasy eye on the door. "Then how am I going to get out of here?"

He was fixing to suggest using the door but stopped himself. This was Hattie Walker standing before him. *The* Hattie Walker. If ever there was a good time to play the hero, it was now.

Back home, Jack had kept his nose in a book rather than play stickball with the boys at recess. But now he was any man's equal. Now he was here to rescue her. Didn't he deserve a little credit?

Warm satisfaction spread through his bones as he found his footing. If he played his cards right, she would be in his debt. He'd rather have adoration, but gratitude was a good start.

"It'll take considerable negotiation skills," he said. "They might not be agreeable. They might demand a payment of some sort." No reason for her to know that the chiefs wouldn't keep her another day if Jack paid them.

Her eyes widened. Finally she was looking at him like a desperate female should. "I can't stay here. I have plans."

"I hope it's nothing urgent," he said. "These treaty deals can be tricky. Could take some time." And the longer it took, the more time Jack had to impress Hattie.

"Please," she said. "Please do whatever it takes. If I have to stay here any longer . . ."

"Chief Right Hand respects me, but you're asking a lot. Let's just pray I can persuade him."

If he wasn't mistaken, he saw respect in her eyes. About time. Jack turned to leave and saw the damp spot in the dirt and the chunks of stew on the ground. Remembering Spotted Hawk's pantomime, he realized that Hattie's bedraggled condition might be due to more than the weather.

"How long has it been since you've eaten anything?" he asked.

"Three days." She wrapped her arms around her stomach. "I think they're trying to poison me."

"Why in the world would you think the very people who went out of their way to rescue you would poison you?"

Hattie's brow wrinkled. "Rescue me? I thought you were rescuing me."

And just like that, Jack had nearly lost his advantage.

"Ransom," he said. "They saved you for a purpose, and now we have to see what they're demanding for your return. While I'm negotiating for your release, I'll see about getting you some supper. It's the least they can do for all the trouble they're causing us."

Then he saw something he'd never thought he'd see — a tear on Hattie Walker's cheek. The confident, vivacious girl of his dreams had shown a weakness. And he was in a position to help her.

Jack wasn't sure what to do. He knew Hattie. She wouldn't appreciate his noticing that she'd succumbed to womanly emotions. While he dreamed of taking her in his arms, he thought better of it. Respect. That was what Hattie wanted more than anything.

Keeping his gaze somewhere over her head, he said, "You've maintained your composure so well. Just a while longer, and everything is going to be fine."

Her voice was flat and tired. "The coach was attacked. I saw him shoot the driver. I . . . I touched dead bodies." She swiped at her face, but not before Jack saw another tear forming.

He had to look away. Had to think of something besides smoothing her hair, now matted and littered with dry grass. Better to keep the conversation on the facts. Facts had always been Jack's friends.

"Ma'am," he asked, "did you know anyone on that stage?"

It was the right question. Her chin went up, and her sorrow turned to outrage. "No. And the two men traveling with me were very disrespectful." She crossed her arms over her chest. Her dirty cuffs exposed hands with red, cracking skin and fingernails split by the cold. "They didn't give me a moment's peace. Extremely rude."

If the report was accurate, they wouldn't be rude to a woman ever again, but he knew better than to tell Hattie that. "We'll find the man responsible for putting you through this," he said. She gave a brisk nod, and the pain in his chest eased. Now that she was ready to fight again, he was ready with his plans. "In the meantime, eat the food Spotted Hawk gives you and cooperate with her. I'll speak to the chief and work everything out."

He had to force his feet to carry him away. Of all the prayers he'd said for Hattie over the years, he'd never thought to ask for her to be delivered to the reservation. It was up to him to make the most of it.

CHAPTER FOUR

"We will have a feast," said Chief Right Hand. "Is that what you want?"

Jack nodded. The sun had gone down. His men were still out scouting the stagecoach massacre scene, and the ambulance wagon hadn't arrived. It looked like Hattie would be stuck in the village for another night. Stuck with him. But once she saw what a good leader Jack was, and how much authority the U.S. Cavalry trusted him with, she couldn't help but be reassured . . . and maybe impressed. And maybe once she got home, she'd remember how brave and handsome he was. And maybe she'd answer a letter of his every once in a while. Or at least once.

"A feast would be perfect," Jack said. "Do it up right. Songs, some of those drums. And can we have a ceremony where you hand her over to me? Something to make my possession of the survivor official?"

Coyote's translation pleased the elders. "A ceremony is necessary," Chief Right Hand replied. "We will have the women prepare." The women sitting to the side began chattering. Many happy glances were cast Jack's way. Jack returned their smiles with a nod. At least these ladies were on his side.

"They like this idea?" he asked Coyote.

Coyote raised an eyebrow. "They've been wishing for this ceremony ever since you started telling us about the Darlington school."

If they'd wanted to have a party, then why hadn't they said so? "If this will convince them to send their children to the school, then it'll be well worth it."

"Lieutenant Hennessey is more determined than we knew," Coyote said. "We'll tell you when everything is prepared."

Jack hoped they didn't rush. After years without Hattie, he wanted to savor every moment before him.

This time when Spotted Hawk brought her a bowl of stew, Hattie fell on her knees as soon as it was in her hands. She greedily slurped the broth, then picked up the chunks of meat with her fingers. Part of her knew she should slow down, but she couldn't stop eating until the woman gently pulled it away from her. Now that the soldier was here and Hattie no longer feared Spotted Hawk, she recognized that the woman was just trying to help. And look how Hattie had acted. Like a spoiled brat.

The little she'd eaten only made her hungrier, but it also gave her strength. Standing, Hattie made her way to the side of the tepee, then began to wipe at the dried stew with the hem of her ruined dress. She'd made a mess, and she would fix it. She didn't expect anyone else to be put out on account of her.

But more women entered the tepee, and they wouldn't let her clean the hides. They pulled her away from her work, but the tone had changed. Hattie understood now that they had been gracious to her, and they understood that she was sorry. Or at least she hoped that they did.

The appearance of the cavalry officer had changed everything. His confidence gave her courage. His protection gave her hope. She hadn't been forsaken. God had sent her a rescuer, and it was no less miraculous in her mind than the jail door falling open for Paul and Silas.

A woman dressed in beaded buckskin presented her with a basin of water and a cloth. Hattie knew what to do with that.

The warm water and calming ritual made her realize how sleepy she was. The sun had gone down, and she couldn't wait to rest. Would she sleep at a fort tonight, or out on the range? The thought of traveling with the trooper should have troubled her. He was a stranger, and yet there was something so familiar, so endearing about him. He was strong and hardy, that much was clear, and she hoped he was as competent as he claimed. She felt confident that he could save her, but she wondered where this confidence in his abilities came from. Who did he remind her of that she trusted him so implicitly?

A younger woman with a baby on her hip handed Hattie a strangely shaped comb. Just thinking about the tangles in her hair made Hattie's head hurt, but she smoothed the comb over the top, knowing she'd have to have some soap and a bath before tackling the snarls.

One of the women approached with a leather dress draped over her arm. Hattie froze. They didn't expect her to put that on, did they? Her fears that she would never get to leave returned.

She shook her head. Spotted Hawk touched the muddy hem of her skirt. Hattie drew her feet in and tucked the hem beneath her. They weren't taking her clothes. If she had to yell bloody murder she would, but she wouldn't get undressed until she was in a room with a lock and key.

Sensing her panic, Spotted Hawk motioned the dress bearer back. But this time she didn't just touch Hattie's dress, she pulled the hem toward her and began picking off the clumps of mud. Spotted Hawk's voice was stern but calm. Seeing what she was about, Hattie and the other women joined her in removing the burrs and mud as best they could. The dress was ruined, but Hattie was grateful they wanted to clean her up. She was going to see the soldier again and, although she knew not to have her head turned by a dashing officer, she might as well look her best.

From outside the tent, children's voices could be heard, and heavy, slow steps passed as if many people were carrying burdens. A drum pounded a rhythm, then stopped and tried a different cadence.

At last Spotted Hawk stepped back, and with her hands on her hips, nodded in satisfaction. Good. Hattie had tired of the attention and wanted to find the soldier again. How was he doing with the negotiations?

Now that she'd had a moment for her

food to settle, Hattie reached again for the bowl of stew, but the young woman took it away. She shook her head and motioned for Hattie to come to the door. Looking at the half-filled bowl as she passed, Hattie stepped through the flap of the tepee.

She didn't remember the tepee that stood right outside. In fact, with women still staking down the bottom of the leather covering, it looked like they were still in the process of constructing it. White puffs of breath followed the men laboring to carry logs inside for a fire. The smell of another spicy meal reached her nostrils. All the activity could only mean one thing: the trooper had planned a feast for her.

Hattie smiled in relief. The women giggled, and two of them took her by the arms as an escort. Hadn't the trooper told her to cooperate, that this was a delicate negotiation? She'd do as she was told. She had to trust him.

The elders of the tribe were crowded in the tepee, men on one side and women on the other. Hattie nearly ran back outside when she saw them all assembled with their layers of colorful adornments and braids spiked with feathers.

But then she saw the officer. He sat among the men at the fire, his back every bit as straight as the chief's, his overcoat with the cape draped from his shoulders and rumpled on the ground around him. He stood when she entered, and every fiber of him spoke of achievement and success. But then a young Indian man in white man's clothing tugged on his sleeve, and the officer returned to his seat at the fire. Under the direction of the women, Hattie sat among them, opposite the men.

The room quieted for the chief. His speech wasn't long but was appreciated by his people. He dragged a boy forward and, with a hand on his shoulder and a hand palm up, made some sort of pledge. Although the scene was not as majestic as she imagined the Rocky Mountains to be, Hattie wished for her box of paints and a canvas to capture it.

She was brought to her feet again, but this time she was led all the way around the circle. When she spotted a kettle of stew, her stomach growled, but the women kept her marching past it. The trooper was also being marched around. He looked solemn, dignified, making her wish that she had clean clothing.

The two groups met at a spot by the fire that had been cleared for them. With a little tugging, their hosts managed to arrange both of them at the fire next to each other. Never had Hattie been so anxious to hear her own language.

"You're doing wonderful," the trooper whispered. "If we play our cards right, we should get out of here alive."

Yet he was so brave, the danger didn't seem to bother him at all.

"Do they do this for all the captives?" she asked.

"This is a first for me." Instead of cowering, he motioned to an Indian wearing an army coat over his fringed buckskin trousers and asked, "Coyote, when can we feed the lady?"

"Soon. Chief Right Hand will have prayer first."

Prayer before the meal. Maybe they weren't as foreign as she'd thought. Hattie bowed her head and thanked God for sending her a rescuer. She prayed for Agent Gibson and Mr. Sloane's families and the family of the driver. She prayed for her parents, that they wouldn't be worried about her, and she prayed that this detour wouldn't prevent her from the success she sought in Denver. Maybe the exhibition directors had been right. She had never experienced hardships like this before. It had certainly changed her perspective.

The prayer was over, but only Coyote moved. "What do you have to give her?" he asked the trooper.

For the first time, her escort looked uncertain. "Give her? I wasn't prepared for a trade."

Oh no. His confusion frightened her, but the tease of the familiar had returned. Looking worried like that, he reminded her of someone. It was on the tip of her tongue. . . .

"How about my overcoat? Will that suffice?" The officer unclasped the navy cape from his neck and removed it. He paused, then draped it over her shoulders.

Hattie kept her eyes down. She must smell like a three-week-old basket of wash left in the cellar, but he treated her as if she were decked out in her finest gown. Why hadn't a man like this been on the stagecoach with her? It would have made all the difference in the world. Then again, considering the fate of the other men, she was glad he hadn't been there.

"And you?" the Indian asked her.

Hattie sat flummoxed. She could give him her coat, but it would be useless to him. She had nothing else. All her luggage, even her reticule, had been on the stagecoach. Thinking quickly, she reached for her earring and slipped it off. The officer blinked in surprise but held out his hand for her to press the jewelry into. The gesture pleased their audience. The women shimmied their shoulders to make their bells jangle. The officer smiled his thanks and tucked the earring into his pocket.

"Aren't you going to wear it?" the Indian asked. "We have a knife, so we can fix that ear."

"No, thank you, Coyote," he said. "I'll just put it in my pocket."

"Then the ceremony is complete. The chief will make an announcement."

The chief stood before them and raised his hands. A brief word with Coyote, and then Coyote whispered to her, "Your name is Hattie Walker, right?"

Hattie tensed. She hadn't told anyone her name, not even the officer. How did they know? Had they found her luggage on the stagecoach? Something with her name on it? She nodded, then waited as Coyote passed on her reply to the chief.

The words slurred over unfamiliar syllables, but then she heard her name. The chief motioned to her, and she stood. When he reached out, she wasn't sure what to do, but she took his hand, more and more sure that with the trooper there, she was in no danger. His wizened hand gripped her firmly as he motioned for the officer to stand.

Hattie's cape was slipping. The officer straightened it before allowing the chief to take him by the hand, too. Thank goodness for the officer. If a simple release of a prisoner was this complicated, then Hattie would have never figured it out on her own.

What came next startled her. Chief Right Hand placed the officer's hand atop hers. The officer covered her hand in a broad, warm grasp. Her eyes flickered up to his, and she was surprised by the emotion she saw. He must have been thinking of someone else, some other time, because she hadn't earned the regard in his gaze.

The words continued while they stood there with their hands linked atop the chief's open palm. He was drawing to a close, or at least she hoped so. She heard her name again, but this time it was followed by something more.

". . . Lieutenant Jack Hennessey."

Hattie's eyes widened. Jack Hennessey? The spindly stretch of a boy she'd gone to school with?

The officer's chin went up as he dared her to question him. And here she was with her mouth gaping open. She snapped her jaw shut and studied his gloved hand covering hers. It was impossible. Not this handsome, manly lieutenant who'd come in and risked his life for her. He couldn't be the know-it-all boy from home, could he?

She fluttered her eyes upward to steal another peek. She'd meant to answer his letters, but he was so clever, and she got intimidated when she picked up a pen. Procrastination took over, and she'd never gotten around to replying. But why would he be here in Indian Territory? And why hadn't he told her?

As the chief's words ended, the women whooped and cheered. The men pounded their staffs into the ground in beat with the drums that had struck up. Again she was being led around the circle of observers, but this time Jack was holding her hand.

Jack? Maybe this was a man who only shared his name, because she could see nothing of the boy she'd known in him. But his gaze was too familiar, too knowing for him to be a stranger. It had to be him. And even as she was coming to terms with that fact, her embarrassment grew. Why hadn't he told her right from the first? It put her at a disadvantage, and she had always been at a disadvantage around him. Other boys flattered her and made her feel superior when they competed in their immature contests to win her favor. Never Jack. He was above all of them. And her. And now she would have to admit that she hadn't even recognized him while he was saving her life.

The Indians broke out into some chanting song. Jack smiled and hummed along as if he'd heard it before. Everyone was looking at her as they marched around in the circle. Just what a woman who had been through the wringer wanted, to be the center of attention.

Still, one thing was settled. She would be safe. Jack Hennessey always passed his tests. She had nothing to fear in his hands. Nothing besides looking inadequate.

CHAPTER FIVE

What kind of ceremony was that? Jack sat on the cold ground, shoulder to shoulder with Hattie. He took the food offered to them, finding it strange that the Arapaho made the guests of honor share a bowl when everyone else had their own. Through all his study on the Arapaho, this had been one of the richest experiences he'd witnessed, yet it didn't have the feel of a usual village celebration. It was too scripted, too formal, too similar to another ceremony — one he didn't dare name.

Instead he let his mind wander to a cold day in Van Buren years ago, when he'd decided to ask Hattie to the Valentine's Day dance. He'd written a very formal, very proper invitation, wanting to impress her with the forethought he'd put into the offer. But when he stood in front of her on the schoolhouse steps, his hands shook too much to read the sonnet he'd composed.

Instead he gaped, unbelieving that anyone's skin could be so perfectly flawless when his own was so besieged. And her eyes sparkled, while his were hidden beneath the reading glasses he'd had to don if he had any hope of making out his sonnet.

All the preparation was worthless, because instead of rivaling Shakespeare with his eloquence, he stammered, "Are you going to the dance?"

And when she replied with, "Yes, I am. Carson McKinney is taking me," Jack could only smile and say, "I hope you have a good time," before running away to berate himself on the botched offer.

Normally, Jack was the first to speak up, ask a question, or share an opinion, but he had always lost his nerve around Hattie. Even here, even now, when it seemed important to know exactly what Chief Right Hand was saying, he had let the ceremony go on. If he had made a mistake, he'd correct it later. Hattie didn't need to know.

One by one, the Arapaho came by to impart a word that Jack had never heard before — *neniiseekuuthi'*. He wished he had a notebook to write it on, but after hearing it a dozen times, he was confident he could reproduce it in his office. He focused on the well-wishers, keeping in mind that he was the official representative for the army and relationships were important. Meanwhile, Hattie could feast on the rabbit stew, which she was doing with relish.

He'd heard from his family that Hattie's artistic talent had continued to mature. He'd also heard when she rejected a proposal, choosing to study painting instead, thus keeping his hopes alive that he might someday have a chance. But she was a different person now. He didn't know her anymore. And he'd changed, too. Or at least he thought he had, until she appeared and made him feel thirteen years old again.

The party continued until midnight. Coyote had shed his agency clothing and was dancing with his tribesmen, unconcerned with Jack. As much as Jack was enjoying seeing village life in this manner, he worried about Hattie. The ambulance driver must have bunked down for the night. They wouldn't see him until morning, but Hattie could barely keep her eyes open. It was time for her to retire.

He motioned Coyote over. "Miss Walker is tired. What accommodations have been made?"

Coyote scrunched his forehead in confusion while Hattie listened attentively. "She's sleeping here. This is your tent."

"My tent?" Jack scanned the hastily constructed tepee. "I don't need a tent."

"It's custom," said Coyote. "They know you're going back to the fort, but for the night after the *neniiseekuuthi'* feast, you are given your own tent." He turned to the group and in a bellowing voice made some sort of announcement. The party began clearing out, women and men picking up the pots and musical instruments as they squeezed through the narrow opening and out into the night.

"I don't mind sleeping at the door to guard it," Jack said, "but isn't someone going to stay in here with her? Spotted Hawk?"

Coyote's skills as an interpreter were unsurpassed, but he seemed to be having trouble understanding now. "No one will guard the tent. You will both be safe in here."

"Jack? What's wrong?" she asked.

It was the first time she'd said his name. The first time in years. Jack turned, ready to give her the world if she wanted it. "Nothing is wrong. We're making arrangements for the evening. Excuse me while I get this settled." He motioned Coyote to follow him a few steps away. "Are you saying that we're both supposed to stay in here?"

"Don't you speak English?" Coyote asked. "She's no longer the tribe's responsibility. You asked them to give her to you. Now you take care of her."

"I am taking care of her. I'm protecting her reputation. We can't stay in here together alone. It's against our customs. You're on the army's payroll, and I'm ordering you to remain with me."

Coyote stepped backward. His hands flew up in protest. "No, sir. I can't do that. I have a reputation as well, and if word got around the Cheyenne and Arapaho tribes that I stayed in the tent after a *neniiseekuuthi'* ceremony, I would be shunned. Stop worrying so much, Lieutenant. You're warm, you're fed, and you have your lady back. Tomorrow you can work. Tonight is celebration."

Then, with a curious tip of the hat, he sauntered out of the tepee and closed the flap behind him.

Jack stood with his back to Hattie. How was he going to explain this? Somehow he knew that the change in circumstances was not going to improve Hattie's opinion of him.

Hattie had never been so exhausted before. She had reached her limit. But even though her eyes drooped, she feared what scenes would play in the dark when she finally closed them.

Jack lingered by the door, but Hattie wasn't fooled. She might be tired, but her ears worked just fine. Jack had always been one of the more cautious boys of her youth, and she could well imagine his dread of staying the night with her. After all he'd done, she hated to be more trouble. He was probably wondering how she'd managed to get herself in such a mess. He probably wondered how soon he could get rid of her.

Despite her embarrassment, Hattie was relieved that he was staying. The rules of society she'd always lived by had vanished when the stagecoach rolled away without her. This was pure survival, and if that meant falling asleep under the watchful eye of a cavalry officer, then Hattie could live with that.

"I'm so glad you're going to be my guard tonight," she said to ease his discomfort. "I know it's an inconvenience for you, but I don't think Spotted Hawk likes me."

His posture softened a smidgen. "I tried to explain to them —"

"Please, if you don't mind." Her face burned with shame at her request. "If you'd stay, I'd be eternally grateful."

The words seemed to do the trick. "I'll remember you said that," Jack said. He pulled a stack of buffalo hides away from the door and arranged them next to the fire. "I apologize for the unorthodox manner in which this was conducted. It seems I don't know as much about the Arapaho customs as I thought I did."

Hattie sank to her knees on the hides. "I can't believe you are Jack. I would've never recognized you."

"The army has changed me, Hattie."

Yes, it had. He'd always been an awkward smarty-pants. Now? Well, the smarty-pants aspect was probably still true.

"Where are your spectacles?" she asked.

His mouth twitched into a smile. "I still have them, but they're only for reading."

"It seems you wore them all the time in school."

"I was in school. Reading." He spread another hide next to the door.

"You don't want to be by the fire?" she asked.

"I don't think it's proper."

Perhaps not, but the truth was she worried that she'd never be able to close her eyes and sleep again. On the other side of darkness was the fear of being discovered, of being cold and hungry, of bad men groping in the blackness, trying to find her.

"At least take your coat back. There'll be a draft." She unclasped it and handed it to him. But she forgot to let go. He stood over her, the cape suspended between them. "And give me my earring," she said. "You have no use for it."

A strange look came over his face. "No. That was part of the ceremony, and it has meaning to me. I think I'll keep it. At least until you're back on your way to . . . where were you going, again?"

She released the cape and tucked her skirt beneath her knees. "I'm going to Colorado. And those earrings were a gift from my father. If he knows I lost one . . ."

"I'll be glad to explain it to him. I always admired your father. Why are you going to Colorado?"

"To study art." She could only imagine what Jack thought of her grandiose aspirations. "I only have two months to be recognized, or else I have to go home."

"I recognized you immediately," he said.

"I suppose I haven't changed as much as you have," she replied.

Hours later, Jack was still awake. He'd lain down mostly to assure Hattie that he wasn't leaving, but as soon as she'd fallen asleep, he sat up and pushed open the tent flap. He wouldn't go out, but his thoughts needed more space than the smoky tepee could afford.

Nothing moved in the camp. The dogs were curled up in tight circles against the tepees to keep warm. The outdoor fires had gone cold. Everything was quiet. Everything was peaceful.

Everything except Jack.

He looked up at the sky full of sparkling crystal stars. Jack knew nothing happened in life that God didn't allow, but that didn't mean that everything had a purpose. Sometimes it was just dumb luck that you spilled your coffee on your uniform and had to change. Or when you misplaced the book you'd been reading and spent the better part of an hour looking for it. God might allow it to happen, but in the grand scheme of things, what did it matter? Bullets flying, prairie fires raging, disease spreading — in situations like that, you hoped God was guiding the outcome. In other things, well, He probably let nature take its course.

For most of his life Jack had been in love with Hattie Walker. Puppy love, infatuation, besotted — no matter what you called it, Jack couldn't think of another woman without first comparing her to Hattie.

Hattie was joyful, courageous, spunky, and generous. Even when they grew up and it became obvious she didn't share his regard, she was still kind. And rather than test her kindness by applying himself again and again, Jack had left Van Buren.

He'd hoped that her memory would fade, but the longer he was away, the brighter her memory seemed to grow, until he wasn't sure what was truth and what was his own conjecturing. It was the courtship of Major Adams and Miss Bell that forced Jack to admit that longing for Hattie wasn't healthy. He had to move on. He had sat under these very stars and prayed about it, asking God to bring him a woman of godly character, common sense, and — if it wasn't too much to ask — a pretty smile. And most of all, someone who'd be able to consider loving him, too.

A gust of wind snapped the hides on the tepee. Was he letting in too much cold air? He closed the flap and looked behind him, but Hattie didn't stir. She looked so small, curled up beneath the heavy robes with her back to him. It hurt to imagine her sleeping uncovered in a cold, lonely gully. How frightened she must have been. What was her family thinking, letting her make this trip alone?

And what was God thinking, bringing her here to him? This wasn't a spilled drink or a missing book. Jack couldn't by any stretch of the imagination turn this into a co-incidence. Something else was going on. Had his prayers been answered? Maybe instead of asking him to give up on Hattie, God was delivering her right to his arms.

The fire had slacked. Moving silently, Jack took the unburnt ends of the sticks and pushed them toward the coals. Hattie stirred. She flipped over to face him but was still asleep. Her brow wrinkled, and her mouth tightened. Her whimper nearly broke his heart. Feebly she pushed against the blankets, like she was trying to claw her way out of a grave. Jack hurried to sit at her side.

He brushed her hair away from her face, and his heart skipped a beat at the feel of her skin beneath his fingertips. She'd been through so much, and yet she still could stand her ground, even surrounded by a whole culture that was strange and frightening to her. He'd always thought her unsinkable, unshakable. But now, in her sleep, trouble creased her face. Her chin quivered, and her hand continued to push at invisible torments.

"Shhh . . ." Stroking her hair seemed to calm her, but what if she woke suddenly?

Would his presence startle her?

Then she did something that startled *him.* Hattie grabbed a handful of his overcoat and pulled it beneath her chin, like it was her most cherished possession. He drew back, but she wouldn't release him. Instead, she took a deep breath against the fabric, and her breathing slowed. The creases on her face smoothed, and everything relaxed except for her grip.

He was caught, awkwardly leaning over her at an angle that couldn't be sustained. What would Coyote or any of the Arapaho think if they walked in? There was only one thing to do. Jack unbuttoned the coat and slid it off his shoulders. He tried to tuck it around her, but she preferred to hold it tightly to her chest.

He waited another moment before moving away. It would be a cold night, but he couldn't complain. They'd made a trade, after all, and he'd had his reasons for keeping her earring. He had to wonder what her reasons were.

CHAPTER SIX

Hattie woke with a start. She shoved off the heavy buffalo hides and bounced to her feet. The cool air in the tepee bit clean through her fogginess. She stood with one hand against the sloped wall, the other hand clutching a wool coat over her chest, and it was already light outside. What had happened?

The caped overcoat was the clue. The troopers had come, and one of them — Jack Hennessey, of all people — had arranged for her release. Last night she'd finally been fed and rested, and today she could continue her journey.

The cedar log on the fire filled the tepee with a sweet scent. Hattie threw the coat over her shoulders and huddled next to the flame. The experiences of the last few days were too frightening to think about, so she tried to focus on her future. What was her plan? Was she ready to give up on her mission and return home? If she did, her parents wouldn't fund another venture. So she'd continue to Denver, then. Get on another stagecoach like the one before and travel with strangers. Hattie pulled the edges of the coat around her and shivered. She'd do what she had to, but she didn't relish the journey. Not with the memories so fresh.

Reins jangling and the creaking of wheels alerted her that someone had arrived. The door flapped open, and a tall silhouette darkened the space. She tucked her chin into the cape. All her hopes hung on Jack Hennessey. She was still having trouble acquainting herself with that fact.

He took off his hat and brushed at his wavy hair. She did remember that brown shock of mess, but it didn't look so out of control now that he'd grown into it. His fresh haircut enhanced his fine dark eyes, just like the perfect frame could anchor a painting.

"The ambulance is here," he said. "There are provisions in the wagon for you — clean clothes and the like — or we can start out on our journey immediately, if you'd rather."

"I'm ready." She had no bags to pack, no items to gather. Only plans to make once she reached civilization.

She followed him outside where, among

the Indians, a knot of troopers stood, each wrapped in his own overcoat. Only Jack was missing his.

"Your coat." She pulled it off her shoulders before the soldiers noticed. "Did you give it to me last night? I don't remember. You must be freezing."

His smile was genuine. "I don't mind."

Hattie didn't miss the look between Coyote and Spotted Hawk. Whatever they were saying amused them greatly. She lifted her chin and threw the coat around her shoulders again. She would follow Jack's lead. He knew how to act here.

The chief stood to the side with the boy from the night before. The boy was dressed warm for traveling, and there was a bedroll on the spirited black pony that paced behind him. From the sorrow on his face and the solemn looks of those around him, Hattie felt that a farewell was in progress.

Jack escorted her to the wagon as she asked, "Is he going with us?"

"The chief has decided to let his nephew, Tom Broken Arrow, attend the Arapaho school at Darlington." Jack stopped at the wagon and offered her a hand. "I hope his decision will encourage more of the parents to send their children."

Jack and school. So he hadn't changed

72

that much after all. She looked around at the Indians, still amazed that Jack was at ease in such a dangerous situation. She would probably never see any of the Indians again, and she had something she needed to say.

"May I borrow the use of your interpreter?" she asked.

Jack's eyebrows rose, and his eyes crinkled in amusement. "As long as you behave yourself," he said. "Remember, these people saved your life."

After a word of explanation, Coyote bowed to her, then followed her to Spotted Hawk and a group of the women who had cleaned her up for the banquet the night before.

Spotted Hawk watched Hattie's approach with eyes just like her namesake. Hattie twisted her hands. "I'm sorry I didn't understand that you were trying to help me. I would have never acted like that if I had."

Her scowl softened as Coyote translated. With a quick nod, Spotted Hawk's words bubbled up faster than baking soda in vinegar.

"Next time you meet, you will be friends," Coyote translated. "She wishes blessings on you and the lieutenant."

Hattie's jaw tightened. Were outlaws likely to cross their path on the way back to the fort? Was that why they needed blessings? That reminded her of others she owed gratitude. She'd fought them tooth and nail, but the men who'd rescued her on the prairie had done her a good turn.

Coyote passed her thanks on to the men and finally the chief. Then, having done her duty and made amends, Hattie was more than eager to get into the wagon and be on her way.

Jack lowered the gate of the ambulance wagon for her and, without waiting for permission, picked her up and set her inside. The old Jack Hennessey might have worn her out with his advice and lectures, but he never would have touched her. This new one took some getting used to, but she wouldn't be around long enough for that.

"Thank you for doing what you did back there," he said. "I've worked for years to convince them that we can trust each other. An apology goes a long way."

Hattie took a seat inside the canvased wagon on the padded bench made for invalids before sizing up her escort. "There's more to you than meets the eye, Jack Hennessey."

His jaw slid over in a crooked smile as he closed the gate. "There always was."

Jack should have been scanning the horizon with his men and watching for danger, but he couldn't stop jogging back to the end of the column to look after the ambulance.

Hattie Walker. He was taking Hattie Walker to Fort Reno with him. Once they reached the property, she would become his commander's responsibility, but he couldn't get over the surprise. One thing did bother him, though. He'd told Major Adams about his girl back home. But he hadn't told Major Adams everything, like how she'd never actually been his girl back home. He needed to make sure his major didn't let something slip that would embarrass him. All that jesting he'd done at Daniel's expense when he and Louisa were courting was starting to look like a bad idea.

Private Morris rode up to him.

"What is it, Private?" Jack asked.

"The lady, sir." Morris motioned back to the wagon. "She asked me to give you your coat. Said you looked cold."

Jack squinted at the ambulance cover, but it was drawn up tight. It was probably cozy in there. He thought of gallantly refusing the coat but decided it would gain him nothing. Besides, a shivering man didn't cut as fine a figure as a caped hero. He put the coat on and thanked the private. He should check in on her and see if she'd forgotten her eternal gratitude yet.

After getting his cape secured, he circled around to the back of the wagon and knocked on the frame beneath the canvas cover. It lifted, and Hattie's tired face peeked out.

"Are you sure you're warm?" He'd gotten his horse close enough to get out of the wind.

"It's comfortable in here," she said. "How long until we reach the fort?"

"It'll be suppertime. No more cook fires and sleeping outside. You've had enough of that." Although why was he in such a hurry to get her back? Then he'd have to say good-bye. "If you don't mind me asking, what were you going to do in Colorado?"

"I was going to paint the Rocky Mountains. It's part of my training."

"And your parents let you travel alone?" He lost sight of her when the wagon hit a rut and she bounced out of view.

"I was supposed to be safe on the stagecoach until I arrived in Denver, and then one of their friends was providing me with board."

Jack shook his head. Her poor parents would be frantic with worry when she failed to appear. "Do you realize how fortunate you are?" he asked. "Surviving the stage-coach attack was one thing, but you could've easily frozen out there on the prairie if White Horse hadn't found you." He didn't want to chide her, but his blood curdled when he thought of the danger she'd been in.

"I had to get away," she said. "Mother and Father are adamant that I get married, but I haven't had a chance to see what I can do with my painting yet. That's why I'm going to Colorado. You probably think I'm fool-ish, but I'm not about to get shackled to whatever man befriends Father this year. I'm too young to give up my painting."

"You're my age," he said, and Jack thought twenty-four was rather late for matrimony.

"Exactly. You're doing what you want to do, so why can't I?"

He didn't have an answer for that, besides reflecting on the opinion his mother had always held that Miss Hattie Walker was a spoiled child who would cause someone a heap of trouble. Jack had always argued with his mother. Hattie was funny and kind, but he did have to admit that she was fond of having her way.

"Are you going on to Colorado from

here?" he asked.

The tiredness came back to her eyes. "My purse is gone. My money and my bags were stolen. If I tell my parents, do you think they'd make me come straight home?"

"I would," Jack said. Then, at her woebegone expression, he added, "You have plenty of thinking time before we reach the fort. Maybe you'll come up with a plan." With a tip of his hat, he rode back to the front of the column where he belonged.

Her dismissal of marriage had left a bitter taste in his mouth, but he shouldn't be surprised. Conversations with Hattie had never gone the way he wanted.

Tom Broken Arrow rode even with the troopers, his proud heritage apparent in his face. Jack thought about asking him if he needed anything but stopped, because even if by chance the boy could understand him, he wouldn't appreciate being looked after like a child. Instead Jack rode next to Coyote.

"Let me know the next time there's a *neniiseekuuthi'* ceremony," Jack said. "That was very impressive."

Coyote grinned. "The people were impressed by *you,* my friend."

"Me? What'd I do?"

"Before the ceremony, Miss Walker was

an angry she-cat, clawing and spitting at everyone who came near. But after one night with you" — he wagged his eyebrows — "she came out as calm as a doe."

Jack nearly choked. "Miss Walker . . . well, that was a misunderstanding. She was scared out of her wits and didn't know they were trying to help her. She just needed someone to explain it to her."

"You are a very persuasive man, Lieutenant Hennessey, but I don't think it was your explanations that tamed her. Even you can't negotiate that well."

Jack had to get the ribald jokes straightened out before Coyote said the wrong thing in front of Major Adams. "The ceremony helped settle her nerves," Jack said. "Seeing everyone there, eating, singing, praying together — that had an effect on her. It was a very nice ceremony." He shouldn't have let Coyote leave them in the tepee alone all night, and he hoped that decision wouldn't come back to haunt him. The last thing he wanted was a reprimand in Miss Walker's company.

"We weren't sure she understood what was happening until she gave you her earring," Coyote said.

The earring? Jack had recovered people from the tribes before and had never had an exchange ceremony like that. Then again, he'd never requested one. As much as he was enjoying his time with Hattie, Jack couldn't wait to get back to his office and record the events of this mission. There was much to ruminate on.

"And for the first time, I feel like Chief Right Hand is agreeable to the school idea," Jack said. "I can't believe he sent Tom to Darlington. That's progress."

Coyote nodded. "He told you all along that they didn't trust a bachelor to advise them on their children. That once you became a married man, then you'd take the responsibility more seriously."

"Yes, I've heard it a dozen times, but why now? Why . . ." Jack looked over his shoulder at Tom, who rode in front of the ambulance. Had Chief Right Hand gotten the wrong idea? Did he think that Jack and Hattie were planning matrimony? "I have no plans for marriage," he said.

Coyote's perfect teeth flashed in a grin. "Too late, friend. She's yours."

"Oh, no. While I think Miss Walker is a fine lady, I'm delivering her to the fort, and then she's going on to . . . well, somewhere else. She has plans."

"You would allow that?" Jack had seen Coyote in some tight situations before, but he'd never seen him so surprised. The Arapaho man leaned forward over the neck of his horse and spoke in a shocked whisper. "You would allow your wife to abandon you and go on to some other man?"

"She's not my wife," Jack said. "Look, I know her from home, and yes, I do admire her, but I have no intention of marrying her."

"She *is* your wife. The *neniiseekuuthi'* ceremony —"

"Is a prisoner transfer. The chief placed her into my keeping." Why did he have to explain this to Coyote? Shouldn't Coyote know such things?

But Coyote was no longer smiling. He looked concerned. "He prayed over you, and you exchanged gifts. You ate from the same bowl. The contract is sealed."

"That's not right. You don't understand."

"*I* don't understand?" Coyote rolled his eyes to the dark, low clouds scudding about overhead. "You are telling me that I don't understand my own people?"

Jack's frustration was rising. Coyote had never carried a jest this far. Checking to make sure that none of his men could hear the conversation, Jack leaned toward Coyote.

"If you're laughing at me, then I appreciate the humor. Very funny. But you'd better start telling me the truth. That's an order."

"This is the truth," Coyote said. "I've been to many weddings in my tribe. Everything was done according to custom. The chief even added the prayers that the white missionaries taught us. You are wed."

Jack could no longer feel the cold, but he felt like he'd just caught a cannonball in the chest.

Him, wed to Hattie? Hattie, the woman who would leave her home and travel across Indian Territory rather than face marriage, was unknowingly married to him?

Of all the stupid things. *Stupid. Stupid.* Despite Jack's extensive vocabulary, all he could manage as he scolded himself was *stupid.*

"I didn't ask for a wedding," he said. "They can't do this to me."

More importantly, they couldn't do it to her. What would Hattie say? Jack ground his teeth. Married? He couldn't face her. She'd be so angry, so disappointed in him. He had to come up with a plan. He had to cover his mistake and make sure that Hattie never, ever learned of it. She might claim that her gratitude was eternal, but Jack knew Hattie would be horrified to find that the Indians considered her to be his wife —

Mrs. Jack Hennessey.

The weight of dread fell on him, heavy as a boulder. He'd been so proud that he was the one to rescue her, but he'd bungled it horribly. He had to get her on a stagecoach and out of Indian Territory before she heard. If Coyote would keep it to himself for a few days, then Jack could deal with the consequences once Hattie was gone.

The smartest man at the fort, and he hadn't realized he'd been celebrating his own wedding.

CHAPTER SEVEN

Whenever Hattie heard about forts, she always imagined them to be tightly guarded strongholds surrounded by stockade fences. Fort Reno was open and visible for miles. The whitewashed barracks and tidy roads cut into the middle of the otherwise uninterrupted prairie. The tall houses along what Jack called Officers' Row were impressive with their spotless white siding and French doors. Besides the houses' green shutters, the only color around was the blue of the cavalry uniforms. Hattie had been riding for days across the territory, first in the stagecoach and now in an ambulance, and her artist's eye felt like it had been deprived of nourishment.

The ambulance driver waved Jack over once they'd reached the buildings. "Lieutenant Hennessey, should I take Miss Walker to the infirmary?"

Jack kept his horse a wagon's length away.

Ever since their last talk about her plans, he'd kept his distance, which was fine with her. Normally, Hattie's appearance gave her enough confidence to cover for her deficient areas, but right now she had nothing to offer.

"I'm not sick, but I'm in need of a wash and some clean clothes," she said.

Jack's eyes cut to the ground.

"The only place she's likely to get any help with that would be at the major's house," Sergeant Byrd suggested for him.

Jack slouched. Then, with a nod of his head, they turned toward the fine houses along the north side of the fort.

Why was he so reluctant? Had he received news that she didn't know about? Was he in some kind of trouble? Hattie fiddled with her ear, the one missing its earring. She hoped she hadn't caused trouble for him. The sooner she got out of Indian Territory, the better off they'd both be.

The wagon stopped in front of the grandest two-story house on the block. It was centered directly across from the flagpole in the middle of the green. A private waiting on the porch helped her out of the wagon. Hattie could appreciate the symmetry of the long barracks lined up on both sides and the buildings arranged opposite of their twin, but she could also appreciate a warm fire. There was no reason to stay outside any longer.

Jack took her arm and led her to the house. Her rescuer might be a classmate, but their warm, familiar relationship had disappeared. Now he was treating her like a stranger.

"Miss Walker." He released her arm and removed his hat. The wind teased his thick hair. "I've got to report to the adjutant's office and see after my work, but I wanted to say that I hope your trip continues without further incident."

Just like that, he was leaving her? Hattie rolled her shoulders forward, stretching her battered coat tight around her shoulders. "Perhaps our paths will cross someday," she said. "Maybe when we're both in Van Buren."

"But you're going to Colorado," he said, "and I can't think of any reason I'd go to Colorado."

Poor Jack. He'd finally caught her attention and didn't know what to do with it. Hattie tucked her hands beneath her arms and shivered. "Colorado or Van Buren, I'd be glad to see you. Now we have a story to share."

His gaze sharpened. "We spent our entire

childhoods together, and only now we have a story to share?" With a shake of his head, he slapped his hat back on. "Safe travels. I hope you find what you're looking for."

He stepped off the porch and started down the gravel walkway just as the front door of the house opened.

It was clearly the major. He was a large man, older and sterner than Jack. His eyes skittered past her and landed on his lieutenant, who was making a hasty departure.

"Lieutenant Hennessey," he bellowed, "where do you think you're going?"

Hattie shrank back from the door. She hadn't meant to intrude on his business, and this man seemed all about business.

Jack turned sharply and made a crisp salute. "I was seeing after my duties at the adjutant office. With you celebrating your recent wedding" — Jack's eyes darted to Hattie, and he turned red — "Captain Chandler will be looking for my return."

The major shook his head. "That's unlikely. Get over here."

Hattie folded her hands together. What had Jack done? She couldn't imagine what trouble goody-goody Jack would have gotten into.

"Are you going to make introductions?" the major asked.

Jack's chin went up, and he looked ever so official. "Major Adams, may I present Miss Hattie Walker? Miss Walker, this is my commanding officer — and sometimes my friend — Major Daniel Adams."

Major Adams bowed with his head tilted to the side. One eyebrow rose as he said, "Miss Walker? That's not what I heard. Please, won't you come inside?" Then, to the man who was trying to disappear, "That includes you, Lieutenant Hennessey. Inside. We have a lot to discuss."

What was going on? Why didn't the major believe she was Miss Walker? Was she supposed to be someone else? Hattie followed him through the door and found herself in a charming entryway with an office at her right and a parlor ahead. A striking blond woman rushed forward to hug her as Jack stepped away.

"Welcome to Fort Reno, Hattie," she said. "And congratulations. I'm Louisa, and this is my husband, Daniel, or Major Adams, I'm supposed to say."

Her use of first names was surprisingly familiar for such a proper-looking lady, but maybe the situation wasn't as formal at a military fort. "Nice to meet you," Hattie said. "But I don't feel that congratulations are in order. The ordeal was nothing to celebrate."

"An ordeal?" Major Adams jabbed his elbow into Jack's arm. "Hardly an auspicious beginning."

"She's talking about the attack on the stagecoach," Jack said. "I hope you haven't forgotten that part."

The major's face sobered. "Of course not. I'm sure the Arapaho hospitality was a comfort after your harrowing experience."

Comforting? Hattie blushed to think of how she'd treated them. But Jack didn't give her time to confess.

"The Arapaho were impressed by her courage and grace," he said. "She conducted herself admirably."

Hattie released the breath she'd been holding and shot Jack a look of gratitude.

"That's good," Major Adams said. "We'll want to get a full interview from her as soon as you feel that she's ready. Have your men written their reports?"

"Sergeant O'Hare will have them first thing in the morning," Jack said.

An interview? Hattie supposed she should have expected to give a record of the attack. So much had happened since then that she'd forgotten there might be a chance of catching the man who was responsible for all her misfortune.

"Are they here?" a young voice called out from the top of the stairway that rose in front of Hattie.

"They're here," said the major. "Come on down."

Hattie took another look at the beautiful Mrs. Adams before she stepped to the side and made way for two young ladies coming down the stairs with a large piece of butcher paper.

They had painted her a picture? How fitting. They reached the bottom of the stairs, and the youngest, who looked about eleven years old, took her end of the paper and walked away from the other girl, who had to be her big sister. The hand-painted banner unfolded to reveal an announcement in big block letters festooned with birds and flowers.

Welcome Home, Lt. and Mrs. Hennessey

"Mrs. Hennessey?" Hattie's eyes opened wide as she looked at Jack. "You didn't tell me your mother was here."

Louisa squeezed Hattie's waist. "Jack's mother is here? How wonderful. Did she come in for the wedding?"

"You're the one who got married," Hattie responded. "I don't know who you invited."

"Sir, we need to talk." Jack motioned toward the office. "The sooner the better."

"When the scout came with the report this morning, we couldn't believe it," Major Adams said. "But it's about time."

"What's going on?" Hattie asked. Not knowing what everyone was talking about put her at a disadvantage.

The major shot Jack a questioning look, then with a flick of his finger directed his daughters to put away the banner. "We shouldn't make any more demands on your time," he said to Hattie. "Not until you've had a chance to refresh yourself. If you'll pardon me, I'll take some time to consult your — Lieutenant Hennessey while my wife and daughters get you settled for the night."

Jack's sigh sounded like a whoosh. "Go with them, Hattie. They'll get you what you need."

Was the military always in this much confusion? Whatever misunderstanding they'd had, Hattie was more than ready to leave it all behind. A warm bath and soft bed were more important to her after a long day of bouncing in the ambulance wagon.

"If you'll come with me, Miss . . ." Louisa paused, and Hattie wondered at her forgetting her name already. "I'll gather some clean clothes for you, and we'll go next door and get some water heated. Won't that be nice?"

Clean clothes and warm water. Things Hattie had always taken for granted, but with them, she'd be ready to face whatever came next.

Major Daniel Adams appeared to be the embodiment of decorum and concern, but Jack wasn't fooled. As soon as the door to his office closed, Daniel dropped into the seat behind his broad oak desk. The epaulettes on his shoulders caught the lamplight, as did his wide smile. He wouldn't miss this opportunity to meddle in Jack's personal life. It was only fair, considering how Jack had conducted himself when Mrs. Adams had first arrived at the fort, but this wasn't fun and games. This was serious.

"As a newlywed man myself, I congratulate you on your lovely bride," Major Adams said. "At the same time, I offer my condolences that she doesn't appear to enjoy the nuptials as much as yourself."

"I can't believe word spread already," Jack said. "You must have known before I did."

"Both tribes are celebrating the union. Chief Right Hand sent a messenger as soon as the ceremony was completed."

"There was no ceremony. The Arapaho

made a mistake."

"But that's Hattie Walker from Van Buren, Arkansas? The young lady from your hometown you've told me about? The one you write to?"

"And the one who never writes me back. It's her, all right. Never in a hundred years would I have expected to find her in Indian Territory."

"But here she is, and what's more, she married you. How could a fellow be so lucky?" The major's smile was stubborn, daring Jack to contradict him, but Jack had no choice.

"She doesn't want to be my wife, sir." The words twisted like an arrow in his gut. "She didn't even recognize me when we stood face-to-face and conversed. I asked Chief Right Hand to arrange a ceremony for the transfer of the survivor. Something happened in translation. Coyote got confused, and the next thing I know, he's telling me that she's my wife."

The major's brow lowered. "The Arapaho have been after you all summer to find a wife. They didn't understand why you wouldn't pick a woman."

"I didn't pick one," Jack said. "They picked her for me, but I can't let it stand. Hattie and I aren't married."

Outside the office door, the house had gone silent. Louisa must have taken Hattie next door to his house. What was Louisa saying to her? He knew the major's wife was good at keeping secrets. He prayed she could keep mum about this one.

"You said the chief's nephew came with you?" Major Adams asked.

"Yes, Tom Broken Arrow is going to enroll at Darlington."

"What changed the chief's mind?"

"Can't you guess?" Jack asked. "He reminded me that only a family man could understand what it meant to be responsible for someone's child. At the time, I thought he was just goading me."

"Did he mention the payment that's due to them? That cash was going to provide them with blankets and beef for the winter."

"The money that was stolen in the robbery? No. The Indians don't know that the cargo that went missing is their payment."

"It's not going to sit well when they hear it's delayed again. And you worked hard to get that money for them." Major Adams's chair creaked as he leaned back into it. "Ever since you arrived at Fort Reno, you've made it your aim to gain the trust of the Cheyenne and Arapaho."

A verdict was coming. Jack could feel it.

"To that end, you've studied their culture and language and strengthened relationships that have kept peace on this reservation. That peace has saved lives, but it's fragile."

"Sir, I can't sacrifice Miss Walker for my career. That's a line I won't cross."

Major Adams swung one leg over the other. "Miss Walker might not have chosen to get married yesterday, but neither did she choose to be attacked by outlaws or rescued by Indians. She has to allow for some complications."

"I'm not a complication."

"No, you're worse. Agent Lee and I have had our fill of white men coming in and marrying Indian women, only to leave them when they've grown tired of living on the reservation. They claim that the Indian ceremonies aren't binding on them — a cruel trick to play on unsuspecting Indian maids."

"I didn't marry an Indian."

"But you're asking me to release you from oaths you made in the presence of the tribe. That I cannot do. You're of age and know more than most. How can we hold others accountable while allowing you to break your vows?" Major Adams lifted an eyebrow as he tapped his chin. "What happened after the ceremony last night?"

"Nothing. The hour was late. Everyone went to bed."

"Where?"

Jack rubbed his head. "Where did they go to bed? In their tepees, I suppose."

"Where did *you* go to bed, Lieutenant Hennessey?"

Jack's hand stopped. His heart rocked in his chest. He peeked up at his superior with guilt crawling all over him.

Major Adams sighed. "So you never protested in their presence, and you left the camp with her in your custody?"

Jack covered his eyes and nodded.

"Good heavens, Jack, what were you thinking? I'm afraid this is on your shoulders. The only thing to do is go home and make the best of it." The major's boot hit the floor with his verdict. "We can't tell the Arapaho that we respect and honor their traditions and then show disdain for their most binding contract. Besides, she's the only witness to a triple murder and the robbery of government property. She must stay here until a marshal from Fort Smith has made a full investigation, and she'll be safe under your care. There's no way around this, I'm afraid."

"You can't do that," Jack said. "You can

order me into a battle that means certain death, but you can't make me live with a woman who doesn't want to be my wife."

"Then maybe you ought to work on changing her mind."

That was a thought, but Jack had been ruminating on how to win Hattie for years. What made him think she'd be agreeable now? Especially in this situation?

Major Adams smiled. "Go home, Jack. It's late. See that she's settled, and maybe you'll be surprised. She might not be as opposed as you fear. If she is, well, then it's a choice you have to make. Leaving your wife would mean leaving this post. We can't have you disrespecting the tribes and their customs."

Leave Fort Reno? This was his life's work. It was more than a career. Jack's efforts meant more opportunity for the people he was trying to help. But Major Adams, newly married to his own bride, didn't understand how humiliating it was for a man to have to admit such a colossal mistake. Especially to a lady as perfect as Hattie Walker.

CHAPTER EIGHT

Hattie ran her finger across the plate, then licked the last of the icing from its tip.

"Do you want more?" Louisa poured Hattie a second cup of hot tea. "I'll run next door and get another piece of wedding cake."

"No. Please, don't go." Hattie didn't know if she'd ever be full again, but she was deathly afraid of being left alone. Even in this comfortably cluttered parlor.

Louisa had helped her wash her hair in the strange kitchen, getting the more stubborn knots out with a comb while Hattie ate cold fried chicken left over from dinner. The wedding cake was just another reminder of the Adamses' happiness and Hattie's misery. But Louisa had nothing to say on the topic. She deftly maneuvered around the confusion and kept Hattie busy, offering her choices of woolen underthings, flannel nightgowns, and blankets to wrap in once her bath was finished. The bath had been barely a dip, because no matter how delicious the water felt, Hattie couldn't relax in the unfamiliar room. She imagined someone looking in at each dark window. She imagined the door bursting open and exposing her, so she hurried into the layers of freshly laundered clothing so she could rejoin Louisa in the parlor.

Louisa had to move a stack of books off the couch in order for them both to sit there. After her rough exposure to the elements, Hattie didn't even mind the dust that tickled her nose. Undoubtedly this house had been abandoned. With the clutter and grime, it was unlikely anyone lived there permanently. But was she supposed to stay alone? She feared that once the darkness settled, her horrible nightmares would return.

"Will I be on my own tonight?" Hattie set her plate atop a leather-bound journal and shivered. "This is an awfully big space for one person."

Louisa smiled and kept smiling. "Have some more tea. It will help calm you. And it does feel cold in here. Lieutenant Jack normally keeps the stove warm, but with him out on patrol, the house has gone cold again. Here, let me get some more fire-wood."

Louisa took a few sticks from the firebox and placed them in the fireplace. The warm red glow of the coals tinted the room and filled it with a homey smell. Hattie could have fallen asleep right there on the sofa if she knew this kind woman wouldn't leave her side. She had to make conversation if she wanted to stay awake.

"Are those your daughters?" she asked.

Louisa beamed. "They are now. I came to the fort in June as their governess, more or less. And yesterday, as you know, I married their father, the major."

"Yesterday? You should be on your honey-moon."

"We're leaving on Wednesday. Daniel was waiting for Lieutenant Hennessey to get back, and then we're taking the girls to Tahlequah for a few days."

"You postponed your honeymoon over me?" Hattie asked. "I don't mean to be any trouble. As soon as a stage comes through, I can be on my way again. And look at me now. It's late, and I'm keeping you from your household."

"Nonsense. We rarely get visitors here, and I've heard so much about you, or at least Daniel has. It's a treat to finally meet you."

Louisa paused as footsteps could be heard outside. She stood and twisted the blond hair that was gathered over her shoulder.

The doorknob turned, and Jack stepped inside, the cape on his overcoat snapping in the wind. "Mrs. Adams, thank you for looking after Hattie for me. I would've left the house in better condition if I'd known."

"This is your house?" Hattie looked at Louisa, who'd snatched her coat off the sofa and shoved her arms into the sleeves.

"Good night, Hattie. Come see me in the morning if you'd like." Then, barely opening the door more than a crack, Louisa slipped out, leaving Hattie bundled up on the sofa with Jack standing before her.

Jack's steps were heavy, as if he carried a burden too great to bear. He unfastened his overcoat, tossed it across the banister of the staircase, and dropped his hat onto the post at the last step. The quietness of the house made Hattie realize how alone the two of them were and how little Jack resembled the boy of her youth.

Ruffling both hands through his hair, he sighed as he went to the fireplace and stood with his back to her.

"Jack, I'm exhausted," she said. "If you need me to fill out a report about the robbery right now . . ."

He turned but didn't quite meet her eyes. "Of course not. It can wait until morning. You need your rest."

"Where am I staying?" she asked. But when he kept his eyes down, she said, "Why do you look like that? Did I do something wrong?"

"No. Not at all. It's just that the fort isn't prepared for guests, especially women. Major Adams's house is full, and he's the only officer here with a wife. I could go to the barracks and let you have the house to yourself, or there are empty beds at the fort hospital. There'd be staff up during the night, so you wouldn't be alone. Of course, none of them are women — just enlisted men."

Hattie hugged the blanket around her. If she was going to be alone with a man, she'd much rather it be Jack than a stranger. Somehow he'd been designated her protector. For the night in the tepee, it made sense. There had been no choice. Here, her choices were a roaring fireplace in a beautiful home or a cold fort of sleeping men.

Poor Jack. Dead grass stuck to his boots. His clothes were wrinkled. Two days' growth of beard sprouted on his jaw. While she'd had dinner and a chance to clean up, he'd had nothing. He didn't need her to make a fuss. His day had been hard enough.

"I'll stay here with you," she said. "According to Mrs. Adams, it's all been arranged."

His jaw dropped like she'd just granted his dearest wish. His eyes darted around the room, and she could almost hear that giant brain of his spinning. Hattie had never seen Jack dumbstruck, and she couldn't fathom what had caused it. He bounded forward and fell on his knees before her. Hattie drew her blanket tighter as he began to babble.

"You've been through the worst trials imaginable," he said, "but from here on out, it's my duty to see that you lack for nothing. I'm going to take care of you. You won't regret this. Thank you, Hattie. You'll see."

Her forehead wrinkled in confusion. She'd never understood Jack. One minute he was dumping her on a stranger's front porch and trying to escape, the next he was groveling at her feet. He was a very handsome man, as far as grovelers went, and because of him, her plans in Denver could be salvaged. Two fine reasons to forgive his strange conduct. But Hattie had to wonder if there was anyone in Indian Territory who behaved rationally.

Jack knew Scripture. He believed in miracles. Blooms on Aaron's rod, a blind man with renewed sight, Lazarus raised — God could do anything. And while Jack was still grappling with the impossibility of Hattie's appearance in the nations, God had taken it a step further and made Hattie his wife. He hoped Louisa's explanation had spared him from blame, but Hattie seemed to have already forgiven him.

Shame on him for not crediting her with more sense.

"I was so worried about what you'd think." He picked up a lamp and motioned her forward. She'd probably want another ceremony. Ladies set store by such romantic moments, and Jack would be happy to oblige.

She followed him up the stairs, running her hand over the wool coat hung on the banister as they went up.

"You might want your own room tonight?" He swallowed the knot in his throat. "Yes, definitely you need your own room." He hoped it wasn't prudish to admit that even he needed some time to think through the momentous events of the last day. On the other hand, if she insisted on consummating their marriage immediately . . . He had to hold the lamp with both hands to keep it steady.

He nodded toward the six-paneled door at the head of the stairs. "I'll be in here if you need me," he said as they passed. He knew the next room was in horrible disarray, so he continued to the one that Daniel had recently vacated. The lamplight showed a worn dresser covered with boxes, and a bare mattress atop a metal bed frame. He nudged the bed. "I stripped the sheets before I left, but I don't have any replacements on hand. I wasn't expecting to bring a guest home. If you give me a minute, I'll go to the laundress —"

"It'll do," she said. "Just get me a pillow. I can sleep on the mattress, and I already have a blanket. After the stack of buffalo robes, it'll feel like heaven."

"You deserve better than this, Hattie. I'm sorry."

What a way to start a marriage! But she was being astoundingly levelheaded, at least compared to how Jack remembered her.

She hugged the rough army blanket around her shoulders. "You saved my life. That's enough."

Even with her chestnut hair soaking the

bulky blanket, her heart-shaped face shone like an angel's. It was all Jack could do to keep from falling on his knees again and kissing her feet. Instead, he poked around the boxes, just to make sure there weren't any rodents hiding in the corners, and fetched her a feather pillow.

Hattie was still wrapped in the blanket, waiting for him to do something, but what? A good-night kiss from her husband? Jack didn't know what else she could be waiting for. He tossed the pillow on the bed and wiped his hands on his trouser legs. He wished he'd had a bath and a shave, but if Hattie didn't mind, neither did he.

His lips were already tingling before he grasped her shoulders. He would have preferred a time when they weren't both so spent and disheveled, but that didn't keep his heart from pounding in anticipation. He'd dreamed of this for years. She was gorgeous despite her dripping hair and the tired lines around her eyes — eyes that grew larger as he bent toward her. He couldn't believe this was happening.

"Jack!" He felt her lurch backward. "Open your eyes."

When had they closed? He blinked a few times to find his focus.

"What do you think you're doing?" she

whispered.

His hands tightened on her shoulders. Holding her this close without his glasses meant that her face was a little blurry, but he could still see her confused expression.

"I'm kissing you good night," he said.

Her mouth dropped open. "What? Why would you think I'd allow that?"

"Because . . ." His eyes narrowed as they gauged her shock. "Didn't Louisa tell you?"

"Tell me what? That you were going to accost me? No, she didn't mention it."

Jack smoothed the blanket on her shoulders as the implications fell into place. It had been too good to be true. She would have never consented. He was just a fool fooling himself foolishly. Yet what Major Adams had said hadn't changed. The penalty for walking away from the ceremony would be severe. He had to tell her.

But not tonight.

He stepped back and clasped his hands behind him. "A good-night kiss," he said. "It's a . . . a fort tradition to wish you sweet dreams."

Hattie looked unconvinced. "Nothing will help with my dreams tonight," she said.

"Yes, well, don't suffer alone. If you need me . . ." But she didn't. His mother had always taught him that a gentleman must know when to end a conversation. He'd already said too much. "Did you leave the hip bath in the kitchen?" he asked.

Hattie nodded. "I'm sorry. I didn't know if I should dump it."

"No, that's perfect. I'll avail myself of it now, so if you're not going to leave the room . . ."

Hattie blushed as she understood his warning. "I'll stay up here. You can have the kitchen to yourself."

"Thank you. Good night, Hattie. I'm sorry for all the confusion." But most of all he was sorry that those few minutes of erroneous bliss were all he'd ever know.

He closed the door and walked downstairs for a cold bath.

Hattie was confused, she was frustrated, but most of all, she was exhausted.

Jack had left her the lamp, but even the light didn't help. As soon as her eyes drifted closed, she heard the wind. Her bones ached, her fingers and toes went numb. The feather mattress turned into a cold wall of clay. She jarred awake, thinking that someone was in the room. The outlaw was hiding behind the boxes. She told herself it wasn't true, that it wasn't even possible, but still she couldn't go back to sleep until she looked. Leaving her blanket, she tiptoed to the boxes, her heart pounding. She lifted the lamp. No one was there. Of course, the room was empty.

She lay down again, shivering from fright. This time she didn't put the blanket over her. What if she needed to get away? What if she needed to fight? She didn't want it holding her down. She huddled on the mattress and watched the flame of the lamp flicker. She wasn't alone; she was safe. But what if Jack left? The house was too big to be in alone. Just like when the Indians had found her, no one would hear her cries. The light dimmed as she drifted asleep, then with another jerk awoke.

It was drums — the Indian drums pounding. Without hearing them, she knew the chants they were singing. Again the fear that she'd experienced all alone in their village rolled over her. Sleep was impossible. Hattie sat up and crammed her fist against her chest. Her heart was running away with her. No matter how tired she was, she didn't want to hurt like this. Maybe it was better to stay awake.

Crawling off the mattress, she pushed her door open and listened in the hallway. Noises came from downstairs. It was Jack in the kitchen. She released a pent-up sigh. A good-night kiss? No wonder Jack had never had any girlfriends. He had the worst timing in the world. And yet, having him near was better than being alone . . . as long as he didn't take any liberties. She thought of the sofa by the fireplace. Maybe there she could rest. It was better than being trapped in a room at the end of the hallway.

With her pillow under her arm, Hattie made it halfway down the staircase before she remembered Jack's warning. She couldn't go into the parlor. What if he'd left the door to the kitchen open? She tapped her fingers against the banister. Jack might be a childhood friend, but the man in the kitchen had nothing of childhood left about him.

She had turned to go back up the stairs when her hand brushed against something warm. It was Jack's coat. Taking it in both hands, Hattie gathered it to her face. Slowly, her pulse calmed. Her muscles unknotted as the sound of the drums faded. She wasn't alone. God had sent someone to rescue her. For now, Jack was her protection from the evils of the wild west.

Hattie sat on the floor in the upstairs hallway. She'd wait here and ask Jack about sleeping on the sofa. He wouldn't be long. As long as she didn't have to go back into the creepy room with the shadows behind the boxes. The spot in the hallway across from his room was warm, and with the coat and blanket, she was comfortable. Comfortable enough to doze off.

The water felt brisk, but Jack made up for it by scrubbing his skin until it was pink and clean. How could he have made this bad of a mistake? Hattie would accuse him of colluding with the chief, and all he could claim in his defense was ignorance.

Not his finest hour.

The water sloshed as he stood and reached for a towel. It was already damp. He paused before resolving not to think about its previous duty. Another good scrubbing, and he'd be dry and ready for bed, although whether or not he could sleep remained to be seen.

Jack wrapped the towel around him, then scrounged the last of the meat off the cold chicken leg left on the table before tossing it into the bin. He blew out the light in the kitchen, deciding against carrying a lamp. He should have thought to bring clothes down, but he was used to the bachelor's life. At least Hattie was asleep in her room.

The fireplace in the parlor gave him light enough to see the stairs, but at the top it got dark again. With one hand holding his towel around his waist, he couldn't check on his guest. Everything was quiet, so she must be doing fine.

And she was, until he stubbed his toe on her.

His knee caught him, and fortunately for both of them, he managed to fall on the hard floor instead of the soft pile of blankets. What was she doing out here? Jack doubled his grip on his towel. Then he saw what she was holding. His coat. He sat back on his haunches.

From what Major Adams had said, Jack had no choice. He was either married to this woman, or he'd have to give up his work with the Arapaho and move to another unit so they could separate without causing a scandal. The Arapaho had been his study, his life's work for years. He couldn't imagine going somewhere else, starting from scratch with another tribe. He also couldn't imagine keeping a woman against her will, especially one as determined as Hattie.

What he could imagine, what he had imagined many times in the past — and experienced so fleetingly before his bath — was that Hattie Walker would by some miracle fall in love with him and consent to being his wife.

And now here she was.

And here he was, an innocent man, trying to decide whether to leave a lady sleeping on the floor or move her to his bed. For an innocent man, he sure found himself in a conundrum.

She whimpered, fighting terrors he could only imagine, and then her eyes opened.

"Hattie?" he whispered. "What's wrong? Why are you out here?"

"I was afraid. It's better out here," she said drowsily. She blinked. "Are you wearing a towel?"

"Are you hugging my coat?" he responded.

Hattie groaned and buried her head beneath his cape. "Can I stay here, please?" she asked. "Your room is right here, next to me . . ."

Those were her last words before fatigue overtook her again.

Weighing his options, Jack finally settled on straightening her quilt over her, then going into his room to sleep. He'd leave his door open, where he could keep an eye on her from his pillow.

And until she woke up, found out what had happened, and gave him the dressing down of his life, he could imagine that she'd come to live under his roof by her choice. Relive those brief moments earlier this evening when he'd thought it was true. It was a sweet dream, but one that would die with daybreak.

Chapter Nine

The next morning, Jack woke up to the bugle sounding stable call. He rolled onto his back and threw his arm over his eyes. Major Adams hadn't required him to report to assembly, but his sleeping in meant he'd missed breakfast at the mess.

If he'd missed breakfast, then why did he smell eggs and potatoes frying?

He had to kick a bit to get his legs free from the sheets. The cold floor against his feet brought him to his senses, as did the empty hallway. Had he dreamed the whole Hattie story? His wardrobe stood open and his clothes hung neatly inside it, but every other horizontal surface was covered in journals, papers, and books. In short, his room looked like it always looked. And he felt disappointed that the sleeping lady hugging his overcoat had disappeared.

Throwing on his clothes, Jack hurried down the stairs before he even had his suspenders over his shoulders. The delicious aromas led him straight to the kitchen, and he burst through the door without giving a thought to the poor girl on the other side.

His sudden appearance startled her. The skillet — Jack had never seen it before — rattled against the iron stove.

"Sorry," he said. "I didn't mean to surprise you."

"It's all right." She took the skillet off the hot part of the stove. "I'm frustrated with myself for being jumpy of late." She reached up and opened a cabinet door. Cobwebs ballooned out, then settled back into place.

He shouldn't just stand and stare, but have mercy, Hattie Walker was in his kitchen. Her thick brown hair had been twisted into some sort of loaf on the back of her head, displaying her elegant neck. The apron tied around her waist cinched her skirt to show that her days of starvation hadn't deprived her of all her womanly attributes. And the quizzical look on her face demonstrated that she didn't have time for his admiration.

"What are you looking for?" Jack asked.

"Pepper? I prefer some seasoning on my potatoes. Do you have any?"

He reached above her head and pulled out a pepper grinder. "I never knew that was up there." He wiggled the crank. "And there's peppercorns already in it."

She hesitated before stepping closer to take it from him. "Plates?" she asked as she cranked the handle. "Cups?"

They had a very important discussion ahead, but Jack would rather shut his mouth and get breakfast going.

"Let me help." He started to the cabinet but nearly shinned himself on the bathtub. Why hadn't he dumped it out last night? Here she'd been cooking around his cold bathwater and his dirty uniform wadded up on the floor. He gathered his clothes and tossed them out the back door. After being worn for his trip out to the Arapaho camp and back, they'd be fine outside until he could get them delivered to the laundress. Next to go was the heavy tub. He strained to get his arms around it. Full of water, it was heavier than it looked. The water sloshed up on his shirt as he dumped it outside.

He brushed at the water on his shirt, then thought to ask about her clothing.

"Mrs. Adams loaned me these," Hattie answered. "She also brought the food, which was nice, but she acted strangely."

"Mrs. Adams is one of the kindest — what did she do that was strange?"

"Instead of inviting me to breakfast, she expected me to stay and cook for you. It doesn't seem very hospitable — or proper, seeing how you're a single man." Using her faded black skirt as a hot pad, Hattie picked up the skillet and carried it to the table. "Even if we used to be friends."

Friends? Jack had always felt more like an overeager puppy that danced around her ankles. And the fact that he wasn't a single man needed to be addressed.

"She's busy getting used to being married, I'd imagine," he said.

He slid a plate in front of Hattie. It might be the heat from the stove, but he'd bet it was windburn that pinked her cheeks and made her brown eyes shine. And the news he had to tell her was going to make her blood boil. He scooped a spoonful of potatoes onto his plate, then added two eggs. No reason to wait any longer.

"Hattie, there's something I have to tell you."

He rarely thought about strategy, preferring to deliver the unmuddled truth straight and clear. But in this case, that approach might leave him with an unconscious woman on his hands if Hattie was the fainting type. It might leave him with a black eye if she wasn't.

"There's been a mistake." He arranged the plate directly in front of him. His nose twitched as she continued grinding the peppercorns. "There's a reason everyone is acting so strangely. The chief meant well. He thought he was solving a problem for me, but I didn't ask him to do it that way. I would've never participated in that ceremony if I had any idea."

The grinder caught on a stubborn shell. Hattie grunted with effort as she broke it loose. "You got me free, didn't you? That's all I care about."

"When learning the ways of a foreign people, even the most experienced ethnographers make mistakes. You look for similarities between them and their sister tribes, but then a difference comes along that is unexpected and you end up looking like a fool." Jack was warming to this topic. He'd much rather talk about his work than something personal. "Just last month, Chief Right Hand gave me a gift —"

"Jack," she interrupted, "what's this have to do with me?" She slid the drawer of fresh pepper open and sprinkled it on her potatoes.

Jack stabbed the eggs with his fork. His stomach turned at the sight, but he recognized nerves when they afflicted him. Best just to say what needed to be said and go from there. "That ceremony at the village . . ." He forced down a mouthful of food before continuing. "That ceremony was a wedding. According to the laws and customs of the Arapaho, we're married. To each other. Ain't that something?"

He lifted his fork but couldn't force another bite. Instead, he left it suspended in the air as she sat stunned, the pepper tumbling out of the drawer and onto her plate like a tiny avalanche.

"That banquet was a wedding?" she asked. Her lips pursed tight. Some tendons in her neck bulged. "The exchange of gifts, the prayers, the feast — all of that was a wedding?"

Jack couldn't bear the look she was giving him. He dropped his fork, then, and seeing some mugs, decided it was a good time to get them a drink. "I was as surprised as you are," he said. He filled the mugs and set one in front of her.

Her eyes had to be burning, because she hadn't blinked yet. "Nobody else knows, do they?"

Jack fiddled with the handle of the mug. "Chief Right Hand," he said, "Coyote, and the whole tribe. And Major Adams and his family."

"They all know? That's why they had that banner — Lieutenant and Mrs. Hennessey. And then last night in my bedroom . . ." Her fist fell against the table. "Jack? The good-night kiss? You thought I already knew, didn't you? Of all the far-fetched —"

"It's not that far-fetched," Jack protested. "We've known each other for years."

"I've known a lot of people for years, and so far I haven't married any of them."

"Technically, you have." Sometimes Jack's quick logic was not appreciated. This was one of those times.

She tucked her chin. "That's not funny."

"I'm not laughing." The table creaked as he leaned his elbows against it. "I'm the ambassador between the army and the tribe. Getting a divorce or annulment will ruin my relationship with them."

"But me being married to you is going to ruin my relationship with, oh, anyone else I might want to marry someday." Her voice was rising, and the look she was giving him was not charitable.

A tight knot began to form in his stomach. "Are you engaged?"

"No."

"That's right. You were running away from marriage, last I heard. Well, you're safe here. Pretending to be married is the best way to keep other men away."

"I'm not staying here. I can't." She rubbed her forehead. "I have two months to prove myself to my parents, or else I have to go home. I'll never get this chance again. Besides, this is the last place in the world I'd want to stay. This prairie nearly killed me." She faltered before regaining control. Lowering her hand, she met his gaze. "Here's what's going to happen. I'm going to finish my breakfast, then we're going to look into getting me on the next stagecoach out of here."

"What about the attack? You're the only witness to a triple murder and the theft of government property."

"A hostile witness." She fell back in her chair. "This is the end of everything I planned for. I'm trading my paintings and art for . . ." She motioned around the grimy kitchen and ended with her outstretched hand pointing directly at him.

Jack's heart dropped, but he kept his chin up. His first prediction had been right. If he'd ever had any hopes that she might someday deign to consider him a spouse, they were squelched. Certainly, she was happy enough to see him when he showed up and saved her hide, but beyond that, she had no use for him. The years hadn't changed a thing.

Time to take it like a man and figure out how to fix the awful mess he'd made.

She wasn't married. She didn't feel married. She didn't feel anything but shock. "It's not right," she said. "You can't do this to me. I'm on my way to Denver. I've got plans."

"I have work to do." Jack stared straight ahead and spoke to the wall behind her. "I have to report at the adjutant's office, but I'll talk to Major Adams. Don't worry. We'll find a solution."

He stood, carried his plate and mug to the washbasin, then marched out of the kitchen.

So much for her future. Hattie waited until she was sure he'd left the house, then ran to his desk and tore a piece of paper out of the first journal she laid hands on. She dropped into his chair and pushed a spot clear from his clutter. Three pencils were visible amid the messiness. The chewed end didn't matter as long as the point was sharpened. Her pencil flew over the page, forming the spine of a mountain range. Dark shadows obscured the face as a towering, angry thunderstorm built above it.

What would people say? What would her

parents say? How could she explain this to them? More than once her parents had teased her about brainy, scrawny Jack Hennessey following her around. If she'd known he was going to do this, she would have set him straight while he was still manageable.

The mountains blurred before her eyes, but the thunderstorm grew more and more distinct. Boiling clouds ready to unleash gallons of pent-up frustration. The pencil lead broke. Without pausing, she tossed it aside and grabbed the next one.

Hadn't she the right to determine her own fate? She'd tried to be traditional. Plenty of boys had come calling, but she'd shown the good sense to see through their foibles and know that she didn't want to settle down to such a tame existence. In fact, for all her protests to Jack, she seriously doubted that a future husband would come along. Not one she could please, anyway. Better to live on her own, but one ordeal after another kept getting in her way.

She was the lone survivor of a stagecoach robbery.

She'd seen to two murdered men without any help.

She'd wintered overnight with no shelter on the freezing prairie.

She'd been rescued by Indians whom she

didn't know or understand.

The Indians had passed her off to cavalry-men who'd transported her to this forsaken outpost.

And now she was being told that she was married to one of their officers and had to stay at the fort to benefit his career. All that was missing was three days in the belly of a whale.

Another pencil broke. She picked up the third.

Another obstacle, another delay, but she could find her way through this. She was after life experience, exposure to culture, and discovering inspiration. Trading the rugged mountains of Arkansas for the majestic Rockies should be enough to get her out of her rut. And if the mountains didn't do it, then all the hardships she'd endured thus far should.

Three weeks to paint something so she could submit it to the curator in Denver. All of her bags were gone, as well as her money and her paints. She was completely at Jack's mercy. She'd been saved by the Indians and kidnapped by the cavalry. That wasn't how it was supposed to happen. And who would save her now?

Hattie held the sketch out at arm's length. The mountains weren't well defined, probably because she hadn't made it to Colorado to see them yet, but the storm clouds felt real. Heavy, wet, and ready to roar off the paper. Her critic's eye approved. Experience more of life to improve her painting? It looked like she'd already benefited, but she was running out of time.

CHAPTER TEN

Walking into the adjutant's office felt like climbing into a lifeboat after nearly drowning. Here was order and reason and duty and progress. Here, between the cabinets of the major's reports and letters, were issues that Jack was equipped to deal with. Regulations and procedures that ordered his days and gave him guidance on what was expected of him. For nearly any question that might arise, he could find a regulation to answer it. On matters not already prescribed, his major would take the responsibility for the decision.

But his marriage decision couldn't be left up to the major.

Their discussion that morning hadn't gone well. When Jack had requested a transfer, Major Adams had reminded him that breaking oaths made before the tribe could result in his dismissal. But Major Adams was also his friend, and even he couldn't be so legalistic not to sympathize with Jack's dilemma. Since the major and Louisa were leaving for their honeymoon, he'd said he would post the request, but he wanted Jack to remain at the fort until he returned. And remaining at the fort meant pretending to honor the Arapaho's ceremony.

Jack tapped his pen against the inkwell and watched the ripples in the dark liquid. This intersection of his military duty and his love life — or potential love life — was a disaster, and there was nothing in the rule books that could simplify the matter at all. He knew how he could correct the situation, but it would cost him. Worse, it would cost the tribe. Without his intervention, the Darlington school would fail. But he couldn't ask Hattie to make that sacrifice for a people she knew nothing about. His shoulders felt heavy with what he was going to promise, but he had no choice. His only hope was that he wouldn't lose his position in the cavalry entirely.

"Lieutenant Hennessey." Sergeant Byrd's glossy black mane appeared in the doorway. "Mr. Clark is here to see you."

Jack didn't have to respond. Everyone knew not to keep Ben Clark waiting. The scout had a long and distinguished career, spoke more languages than Jack could name, and was a fixture at the fort with his Cheyenne wife and their seven children. If Ben bothered coming in to tell you something, you'd better listen.

Ben walked through the doorway in his knee-high slouch boots, his slouch hat, and a mustache and goatee that slouched all the way to his chest. As rumpled as his clothes were, his eyes were just that sharp. He pulled off his gauntlets and dropped them on his lap.

"I heard those Arapaho pulled one over on you," he said.

Jack felt like a schoolboy in front of the wise old scout. "I wish you had been there. Then I wouldn't be in this mess."

"Horsefeathers. Marriage makes a good man better. 'Course, it makes a bad man worse, so now the burden is on you to prove what kind of man you are."

Everyone expected Jack to live up to his vows, when he hadn't realized that he'd made any.

Sensing his helplessness, Ben mercifully changed the subject.

"I came because I heard a nugget that I thought you'd be interested in. The Cheyenne have bedeviled some poor wayfarer. Shot his horse full of lead and nicked him a time or two for fun."

Jack looked up from his inkwell. Here was something he might be able to fix. "Do they have him?"

"They claim he got away. Last they saw, he was limping east off the reservation."

"I would've heard if he'd reached Darlington," Jack said. "I'll send out a party to find him." He called for Sergeant Byrd and passed word along. Ben waited as orders and questions flew above his gray head. Satisfied that the search would be started immediately, Jack returned to the question at hand. "What do you make of it?" he asked. "Why would Cheyenne Dog Soldiers shoot him up and then let him go? We both know the Cheyenne. That's not their usual dance."

"They have incentive to behave," Ben replied. "They and the Arapaho have a big payment due them from the government. The Dog Soldiers attacked, but cooler heads called them off. They reckoned it was better not to do anything to jeopardize the payment."

The payment that had been stolen when Hattie's stagecoach was attacked. Jack scratched his ear. "You know about that payment, don't you? It's gone."

Ben's eye twitched. "With the stagecoach

robbery? I was afeared of that."

"What will the Cheyenne do when they find out the money isn't coming?"

Ben groaned as he got to his feet. "You don't want to know. Why don't you wire Washington for more funds? Tell them it's a matter of life and death."

And a matter of jeopardizing the future of the tribe. The relationships were already strained enough. One more promise broken by the United States, a few more students returning home, and the schools would close . . . along with a door of opportunity. Jack had to find the money, and it might be that the only witness to the crime could help.

"Couldn't I ride on the outside? I don't mind, really." Hattie twisted a handful of her skirt as she tried to keep the panic out of her voice.

Louisa bit her lip and glanced at the stack of trunks on her porch. "I'm afraid with the four of us and all our luggage, the coach is already full, even the top."

"I'll make room," Hattie replied. "Or I'll sit with the driver. If this is the only coach for two days, I don't have a choice."

"But we're going to Tahlequah. That's the opposite direction from Denver, dear. I don't understand how it's going to help — oh, here comes Lieutenant Hennessey. Maybe he can explain." Louisa's smile spread with relief as she spotted Jack. "Lieutenant Hennessey, won't you join us?"

Hattie's shoulders slumped. She'd been caught. She didn't even bother turning around as his boots echoed on the wooden porch.

"Good morning, Mrs. Adams. Can I help you?"

"There's some confusion about the stagecoach schedule. I was just explaining to your wife —"

"Thank you," Jack interrupted. "Surely you're busy with your plans. I'll be glad to answer her questions." He tipped his hat. With an apologetic shrug, Louisa shut the door, leaving Hattie with no ally in this battle.

Jack nudged Hattie with his elbow. "Please take my arm. I think a stroll might be the best thing to clear the air."

It was only because he seemed as agitated as she was that she agreed to accompany him. He directed her to the gravel road that ran along Officers' Row and began a slow walk to his house next door.

"Major Adams was not as helpful as I'd hoped." He walked stiffly, his arm flexed beneath her fingers. "He is adamant that the ceremony is binding and must be respected on the reservation."

"If adamant means what I think it means, then I'm adamant that the army can't force women to marry against their will," Hattie said.

"You understand the word perfectly," Jack said, "but I promised you a solution, and I hope I've found one. Major Adams has agreed to assign me to another unit. He's requesting my transfer today before he leaves. Once I'm officially moved away from the Cheyenne and Arapaho tribes, then I'm free to continue life as a bachelor. You would be free to go on with your life. Both of us could pretend that this never happened."

Hattie slowed. For the first time since the attack, she felt like she could see the fulfillment of her journey. "That's it, then. Problem solved. We can end this charade —"

"Not quite. For this to work, I need your cooperation for a bit longer." Jack nodded to a small band of troopers riding out with their supplies, but his eyes remained tight.

"Cooperation in what?" she asked as they passed.

"In pretending that you're my wife. I'm in

133

command until Major Adams returns from his honeymoon. While we're here, we must uphold our roles of a happily married man and wife — at least in public. Let the Indians see that we honor their ceremony. If you'll do that, I promise you'll be free and on your way when Major Adams returns and I'm reassigned. In fact, I'll even accompany you to Denver and see that you have the funds you lost so your plans won't be interrupted."

Pretend? Hattie didn't like the sound of that. "And if I don't accept this offer?"

Jack turned to face her. "Once you give a report of the attack, I can't stop you from leaving. Wire your parents for more money, buy some clothes, some paints, get on another stagecoach, and take out across Indian Territory on your own again. Chief Right Hand and the tribe will wonder why my wife left me, but after keeping you for a few days, they understand how hard you are to control." He gave her a weak smile.

Hattie's gaze traveled past the barracks, past the stables to the endless prairie beyond — the land of her nightmares. She couldn't close her eyes without being overwhelmed by terror. Perhaps she'd recover after another night of safety. Perhaps she'd feel braver once she had a few days of rest. But as she considered the daunting journey ahead of her, leaving alone didn't have the same allure. Having Jack's company on the trip would make all the difference.

"If I agree to your bargain, I only have to pretend in public, right?" she asked.

"That's right. No pretending at home." They'd reached the house. Jack escorted her up the steps of the porch and opened the door.

Hattie paused in the doorway. "No more good-night kisses?"

His eyes flashed at the mention, but he recovered nicely. "I'm willing to break with the fort's tradition if you are."

"Fort's tradition?" Hattie raised an eyebrow. "I didn't believe it the first time you said it, and I surely don't now. You're acting so smart, Jack, but I caught you this time."

"Traditions have to start somewhere," he said. "And if anyone ever asks you about your time at Fort Reno, tell them that you worked as a housekeeper on the post." He looked around at the messy parlor. "How seriously you want to take that role is up to you."

"I thought I had it bad in Van Buren," she said. "What about the report? Don't I have to get that done before I can go?"

"The longer we wait, the more chance

there is that you'll forget something."

As if the memory would fade. She couldn't close her eyes at night without hearing the gunshots and reliving the terror of being left alone and feeling hunted. "Will I be under oath?" she asked.

"You won't be sworn in, but you should tell the truth."

"What if I'm asked about my husband? Then what do I say?"

Jack rolled his eyes. "Excuse me while I call for my assistant."

She must have nodded, because Jack went to the front door and called out an order. Before Hattie knew what was happening, he had her arranged in a chair in his office and was sitting next to her. A man entered, introduced himself as Sergeant O'Hare, and sat behind Jack's desk with a pad of paper. The cold had blended his freckles and his rosy cheeks into a swirl of red. Such details kept her excited for the day she could paint again.

"Nice to meet you," Sergeant O'Hare said. "I'm much distraught over your treatment here in the nations. I want you to know that me and the boys are going to find that man who affronted you, and when we do, we're going to take him by the —"

"Thank you, Sergeant," Jack interrupted.

"Getting her testimony will aid in our efforts."

"Yes, and congratulations, as well," the sergeant said. "We hope you enjoy the fort, Mrs. Hennessey."

Hattie paused at the use of the name, but with a glance at Jack, she drew in a slow, deep breath and tried to remember their bargain.

"Thank you, Sergeant O'Hare. I'm sure it's a lovely place when the weather is more cooperative."

"Well, those days are as rare as hen's teeth, but you keep up that wistful thinking."

"Let's not waste Mrs. Hennessey's time," Jack said. "Are you ready to commence?"

Sergeant O'Hare nodded. "But it does feel strange taking notes for you. You're the journalist around here."

"The interview might stand up better in court if conducted by someone other than Mrs. Hennessey's husband," Jack said.

"Court?" Hattie turned in her chair. "I won't have to testify in court, will I?"

"Very likely. Consider your words carefully." Jack leaned over the arm of his chair. "Now, tell Sergeant O'Hare about your journey. Who was traveling with you?"

"Sir, I thought I was doing the interviewing," O'Hare said. "Mrs. Hennessey, please describe the people traveling with you during this journey."

"Agent Gibson," she said. "He had a large, heavy traveling case that he kept at his side. Maybe he was sick, but he seemed to be melancholy on the journey."

"That wasn't unusual for him," Jack said. "But he didn't seem nervous?"

O'Hare frowned at his superior. "He didn't seem nervous?" he repeated.

Hattie shook her head. "Only concerned about his traveling case. And then there was Mr. Sloane. He got on in Fort Smith, same as me. He was a very handsome man, with a beguiling smile."

Jack cleared his throat. O'Hare dropped his gaze to his paper, but his pencil had stopped moving.

Hattie rolled her eyes. "He looked mighty fine, but he was a pretentious bore. Always checking his big gold watch and lifting the curtain, which let in the cold. He certainly put on airs for a working man."

Was it her imagination, or was Jack breathing easier? "And the driver?" he said.

"I never caught his name," she replied.

"What were you doing when you first heard or saw the outlaw?" O'Hare asked.

Hattie folded her hands and tried to be as

objective as her colorful imagination would allow. "I was down in a gully when I heard a horse approaching."

"Where was everyone else?" O'Hare asked.

"In the stagecoach."

"And you were the only one outside? Why?" His florid face scrunched in confusion.

Hattie wanted to hide. "I just needed a breath of fresh air."

O'Hare laughed. "That's all we've got here is fresh air."

"You don't seem the type to lollygag," Jack said. "Getting to Colorado was important to you, so why delay?"

"Colorado?" O'Hare's forehead wrinkled. "I thought she was coming here to get hitched to you. Why was your fiancée going to Colorado without even stopping by for a howdy?"

Hattie arched an eyebrow. "You should've let him do the interviewing."

Jack leaned back in his chair and motioned for the sergeant to continue.

"I got out of the stagecoach because of nature," Hattie said. "I think that's as specific as I need to be."

"That won't answer in a court of law —"

"O'Hare," Jack barked. "Move on to the

next question."

"Alrighty, then. You were down in the gully, and then what happened?"

Hattie closed her eyes to blot out the cozy office and the two men in blue. "I heard shots. I don't know who shot first. I looked over the edge of the gully, and the driver told me to get down. I ducked. The two men in the stage, Agent Gibson and Mr. Sloane, both had their guns drawn. They were shooting out the windows at a man who was riding up behind the stagecoach. Agent Gibson had opened the door of the stage and was using it as a shield. Then the horses took off, and the coach was just beginning to roll away. The driver was urging the horses forward, but then he was hit and fell out of his seat. He didn't catch himself when he fell, so when he hit the ground . . ." She dug her fingernails into her palm.

Funny how she could tell it now, and it seemed distant, like she was repeating someone else's story. But Hattie knew that when night fell and she heard the Indian drums again, it would come back with startling clarity.

"What about the outlaw? Could you describe him?" O'Hare asked.

She tried to turn her mind's eye toward him, but every time she directed herself that way, she wanted to duck. "I yelled to disrupt him, but when he turned, I couldn't let him see me," she said. "I can't let him see me. If he sees me, then he'll come over and —"

Jack took her hand. The gesture was unexpected, but appreciated.

"He didn't get me," she said at last, fighting the tightness in her chest. "I'm safe now."

"Was he white? Indian? Thin? Thick?" Sergeant O'Hare asked.

Drawing up the memory of his face made her stomach churn. "I don't know. I don't have the words." She looked to Jack, as if her eloquent friend could help, but he had no comment.

"How long did you wait before the Arapaho found you?" O'Hare asked.

Hattie's hand trembled. Jack renewed his warm grasp. "I think we have enough for now, Sergeant," he said.

Hattie could only sit mute as they discussed getting their information to the marshals. She was so confused. She was frustrated by the position Jack had put her in, but when faced with the reality of her situation, she knew that without him, she was in danger of losing her sanity. As someone who prized her independence, it was a bitter pill to swallow.

"If that's all" — Sergeant O'Hare gathered his paper and stood — "thank you, Mrs. Hennessey. Lieutenant, I'll send word back to the marshals and see if they can piece together any more information."

"What about my belongings?" Hattie asked. "Were they recovered?"

"We haven't found the stagecoach yet, but if you'd like to make a list, it'd help us identify them if something does show up," Jack said. "Did you lose anything of value?"

Anything of value? That trunk contained her whole life. "No. Just my clothes, my money, my sketchbook, my oils and water-colors. Nothing that couldn't be replaced." She ducked her head. *Nothing except my freedom.*

CHAPTER ELEVEN

It was her second day as his wife — or at least the second day since she'd found out that she was married — and Hattie and Jack were at an impasse. He stood at the front door, decked in his full uniform with a wagon waiting behind him. The cold wind gusted between them and snapped her dreary skirt around her legs.

"I can't go to town wearing only one earring." Hattie's teeth would have chattered had she not clenched them. "I'm not accustomed to appearing in public half dressed."

The set of his jaw could only be called stubborn. "Then don't wear any earrings. Makes no matter to me."

"Why don't you give it back? You know I never meant for you to keep it."

"I'm keeping it." When had Jack grown so determined?

"Why?" Hattie asked.

He opened his mouth. Then, with a narrowing of his eyes, he looked away.

Hattie could have asked Mrs. Adams for the loan of some earrings before she and Major Adams had left on their honeymoon, but she was standing on principle. She'd given him back his coat. It was only fair that he return her jewelry.

"Come on, Hattie," he said. "Darlington is a tiny town full of Indian students and Mennonite missionaries. No one will even notice what you're wearing."

Which was precisely her objection. Hattie had always been able to convince her parents to keep her dressed in the latest fashions. Her darling traveling gown had been ruined by the night in the gully. Her other clothes were in the possession of a bloodthirsty murderer, and now her pretend husband was hoarding her jewelry.

"If you don't want to go, I could pick out some clothes for you, I reckon," said Jack.

"You know a lot of things about a lot of things, but I doubt women's clothing is your fermata."

"Forte," he corrected. "C'mon, you look beautiful in faded black. I'll ask around if they have some more. Or maybe buckskin. I know how you admire the Arapaho fashions." His mouth twitched. If he wasn't so

144

infuriating, Jack would be a decent-looking man.

Hattie closed her eyes. How long was she stuck here? "I'll get my coat." Although the battered garment looked even worse than wearing one earring.

Jack moved to the wagon while Hattie pulled the coat over her too-loose blouse. Her eyes darted over the cluttered entryway and parlor as she thought about what items she needed to replace. Besides clothing, she needed food, since she wouldn't be eating in the officers' mess with Jack, and she insisted on replacing her paints and canvases. She hadn't held a brush since leaving home, and she had a painting to paint, although what she could find to inspire her here was beyond her imagination.

She joined Jack outside, prepared for the trip. Providing her with food and clothing was the least he could do, since he was withholding things like freedom and liberty. Her shoulders tightened as they left Fort Reno behind. She would master this fear that lurked at the corners of her mind, waiting for an unexpected moment to attack. Nights were the worst. She'd stayed in her room the night before, but comfort and sleep had eluded her. Would having Jack's coat in her arms have made a difference? She was too embarrassed to ask. Even now in full daylight, she couldn't hide from the feeling that she was being hunted.

"Darlington is just ahead," Jack said. "The two miles between the fort and the agency are the safest two miles on the reservation."

Why did he have to notice her distress? Hattie slipped her gloved hands into her coat pockets. "Thank you for that information. You always were a walking almanac."

Jack stared at her, dead even. Then, as if deciding not to say what was on the tip of his tongue, he turned back to watch the horses. Had she offended him? Maybe riding in silence was the best option. Though he was better company than Agent Gibson and Mr. Sloane had been — one of them studiously ignoring her as if her mere presence was offensive while the other taunted her with mocking chivalry. They were both dead now, unable to redeem themselves. Hattie would rather not think of them at all. She'd rather forget everything that had happened since that blustery day, but the new Jack was hard to ignore. Especially since he kept glancing her way.

"We need to get our story straight," he said. "I can't have you going to town and telling everyone how I ruined your life."

"You didn't ruin it. You only messed it up

146

temporarily."

"And as generous as that sounds, maybe you can prevent yourself from saying it."

"I want to help," she said, "but exactly what is it that you're asking me to do?"

Jack drew in a long breath before answering. "First off, don't faint when I introduce you as Mrs. Hennessey. Try to act like a new bride might, happy to spend time with your husband. I've seen you pour on the charm. I know exactly how you act when you want to impress someone. Act like that, and everyone will be too enchanted to bother asking about our engagement."

Hattie felt at a disadvantage. Jack seemed to know everything about her, while she was constantly surprised by him. While Jack was nothing to sneeze at now, she couldn't shake the image of the bookish adolescent who always seemed ready with a helpful, unsolicited suggestion. If people back home heard about their union without knowing the real story, how they'd laugh.

"I can promise you silence," she said. "That's as far as I'm willing to go."

"Silence? I should be used to that from you." He raised an eyebrow. "Never did have much to say when I was around."

"Because I didn't enjoy my grammar being corrected. Other boys acted delighted with everything I said. Tommy Dupree never told me that my subject and vowel weren't in agreement."

"Subject and verb. So why didn't you marry Tommy Dupree?"

She snorted. The thought was ridiculous. Tommy Dupree wasn't the least bit interesting now that he'd grown up. Or maybe since she'd grown up. Hattie shook her head. "He asked. I declined. Nothing further to report. If you'll remember, I took this journey to win my freedom. I never thought that I'd end up . . ." She paused to look at her companion. Jack shot her a sideways glance. "Jack, what exactly did you tell the Indians to do for that ceremony?"

"I made a mistake. My Arapaho isn't as good as it should be. Simple misunderstanding."

"Do you have any idea how many times you told me that I had made a mistake on my papers, how many times you pointed out that I wasn't quite as clever as you?"

"I was trying to help you with your homework. I was looking for an excuse to talk to you. I wasn't trying to make you feel bad."

"By sneaking looks at my homework so you could discover my inadequacies? Not exactly a charming trait, Jack. If you think I want to spend the rest of my life married to the boy who stopped my speech on David Livingstone to correct me, then you're wrong. Wrong. You didn't pass this test."

"You claimed Livingstone was English. He wasn't! He was Scottish! How could you make that mistake?"

Hattie almost laughed at his indignation. "Another reason why we can't be married. We'd make each other miserable." He looked so crestfallen, she felt guilty. She dipped her head and smiled at him from the corner of her eyes. "You never answered my question about the Arapaho banquet. Hadn't you ever seen that ceremony before?"

"You look cold." He buttoned the top button of his coat to keep out the prying wind. "We should've brought you a blanket. Hopefully we can find a new coat that fits you."

"Get one that is made for traveling, and work on that story of yours. You owe it to me."

The white tepees along the river didn't interest Hattie in the least. She'd seen a camp up close, and now they only reminded her of her mislaid plans. She looked to the heavens and all but cried, *Why me?* But then another thought hit her. She could have been one of the bodies left on the cold ground. She could have been found by men who were not as chivalrous as the Arapaho. She could have been in the same situation with another man who wasn't Jack.

New perspectives. That was what she was supposed to learn from this adventure. Maybe when it was all said and done, God would bring something positive out of this. But it was too late for Agent Gibson, Mr. Sloane, and their driver, whom she'd nearly forgotten about when faced with the inconvenience of Jack's proposed delay. Could it be that the gallery owners were right? Could it be that Hattie was shallow and selfish and didn't know how to sympathize with people?

It was an unsettling thought.

And what about Jack? How was he affected? She hadn't spent much time thinking about what his life had been like before he'd encountered her, or what would happen to him after she left. Hattie shot him another glance. He'd saved her life and, the earring notwithstanding, had provided for her needs ever since. It wouldn't hurt to show him some understanding. Besides, he'd promised to help her get to Denver, which was as generous of him as it was necessary for her.

"What are you going to do, Lieutenant Hennessey?" she asked. "If I'm lucky, I'll be able to hide this humiliating episode from my acquaintances, but what about you? How are you going to explain it to your fellow soldiers when I leave?"

"I haven't figured that out yet. I'm hoping Major Adams will reverse his decision. If not, then I'll have to leave Indian Territory, as well." His eyes tightened. Was there some danger ahead? But then he looked away. "As far as most of them will know, my lovely bride and I were reassigned to live out our marital bliss at another location."

"But won't they find out sooner or later? I mean, it's not like you won't cross their paths someday. It'd probably be best if we told everyone at Fort Reno exactly what happened. Then they won't think ill of me when I have to leave."

"That would be counterproductive. If our objective is to show the Arapaho that we're honoring their marriage ceremony, then we have to be consistent. Strong marriages have been built on shakier foundations."

"But not when both parties opposed the union."

He sighed. "By the rules of the Arapaho, in whose reservation we are abiding, we are man and wife. There's no further explanation needed for anyone — American or Indian."

Hattie disagreed. She wanted to explain to everyone that the man at her side, however gallant, was not her choice. That he was the result of a series of unmanageable circumstances, and she couldn't be held responsible.

His gaze saw right through her. "Hattie, please just follow my lead," he said. "These people have been moved from their homeland, their movements are restricted, they are surrounded by a society that has done them harm, and now they are being told that their best hope for the future is to embrace the changes and adapt. Can you imagine?"

"Taken from their home, their travel restricted, and told to embrace the changes? Yes, I think I can imagine."

Jack's begrudging smile was almost attractive. "While you have a good point, mine is equally true. For years, the Arapaho and Cheyenne have claimed that sending their children to school was a hardship that I couldn't understand. They blamed it on me not being a father. Now, whether they truly misunderstood or if they decided to fulfill my lack, the fact that a lieutenant in the U.S. Cavalry was married by Chief Right Hand is being told in every village. It means something to them. We have to keep up appearances."

"But only in public?"

"Only when we're in public. Back at the house, you are free to completely ignore me."

"Can I rail at you, berate you, and order you about?"

"Certainly, but I thought you *didn't* want to pretend that we were married."

Hattie had to smile. "Your behavior could help me get into my role."

"It's about time I turn ornery. The nice guy never gets the girl."

He had her now, she thought, and he didn't know what to do with her.

They crossed a river on a metal bridge. Ice frosted the banks white, but the water flowed sluggishly down the middle. Once on the other side of the river, Hattie strained her eyes to make out the strange shapes that littered the ground. Like bizarre sculptures, the white prongs emerged off the flat plain.

"What are those?" She thought about pointing, but they were scattered everywhere. Besides, it was too cold to pull her hand out into the wind.

"Bones. On distribution day, every Indian family gets a steer from the agency. They chase them out of town and butcher them here."

The shapes were beginning to make sense now. Piles of bones? Not exactly the warm welcome she'd hoped to meet outside the nearest town. Then she saw dark forms darting among the piles of bones. They were stray dogs fighting over a recent kill. She thought of her beloved Saint Bernard, Nero, who was furry, patient, and gentle. How could these rangy, mangy animals be the same species?

"Those are the ugliest, meanest dogs I've ever seen." Their savage, lean bodies gave her chills. Did this wild spirit lurk in every canine pet? It was worth exploring on canvas. Maybe her sweet Nero hid a vicious temperament, too. She was too quick to judge on appearances.

"The dogs have to be mean if they want to survive," Jack said. "At night the wolves come out, and the dogs seem like puppies."

"You're teasing me."

He smiled as he held her gaze. "I'm not teasing, but don't worry. We'll be safely home before nightfall."

Safely home? His home, not hers.

The town grew as they approached. From a distance, she'd seen two hulking buildings, but as they got closer, the buildings seemed to expand. They were three stories tall and as long as ten wagons. She hadn't expected to see anything that massive one hundred miles from the nearest railroad.

"Those are the commissary warehouses. They are nearly eight thousand square feet per story. They hold the supplies that are distributed to the families, as well as the supplies for the Cheyenne and Arapaho school."

"Is that the school that the boy who came with us will attend?"

"It is. And we'll stop in to see how he's doing. The school is my favorite place on the reservation."

"That's no surprise," she said. "I'm shocked you didn't decide to be a professor at a university."

Jack rolled his eyes. "Too predictable. I did a thorough study of my character and determined that I had some underdeveloped areas. The cavalry seemed like a good solution."

Oh yes. Hattie truly appreciated the areas Jack had developed since she'd seen him last.

"It's good you figured that out for yourself. I had complete strangers identify my deficiencies," she said. "The galleries I submitted my work to told me that my paintings lacked depth. That I needed to experience more of life to be able to paint with true emotion."

"They said that to you?" Jack whistled. "That's a low-down thing to say."

"Actually, it was even worse. I think the words *immature* and *shallow* were uttered." She shrugged, not sure why she was telling Jack in the first place. "But if it's true, then I needed to hear it. How can my painting improve if I don't know what's wrong?"

The approval in his eyes anchored her. "Sounds like you're serious about painting."

"That's what I've been saying." Maybe he was finally hearing her.

They came into the town of Darlington, the headquarters of the Cheyenne and Arapaho Agency. Jack pointed out the neat houses with their empty winter gardens, telling her that most of them were owned by the government employees who worked at the commissary and the agency. Besides them, the town was heavily populated by the Mennonite missionaries who assisted with the education of the tribes. Since white outsiders weren't allowed to own property in Indian Territory, everyone had to have permission from the government or the tribe to be there.

A woman walked with her hand against the crown of her head, holding on to her hat as she made her way down the red dirt road to an office. Two Indian men exited a business and walked into what appeared to be a hotel. Another man stood at the hitching post and checked his horse's shoes. Jack didn't recognize him and quickly asked Hattie if he looked like the killer. She had to assure him that he didn't before they could continue to the general store.

The storefront shone bravely with red trim and green lettering, a welcome splash of color in the colorless landscape and the perfect tone for the Christmas season. The buildings were so new that had her nose not been frozen, Hattie could have probably smelled the fresh paint. Jack parked the wagon near the hitching post and set the brake.

"Are you ready for your first appearance, Mrs. Hennessey?" His eyes sparkled as if he might have found the nerve to enjoy their predicament.

"I'm not sure I can even spell *Hennessey.*"

"True. I remember you getting whupped in the early rounds of the spelling bee, but happily, spelling skills are not required."

She considered telling him that the only requirement necessary for a wife of his was to be too scared to ask questions during an Arapaho ceremony.

He offered her his hand. She took it, not

able to stop thinking about how warm she would have been under his wool cape.

"Remind me again, what is my reward for participating in this maneuver?" she asked as she disembarked.

"Clean clothes, hot meals, and a roof over your head. Otherwise, I suppose you could set out for Colorado on foot."

"But you won't let me."

He smiled as he tucked her hand in the crook of his arm. "Correct. The best place for you right now is by my side."

"Congratulations, Lieutenant and Mrs. Hennessey." A slight, balding man appeared in the open door of an office across the street and started toward them. "The chief told me that you'd finally taken his advice."

Jack covered her hand with his own, easing her along the walkway. "Yes, sir. Chief Right Hand is quite pleased with our news." Then, remembering his manners, he gestured to the man. "Hattie, dear, this is Agent Lee. He's responsible for the well-being of the tribes as well as working in conjunction with the missionaries and the school."

"Nice to meet you," Hattie said. How far would she have to go to convince people of this marriage? It wasn't as if married couples had to walk around intertwined. Not everyone was demonstrative in public.

Evidently Agent Lee was. He leaned forward to kiss her on the cheek. "A bride is a woman at the height of her beauty. I can always spot one immediately from the radiant glow she emits."

Not knowing what to say, Hattie just forced a gritty smile.

"Well, you must have a wonderful day planned, so I don't want to interrupt you. See you later." Agent Lee tipped his hat as he ambled away. Then, turning suddenly, he said, "And congratulations on getting the chief's nephew to come to the school. If we don't get more students, it might have to close its doors."

"That's why we're doing this," Jack whispered as the agent moved out of earshot. "Right now the families are deciding if they want to send their kids, but soon they won't have a choice."

"What will happen if they close the school?" Hattie asked.

"Before they opened the school here, Indian students had to apply for limited spots at the Carlisle Indian Industrial School in Pennsylvania. It's far away from their families and a very difficult transition for them to make. That's why we can't let the Darlington school close. That's why Chief Right Hand's nephew needs to have a good experience there." He held the door of the general store open for her. "And now your work begins. What all do you require to make your lot bearable?"

"I doubt this mercantile has any Rocky Mountains available for purchase."

"Yes, but you have to purchase them one rock at a time and assemble them yourself."

She tried not to smile as she headed first to the counter.

"Excuse me," she said to the storekeeper. He wiped his massive hands on his apron and leaned in for her request. "Do you have any paints?"

"Paint? Why, sure. I have whitewash and blacking. Then I have half a can of the green I did my lettering in and a tad of red left."

"I'm looking for artist's paints — water-colors and oils. And canvases."

"I have some pastels and a few canvases on frames for my artistically inclined cus-tomers, but no paints. I could order some. They'd be in by the end of January."

"That'd be too late. I'll be gone by then."

"Gone?" The storekeeper's eyes darted to Jack. "Where y'all going?"

Jack stepped up to the counter. "We'll take the canvases. And why don't you go on and order those paints? Mrs. Hennessey will be grateful whenever they come in."

Hattie bit her lip. She'd promised to help him, and here she was messing up again. She pawed through the clothing they had for sale to keep herself from making another mistake. Thankfully, there were some ready-to-wear blouses and skirts, and Louisa had promised that Hattie could borrow her sewing machine while she was away to alter what she found. "This could get expensive," Hattie said. "I need hats, gloves, shoes — everything must be replaced."

"My money has been accumulating at an indecent rate, so I appreciate your help distributing it." Jack picked up a fan and fluttered it in front of his face. "Did Agent Lee say that you are at the height of your beauty?" He tsked. "I guess it's all downhill from here."

Hattie groaned. "I've been afraid to look in a mirror ever since you found me. I can guarantee I've paid a toll for my adventures."

Jack lowered the fan. His dark eyes took on a serious cast. "Anytime you want to know how you look, you can ask me."

Hattie's heart skipped a beat. She yanked the fan from his hand and dropped it on the counter. She hadn't expected timid Jack to play his role with such flair. He'd better be careful acting like that. You never knew when someone might get confused and think he meant it for real.

Half an hour later, she was still shopping. Jack carried a buckskin coat through the stacked canned goods to where Hattie was riffling through some lacy fabrics. "I'm not sure it's a fashionable cut," he said, "but the leather will keep you warm." He held it out by the shoulders. "Do you want to try it on?"

She looked doubtful, but Hattie was a practical sort. She shrugged out of her ragged coat and slid her arms into the buckskin. Jack pulled it up on her shoulders, and when he let go, the weight of it took a full inch off her height.

"It's heavy," she said. "Are you sure they took the deer out of it?"

He began to button the coat at her neck, and she slapped his hand. Jack stepped back in surprise. "What?" he asked. He was just doing what needed to be done. "We have to see if it fits."

"I can dress myself, thank you." She turned her back to him and tested the buttons.

Jack's face warmed. He hadn't meant it as an intimate gesture, but he was in an impossible situation. Ignore her, and he was a churl. Be helpful, and he got his hand slapped. He looked about the store, but no one else seemed to have noticed the embarrassing moment for the newlywed groom. He leaned against the counter, his hand crushing a lacy pile of softness.

"What are you doing now?" She bustled to the table, the thick buckskin coat standing stiff and foreboding around her. "Don't touch my things." Her hand swept along the counter as he jumped out of the way. She gathered the white items and hid them inside the coat, all the while pinning him with suspicion.

"I didn't know you were buying those types of things," he said. The blood was rushing to his face.

"*All* of my luggage is gone."

"I understand." He cleared his throat. "Excuse me." White lacy things both terrified and intrigued him.

Jack moseyed to the canned goods and began to set aside a hearty pile. Until now, he'd always eaten in the mess hall with his men, but he could hardly leave Hattie to fend for herself. Besides, she might turn out to be a better cook than Colonel Nothem. Jack wouldn't mind putting some meat on his bones to stave off the winter cold.

While he set aside foodstuffs, he pondered

the disclosure Hattie had made on the way here. It was impossible to fathom a man looking Hattie in the face and telling her that she was immature or shallow, or lacking in any way. The only flaw he'd ever noticed had been her failure to admire him. Then again, he'd been young when he'd decided to win her. Perhaps that goal could have used some critical reevaluation in the last decade or so.

An Indian couple entered the store. It was Red Cloud and his wife, Fawn Who Stays, there to buy the strong needles that she needed for the beadwork on her leather goods. Jack tipped his hat to the lady. She stared at him, unblinking, and spoke words that with effort he understood.

"That's your wife?"

Jack looked over his shoulder at Hattie, who was smelling a bar of soap. Red Cloud and Fawn Who Stays were from a village farther from the agency than the one Hattie had been in, yet even they knew of the wedding ceremony. "Yes, ma'am, that's my wife."

"What is her name?" Red Cloud asked.

"Hattie Walker. Formerly Hattie Walker. Hattie Hennessey now." Jack pronounced the syllables slowly, knowing how hard it was to catch foreign words the first time.

Fawn Who Stays's eyes sparkled. "That's better than her Arapaho name."

Jack drew in a long breath. He didn't want to know, but it would be rude not to ask. "Which is?"

She beamed. "One Who Spills Stew in Anger."

"That's an awfully long name, isn't it?" They might have fooled him with the wedding, but he didn't believe this.

Fawn Who Stays shrugged and returned to digging through the sewing notions.

"We sent Sweet Water to the Christian school," Red Cloud said. "Fawn Who Stays doesn't know how she'll manage without her oldest daughter to help with the younger children, but we want her to learn the new ways."

Finally, something was going right for Jack. "Someday she'll thank you," he said. "At least I hope so."

Red Cloud tested the sharpness of an ice pick on his palm. "Everyone says they know what is best for us, but you . . . you learned who we were before telling us what path to take. We trust you will know our children, too. You will know who they can be in the new world because you know who they were in the old world."

But Jack wouldn't be here to help them

anymore — not if Hattie was going free. He watched the man and his wife walk away, and Hattie was watching him.

"Was that Arapaho you were speaking?" she said. "Funny how you understand it now, but three days ago at the ceremony —"

"Have you got everything you need?" Jack asked. "Then let's go to the school."

CHAPTER TWELVE

They stopped the wagon at the imposing school. Hattie could hear children's voices from the field behind the building. It brought back memories of her own school days, when she was insecure, looking for approval from anyone who would assure her.

Now she knew better than to rely on a man for her worth. She had her art to prove her accomplishments, but that door would close if she didn't get a painting into the exhibit. Jack might insist on her staying for a while, but she had to be painting. She was running out of time.

Jack tossed the reins over the brake handle and turned to look at her. "These children can be rambunctious. Just last May, one of the older boys pulled a knife on Superintendent Seger, but he was brought to the guardhouse immediately. They aren't going to try to stab you — I don't think — so try to treat them just as you would any other group of children." He offered his arm.

She hesitated, but remembering the comment about the knife, she relented and took his arm as they entered the double doors.

The high ceiling towered above them, and the black-and-white tile floor made the room feel colder than it should have, with the giant iron stove puffing out heat. Jack walked briskly to the plainly built front desk, nearly dragging Hattie behind him.

"Good morning, Mrs. Lehrman. How are you?"

Despite the woman's tightly coiled hair and somber dress, her smile was as extravagant as a Rococo painting. "Lieutenant Hennessey, how nice to see you." When she grinned, her chin melted into her thick neck, but her eyes sparkled playfully. She turned her attention to Hattie, and Hattie didn't know whether to be flattered or afraid. "I don't believe I've had the pleasure," she said. "I'm Maria Lehrman, the headmistress here at Darlington."

Hattie managed to smile. "Nice to meet you, Mrs. Lehrman. I'm Hattie" — she felt Jack tense next to her — "Hennessey," she choked out.

"Mrs. Hennessey?" Her eyes darted to Jack and back to Hattie. Hattie felt guilty for causing such joy by dishonesty. "Congratulations, Lieutenant! I'd heard a rumor, but I didn't credit it. If you've been spoken for all this time, you should've told someone. Certain teachers here have wasted many lonely hours planning how to get your attention."

Hattie took another look at the man next to her. When he had first walked into the Arapaho tepee, she'd thought him dashing. That was before she knew he was Jack. Before he accidentally married her.

Still, she couldn't be too surprised that the ladies here had taken a shine to him. The headmistress certainly wasn't.

"I can't believe you've kept this to yourself, Lieutenant Hennessey," Mrs. Lehrman said. "Was it a long engagement?"

"No, ma'am. It was quite sudden."

"I was looking for you after Major Adams's wedding, but they told me you were headed out to look for some stagecoach robbers. Was it a secret elopement?"

"You know me better than that, Mrs. Lehrman. I wouldn't mislead Major Adams."

Her eyebrow rose as she swayed back and forth. "And yet I don't feel like you are being forthcoming with your story at this minute."

Jack's neck turned pink above his blue collar. Was it wrong that Hattie was amused by his discomfort? "I beg your pardon, ma'am. Your curiosity will have to remain unfulfilled."

Hattie gripped her skirt and half turned, certain that Jack's refusal signaled an unpleasant end to a sticky conversation, but to her surprise, he didn't move.

"Not yet, dear," he said. "You'll want to hear about the Christmas plans."

Christmas? Hattie had already prepared herself for being away from home on Christmas, but she hadn't counted on celebrating it in Indian Territory.

"Christmas in Darlington is spectacular." Mrs. Lehrman gestured wide. "Most of our students have never celebrated Christmas before, and it's a joy to see their excitement as we begin to assemble the decorations and the materials for the Christmas performance. Sometimes I forget the wonder of Christmas and what it means. It's special to experience it with people who have never heard the story before."

Maybe that was something to consider. Hattie couldn't think of a time she didn't know about Christmas. She tried to imagine what kids who had never heard the story might think about God sending His Son as a baby to earth. With her parents, siblings, and cousins gathered around the tree at her grandparents' big farmhouse by the river, it seemed so traditional, but how strange it must feel to the students.

"I hope you feel safe during the celebrations," Hattie said. "But I guess you have the troopers to guard you when the children are together."

"Guard us?" Mrs. Lehrman's brow wrinkled as she looked at Jack. "Why would we need to be guarded from the children?"

Hattie pulled her arm away from Jack's. "Just something Lieutenant Hennessey said that gave me that impression."

His mouth quirked up at one corner. "Let us know if you need some help with the pageant. There's not much to do in this cold weather besides sit around the house."

"Seems like that's exactly what a newlywed would want to do," Mrs. Lehrman said.

Jack's hand slipped around Hattie to rest at her waist. The familiarity shocked her. Who did he think he was? Her husband? Before she could shrug him off, he pulled her against his side.

"I'm trying to spare my blushing bride from any embarrassment," he said.

"Nothing to be embarrassed about." Mrs. Lehrman beamed. "God ordained marriage. Nothing would please me more than knowing that you are happily wed."

"I'm happy," he said. The flash of teeth was probably supposed to be a smile. He kept the carnivorous grin as he turned to her. "Aren't you happy, dear?"

He'd said silence was all he required, so that was all he got. Hattie returned his endearments with a blank stare as she tried to comprehend why she felt so right against him.

Nonplussed, he squeezed her waist and laughed. "Capital! Then, without further ado, let's go see the children at work." Releasing her, he marched to the interior doors and held one open wide for her to pass through as he waved good-bye to Mrs. Lehrman.

For a while, the only sound down the long corridor was the clopping of their heels against the black-and-white tile floor. Finally, Jack's chuckle broke the impasse. "It's surprising how easily people believe that we're a couple. Mrs. Lehrman saw nothing unusual about us being together."

It was times like this that Hattie had a hard time remembering this was the same boy from back home. She didn't quite know how to handle this man, and it was a troubling realization.

"You lied about the knife," she said. "Mrs.

Lehrman didn't act like there was any danger at all."

"I didn't lie. A student did pull a knife on the superintendent. It was even in the *Cheyenne Transporter* newspaper. And I told you that you weren't likely to get stabbed."

"But the way you said it made me think that I'd be in danger if I didn't take your arm."

"You would be in danger. In danger of missing the opportunity to be escorted by your charming husband."

She grunted. "My husband? The last thing in the world I was looking for on this trip."

"Happiness often catches us unaware." He'd always been ready with a smart remark, but they were more effective coming from this grown man than a spindly boy.

A woman's voice could be heard ahead. Light filtered into the shaded hallway from an open door. *"R says errrr. . . . S says sssss. . . . T says tuh."* Then a chorus of children's voices dutifully repeated the information.

Hattie slowed as she approached the door. Peeking around the corner, she could see the Indian students at their desks. Although the class sounded like a primary level, there were children of all ages sitting in the rows. Boys with stern brows and freshly cut hair, girls with high cheekbones and almond-shaped eyes. Perched with the same posture that Tom Broken Arrow had on horseback, they carefully enunciated their lesson, but their quick eyes darted about as if trying to find some meaning in the nonsensical cadence.

Instead of waiting at the door, Jack strode inside. He tipped his hat at the flustered young teacher holding a yardstick and pointing at the letters on the chalkboard. She only had time to wet her lips and brush back an errant strand of blond hair before her eyes fell on Hattie. Her knuckles went white around the yardstick she was holding, but by the time Jack had closed the door behind them, she'd covered her shock and looked as sweet as a confectioner's mixing bowl.

"Why, Lieutenant Hennessey, how nice to see you today. Class, let's greet Lieutenant Hennessey." She cleared her throat. "How are you doing today, Lieutenant Hennessey?"

The students got the words right when they repeated them, and even did a fair imitation of her high-pitched, flirtatious tone. Hattie bit her lip to keep from laughing. If Jack had missed her simpering the first time, he could hardly ignore it when it was amplified by two dozen students.

"I am doing fine," he said clearly and slowly while facing the class. This time his smile was genuine. *"Koonííni'ííni?"* he asked.

"Lieutenant Hennessey." The teacher put her hand on her hip. She had an easy, natural grace. Then again, one had to be confident to take a teaching assignment in Indian Territory. "We speak English in this classroom. It's the only way they're going to learn."

Jack's smile grew as the class shouted out various answers in their native tongue, causing Hattie to wonder again exactly how much of the Arapaho language he understood. And how could he carry on a conversation and not realize that he was being married off to her?

Finally, he ducked his head and held up a hand. With some carefully spoken words from him, the class settled down. "I apologize, Miss Richert. I didn't mean to distract your class. Please continue."

Miss Richert's jaw scrunched to the side as Jack directed Hattie toward the last row of desks. Obviously, not being able to place Hattie was eating away at Miss Richert, but for some reason Jack didn't feel obligated to introduce her. Could it be that this was one of the teachers who had set her cap for Jack?

Could it be that he wanted to keep his marriage a secret from at least one person?

Hattie chewed that thought over throughout the rest of the alphabet. Maybe the marriage had thwarted Jack's plans, as well. What if he was in love with this woman? What if Hattie's appearance would ruin their chances of being together? Was he as devastated by the arrangements as she was, or was he a tiny bit hopeful? He seemed to have been surprised, but it would be helpful to know whether there was a shade of acceptance on his part.

It would also be helpful to know if her so-called husband was going to allow the spunky schoolteacher to continue her attempts to gain his attention. Even a pretend wife didn't appreciate a husband who allowed women to fawn over him.

"Very good, class," Miss Richert said. "You are making Miss Richert so proud of you. No wonder it's such a blessing to work with you children. You all are so clever."

Heads turned toward Jack in confusion, eyes questioning if they were supposed to do something. Had Miss Richert already forgotten that they didn't speak English? Jack nodded at the students, and it seemed to reassure them.

A little girl braved a wave at Hattie. She

was missing a few of her baby teeth, but her smile was prettier than anything Hattie had ever painted. Hattie wiggled a finger in her direction. The approval in Jack's eyes embarrassed her. What was he smiling at? All she'd done was wave at a child. Nothing remarkable there.

"You may be excused for recess," Miss Richert said, but no one moved. Forgetting the students glued to their chairs, she approached Jack and Hattie again.

Jack spoke a few words to the class. There was a mad scramble as the students jumped out of their chairs and raced out the door. A shrill whoop sent shivers down Hattie's spine. Jack stepped closer to her, hands clasped behind his back but giving her the security of his nearness just the same.

Even Miss Richert noticed. "So, Jack, are you pleased at the progress they've made?"

She called him *Jack,* and Hattie already guessed that he wouldn't correct her.

"You're doing a fine job with them," he said. He gave a quick salute as Tom Broken Arrow paused before him. Some words were exchanged between them, and then Tom left, looking ill at ease in his school uniform. "Where's Cold Rain?" Jack asked as he scanned the remaining students.

"She's in detention," Miss Richert said.

"She stole the blanket that was on her bed. We hope she'll confess and tell us what she did with it. Until then . . ."

Tom had stopped and was listening intently. Did he understand the conversation? He must have felt he had something to contribute, for he spoke to Jack in Arapaho again, repeating the words slowly for Jack's benefit. Jack asked another question of Tom. When the boy answered, he cut his eyes toward Miss Richert.

Jack patted him on the back and sent him with the rest of the class.

It was past time that Hattie be introduced, but Jack was clueless. In fact, he didn't seem to notice how badly Miss Richert was trying to get his attention, either. Instead he continued to greet each child by name. The longer he waited, the more this teacher fretted over Hattie's presence, and there was nothing Hattie could say to ease her anxiety.

Stiffening her spine, Hattie flashed Jack a smile. "I'm sure you and Miss Richert have a lot to talk about. Would you like me to wait in the hallway?"

His forehead wrinkled. "Why would you do that?"

Miss Richert cleared her throat. "Jack, I'm so happy to meet your . . . sister?" Her eyebrows rose with hope.

178

"This isn't my sister," he said. "This is my wife, Hattie."

"Your — what?" The end of the yardstick bounced against the ground. "What an unexpected . . . When? Who is she?"

"Mrs. Hennessey is from Van Buren. She's a childhood friend."

"You've known her all along? The whole time you've been here, and you already knew her?"

Hattie feared for Jack's safety. Miss Richert might be lean, but she looked capable of wielding the yardstick as a weapon.

Jack looked back and forth between the two women as if not sure what was happening. How could he be so naïve? Hattie decided right then and there that if Jack managed to get her out of this mess, she'd do what she could to help him with Miss Richert. Jack married to a schoolteacher? What could be more perfect?

"We won't take any more of your time," he said, "but you'll be seeing more of me in your classroom. I promised the chief I'd keep an eye on his nephew."

Jack seemed confused when Miss Richert didn't answer. Hattie pinched the sleeve of his uniform and led him out of the room. Again, they made their silent way through the corridor, Hattie looking at the man at

179

her side with more puzzlement than ever. It was no wonder that Miss Richert had her heart set on him. The way he cared about the children at the school was endearing. And then there were his looks. His deep, intelligent eyes now belonged to a strapping man, capable and rugged. But one thing remained unchanged — he couldn't figure out what a woman wanted.

It wasn't until they were in the wagon and passing the open window of the classroom that Hattie heard the sharp snap of a yardstick being broken in two.

CHAPTER THIRTEEN

"Something is wrong," Jack said. "Cold Rain shouldn't be in detention." He darted a glance at the silent woman riding next to him, nearly hidden by the buckskin coat. "Tom Broken Arrow told me that the girls all swear there's an evil spirit in their dormitory causing mischief. Cold Rain's blanket is just one of many things to have gone missing. They are also losing food from the kitchen regularly. The girls swear none of them are leaving the room."

"Why didn't you tell Miss Richert?" Hattie asked. "Wouldn't she need to know?"

"I might tell her later, but I didn't want to contradict her in front of her class. It would embarrass her."

"Just like you didn't want to introduce me? That made her uncomfortable, as well."

While Jack thought their day had gone well, Hattie seemed to be stewing over something. True, deciding what to say about his wife and what to keep hidden went against his usual candor, but he hadn't expected it to weigh so heavily on Hattie.

He shook his head. "I was busy talking to the kids. I didn't think you needed my help to speak to a teacher."

"But you should have prepared her, Jack. The poor woman obviously cares about you, and you show up with a wife. Can't you imagine how that made her feel?" Hattie took a deep breath and forced the air through her nose. "If there's anything I hate, it's breaking someone's heart."

Jack jangled the reins to speed up the horses before he made a telling remark about Hattie breaking hearts. "Miss Richert doesn't feel anything for me. She has more important matters to concern herself with."

"Oh, Jack. You are hopeless," Hattie said. "If this marriage were real, you would owe her an apology. As it is, you'll have to see what you can do for her once you're free from me."

His neck tightened. "When you leave, I leave. That's the only way."

Hattie looked him over like she was appraising him for auction. "Miss Richert doesn't know what an insufferable boy you were. You might have her fooled, so don't be surprised if she opts to go with you."

Why, oh why hadn't he sent Sergeant O'Hare to recover the missing woman from the stagecoach? Then he wouldn't be in this mess.

The trip from Darlington had never taken this long. Instead of good memories from his visit — like how well the children were progressing and how he appreciated the Mennonite missionaries and their work — Jack was questioning his own behavior. According to Hattie, Miss Richert's conduct was proof that somehow he'd misunderstood, or she'd misunderstood, or something had gone wrong.

This was why he preferred books. You just wrote down what you wanted to say, and there could be no miscommunication. Perhaps he should try that method with Hattie. Only he had tried to write her, and she'd never answered his letters.

Slowly but surely, his long-standing fascination with Hattie was changing. She was still beautiful. He couldn't look at her without his gut twisting. Her mannerisms, her voice, her deportment had only grown more graceful, yet she wasn't the perfect image he'd worshiped over the years. There were misunderstandings. She was more reserved than he'd wish, especially to his friends. She varied between strongly opinionated and indecisive. Also, she seemed more concerned with getting to Denver to paint some overrated mountains than about his career, or the Arapaho and Cheyenne, or what would happen if Jack was no longer there to reconcile the situation.

It was possible that he had a personal bias in the last instance.

Yes, he should have sent Sergeant O'Hare on the mission and stayed for Major Adams's wedding.

By the time they pulled up to his house on Officers' Row, Jack was ready to get back to his duties as Major Adams's post adjutant and forget about his women troubles. The troopers who appeared to return the wagon to the livery and the horses to the stables were instructed to help Mrs. Hennessey unload the foodstuffs and to perform any more tasks she might require of them.

Hattie didn't move when Jack extended a hand to her. She just sat on the bench, muffled and bundled up, staring straight ahead. If she didn't straighten out, her behavior was going to attract attention.

With a step on the wagon spokes, Jack pulled himself back onto the wagon bench. "This isn't the place for a statement." He tried to keep his face pleasant, as if there was nothing amiss with having to talk his wife out of a wagon. "If this is about Miss Richert, we should talk about her in private. We can't make a scene in front of my men."

"It's something that Louisa mentioned," Hattie said. "She said she and Major Adams had heard a lot about me. Why would she say that?"

Private Willis walked by carrying a crate of supplies. He paused long enough to let Jack know that he was listening.

"Major Adams left this morning, and I'm responsible for answering all of his mail and sending his reports. There are things I must attend to, so if this could wait —"

"It seems to me that you had a sweetheart somewhere that Louisa is confusing me with. Was there more than one woman? Were you stringing along Miss Richert as well as others?"

If only she knew. Jack wiped a hand over his face, then remembered to smile patiently. "It doesn't matter right now, dear. My concern is getting you out of the cold. Why don't you go inside so the troopers can take the wagon back to the livery?"

"When we struck our bargain, I didn't think it would be this complicated," she said. Avoiding him, she climbed out the opposite side of the wagon. Private Willis stood by, ready with a box of goods, and followed her into the house.

Jack climbed out of the wagon with a groan. He respected Miss Richert and hated that he'd hurt her, but there was nothing he could do to correct the offense. No explanation possible.

On his way to the adjutant's office, Jack walked past a unit of new troopers practicing their flanking movements on horseback. The whinny of a rebellious steed carried on the cold air. Jack understood the frustration. He ducked his head low into the warmth of his coat and hurried into his office.

Sergeant O'Hare saluted when he entered, then handed him the dispatches that should have gone to Major Adams, had he been around. Jack scanned the quartermaster's report. Was it always this disorganized? How did Major Adams stand it?

"Send for the quartermaster," he said. "I want to talk to him about this report." Numbers on paper should be in neat columns that were clearly labeled. Whatever shorthand the quartermaster was utilizing was not sufficient.

O'Hare waved Private Gundy out the door with the message.

Jack stepped behind his desk, but his eyes never left the dispatches. He started to sit and had to thank O'Hare for quickly moving a chair beneath him. A tumble in the crowded office would have been the perfect cap to a miserable morning. The dispatches contained a few telegrams from Washington with general information about the moving of troops, which units would be coming in the spring and which would be moving out. There was nothing about his request to change locations, but that would probably require a more discreet communication.

"Lieutenant." Private Morris stepped forward with a letter in his hand. "Just got this from Washington. Thought you'd like to see it."

The letter was from the Office of Indian Affairs regarding their request for gold to replace what had been stolen. The bureau thought that greater effort should be put into finding the lost money before more was requested. It also questioned why troopers weren't sent to Fort Smith to accompany the agent when an escort had been requested.

"That bad, huh?" O'Hare shifted nervously.

Jack's mouth tightened. "Did we receive a request for an escort on that distribution payment?"

O'Hare hit the spittoon with a well-aimed

missive. "No, sir. Not that I saw."

"Me either." And everything that Major Adams saw came through Jack's office first. "Get in touch with Fort Smith. See what happened to the request," Jack said.

A simple mistake was possible, but something about the situation didn't add up.

Hattie walked ahead of the young private carrying the crate to direct him into the kitchen. Once she stepped through the cluttered parlor and into the dining room, she backed out of the way to let him pass her. Her skirt bumped against the dining room table, causing a stack of books to crash to the ground.

Private Willis popped his head out of the kitchen. "If I wasn't seeing it with my own eyes, I wouldn't believe it. Lieutenant Hennessey is so particular about our uniforms and drills. Everything has to be sharp as a tack. And then he keeps his house like a family of pack rats lives here."

Hattie gathered the musty-smelling books and returned them to their place on the table. She ran her finger between the stacks and held up a smudged glove as proof. "I'm as surprised as you are."

Willis whistled. "And now you're married to him? You've got your work cut out for you. To tell you honestly, all us men are downright surprised by the marriage business. We knew he had a girl he was sweet on, but we didn't know he was ready to jump the broom."

A girl he was sweet on? Hattie could feel her throat tightening again. But why should she feel guilty? It wasn't her fault they were in this mess.

"Now, me, I've got a sweetheart of my own. She lives down in Texas, and as soon as I . . ." Private Willis's voice droned on from the kitchen, where he was unloading the crates.

Hattie felt awkward hearing about some stranger's courting plans, but if he wanted to talk, it took the pressure off her. The house was a mess. And while it wasn't her fault or her responsibility, she'd rather have some order imposed if this was going to be her prison for the next few days.

Weeks? Months?

Hattie ripped off her gloves and tossed them onto the table. First she'd get her goods put away, and then she had some drawing to do.

Private Willis proved to be able help when it came to toting heavy bags and crates around. He did drop a paper-wrapped package when he tried to walk across the house while balancing it on his head, but it was only clothing, so no harm was done. And although he shared his opinion on everything from green apples to camels, he didn't require Hattie to respond. Her efforts were focused on arranging the vacant kitchen shelves to her preferences. Once all the heavy lifting had been completed, Private Willis left with a tip of his hat and a spin on his heel, leaving Hattie alone with her thoughts and a pack of pastels she'd picked up at the mercantile.

Here, with a blank piece of journal paper and the thin winter light streaming across the kitchen, Hattie could pretend that her plan was still viable. If she'd had her paints, then this house would suit much better than a peopled boardinghouse. Would the boardinghouse have had a kitchen this spacious? Honestly, the house on Officers' Row was much nicer than she'd expected in Denver — even nicer than her parents' house back in Van Buren. If it weren't for the strings attached, she could be content here.

She hurriedly sketched Jack's house. Instead of showing the homes on either side of it, she showed it alone, the sole refuge in a hostile territory. The angle she portrayed, coming down from on high, made the large home look fragile but safe. A safety that she couldn't guarantee would last. Most of the page was filled with light brown scratches to color the plain surrounding the haven.

Hattie looked out the window. She'd left home to feed her soul on the beauty of God's creation. Instead she was stuck in the most dismal landscape God's infinite mind could devise.

She sat staring out the back of the house at nothing. Thin, wispy clouds feathered high up in the blue sky. With such a massive sky, such big space surrounding her, Hattie felt tiny, insignificant. The world had never felt this large, nor she this small. How easily she'd been lost on the plains, just one warm heart beating in miles of cold, dead fields. And now, even though she had a roof over her head, she still had trouble believing that God was taking any notice of her plight. How could He, when she could completely disappear in the emptiness and not cause one ripple?

"I don't know if You've forgotten me," she said, "or if You are just too busy to bother right now, but I've never felt so alone before. It'd be nice if I could just have a sense of You every once in a while. Just a sign that You see me. That You haven't forgotten me. Or, if it's not too much to ask, that You'd send a friend."

"Hattie?"

Her fingers tensed on the pastel. It was Jack. How long had he been listening? She rubbed her neck. "Do you need something?" she asked.

"I came to check on you, see if you needed any help putting things away." His boots creaked as he shifted his weight. "It looks like you're doing a fine job setting up the kitchen. I usually eat in the officers' mess, but it'll be handy having food in the house."

Instead of honing her painting talents, she'd be cooking. The implications kept getting better and better.

Poor Jack. She'd always imagined that he was impatient with her dullness when it came to school, and here she'd been berating him for his lack of social acuteness. Everyone had their strengths. Dealing with ladies wasn't Jack's.

"It's a nice kitchen," she said.

"Is there anything else you're planning to do today?" he asked.

Hattie smiled. "Now that you mention it, I was thinking about taking a hike up in the mountains with my easel this evening to catch the best light of the day. But while I wait for the sun to get at the right angle, I'm hankering to find a soda fountain, and after that I'll attend an art exhibit at the museum. I'm sure the Darlington museum houses a grand collection."

She stopped herself before she went any further. He stood watching her, the same striking man who'd rescued her. Instead of sounding funny, now her words left her ashamed.

"I'm sorry." She rubbed at a spot of color on her finger. "I need to keep my thoughts to myself."

"No." His dark eyes held enough sorrow for both of them. "I'm asking a lot of you — telling you what to say and how to behave when we're in public. You deserve a place where you can say what you want and be honest about how you feel. You don't have to pretend here."

"I'll just make you miserable."

"Then it's a fair turn," he said. "What are you drawing?"

Hattie turned the paper around so he could see. "Just getting started. I removed the other houses to capture the sense of isolation here."

"It's not that isolated," he said. "And the shutters are darker green, too."

She looked at the picture again. Was he really going to correct her drawing? "It's the right shade. Light, like a mint leaf."

"No. Closer to basil. I remember when

they were painted."

"I saw them today. Light green."

"We could go outside and look," Jack said.

She shook her head. "You can go on your own, because I know I'm right. Come back and tell me when you see."

"Later. First, the stove's almost gone cold. If you're going to be cooking, we'll need to have firewood delivered to the kitchen door." He reached up to the top shelf over the window and retrieved a box of matches.

Hattie arranged the picture before her. One warm, safe place. That was all she had at the moment. "I'm going to write my parents today, but I don't know what to say. If I mention the robbery or the Indians or the wedding, they'll come after me and drag me home."

"That's going to be one short letter."

"What can I say? Just that I'm at the fort — safe and warm for the winter." The smoky smell from the stove made her nose itch. She rubbed at it with a vengeance.

"And that you happened to run across a childhood friend." He reached a hand toward her face. Hattie drew back. "You've got a smudge," he said. He rubbed his thumb along the side of her nose.

Their eyes met. He dropped his hand but didn't drop his gaze. Hattie turned away before he could see the questions in her eyes.

Childhood friend? He'd never been that exactly, but he was a friend now. And the more time she spent with him, the more she realized that she'd never known him at all.

CHAPTER FOURTEEN

Jack's coffee cup rattled as he set it down in the saucer and scanned the dispatches that had come in that day. 'Twas a pity that filling in for Major Adams meant that his schedule would be full, with little time to escort his wife around. Did Hattie prefer him gone and busy, or did she think he was being rude if he wasn't there to attend to her? Either way, he wanted to spend all the time he could with her before they parted ways.

His daydreams were interrupted by the words on the missive before him. According to the onionskin paper, Fort Smith had requested an additional escort for the gold shipment. They'd sent a telegram to Fort Reno before the stage had set out. Jack adjusted his spectacles. Had the message been received, but mislaid? Mistakes did happen, but it was unlike the major or himself to be negligent — even amid wedding plans.

"Lieutenant Hennessey, there's a lady here to see you."

"Send her in," he said. He should have brought her around and introduced her to everyone, but he didn't want to vex her. He only had time to smooth his hair and stand before she entered.

Her chestnut hair was thick and plentiful, hanging in a heavy mass at the nape of her neck. Hattie had the winsome habit of focusing completely on whomever she was conversing with, but his office must have caught her off guard. Jack gave her a moment to take in her surroundings.

"I didn't expect your office to be so vital," she said. "It seems like the heart of the fort."

Jack didn't know what to do with her praise. "It is," he said. "All expenditures and correspondence pass through here."

"Including reassignment requests?"

Jack laid down the report from Fort Smith. "Yes, but I can hardly request my own transfer. Major Adams sent that before he left."

"Thank you," she said. "Time is getting away from me if I want to succeed in my painting challenge." She tugged on her earring — her only earring. "But that's not why

I'm here." She dropped an envelope on his desk.

Mr. and Mrs. Carl Walker. Jack gazed at the address. How many times had he lingered on the street outside the brick two-story home, hoping to catch a glimpse of her?

"The post has already gone for today, but I'll send it out tomorrow." He placed her letter on a stack of envelopes on the credenza. "Do I need to write my parents?"

She cocked her head. "Why would you do that?"

"If you made any mention of me, word might get back to my folks. I wouldn't want them to hear something significant second-hand."

"Why in the world would I tell my parents that I'm staying with you? Don't you think that would obligate us, in some way, to . . . you know?"

She played dense when it suited her. Now it suited him. "Obligate us to what?"

Hattie squirmed under his gaze. Her hand brushed her cheek as she looked behind her to see if anyone was listening. "I've already spent several nights alone with you," she whispered. "If that becomes known, then we might as well resign ourselves to the fact that we're married."

"I agree."

"What?" Her startled expression put him on the defensive.

"If it gets out, I mean. But I thought we were going to tell people that you worked for me. You were my housekeeper for a few weeks, or my cook, if you'd rather."

"Who's going to believe I left home to become your housekeeper?"

"Who's going to believe you married me?" he replied, and she acquiesced the point much too easily. Jack took his seat and gestured for her to do the same. "All I'm asking is whether your letter invoked my name."

Hattie perched on the edge of the rickety wooden chair with her hands on her knees. "I told them that I hadn't made it to Denver. That the weather had turned cold, and I was going to stay at a little town in Indian Territory until travel became more convenient."

"No mention of me?" He looked at her over the top of his glasses.

"Why does it matter?"

"It doesn't matter."

Hattie's face contorted, and she covered her mouth with her hand as she tried to hide a yawn. "It's been a long day, and I didn't sleep well last night."

Because of her nightmares. The little

frame bed squawked when she tossed and turned. He could hear her voice at times, which led to his waiting outside her door as he debated at what point to intervene. So far, he'd restrained himself, but there was a limit to the agony he'd let her endure. He wished there was something he could do.

"Do you have everything you need?" he asked.

"Besides paints, yes. I cleaned out my room and moved those crates to the spare bedroom, but it's chock-full of furniture. What do you have all that for?"

"It's not my furniture. It came with the house. The army doesn't want to cart around tables and chairs for us, so they keep the officers' homes furnished. There's even a crib, just in case."

Her brown eyes flashed up to meet his.

"Just in case," he repeated, "the next officer who lives there has a family."

"Sir — oh, sorry," Sergeant Byrd stammered. "I didn't realize you were entertaining. I'll tell the quartermaster you're occupied."

Jack was just about to agree when Hattie spoke up. "No, please send him in. I don't mind."

He studied her with surprise. No one met with the quartermaster if they could avoid it, and she wanted to stay? Could it be that she was interested in what he was doing?

Jack nodded to Byrd, and before he knew it, he was going over accounts, pointing to areas that needed clarification, and jotting notes on projected expenditures — all under Hattie's gaze. If Jack was a tad too complimentary of the quartermaster, it was for Hattie's benefit. He wanted her to see that he wasn't overly critical. It didn't stop him from pointing out areas a person could improve, but he could do it in a positive manner.

Before he knew it, the sun was going down, and he had spent more than an hour working beneath Hattie's full attention. He felt like floating when he closed his ledgers and took up his hat.

He escorted her home, just like he'd always wanted to do back in Van Buren, but the situation still troubled him. What was he going to do? Even if they could somehow secretly get away from Fort Reno without anyone from Van Buren hearing about their shocking living conditions, there was always the chance that somewhere, someday, it would come back to taint her reputation. Twenty years from now, Hattie could be a well-respected artist and mother, but what would happen if she crossed Miss Richert's path? What would she say? How could Hattie defend herself?

He saluted Captain Chandler as he turned onto the walkway that led to his home, then stopped in his tracks. "Well, what do you know? I could've sworn that we painted the shutters a darker green."

"I tried to tell you. You might have painted them dark green, but paint fades." Hattie dimpled. "As do bad memories of unbearable boys."

"I hope you don't forget this one altogether," he said. "Maybe that's why God brought you here. So I could make amends for my insufferable behavior from years past."

"Just saying *I'm sorry* would've been less trouble."

And the longer they were together, the more Jack had to apologize for.

Once they got to the house, Hattie disappeared into the kitchen to set about supper while Jack organized his papers in his study. The only way he saw to safeguard Hattie from further gossip was to stay married to her. Wasn't that the gentlemanly thing to do? But Hattie wouldn't see it as gentlemanly. She'd think he was taking advantage. He opened his journal — a daily habit to record anything new he'd discovered that might warrant further contemplation — but he had nothing he could put on paper.

If only God would appear and fix everything. God knew his mistake was honest. God knew that Jack would rather lose Hattie altogether than have her think he'd manipulated her into this. But here they were, and Jack didn't like the thought that they would both be living the rest of their lives with a secret that any one of a hundred people could disclose.

He closed the journal and went in to supper. God wasn't showing him an easy way out, so all he could do was stay the course, take care of Hattie, and pray that nothing they did would bring shame to them in the future. He hoped that someday he could look her husband in the eye, knowing that he'd done nothing to harm her.

But his resolve was to be tested that night.

After supper, Jack sat in his reading chair in the parlor and tried to ignore Hattie's movements in the kitchen. He tried not to think of her cheeks flushed by the heat of the stove, of her bending and reaching to clean the table, or of her graceful hands covered by soap bubbles and warm water. There were so many things he was trying not to think of, he couldn't concentrate on his book at all. When she passed through and wished him good night, he exhaled a sigh of relief. Just a few minutes, and then it would be safe to go upstairs.

By the time Jack got to the second floor, the door to Hattie's room was closed. He hoped she would finally be able to sleep soundly. He couldn't stand the thought of her suffering when he could do nothing about it.

He went into his room and undressed with the door open before he realized his mistake, but by that time all he had to do was slip under the covers, put on his glasses, and take up another book.

Actually, it wasn't a book as much as a collection of writings left for him by the previous Darlington agent's wife, Mrs. Ida Dyer. As she'd traveled with her husband from post to post, she'd become a student of the different tribes. Her insights from the Quapaw, Shawnee, and Modoc Indians were helpful in contrasting what he was learning with the Arapaho. Together with the missionaries, he hoped the tribes would be able to retain their culture while still learning how to operate in the new world they were faced with.

So engrossing were the essays that Jack dismissed the first noise he heard as the wind howling. The pane in the back bedroom always vibrated when the wind hit it just right, and the wind was blowing now. But the second time he heard it, he recognized it for what it was: a sob.

Jack lowered the book. Hattie was crying again. It wouldn't be right to go to her. It wouldn't be proper, but how many nights could she endure this? He couldn't ignore her pain any longer. Getting out of bed, he set his glasses on the washstand and reached for his trousers.

Just then a door opened down the hall. Jack froze with his pants up around one leg. Hattie was leaving her room. Quick as a territorial cyclone, he blew out his lamp and dove into bed. Pulling the covers up, he lay on his side and waited, praying that she'd assume he was asleep.

The house was so silent that he wondered if he'd imagined the creaking hinges, but then she appeared. Her white nightgown glowed in the dark hall. Her hair fell down her back in a long braid. The only noise was the rasping of her blanket against the ground as she dragged it behind her. Then came a soft *pouf* as she dropped her pillow on the floor in the hall, right in sight of him. Could she tell that he was awake? Should he let her know? She arranged her blanket as well as the extra blanket that he'd lent her the night before, then lay down in the hall, curled up beneath the covers.

She wanted to be where she could see him. Jack wished it meant more than it did, but after her ordeal, he knew she didn't want to be alone. In fact, her presence in his office earlier was probably more on account of her fear than any desire for his company.

Hattie shivered as she clutched at the edges of her blanket. Was she not warm enough, or was she trembling from something other than the temperature? Jack couldn't be silent any longer.

"Hattie?" he whispered from the safety of his bed. His pants were still caught around one ankle, so he'd play it safe and not move.

"I didn't mean to wake you." From her voice there was no doubt she'd been crying. The blanket tightened beneath her chin. "I haven't been sleeping at all. It's horrid. And tonight . . . I don't know what I'm doing here. I'll go back to my room —"

"Wait," he said. "My coat is hanging there on the balustrade."

Jack closed his eyes and grimaced. Why had he said that? Why would she want his coat? But instead of laughing, she sat up and snagged it off the rail. She gathered the fabric in her arms and buried her face in its folds. She lay tense, as if ready to bolt.

"Jack, do you think they'll ever catch the man who robbed us?"

He rose up on his elbow. "The marshals in Indian Territory are a fearsome bunch. I can guarantee they are already on his trail."

"But they might not catch him, and if they don't, will I ever be safe?"

Something inside him melted. No, she wouldn't be safe. As a witness to a crime like that, she would spend the rest of her life looking over her shoulder. Jack could offer protection, but what he wanted to give would interfere with her plans.

"You're safe here, and we'll have that good-for-nothing caught by the time my transfer is approved and you go to Denver. Until then . . ."

Until then he'd stand guard over her fearful moments in the safest spot in the nations — his house on Fort Reno. Jack could spend all night detailing how he would fight to the death for her, but he'd said enough.

Her arms seemed to relax, and her breathing grew deeper. She wasn't going back to her room. His not-wife couldn't sleep unless he was in view.

Another trait that proved she wasn't flawless, and another problem he didn't know how to solve.

CHAPTER FIFTEEN

She wasn't used to sitting around, doing nothing. That was why Hattie couldn't wait for Jack to leave the house that morning. Another day had slipped away. Each day a missed chance to paint for the exhibition, and if she couldn't make progress on that goal, she wanted to attempt another. The impossible task she'd chosen was none other than the mess of a house she was resigned to live in.

She set beans soaking for the midday meal while Jack loitered, looking for an excuse to stay. After asking for the third time if he could bring her anything and reminding her for the second time that if she needed him, all she had to do was open the door and ask the first trooper she saw to fetch him, Jack reluctantly took his hat and coat and left. Hattie swung the door closed, then collapsed against it, trying to get her bearings.

Wasn't it something that scrawny Jack was

such a bigwig here at the fort? Hattie had enjoyed watching him study the page of numbers the quartermaster had produced. It reminded her of the young boy who had stood in front of the blackboard, studying an impossible arithmetic problem. He'd even chewed on his pencil, just like he used to. What a mess he used to make when he forgot and put the chalk in his mouth. Some things had changed, but others . . .

Jack had been the epitome of generosity and chivalry since she'd been at the fort, but Hattie had the horrible suspicion that his kindness was related to her hysterics every evening. She was more than frustrated with herself. It was humiliating. By morning light, she didn't want to face him. How could she, after shamelessly crawling right up to his door to sleep? And every night when he offered her his coat, she didn't know whether to cry in relief or shame. It had been only a week since she was hiding from a murderer in a freezing ditch, she reminded herself. With time, the memories would fade. With time, her need for him would, too.

Until then . . .

Hattie surveyed her new domain. Books stacked beneath the tables, books shelved on windowsills, books scattered across the dining room — every flat surface was covered with them. Her artist's eye would love to see the pretty, leather-bound volumes adorning his study in clever arrangements and groupings. At the very least, she needed to get some of the dustier tomes hidden away in the upstairs bedroom.

She started in the parlor, sweeping up as many books as she could in her arms. If a particularly handsome volume caught her eye, she left it behind, but the rest were carted up to the vacant room.

No wonder Jack had never had any girlfriends in school. No one who spent so much time looking at words could have anything interesting to say. Or at least he hadn't back then. Now, well, he was Prince Charming when they were out and about. Back at the house, he was as silent as a portrait.

She trudged up and down the stairs, her footsteps thudding louder with every trip, until she dropped the last armful of books on the bed. The frame squawked, and dust clouded the air, but Hattie wouldn't be deterred. She had to get that parlor downstairs tidy before Jack returned for the noonday meal. Otherwise the only thing they'd have to discuss would be her embarrassing habit of crying at night until she had his coat in her arms.

Jack didn't have many decorative objects, but she gathered items that deserved a better placement in the floor-to-ceiling bookshelves that flanked the fireplace. Candlesticks, a nice platter from the kitchen, a feathered pipe, and a clay pot painted with an Indian pattern were all gathered on her first round.

On her second pass, she spotted an oddly shaped box among the notebooks on the credenza behind his desk. It was a waste for the red leather case to hide in his office where no one could see it. It was the perfect size and would add some color to the shelves in the parlor.

She tucked the leather box beneath her arm and bustled back to the parlor. It rattled as the items inside shifted. Hattie paused. Was this a treasure chest of Jack's? What could he be hiding? Her earring, perhaps? Carefully, she turned the box over to fiddle with the buckle and remove the lid.

There were some marbles, a gold coin, a small card with a picture of Jesus that she remembered Jack earning in Sunday school for memorizing the most verses in their fourth grade class. Then there was a jack with one prong broken. She'd meant to look for her earring, but she'd forgotten how much of their history they'd shared. This was the broken jack she'd given to him when he'd broken his arm falling out of a tree. Only Jack would have tried to read a book in a tree and gotten so engrossed in the story that he fell out. She'd felt bad for him with his sling in the middle of summer, and when she found the broken jack, she'd thought it was an appropriate gift for the broken Jack she knew. She smiled as she held the memory in her hand. He'd kept the silly thing all this time?

Pieces of his childhood, of their childhoods, lay scattered before her, but for all the treasures there, her earring was not one of them. Hattie was gathering the last of the scraps when one of the papers caught her eye. It looked like an early drawing of hers — before she'd perfected shading and proportion. With a nervous glance at the front door, Hattie unfolded it. If she'd drawn the picture in the first place, it couldn't be wrong for her to look at it now, could it?

She recognized the landscape immediately. It was the valley outside the schoolhouse. Prone to daydreaming, Hattie was never assigned a seat by the window, so she'd had to draw from memory. Had she not doodled, Hattie might have learned rhetoric better, but she was content with her choices.

The picture was set in autumn. Leaves littered the ground, and a rock house on the other side of the valley was visible through the scantily clad branches. Hattie stared. That was Jack's house. Every day he'd tossed his strapped books over his shoulder and set out across the valley. No wonder he'd kept this picture. It was of his home.

Hattie flipped the paper over, but the other side was blank. A vague memory danced just out of reach. Someone had asked her to draw the valley. Had it been Jack? She didn't quite remember, but it was possible. But why had he wanted it? Had he known how far from home he would travel?

Hattie shoved the picture in with the other treasures, then placed the box on a shelf to balance the effect of the platter. Surely after Jack saw the improvement to the parlor, he'd understand the importance of culling down his library. One could never have a parlor that was too fashionable, but one could definitely have too many books.

The last volume was placed just in time for Hattie to rush to the kitchen, wash the brittle book dust off her hands, and drain and rinse the beans before setting them on the stove to simmer. In no time at all, she heard the front door open and Jack's voice call out, "Honey? Are you here?"

Hattie paused with the wooden spoon in hand. *Honey?* Why would he say that? No one was watching them here. Was he teasing her? Her eyes narrowed, and just to be on the safe side, she sucked in a deep breath, then answered in a melodious tone, "I'm in the kitchen, darling."

She wagged her head at the ridiculousness of the situation. Her younger self might have found it fun to play with romance, but grown-up Hattie had learned a lesson or two. The reward was rarely worth the effort.

"Could you come out here, please?" Jack asked.

She gave the beans one last stir, then abandoned the spoon to touch up her hair. She found him waiting by the front door, and her eyes lit up at the sight of the strapping cavalryman. The cold had heightened the color in his face and made his eyes shine. But the man standing next to him was a total surprise.

"Chief Right Hand?" Hattie stopped dead in her tracks. She threw Jack a worried look. He wasn't going to give her back to the Arapaho, was he? She clasped her hands together to keep them from shaking.

Jack noticed immediately. How he got to

her so quickly without looking like he was in a hurry was a mystery to her.

Blocking the chief from her view, he took her hand and willed her to face him. "Honeybee, I should have sent word that I was bringing a guest, but I knew you wouldn't care if the chief eats with us. He's anxious to see how my bride and I are doing."

"Your bride?" She knew what he meant, but no other words would come.

"Yes. And we need him to see that you are here and you are taking care of your husband."

Hattie released a shaky breath. She stiffened her spine as she met Jack's gaze.

He nodded. "Good girl," he whispered and released her to meet their guest. "The chief has come for dinner." With a hand at her back, Jack escorted her forward. "Mrs. Hennessey, you remember Chief Right Hand."

"Nice to see you again, Chief," she replied.

The Arapaho man was no less dignified standing here in her parlor than he'd been at the ceremony with his people. His sharp eyes studied her with a directness that a white man wouldn't have dared. He spoke words to Jack. Jack stumbled in his reply, but was evidently making some headway in the language.

Jack turned to her. "He says that you look a lot better than when they found you."

She had to smile at that. It had taken hours and several washings to scrub all the prairie from her skin.

The chief added something. Jack nodded. With a finger, the chief motioned for Jack to pass his message on.

This one wasn't as easy for Jack. "He says that marriage is good for you." His eyes didn't meet hers, just stayed focused on her collar. "That he knew I would be a good husband, and he expects I'll have a son by harvest in the fall."

Her smile disappeared. "So much for only having to pretend when we're in public," she said.

Jack shrugged apologetically. He raised his head and for the first time saw the parlor. He stepped backward as his eyes took in everything from the beautifully balanced display of his artifacts on the shelves to the colorful carpet that probably hadn't seen daylight for years.

"Doesn't it look magnificent?" Hattie clasped her hands behind her back.

Chief Right Hand squinted at the room, probably curious what they were looking at.

"Where are my books?" Jack asked.

"Well, there are a lot of them on the shelf,

as you see. The extra ones went upstairs so they'd be out of the way."

"Extra ones?" he repeated.

"There's not room for all of them."

"There used to be." He strode to the wall and examined the shelves. "You've put Washington's biography next to poetry. And what's this? *The Pilgrim's Progress*? It goes in the stack with my devotional books, not with history."

"Was that the stack that was under the chair, or the stack I tripped on next to the window?" she asked.

"Devotional books are next to the window. That's where I go in the mornings. Now I don't know where anything is."

The chief stepped between them, holding up a hand. Hattie rubbed the back of her neck, pulling a strand of hair loose from her braided bun.

"Peace," the chief said, before adding more words that only Jack could understand.

"We'll talk later," Jack grumbled to Hattie. Then, with artificial lightness, he added, "Dinnertime."

Hattie had been so convinced that Jack would be thrilled with the progress she'd made that she hadn't put much effort into the meal. But here he was, unhappy, with a guest, and she only had some beans and cold corn bread.

Taking three china plates, she started toward the dining room, but Jack caught her by the arm.

"He'll feel more comfortable in the kitchen where the food is made. Don't worry about the china."

"It's what we have," she said. The dishes clanked against the smaller kitchen table.

Jack disappeared only long enough to pull in an extra chair from the dining room. "I see you cleaned off the dining room table, as well," he said. "European history and encounters with the Plains tribes, gone."

"They aren't gone. They're upstairs." She tugged on her unadorned earlobe. "Maybe they're hidden with my earring."

Jack motioned the chief to his seat. "I know exactly where your earring is at all times," he said, "and if you didn't look so fetching wearing only one, I probably wouldn't be able to keep my temper right now. Let's eat."

Jack had always been head over heels for Hattie, but he'd never imagined how she could disrupt his life. Here he was, feeling like a stranger in his own home. He didn't want a pretentious house. He didn't want people to feel ill at ease when they visited. Having books stacked all over wasn't just convenient, it was also welcoming. At least, it made him feel welcomed.

But he needed to focus on the task at hand. Chief Right Hand had come to talk about his nephew at the school. Judging from his unusual request to join them for a meal, Jack figured the chief had more on his mind than Hattie's beans. And while Jack never felt adequate conversing without an interpreter, the chief didn't seem bothered by the lack.

The chief ate slowly, as if savoring each bite. After the first bowl, he removed the blanket from around his shoulders and loosened the leather thong on the neck of his tunic.

"It's warm?" Jack said in Arapaho. At least that was what he thought he said.

"Yes. The fire is good," the chief replied.

He didn't speak again until the second bowl of beans had been consumed. Once Jack saw how little Hattie had prepared, he'd contented himself with pushing his food around in his bowl so there would be enough for their guest. Hattie was doing the same. She'd done everything he'd asked, even welcoming the chief to her table, and Jack had shown her no gratitude. They'd talk about it later. For now, they needed to put on a good show for the chief.

"We heard that the Cheyenne shot an intruder," Jack said, "but he got away. Have your scouts seen anything?"

"No. No one has been found. If we find a body, we always tell you."

"And I appreciate your help," Jack said.

Hattie left the table to go to the pantry. She opened the door and began digging into the middle shelf.

"Need some help?" Jack half rose from his seat.

"No, I got it" — she turned around and waved a can of peaches in his face — "dear." Then she opened the drawer for the can opener.

Jack dragged his attention back to the chief. "You visited with Tom Broken Arrow?" he asked. "How is he doing in the school?"

The chief politely laid aside his spoon before answering. "The lessons are not hard, but he misses his land. He doesn't get to ride his horse. He doesn't get to hunt. He is a slave. The only joy in his day is learning to care for the animals."

Jack knew plenty of his friends growing up in Arkansas felt the same way about school, but this was a serious issue for the

Arapaho.

"It's hard for strong young men to sit at desks all day," Jack said, "but that's how white men pass on their wisdom."

The chief scoffed. "Marks on pages can't teach you to be a man."

Jack thought of his Bible, which was now missing somewhere upstairs. "A boy needs a good man to teach him how to be a man. But a good man can make those marks on a page, and then his lessons can be shared for generations. Think of your wisdom and the lessons you want to pass on to your children. We could write your words down, and then your children's children could learn from you, even after you have . . ." He couldn't think of the nice expression, so he went with what he knew. ". . . died."

The aged chief thought this over. "There can be goodness there. That's why Tom is at the Darlington school. But I don't want him to forget the lessons he learned with his hands and with his heart."

"I understand," Jack said. He leaned back as Hattie pushed bowls of peaches in front of them. He smiled at her, but she didn't seem to notice.

"There are other problems at the school," the chief continued. "The children are frightened. Three from another village have

222

gone home."

"Frightened?" Jack stabbed a slippery peach. "Frightened of what?"

The chief shrugged. "They say there's an evil spirit at the school. It rises up from the ground and steals their dreams while they are asleep."

Jack cast a nervous glance at Hattie. She couldn't understand a word the chief was saying, and that was for the best. Not all aspects of the Indian culture would be reassuring to her.

"The school is a Christian school," Jack said. "Evil spirits have no power there, but I've heard the stories, too. And things have gone missing. Blankets?"

The chief nodded. "Could be older students telling tales to scare the younger and hiding their things? I don't know. But three children were troubled. Didn't eat during the day, couldn't sleep at night. Their parents took them home."

Jack's heart sank. The school couldn't stay open if they lost many more students. What would that mean for them? For the tribe?

"Just as you say. The older kids must be telling ghost stories. I'll go and talk to them."

The chief finished his last peach, then picked up the bowl and drank the sweet syrup out of the bottom. "It's good if you go," he said. "If you find there's nothing to fear, the leaders will listen to you." His eyes sparked with mischief. "A family man like you has our respect."

Hattie paused with her spoon halfway to her lips. It wasn't hard to guess that the chief was talking about her. Jack thought of his missing book collection and responded, "Yes, Chief. And I have you to thank for bringing me such a helpful wife."

Chapter Sixteen

She'd never imagined that anyone could be so appreciative of canned peaches. Chief Right Hand licked his lips and nodded courteously as he left the kitchen with the air of one who had many appointments for the day and couldn't be delayed.

"I'll be right back." Jack tapped the table but avoided the glare she was sending him. It would serve him right if she carried all those books back down the stairs and dumped them in the middle of the parlor rug. Then again, that might be what he was planning to do when he returned.

Hattie stacked the bowls and utensils and carried them to the sink. To think that she'd been terrified of Chief Right Hand not too long ago. He'd sat in her kitchen and eaten with them, just like any other gentleman.

Her kitchen? Well, as long as she was the only woman living in the house, it should, by rights, be her kitchen. She had nothing else of her own.

By the time she was hanging up her apron, she heard the front door open again. Hattie paused, trailing her hand slowly down the hanging fabric. She might have messed up Jack's books, but she'd meant well. Didn't that count for something?

Slowly, she walked through the dining room to find Jack in the parlor, fists against his hips, like he was observing a contested battlefield. His mouth was twisted to the side and his nose wrinkled — hardly the response she expected. Frustration bubbled up inside her as she waited for his verdict.

But instead he asked, "How much of your life has changed since you arrived?"

Hattie blinked. "What?"

"Life here is different than it is in Van Buren. It's also different than what you had planned in Denver. How is it different? Tell me what changes you've endured."

Hattie crossed her arms over her chest. This was a topic she could go to town on.

"First off, I never wanted to live at a fort. Soldiers and troopers everywhere. Bugles telling what hour it is. No women to visit with until the Adams family returns. Secondly, living in Indian Territory is awful. There's nothing to do, nothing to see. Now, as far as my personal experience, well, I'd planned to live in a boardinghouse, which would mean that I was free to paint, and paint I must. If I have any hopes of being included in the exhibition, I must have a work to submit in two weeks, although what I'd paint here, I have no idea. But instead of painting, I'm cooking for you and whomever you bring home. I'm sharing a house with someone who, no offense, is little more than a long-lost acquaintance, and I don't even have my own clothes. Everything I thought I was going to have in Denver has been lost, and it's not easy losing something as big as the Rocky Mountains."

Jack couldn't tear his eyes away from the room. His chest stretched with a sigh. "You've lost a lot. I suppose it's only fitting that I sacrifice some books."

"Books? You call that a sacrifice?" She had about determined that he'd lost his head when she realized he was laughing at her.

He dropped his hand to her shoulder and gave her a playful shove. "What I'm trying to say is thank you for doing all of this, and I don't just mean arranging the parlor. I mean thanks for everything you gave up. You might not have intended to do it, but you could've made this more difficult than it is."

"Just because I'm tolerating you today

doesn't mean that I will tomorrow. I reserve the right to throw a tantrum at any point."

"I'm feeling up to the challenge today," he said.

Times like these made Hattie wonder if she'd ever known Jack at all. To keep herself from gazing at him in wonder, she said, "What did the chief say? Do you think he'll let us off the hook soon?"

Jack shook his head. "Chief Right Hand said there's trouble with the students. They think the school is haunted. I think it's time they get a little treat as a reward for their hard work. I'm going to head there right now."

"Right now?" Hattie looked past the dusty curtains at the cold prairie. She was starved for company, for color, for anything exciting. While she didn't want Jack to get the wrong impression, another trip to town would break up the long day. "I could go and visit with the kids. I don't know if I'd be any help, but . . ."

Jack's eyes lit up. "Come with me," he said. "There's something I've always been curious about."

That statement made Hattie all the more curious, too.

The last time Hattie had gone to Darlington, she'd been dressed in Mrs. Adams's clothes, still shaken from her rescue, and not sure where she was. This visit, she would put on her best ensemble from the mercantile, fix her hair, and know the lay of the land. But she was still missing her earring.

She smiled at her reflection in her hand mirror. While the simple mercantile clothes weren't anything to be proud of, Hattie had outgrown being the victim. Today she was going because she'd chosen to go. Because there was more chance of something interesting happening in town with Jack than if she stayed behind cleaning his study. What was it about Jack? Being with him filled her with anticipation, like they were always on the verge of a fascinating discovery. Like there was treasure locked up inside, and sooner or later Jack — or maybe she — was going to find the right key and surprise everyone. And Hattie wanted to be there for that moment. What that surprise was and why she instinctively knew it would involve her, Hattie didn't question. It was enough that being around Jack was fun, exciting, and sometimes exasperating.

And if Jack didn't provide enough diversion, maybe she'd find something to sketch, even if it was a study of the mule skinner's wagons that delivered supplies to the agency.

She came down the stairs, carrying her sturdy buckskin coat. "Thank you for waiting," she said to Jack.

"Yes, ma'am. The wagon is ready."

He opened the door and escorted her outside, where she faced five troopers who looked like they'd been waiting on their horses for an hour. Because they had.

Jack gave her a dazzling smile. While he'd avoided eye contact earlier, his eyes lingered on her now, even traveling her face as if suddenly free to do so. He hopped off the porch and held out a hand to her. "Your chariot awaits."

Hattie paused. He'd retained the playful spirit that he'd had in the parlor, but now he had an audience. They'd been getting on so well, but was it part of his act?

He climbed up into the wagon next to her once she was seated, but his voice was less sure. "If you don't want to go . . ."

Deciding to play along, Hattie tucked her hand under his arm. Jack's charming manner didn't fade, even when the other troopers were out of earshot.

A muscle flexed on his freshly shaved jaw. "I want to talk to the kids, but I don't know if I'll get a straight answer from them.

Besides the language barrier and the distrust they have of us, they are kids, after all. It could be a case of childish imagination."

"I pretended to be sick so I could miss school once," Hattie said. "I didn't want to do the recitation."

"I remember. You pinched your cheeks and put a hot water bottle against your face to convince your ma."

How was it that he remembered every little incident of their childhood? She knew he was smart, but that was ridiculous.

"My point is, maybe they're making up stories so their parents will let them come home," she said.

"That's why we're going to give those who stayed a treat today. Why make them wait until Christmas for a reward?"

Christmas was coming. Hattie grinned at the thought of his tidy parlor decorated for the holiday. And the dining room. How elegant she could make it look with red tapers and an arrangement of holly as a centerpiece. If she didn't have paints, she'd use his house as a canvas.

It took less than an hour to arrive at the school. Unlike their earlier visit, no children played outside. They were probably working at their lessons with the heartbroken Miss Richert — whom Hattie hoped to avoid.

While they found a place to tie up the wagon, Jack sent the troopers to prepare the warehouse. For what, Hattie didn't bother asking. She had other concerns.

"Remember to treat Miss Richert kindly, Jack, but not too kindly, if you have no interest in a future relationship with her."

"Really, Hattie? I don't know why you persist with this."

"Because you're blind." Hattie smoothed a bonnet ribbon beneath her chin so it didn't flap in her face. "You need to be careful. You don't realize how easily a woman could fall for you."

"That's not been my experience," he said.

"Or maybe it has been, but you're too thickheaded to see it." Hattie laughed. "In this I'm smarter than Lieutenant Hennessey, but there is one mystery you could help me with. If you're not in love with Miss Richert, then who is she? As far as I can tell, there are no other ladies within fifty miles of here."

"Who is who?"

"Who is this sweetheart that you told everyone about? People seem to have me confused with someone else. Private Willis said you've carried a torch for a lady for years. Is that true?"

Jack's eyes fluttered.

Hattie gasped. "It *is* true. Then how can you pretend to be in love with me? Doesn't it feel like a betrayal?"

"There's only one woman I've ever pined over, and I didn't meet her here. In fact, I've known her most of my life."

"Oh, stop it. This act of yours is going too far, and you can't fool me. So who was she? Ida Monroe? She was the quiet sort. Smart, like you."

His Adam's apple jogged. "Hattie, why are we having this conversation? We have a fun day ahead of us. Let's enjoy it."

She studied him for a moment as he got out of the wagon. "I want to be as honest as possible," she said, taking his hand to disembark. "We shouldn't pretend to feel something we don't. Especially when there are others' feelings to consider."

Something about the way his eyes lit up made her feel lighter on her feet. "I'm going to be honest today," he said, "and you will be amazed."

Even though he stood straight and proper in his uniform, facing down the sharp wind, the shine in his eye evidenced that he'd just issued her a personal challenge. Slowly, Hattie was coming to a conclusion. Jack had always been the competitive type in school. Not in the schoolyard, mind you, but at his studies. If he ever missed a math problem, you could be sure he'd come back the next day having already mastered the next three lessons. If he answered a question wrong before the class, whether it be in geography or history, he'd return as an expert on the subject so he wouldn't embarrass himself again. That was what this was. This was Jack not wanting to fail at his mission.

Jack held the door open for her, and they walked the empty hallway together. Through the glass-paned doors, the desks sat empty. An American flag waved slightly in the heat rising from the potbellied stove next to the teacher's desk.

"They didn't all go home, did they?" Jack looked sick. Poor man. He really did hate to fail.

She placed a sympathetic hand on his arm while he scanned the bleak room. Bleak until Miss Richert appeared from the room across the hall, and Hattie saw a chance to brighten his day.

"Miss Richert, I understand that you've lost some students."

There. He'd greeted the teacher and made a coherent statement. If what Hattie said was true, he wouldn't risk speaking any more than necessary.

He watched as Miss Richert directed her answer to Hattie, giving him the cold shoulder. So it was true. She'd liked him, but he'd never noticed. He looked at Miss Richert with new eyes as she and Hattie discussed the rumors that the children were spreading about ghosts. Miss Richert stood with her primer held tightly against her chest, while Hattie leaned forward and listened as if every word was a treasure. It was amazing how Miss Richert's posture softened. Her face registered relief when Hattie expressed her delight with the students she'd met so far. He found that instead of studying Miss Richert, he was again appreciating Hattie. How did she manage people so well?

She was right. In this way, she was smarter than he was.

"Well, are we going?" Hattie asked.

How long had he been standing there? "Yes?" he said and grimaced until Hattie nodded that he'd answered correctly.

"Thank you, Miss Richert," Hattie said. "We'll head to the mission house now."

The mission house? Jack hurriedly tipped his hat as Hattie dragged him from the room.

"It's going to be difficult, but there's a way," Hattie said as she strode down the hall. "After this whole mess is behind us, there's got to be a way you can come back and explain to her."

"Just stop," he said as they hurried down the empty hallway, their footsteps echoing off the newly painted walls. "I'm not in love with her. I never have been, and I never will be. Now, why are we going to the mission house?"

"That's where the students are practicing their Christmas pageant. How did you not hear her?"

He escorted Hattie out the big set of double doors. "I have a lot on my mind," he said. He'd always known Hattie would keep her man on his toes. He'd never believed it might be him.

Even from the street, the students' cheerful voices could be heard coming through the closed windows of the mission house. Festooned with red sashes and pine boughs, the room already had a festive mood. Add the dark-skinned boys pretending to count coup with their shepherd's crooks and the girls swaddling rag dolls with linen bandages, and the room was barely contained chaos. Mrs. Lehrman sat at the front, a crying girl from the primer class curled up on her lap.

"There, there, Francine. No one is going

to steal you away while we're practicing. You're in plain sight on the stage."

"I want to go home," the girl sobbed, "before he comes out of the ground and gets me."

Jack approached. The group of children split, eyes wide, as he passed. Even the coup counters halted their contest. He knelt next to the headmistress as she turned the child toward him.

"See, Francine, here's Lieutenant Hennessey. He keeps bad men away from the school."

Bad men, yes, but he wasn't sure what he could do about mythical monsters.

"Why are you afraid?" he asked.

She studied him solemnly but didn't speak.

Maybe she hadn't understood. "Where did you see the scary person?"

At this she turned away from him and buried her face in Mrs. Lehrman's shoulder.

"I'm sorry you're frightened," the headmistress said, "but you can't interrupt the practice. We have a lot of work to do. Now, let's be a good girl and get up."

You would have thought the child had suddenly been struck with a palsy. Mrs. Lehrman tried to pry her arms from around her neck, but the girl held on.

Just then a miracle happened. Hattie squatted behind Mrs. Lehrman and tapped Francine on the arm. The girl braved a peek through her thick lashes.

"I've never been in this building before," Hattie said. "Is this your first time, too?"

The girl shook her head. "We go to chapel," she said, "for Bible and song. Every day."

"You come here every day?" Hattie looked at the high ceiling above her. "Do you get to stand on the stage or do you sit out there?"

Without a word, the girl pointed out toward the pews that stretched in not-so-straight lines. The jousting shepherds dove between them, darting to avoid being hit by an opponent's staff.

Hattie stood. "Where do you sit?" She sounded so genuinely curious that even Jack was almost fooled. Her smile had always been irresistible to him, and evidently it was to Francine, too. She watched as Hattie walked to the first bench. Hattie spun and, with her back straight, perched pertly on the edge of the bench. "I bet you sit here."

Francine shook her head and giggled. The headmistress loosened her arms and was able to stand while still holding on to Francine's shoulder.

Hattie popped up so suddenly that all the kids laughed. She gave a funny little frown and took a big step to her left. "Is your seat this one?" She dropped onto the pew, and the ribbon on her bonnet bounced.

Forgetting all about Mrs. Lehrman, Francine ran off the stage to a bench on the second row. She crawled up onto the bench, stomach first, then raised both hands over her head. "Mine!" she crowed.

Hattie dropped her jaw like it was the most amazing thing she'd ever heard. "Are you pulling my leg?"

Francine only giggled, probably not familiar with the saying, but Hattie had achieved what she'd set out to do. Mrs. Lehrman was free to continue practice, but right now the headmistress was watching Jack with eyes that were too knowing.

"God did something remarkable when He brought her to you," she said.

Jack watched Hattie play peekaboo over the back of the bench with the laughing child. "Indeed," he replied. "And I don't understand why."

CHAPTER SEVENTEEN

Hattie had never seen a Christmas pageant rehearsal like this before. Francine cuddled up next to her, smelling like strong soap and chalk dust, and together they watched as the students learned their lines. A few of them spoke the syllables haltingly. When Mrs. Lehrman gave them direction, another student would translate.

Their school clothes were creased sharply, starched and proper. Round brown faces contrasted with stiff white collars. The older girls' shiny black braids coiled around their heads elegantly, while the younger girls' braids hung down their shoulders. The boys all had short haircuts, all but Tom, whose braids marked him as a newcomer to the program.

Hattie caught Francine smiling up at her. The girl seemed content enough at the school. It would be a pity if the doors closed and she could no longer attend. Hattie might as well see if she could help Jack in his work while she was here.

"Francine, you said there's a scary man about. Can you show me where you saw him?"

Francine's smile disappeared. She lowered her eyes and pulled her feet up on the bench to hide them beneath her long skirt. "I didn't see him. It was Cold Rain who saw him."

"Cold Rain? Where is she?"

"She went home. Her father came and got her when they found out. The man had already stolen her blanket."

"But you haven't seen anything?" When the girl shook her head, Hattie scanned the faces of the children on the stage. What was behind this rumor? Childish imagination or something more nefarious? But there was another question. "How did Cold Rain get word to her father?" Hattie asked. The children were learning to read and write, but the parents couldn't.

Francine shrugged. "Boys run away to the villages. Girls, too. They get a special meal and honor for bringing messages for the families, then they come back to the school. Maybe Cold Rain told the messenger that she wanted to go home."

Hattie looked at the assembled students

with newfound respect. They might be singing English songs and celebrating a Christian tradition, but they had their own ways and their own system of communication that their instructors knew nothing about. "Do you want to show me where Cold Rain saw the spirit?"

Francine's eyes grew wide. "It was by her bed. She woke up, and it was floating over her."

"C'mon." Hattie stood. "I'll ask the headmistress if we can go back to the school —"

Francine hopped up. "I want to sing." Running from Hattie like she'd suddenly threatened her life, Francine bounded onto the stage and wormed her way into the line of the choir between two girls her age.

Hattie snorted.

"I was just going to compliment you on your skill with children." Jack stood in the aisle, blocking her end of the row.

"Evidently it expired."

The lines of the choir split, and Tom and one of the older girls walked through.

"Joseph and Mary," Jack said.

"Where is Baby Jesus?" Hattie asked. But then the couple turned to start the procession, and she saw a rag doll strapped onto a cradleboard hanging from the girl's back. She and Jack looked at each other and laughed.

"Why not?" Jack said. "It's the best way to carry a baby on a donkey."

"I wouldn't know," Hattie replied. "My skills with children don't extend that far."

The a cappella singing grew louder as the holy family made their way across the stage to where the shepherds had finally ceased their fighting and were kneeling. Turning, Jack eased his way between the benches and motioned for Hattie to sit.

"Did you learn anything from your little friend?" he asked.

He'd removed his overcoat, and as much as Hattie was attached to that piece of wool, she had to admit he cut a striking figure in his uniform. "Francine was scared," she said. But at Jack's wrinkled brow, she realized he couldn't hear her. She scooted closer on the bench. "She said that Cold Rain woke to see the spirit floating above her bed. Francine didn't see anything herself, though."

He put his arm on the back of the bench and leaned in. "The same Cold Rain who was punished for losing her blanket?"

"She isn't here anymore. She's one of the students who returned home."

"From which village?"

Hattie could only shrug. And marvel at

how his proximity made her heart feel bigger.

"Oh, and Jack?" The song had ended. The students began gathering the props from the stage, but Hattie and Jack barely noticed. "Cold Rain's father knew to come get her. The students take turns running away from school to get messages home to their folks. It's organized by the tribe."

Jack blinked in disbelief. "The chief knows they're going to leave?"

"The way Francine told it, everyone knows. They're given a big meal and sent back to the school with messages for the other students."

"All this time we're tracking them down, scared that we've lost a child, when really their parents know exactly where they are. They need to think of a better way. Every time a student leaves, he misses a week of classes at least."

"Why couldn't you or one of the soldiers take messages for them? If it would help the children stay in their classes?"

She'd turned to face him. He was so close. She'd never been this close to a man before. Not without kissing him, anyway. So, yes, she had been this close to a man, but not Jack.

"They wouldn't trust us, especially if the

messages are criticisms of the school, teachers, and various spirits that haunt the dormitory. I wouldn't want to deliver those messages anyway, so maybe they shouldn't trust me." His eyes held hers with a delicious slow burn that completely surprised her. "Maybe I'm not trustworthy," he said.

Those last words had slowed. She couldn't keep gazing into his eyes. Not without doing something she'd regret. Instead she spotted a rough patch on his jaw. With her thumb, she scrubbed at it.

"You missed a spot shaving," she said.

He held very still as if she could wipe it away. "I was in a hurry this morning. There was a beautiful woman downstairs fixing me breakfast."

Something in Arapaho was said loudly, and all the kids huffed out their laughter. Hattie scooted away from Jack and sat with her back flat against the bench. There was pointing, smiling, and dancing.

"Are they laughing at us?" she whispered. She'd forgotten that she and Jack weren't trying to playact for anyone.

He stood and bowed to the students. "Go on," he said. "I'll be there in a second."

Those who understood raced through the room, the first ones hitting the heavy wooden doors and making them fly. Those still learning English were only a few steps behind. Whatever had transpired, Jack was taking credit for it.

He took Hattie's hand and raised her to her feet. "Remember the treat I've been working on? Mrs. Lehrman informed them that they will get to skate today."

Hattie had only been ice skating a few times. It took a hard winter to freeze the ponds in Van Buren, and it sure didn't feel cold enough here.

"They like skating?"

"Don't all children? Let's go." But instead of heading off to a frozen pond, Jack walked her down the street to a massive three-story warehouse, the commissary.

"Is there a pond around back?"

He frowned, then understanding lit his face. "Ahh, you're in for a surprise." He hummed a quick tune as he escorted her inside and then up two flights of stairs.

This was so much better than staying home and rearranging Jack's library. Being with him made her feel special.

If only what she was experiencing were real.

The noise grew as they neared the top of the staircase. The doors opened onto a gigantic room with children whirling throughout. Hattie drew back from the speeding children to get a better look. Roller skates were strapped onto their feet over their sturdy government-supplied shoes. The rhythmic thumping of the skates on the boards sounded like one hundred muffled drums. The excitement in the room was overwhelming. Hattie's pulse raced. Jack's face lit up like a boy's.

"How long since you went skating?" he asked.

"Never on roller skates. Isn't this the commissary?" Stacked crates lined the walls. Those children without skates sat on barrels like statues on pedestals, while the troopers who had accompanied them helped unsteady skaters keep their balance.

"Usually it's pretty empty. That's why I sent the troopers here early to push all the goods to the side and oil up the skates. We haven't done this in a long time. Most of the students have probably never tried it before."

But they were quick learners. Even Tom was scooting around stiff-legged with his hands held out to his sides. Hattie wished she had her paints to capture the new learners' efforts. The angle of the young Arapaho bodies bending at the waist and leaning forward, the intent concentration of their eyes, the fingers held out even though there was nothing to catch but air — the scene was irresistible.

Already, Hattie could feel a shift in her appreciation. Before, she'd looked for beauty when choosing a subject — a sunset, a butterfly wing, a mountain. But she was finding herself more drawn to the emotion, the action of the scene. Because that was where she could most clearly see the character, and somehow character was becoming more interesting by the minute.

Was this what the critics had meant? Was this change what the curators were looking for? Perhaps, but the criticism no longer hurt. Hattie couldn't be anything but happy watching the youngsters' exuberance.

She bounced on her toes. The chase was so entertaining. Two boys zoomed past her, and Jack put out a protective arm.

"Maybe we should wait behind the barrels," he said.

She obediently found a more protected place. She had to squeeze in between the barrel and the wall amid some sacks, but she wanted there to be enough room for Jack, too. She wanted to hear more stories and information about the Indians.

Jack nodded at a set of double doors at the end of the room. "Those doors are for loading and unloading the crates," he said.

"They open to a pulley above them and nothing below. Excuse me while I make sure they're locked down into the floor. If a kid slams into them and they open, it'd be a tragedy."

She shuddered to think about the height they were at on the third story, but the chaos of the skating students soon distracted her.

A trooper stepped forward, inserted two fingers in his mouth, and blew a sharp blast. Groans filled the air from those skating. Those sitting on the barrels hopped off and began chasing down a skater.

"Now the others get their turn," Jack said as he returned.

The skaters were sprawled across the room, their skates being hurriedly removed by their impatient classmates. A few still skated, trying to outrun those waiting, but the waiters were organized. They spread out, cornered them, and pulled them to the ground.

"Watch an expert at work," Jack said.

She watched as he went from student to student, studying their discarded skates. Sometimes he would give a wheel a spin. Finally, he found a pair that met his approval. He dropped to the floor next to a long, lean boy with a mischievous grin, and

Jack began strapping on the skates right over his cavalry boots. He stood slowly and tested first one leg, then the other, with the same concentration she'd seen him expend at the blackboard over a challenging arithmetic problem. Then, satisfied, he gave her a triumphant grin before launching into a race.

Hattie hadn't meant to laugh so loudly. She covered her mouth, shocked as Jack's long legs powered him quickly around the circle. The boy he'd sat by knew he was being chased. He glanced over his shoulder, both his smile and his eyes growing wide as Jack closed in on him. But the boy wasn't an easy catch. While Jack was bigger and stronger, the boy was nimble, and in a room full of skating children, he could dart and dodge better than Jack.

The other boys saw what was happening. Their war whoops nearly made Hattie's heart stop, but she couldn't be afraid. Not here. Not with all the innocent laughter and high spirits. The children were scattering. Taking to the sides, they watched as Jack chased the taunting boy, but the clearer the floor, the fewer places there were for him to hide. Instead of going in circles, now it was a game of tag. The boy cut one way, then another. Jack needed more room to change directions, and that kept the boy just out of his reach.

But the boy was running out of people to dodge through. He was trapped on one side of the room. When he started left, Jack edged that direction, all the time closing in on him. The closer he got, the more Jack grinned. They were laughing, taunting each other in a language she didn't know, but she could easily understand the gist. The boys and girls along the walls yelled their encouragement, some to their classmate and some to Jack. Seeing that the noose was tightening, the boy made a desperate dash to get past Jack and back into the open room. Once he committed to his direction, Jack picked up speed to head him off, but just as the boy passed a group of his classmates, a small wooden crate tumbled out of the crowd and into Jack's path.

He didn't have time to stop. Was he agile enough to dodge it? Hattie's hand covered her mouth. Right when it looked like Jack was going to crash into the crate, he bent and, with a mighty leap, jumped over the box.

Hattie cheered along with the students, but they were premature. Jack did jump over the crate — he even cleared it — but when his skates hit the ground on the other side, he lost his balance. Like a tall tree being felled, Jack went down, limbs waving in the air until he hit the ground with a mighty crash.

The boy turned, now worried for the lieutenant. The girls were scolding the younger boy who'd thrown the crate into his path. With open palms, they slapped the fellow, who flinched away from the punishment he was facing. But Jack just rolled over, flopped on his back, and laughed like he'd never had so much fun before.

Hattie found herself trying to get to him, but her foot was tangled in the drawstring of an old sack. Kicking to free herself, she watched as the boy skated back around and offered Jack a hand up. Jack clasped his hand and got to his feet. There was a lot of good-natured ribbing and slaps on the back as Jack congratulated the boy, and then he was surrounded by his classmates. Hattie waited by the barrel as Jack skated to her, looking every bit as mischievous as the students.

"I need more practice," he said.

"I'd say you presented yourself well." Hattie took him by the arm and turned him to dust him off. A few slaps on his back knocked the white dust off the blue. His britches needed a dusting as well, but that was his problem. She was still smiling when he looked over his shoulder.

"What's so funny?"

"Seeing you bested by a boy made my day."

"I've got to figure out how to maneuver better. Perhaps if I ordered some skates in a bigger size? These skates don't distribute a man's weight properly."

Hattie pinched his arm before releasing him. "Don't you dare. The boy deserved to win. He's a better skater."

"They worked together to beat me, just like the buffalo hunters," Jack said. "Not that any of these kids are old enough to remember, but their parents would be proud."

"After listening to their Christmas practice, it's good to see them doing something that comes easier," she said.

"They can sing, believe me. It's just the language that's getting in the way. Mrs. Lehrman will have them ready in two weeks."

In two weeks? Was Christmas coming that fast? Hattie knew she wouldn't be able to learn an Arapaho or Cheyenne song in that time.

"Now it's your turn," Jack said. Hattie could never predict what he'd come up with next, but she was delighted.

The whistle blew, ending the turn for the second round of skaters. Only a handful were left who hadn't skated already. A few teachers appeared to escort the kids back to the classroom, except for those who had patiently waited their turn. Several students came by to be acknowledged by a wink or smile from Jack before they went back to class. Once the room was mostly empty, Jack fetched two more skates and headed back with them dangling from their straps.

If she ever thought her face could split from a smile, it was fixing to.

"You're going to make me try it?" she asked.

"You've been dying to." He handed her the skates. "You can't fool me."

With a little instruction, Hattie finally got her skates attached to her boots. When they'd first arrived, the room had been cold. It was still cool, and her cheeks felt tight and rosy, but all the activity had warmed the air enough that it was very comfortable.

Hattie reached for a nearby barrel and walked her hands up it until she stood at her full height. With a dozen tiny steps, she turned herself around.

"It's now or never," Jack said.

As she released the barrel, the skates took off on her, rolling forward. With a squeal, she grabbed Jack's hands, but as she tried to straighten, she ended up leaning back farther and farther, and the skates shot forward faster and faster. If it hadn't been for Jack's skates getting in the way, she would have landed on her backside.

"Upsy-daisy." He laughed as he blocked her skates with his own and hauled her upright. "I had no idea you were this clumsy. You aren't going to blame me if you get hurt, are you?"

"One hundred percent, Jack Hennessey. You will have to pay for every scrape and bruise I get today." She was so out of breath from laughing, she could barely talk.

"If you're too chicken —"

"Not on your life." She kept a strong grip on his forearm with one hand and let go with the other. Then, with one hand outstretched, Hattie inched forward. Jack remained in place, allowing her to work a shuffling circle around him. "The skates are steadier than ice skates," she said, "but they're harder to propel."

"You're doing beautifully."

She was prepared to argue, but he spun her around and pulled her into his arms.

"Are you feeling steadier?" he asked.

Not hardly. Hattie clasped his wool uniform, glad for something to hold on to.

"Ready to try a little faster?" he asked. A tint of pink had colored his face. Were she painting him, she would have had trouble finding the right shade.

"Hattie?"

She took a deep breath and forced a sunny smile. "Sorry, I was just thinking."

He watched her too intently. If he kept gazing at her like that, people were going to think . . . exactly what he wanted them to think. Hattie pulled out of his grasp. "My goodness, you're a better actor than I thought. I didn't realize how far you were willing to go to fool everyone."

"I challenge your suggestion," he countered. "I'm being honest, remember?"

Not knowing what to say, Hattie decided to walk away, but it wasn't that easy. It took about a dozen steps to turn around, but she finally had her back to him and was headed toward the middle of the room to join the skating students. A girl with short black hair and her blouse untucked sped by, cutting close to Hattie. Hattie swerved out of her path, but the sudden movement set her wobbling again. Jack took her arm and slowed his pace to match hers.

"I read a lot of books, you know. I write about other people, study them, always living in other people's words and in my own words on paper." He paused as she flailed her arms to get her balance, then continued. "I want to live my own life today, Hattie. I'm not going to waste this time trying to fool anyone. It's already been amazing. Do I have your permission?"

Permission to drop their act? She was having so much fun. She didn't want their time to end. Especially now.

"Will you help me back to the wall before you stop acting your role?" she asked.

He raised an eyebrow. "Absolutely not. I'm going to skate with you until neither of us can walk tomorrow."

Had she misunderstood? He kept her arm as she found her pace. Once her feet really did leave her, but by holding her arm, he was able to keep her from hitting the floor hard. More than a few children laughed along with her.

"I'm never going to be as good as they are," Hattie said.

"Nothing to do but get up and try again," Jack said. And true to his word, he hauled her back up.

"Easy for you to say. You've already got it figured out."

"Let's try something new. I haven't mastered backward yet." His tall boots looked odd with the silver skates strapped on the bottom. He spun around in front of her and held out his arms. "May I have this dance?"

Wait. She thought he wasn't trying to convince anyone of anything today. But she couldn't deny that the idea sounded splendid . . . and likely to get them both hurt. Gingerly, she lifted her hands to his shoulders. He just as carefully took her waist.

"Are you ready?" he asked. "Here we go."

He stepped backward, pulling Hattie forward. "We need some music," she said. A dark-eyed boy skated by, watching curiously.

"Music would distract me." His hand flexed on her waist. "I have enough distractions as it is. You're . . . you're —"

His heel caught on something, but Hattie was still moving. She slammed against him, and it was enough to send them both to the ground.

Jack landed on his back with Hattie on top of him. The look of surprise on his face was priceless. She started giggling and dropped her forehead against his chest. She could find much to admire about her current situation, yet something was wrong. A tough little knot marred the smoothness of his chest and nearly put a crease in her forehead.

She rolled off him, sat up, and asked, "What do you have in your pocket? A rock?"

His mouth tightened as he covered his pocket defensively. "It's nothing."

"Nothing? Then why don't you tell me?"

A whistle sounded. Skate time had ended for the last batch of children.

"Better get out of the way," Jack said as he stood.

The troopers gathered the skates as the students removed them and ran out the door back to the school.

Hattie reached for the buckles on her skates. "That was fun," she said.

"We're not done," Jack said. "Private Willis, I'm taking a detail here to reconnoiter the skating campaign. Can you lead your unit in a general survey of the area until I'm done?"

Willis answered with a sharp salute. "Yes, sir. We'll escort the children to the school and find something to keep us busy until you complete your mission."

Hattie's mouth dropped open, and she pulled on her bare earlobe. "Lieutenant Hennessey, are you abusing your position?"

He grinned, looking more boyish than he ever had at twelve years old. "I can't have those little kids outmaneuvering me. They're cocky enough as it is. Now, come on. We can do this."

Just standing up was comical enough.

Hattie was laughing so hard that she had trouble catching her breath. Jack didn't seem to care that she was still tickled. He took her by the waist and started pulling her as he tried to pick up some speed going backward. With each stride, he lifted a leg and set it behind him awkwardly, like he was walking through thick mud backward.

"I'm afraid to go any faster," he said.

"Would it help if I did the pushing?" she asked.

"Be my guest."

Hattie strengthened her grip on his shoulders and took a step. They wobbled as she found her pace, but Jack's help steadied her.

"If I'd known this was so much fun," he said, "I wouldn't let the kids do it anymore. I'd just bring you here every day."

Hattie lifted her head. "Shame on you, Jack. No one can hear you now, so you don't need to talk like that."

"Hattie." He moved his hands higher on her waist. "Don't correct me again."

She looked up, and what she saw surprised her. Jack was looking at her with more than just the warm, friendly gaze he'd shared since leaving the house. There was a possessiveness in his eyes that sent a jolt through her. With a tug on his shoulder, she rolled closer into his arms. She had to admit, they were having fun. At the moment, skating with Jack was what she wanted, too.

Besides crates, barrels, and sacks, the room was empty. Hattie's attention moved to avoiding Jack's feet as she helped propel them around the room. One step too far was all it took.

Her foot brushed against the side of Jack's skate. The wheels on his skate stopped spinning, and once again he pitched backward. This time he thought to let go of Hattie before dragging her down with him, but it didn't matter much. She still ended up tumbling on top of him.

"You're going to be flatter than a pancake," she said. She flopped to her back and crawdad-crawled a decent distance away. "You hit the floor hard again, and you don't have the padding I do."

Jack rose on his elbow. "Mrs. Hennessey, I find your statement shocking."

She cackled. "I'm talking about my skirts. My skirts and petticoats compared to your trousers, you cad."

"Oh." He smiled wickedly as he stood. "You had me confused." He pulled her up and took her by the waist.

"Again?" she asked.

"I'm determined." Focusing on the far wall, he said, "But this time you're going to go backward. It might be easier." Without waiting for her answer, he pushed off, and they were moving again.

She was running blind. Nothing to look at besides him. "Are you sure? I can barely stand up."

"All you have to do is hold on to me," he said. "Don't move your feet and let me lead."

They certainly were picking up speed. Where before Hattie had felt responsible for directing them, now she only had to hold on to Jack and feel the seams of the floor vibrating beneath her feet. But that wasn't all she was feeling. Her pulse raced. Her skin chilled as the air blew against her damp neck. Who knew skating was so much work? Who knew skating could be so intimate?

Jack had been right. Letting him do all the work was proving to be their best attempt yet. In fact, they were so successful that Hattie began to worry. "We're going so fast," she said.

"And we can go faster."

"But should we?" The crates that lined the room passed by in a blur.

He looked more than a little reckless. "We can do this. Just one more turn, and we've set a new record."

He was trying to turn her. Hattie could

feel added pressure to the outside of her left skate. Jack leaned that way, his right hand bearing down against her waist like she was the tiller on a ship. She should probably lean to take the turn, but she didn't trust her balance. And the speed Jack was going —

"Don't think about it, Hattie. Just let it come. Trust yourself."

"I'm trying," she said as she closed her eyes. "I'm trying."

"That's right. I've got you. Just hold —"

But once again, his skate bumped into hers. One of her feet left the ground. Jack flew forward. He tried to get an arm beneath her to cushion her fall, but it did little to help. Hattie landed flat on her back with Jack sprawled over her.

She lay there with no air at all. Slowly her lungs expanded, and she surprised herself with a throaty chuckle.

Jack was holding most of his weight off her with his arms braced on both sides. His dark eyes searched hers intently. "Are you all right?"

Her blood still pulsing, her hair awry, and her nerves tingling — she'd never felt better. And there was Jack, so close that she could see his pulse bouncing just below his jaw. If it hadn't been good old Jack, she might mistake this breathless feeling for attraction. But it couldn't be that. Besides, he didn't know the first thing about girls.

Or did he?

She was fixing to find out, because the impossible was happening.

Jack leaned down. His breath was sweet, his eyes captivating. What would it be like to be kissed by the handsome officer? His scent was the same as the coat she'd slept with last night, but to her mind, he was someone new, exciting, and strange. No dusty scholar could make her heart run out of control like this.

Placing his weight on one arm, he searched her face. "You never answered me," he said. "Are you all right?"

All the awkwardness over misunderstood ceremonies and childhood regrets had vanished, leaving two people with infinite respect for one another lying in each other's arms. Her eyes were drawn to his sensitive lips as she wondered what they were capable of.

"I feel dizzy," she said.

He paused, so close as he considered his options. For Pete's sake, why couldn't Jack ever do anything spontaneous? Her heart sank as he rolled away, then took her hand and helped her sit up.

She dusted off her hands while trying to

shake away the tingly feeling that had gone unresolved. She knew what would come next — the apology for playing with fire, for imposing on her, because cautious Jack would never have allowed himself the familiarity they'd shared.

Instead he asked, "Did you hit your head?"

"What?" The air between them was cooler than she remembered. It made her skin prickle all the more.

"When you fell. Dizziness and memory loss are symptoms of a concussion. We were skating and we fell. If you can't remember that . . ."

Hattie rolled her eyes. After that moment, the looks they'd exchanged, he was worried about her medical condition? She crooked her knees and began to unfasten her skates.

"I'm not injured, if that's what you're asking." Honestly! Why did he take everything so literally?

"That's good." Silence filled the room like a steam boiler about to blow, but Jack seemed unaffected. "We made it all the way around the room," he said. "See, if you set your mind to something, it's surprising what you can accomplish." Finally, free of his skates, he gathered all four of them and offered her his hand.

Hattie hesitated before taking it to stand.

"We beat a record?" she mocked. Unbelievable. Was he made of stone? "Congratulations to us, then." No wonder it had never worked out between them. He wasn't the man for her.

Jack studied her with that inscrutable expression. Then, with a swing of his arm, he gestured toward the door.

He might be book smart, but when it came to women, Jack Hennessey was flunking his exam.

CHAPTER EIGHTEEN

He'd nearly kissed Hattie Walker. Jumping Jehoshaphat, he'd nearly kissed Hattie Walker. Of course, she might have been suffering from a head injury and unable to read his intent, but it could have happened. She hadn't tried to stop him. Only his good sense had pulled the reins quickly enough to save him.

Jack followed Hattie down the stairs of the warehouse, hoping she knew the way out, because right now he wasn't thinking straight. He had thought that he was growing immune to her — that noticing her flaws and having disagreements nearly every day meant that he couldn't be in love. On the contrary, the strengths she displayed — her ability to calm Francine, befriend Miss Richert, and persevere during the day even though she spent every night terrified — far outweighed her flaws and only increased his admiration. Unfortunately, his admiration was forbidden. He'd made her a deal — pretend to be married, and he'd let her go. It wasn't fair to take advantage of her compliance, and it would hurt too much when she left.

He'd walked straight by Bradley Willis before the private stopped him. After a few hurried instructions on rearranging the commissary room, they headed back to the school.

The school. That was what was important. Saving the school meant everything, and until he was reassigned, he'd do what he could to help them succeed.

They reached the schoolhouse door. Jack didn't have the heart to take Hattie's arm. He held the door open and let her pass. Her jaw was set, her face pale. No more laughter. Was she angered by his familiarity or still suffering from the fall? He might take her by the post hospital just to make sure.

Mrs. Lehrman was greeting Tom when they passed through her office. Tom's usually erect posture was even stiffer. After the skating, Jack was surprised to see him so solemn. With no translator available, Jack used his Arapaho to ask how he'd liked the skating. Tom said it was fun, but his eyes never left the headmistress's desk. What could be bothering him? Jack didn't see anything sinister.

"Tom is settling in here at the school," Mrs. Lehrman said. "Superintendent Seger is on his way over to get him that first haircut."

A lump formed in Jack's throat. It might only be a fraction of what Tom felt, but he shared his anguish. Although Tom was at the school with his chief's blessing — in fact, he was there at his chief's command — he would still feel like he was betraying his people. Cutting those braids was an act of shame. Scalping an enemy meant total domination of your tribe over his. While this haircut wouldn't cost Tom his life, it would cost him his pride. And yet the school and missionaries deemed it an important step in embracing their new culture.

Superintendent Seger entered with the barber. "Good afternoon, Mrs. Lehrman," he said. "Is this the fine young man we're going to give a trim today?"

The superintendent knew well enough the agony the young man was going through. Perhaps it was best that he kept his tone light and efficient. Perhaps it was easier if Tom could pretend to have no qualms.

"Where should we set up?" The barber unfurled an apron. "Right here at the desk?" His thick, curling mustache waggled like

269

mouse whiskers.

"That would be fine," Mrs. Lehrman answered. She closed a ledger and removed a stack of books from the desk. "Mr. Broken Arrow is already a handsome man. This will only make him more distinguished."

Jack knew the words were kindly meant, but they would mean nothing to the boy. Only acceptance from his own tribe mattered, and there the results were mixed. So far, most of the children who'd quit the school had gone back to their old ways in a hurry to prove they hadn't changed. Wearing a school uniform and hard-soled shoes and keeping a short haircut wouldn't earn them any respect in their villages. But those who had finished the upper grades in Darlington, or who had gone on to further schooling at the Carlisle Indian Industrial School, learned to be comfortable in white culture. Some were able to help their tribe through the skills they'd learned, like farming or commerce, or through legal means once they understood the importance of the contracts and treaties signed by the tribe.

Would Tom Broken Arrow regret his decision to come to the school? Would all that he learned here be rejected as soon as possible, or would he find some benefit to the lessons and the language they would teach him? From the look on his face as he sat in the headmistress's chair, Tom had his doubts.

Hattie leaned against the half wall that separated the headmistress's office from the waiting area. With the entrance of the superintendent and a barber, she could hide in obscurity. Truthfully, she didn't know what to make of Jack's actions and wasn't as composed as she would wish. Especially before the knowing eyes of Mrs. Lehrman.

Instead of apologizing, when Jack looked at her now, he watched her like he was evaluating her for treatment. What was wrong with him? Why couldn't he react like a normal man? On the other hand, Hattie had been courted by several normal men. They were so predictable. And none of them had ever tempted her away from her independence. This was something else altogether.

She knew the Indian boy. It was Tom Broken Arrow, and from the looks of it, he was going to get a haircut. Someday she would paint children with that particular combination of the school uniform with braids. Very few of the boys had that. None besides Tom, now that she thought of it. He was the only one. And that was going to change in a matter of seconds.

Hattie looked the boy over. In the village, she hadn't seen one Arapaho man with short hair. They just didn't do it. Would Tom be an outcast when he went home? Would he even be allowed to go home? Leaving her spot against the wall, Hattie stepped forward.

Tom took his seat bravely, avoiding eye contact with anyone. While the barber and superintendent spoke encouragement as they draped a cloth over his wool jacket and white dress shirt, Tom didn't understand their words. Not that they would have been much comfort even if he could.

Hattie was transfixed. The light hit his soft bronze cheeks and reflected into his eyes. What did those eyes see? Did they see a future more glorious than he could imagine, or did they see sorrow at what he was leaving behind? He was determined. His hands clutched the arms of the chair as if they were all that kept him from darting out the door. Determined, but what else? Fearful? Maybe a touch of hopefulness, too? All this Hattie saw, and she knew she could get it on canvas.

She jammed her hand into her reticule and felt around until she laid hold of a pencil. Then, flipping the headmistress's ledger to the back, she ripped out a blank piece of paper. Blue lines sliced it up into columns, but Hattie wouldn't be bothered by them. They might even come in handy as a graph for her next attempt, and she was already convinced that this portrait was worth a more permanent canvas.

Quickly her pencil skimmed over the page, catching Tom's narrow face with the cheeks still rounded from childhood. The apron added nothing to the picture. It would be better to paint him in his school uniform. Who didn't remember the pride and optimism that went along with their new school clothes in the fall? She had to hurry to get his braids. Of course, her pencil couldn't catch the opaque sheen that reflected blue, but she wouldn't forget.

Lastly, and most importantly, was catching the spirit of the moment. The fear and hope warring inside of him. The questions of who he would be once this change took place. Where would he fit in?

Hattie understood his conflict. Before coming to Fort Reno, she was committed to success in Denver. She was convinced that she would only be happy when she'd proven herself with her art, and if the majesty of the Rocky Mountains couldn't inspire her, then nothing could.

But here was a boy who challenged her thinking. The mountains were beautiful works of a mighty God, but was there anything that showed His loving creativity more than people?

The barber picked up a heavy pair of scissors. Hattie's pencil lifted, and her hand stilled. The boy's eyes darted to the side, catching sight of the metal. His braid was tugged out to the side, away from his head, and the scissors slid against his ear. Hattie could imagine the feel of the cold blades. The boy's chin wrinkled, and then just like that, the braid was cut and taken out of his sight. Tom's hand lifted as the barber went to his other side. Hattie watched intently, trying to record every emotion that passed on his face. His fingers combed through his hair, then flicked free where the braid had always been. He passed over the spot again, this time going back up and ruffling the bluntly cut hair that had been tied down before. The cut on the other side was just as quick. Mrs. Lehrman exchanged a relieved look with the superintendent once the braids were dropped in the dustbin.

Tom started to stand, but the barber stopped him with a hand at his shoulder. "We're not done yet, son. Still have to trim you up."

"He doesn't understand," Mrs. Lehrman said. "Lieutenant Hennessey, can you help?"

Tom turned to look at Jack. His eyes were worried. His tightly controlled emotions had nearly broken free.

Jack knelt in front of him, and after a few words, Tom seemed to relax. Jack's honest face remained calm and reassuring, much as it had when he'd found Hattie huddled inside that tepee. It struck her again how valuable her friend had become for the people at the reservation. His ability to mediate and his respect for them had the power to smooth over many hurtful situations.

"Go ahead," Jack told the barber. "He's fine."

With a comb and scissors, the barber worked his way around Tom's head, straightening up the ragged places. Dark, straight hair dusted the apron. He didn't frame the boy's face but left the hair one length, with the front locks long enough to push behind his ears.

"I think I've done enough," the barber said at last. He brushed off Tom's shoulders and untied the apron. His shoulders sloped. "There's another one fixed for you."

While they were morose, Jack seemed determined to brighten the mood. Hattie couldn't understand the words he said, but she could read him like the books he loved so well. The corners of his eyes crinkled up, and his eyebrows lifted a fraction of an inch. Jack was squatting at Tom's knees and leaning forward. Whatever he was saying, he said it with warmth and gentle coaxing. A crease appeared in Tom's smooth cheek. Although not happy, his eyes settled into acceptance. The ordeal was over. It was time to get back to class. With all the other boys in the school having undergone the same initiation, he had no reason to feel alone. In fact, he would stand out less now. The true test wouldn't come until he returned home.

Somewhere during their conversation, Hattie had picked up her pencil again. The tone had changed, and so had her subject. This time she wanted to capture the bridge, the one who filled in the gap between the two cultures so they could better learn to understand each other. True, he might be bound by his oath to don a uniform and serve in the military, but there was no doubt that Jack's heart was with these people.

And these were the people he would have to leave, because of her.

Chapter Nineteen

Jack should have been taking advantage of the last half hour of their ride to tell Hattie what was on his mind, but instead he sat on the wagon bench next to her and silently watched the clouds scurry across the sky as they rode back to the fort.

This was torture, and it was time for it to end. Jack cared about Hattie too much to derail her plans, and after nearly kissing her, he didn't trust himself to keep his distance. He'd transgressed against her for too long. He had to let her go for both of their sakes. The sooner she was gone, the better.

If only he could be assured that she was safe.

Their evening meal at the restaurant in Darlington had been a quiet affair. The troopers waited in the warehouse, eating whatever they'd frittered away in their knapsacks, until Jack gave them word it was time to head back. He'd miss these men.

He'd miss all of it. Who could have guessed that finding Hattie would put an end to his career? But surely God had other plans for him.

They reached the fort as the sun went down on the early winter evening. Jack turned the wagon toward Officers' Row and noticed that the lamps in the Adamses' house were lit. Had they returned? His gut clenched. If Major Adams was back, there was no reason to delay his departure. And knowing Major Adams, he'd have all the paperwork in order already. This period of confusion and heartache was about to come to an end, and hopefully peace would follow. Hopefully Jack could set aside his fruitless daydreams now that he knew Hattie had no room for him in her life.

Jack stopped the wagon and helped Hattie disembark. He paused at the door to his house. "I'll be back in a bit. You don't need to wait up for me."

"After such an exciting day, I couldn't sleep yet."

Ten-year-old Daisy's raised voice could be heard from next door. Major Adams was definitely home.

"There's something I have to check on," he said. "Excuse me." He ushered her into the house, closed the door on her confusion, and marched next door.

Maybe etiquette would say that one didn't interrupt the post commander the night he returned from his honeymoon, but Jack had questions that needed answering. His breath steamed in the cold air as he waited at the door after knocking. The youngest Adams girl's voice could be heard as she twisted the doorknob and swung the door open.

Jack blinked into the brightly lit parlor. "How are you, Miss Daisy? Did you have a nice trip?"

Daisy swung the door open wide and motioned him inside. "Lieutenant Jack! I have so much to tell you. We rode a stagecoach all the way to Tahlequah. It was so cold. And Grandmother and Grandfather met us there. We went shopping with Grandmother, and I wanted to buy you a book about Napoleon for Christmas, but Grandmother said it wasn't becoming for a lady to buy a bachelor a Christmas present. I told her that you were married now, and she said that made it even worse, but I think she didn't want to pay for it. You see, I had no money —"

"Daisy, is your father home?" While Jack was fond of Daisy and her big sister, Caroline, his mission burned with urgency.

"Pa!" she yelled up the staircase. "Lieutenant Jack is here to see you."

"Jack?" Major Adams moved into the hallway at the top of the stairs. He had to step over an open traveling case in the hallway before descending. "What's the matter? It must be important if it can't wait until morning."

It was odd seeing Major Adams in civilian clothes. Just another reminder that Jack was intruding on family time.

"It is important. My transfer request — where are they sending me?"

Major Adams's eyes shifted. "Let's go in my office." He laid a hand on Daisy's shoulder as he passed. "Tell your mother that we have company."

"Yes, sir." She saluted. Then she bellowed with all the strength of her healthy lungs, "Mother, we have company!"

Major Adams merely shook his head. "Louisa is doing wonders civilizing the girls, but it's going to take some time. They were left without any feminine influence for too long."

They entered the major's office, which was nearly as familiar to Jack as his own. Major Adams took his seat behind his desk, while Jack tried not to wear a hole in the rug as he waited for his answer.

"Now, about that transfer —" Major Adams said.

"Everything has been calm since you left. There are troops still out hunting for the bandit and we haven't tracked down the lapse in communication between the two forts concerning the escort for the payment, but the tribes haven't demonstrated against the delay yet. The only negative news is that enrollment at the school continues to diminish. The Cheyenne and Arapaho have no reason to doubt that Hattie and I are man and wife, but it's only a matter of time before that falsehood is exposed. It would've been good if we could've waited for the marshals to talk to her, but I've gotta get Miss Walker on to her destination before we ruin everything."

Major Adams's forehead wrinkled while a ghost of a smile haunted his face. Perhaps Jack was being immature, showing up at this hour and blurting out everything just as carelessly as young Daisy had, but it was better this way. The sooner he could learn his fate, the sooner he'd be reconciled to it. And the sooner Hattie would be off his hands.

"Have you shown them a convincing picture of marital affection while I was gone?" Daniel asked.

"Yes, sir. From our behavior in public, no

one could doubt our love." Especially if they saw them skating together earlier that day.

"And what about your behavior in private?" It wasn't a tease. Major Adams was gathering information before he decided his course. Jack knew him well enough to expect it.

"My behavior has been that of an exemplary gentleman."

"That's a pity."

Jack narrowed his eyes. "You have no idea the strain I'm under. I'm going to lose my mind. The only thing keeping me sane is that you said you would get me reassigned, and I would be dismissed as soon as you returned."

"I may have overstated the case," Major Adams said. He dropped his pencil to the desk. "I thought by the time I returned, you'd have this all straightened out."

"How am I supposed to straighten it out? You ordered me to stay here and honor their ceremony."

"And you're doing a poor job of it."

Jack gripped the back of the chair in front of him. He didn't want to be blunt, but something drastic had to be done. "Has my transfer been approved? Yes or no?"

Major Adams grimaced. "There hasn't been a transfer request made, exactly. If I had known how adamant you are about separating from our guest, then I would've taken the request more seriously."

Adamant? Major Adams had yet to see how adamant Jack could be.

Hattie held the curtain aside in her lonesome bedroom. Every room in Major Adams's house next door was lit. Louisa Adams and Caroline could be seen in the parlor, hanging Christmas greenery, while the youngest girl danced around with an Indian doll. The scene looked warm, homey, and much different than the silent house Hattie was standing in. She reached for her coat. Why should she be alone while Jack visited with their neighbors? The ladies would welcome her.

She barely had to knock before the front door swung open. Daisy clapped her hands together in delight. It was the best greeting Hattie had received since leaving Van Buren.

"Welcome home," Hattie said.

Instead of answering, Daisy put her finger to her mouth and shushed her. "Father and Lieutenant Jack are having an important meeting. You can come help us decorate the parlor. Tomorrow, Father is going to get us a Christmas tree. Caroline says it's too late in the season and that we'll just have to take it down again, but Father said that it's our first Christmas all together, and we're going to celebrate it properly." Taking Hattie by the hand, Daisy dragged her past the office where Jack and Major Adams were involved in a heated exchange. Thankfully, they were both too busy to notice her passing outside the door.

"You have no idea how loathsome this has been," Jack was saying. "The pretending is wearing me slick. You promised that you would end it when you came back, and unless you want me to desert, you'd better see to it."

Loathsome? Hattie's stomach plummeted. She'd felt bad about invading his house, but if she'd known how strongly he resented her, she would have bought a ticket on the first stagecoach out of the territory. At the very least, she wouldn't have accepted his coat when he offered it.

Sweet Daisy continued pulling her along. Trunks and bags lined the wall, with a pile of dirty laundry waiting in the basket for the wash. These little details were what Hattie would focus on to keep her composure. Otherwise, she would be a sobbing mess. Who would have thought that Jack could hurt her feelings so badly?

"Hattie, what a pleasure." Major Adams's

new wife looked a little uncertain. Although a great beauty, Louisa seemed uncomfortable in society, even here in her own parlor.

"I'm sorry to come over uninvited. I wanted to welcome you home."

Half of Caroline's red hair had escaped her chignon, but she had all the confidence her stepmother lacked. "Are you looking for your husband?" she asked. "He's only been here a few minutes, but I'm sure you miss him terribly."

Hattie could only pray that they mistook the flush on her cheeks as a bride's embarrassment.

Louisa dropped a green bough onto the hearth to come closer. "I apologize for leaving Jack in charge so soon after your wedding. When we planned our nuptials, we had no inkling that he'd follow so soon. I hope you were able to spend time together, despite his duties."

"I've seen him more than I expected to, but sometimes I think he'd rather be alone." Hattie hadn't meant to let that slip, but she was so confused. If Jack couldn't stand her, wanted to be rid of her, why did he find reasons for them to go places together? Why would he swear he wasn't being false?

Worry lines appeared between Louisa's eyes. "Marriage is a hard transition," she said, "even under the best of circumstances. As long as the two of you love each other and are willing to work together, everything will smooth over."

There was a commotion at the front of the house. Whatever Jack was saying to his commander, he was saying it loudly.

"I should go," Hattie said.

"Caroline, tell your father that Mrs. Hennessey is here," Louisa whispered. "Hurry."

"I don't want to interrupt them," Hattie protested. Especially when they were fighting about her. "You don't need to tell them I was here."

But Louisa looked like her tail feathers were getting ruffled. "Nonsense. Men should know better than to carry on like that. If I was back at the Cat-Eye, I'd have them both thrown in the street."

The Cat-Eye? What was Louisa talking about? Hattie started toward the door, but there was no sneaking past the office this time.

"Mrs. Hennessey?" The major had spotted her and was looking at Jack with a warning in his eyes.

Jack's head bowed so low that she could see the crooked part in his hair. He came out of the office looking like a puppy caught chewing his master's shoes. "Hattie, I didn't expect you here."

"Evidently not." She'd used this cold look when she was in school and thought someone was mocking her, but it had never hurt this much before.

Major Adams, all pomp and propriety, stepped forward. "Mrs. Hennessey, may I say how pleased I am to see you again? Jack tells me that you are adjusting to life on the fort."

"Is that what he tells you?" she asked.

The major had the grace to look ashamed. "If there's anything I can do to make your stay more comfortable . . ."

Hattie didn't answer. She was too busy staring at Jack and hoping he'd wither away under her burning gaze. Instead he stepped forward as if to take her arm.

"Thank you for looking after the matter," he said to Major Adams. "I think it's time I take my wife home for the evening."

"Look," Daisy called. She pointed above their heads to the chandelier in the entryway. "Lieutenant Jack and Mrs. Hennessey are standing under the mistletoe. Now they have to kiss."

Hattie's skin prickled. And then Jack had the nerve to look at her — really look at her — with some sort of sickly longing in his eyes. For whose benefit? Did he think the major's daughters were part of the audience? Hattie had reached her limit of hypocrisy for the day, and seeing that he was leaning forward as if he might actually touch her, she swung her arm to shove him in the chest.

She hadn't meant to swing so hard, but she was furious. And she hadn't meant to aim so high, but at the last minute, he bent as if to kiss her hand. The combined effect resulted in a punch straight to his jaw.

Everyone in the room gasped. Hattie felt the impact in each knuckle. Jack stepped back and stood with his chin high, refusing to react even as his face turned red.

"Girls, it's time for bed," Louisa said. "Let's go upstairs and get ready." Grabbing the arms of her daughters, she herded them up the stairs.

"It's getting late," Major Adams said. "I'll leave the two of you to find your way out."

But Hattie wasn't waiting to hear any more. Ducking her head, she ran past the stunned men and straight to her bedroom next door.

CHAPTER TWENTY

Had she heard him begging for relief? Had she witnessed his anger when told that he had to spend more time with her? If she'd arrived any earlier, then she might have realized that he was pleading on her behalf. The pain in his jaw told him that whatever she'd heard, Hattie hadn't appreciated it.

She'd left his front door open a crack, and her coat lay crumpled on the floor in the doorway. Jack picked up the heavy buckskin and hung it on the banister. Hattie was usually the tidy one, but in her hurry to hide from him, she'd abandoned all her habits.

Hadn't they talked this through? She wanted freedom, and that was what he was trying to give her. But what was important right now was that Hattie was hurt, and Jack had caused it. He had to make amends, but this time he'd be ready to duck when she swung a fist.

He paused as he reached the top of the

stairs and saw the light spiking out from beneath her bedroom door. He knocked gently. "Hattie, do you want to talk?"

There was no answer.

"I don't know exactly what you heard, but I'm trying to do what's right for you." He leaned against her doorframe, ruing every inch of space between them.

"Leave me alone," she said.

If there was anything Jack knew, it was how to obey orders. "Yes, ma'am. I'm going back downstairs for a bit, but I won't leave the house tonight. If you get scared with the nightmares, find me. Don't suffer alone." The very least he could do was leave his overcoat within her reach, but with the way she'd responded to the mistletoe, he didn't want to suggest it.

He told her good night, then went downstairs. He selected a book from the shelf in the parlor, grabbed his eyeglasses, stretched out on the sofa, and dropped the book unopened on his chest. The sooner she was gone, the sooner he could get his life back to normal. He could journal about the tribes and record new information. He could eat in the mess hall with the troopers. And at the end of the day, he could sit in his half-lit house alone every evening, read his books, and daydream about the girl back home. The girl he'd let get away without once telling her how much he loved her.

No. When she left, he had to leave all this behind, as well. Nothing would be the same.

It was funny how dignified the parlor looked with the books arranged like that. Instead of a dusty mess of information, his house looked respectable. So what if he had to go upstairs to find a certain volume? He'd get used to it. Maybe he should let her organize his office, as well.

Giving up on the book, he extinguished all the lamps downstairs and pulled the shades. She didn't want to stay, and he'd do his best to give her the freedom to leave. He'd sacrifice everything for her to have her choice. He didn't want her to ever think he'd chosen this mess. Caused it accidently, perhaps, but not chosen it.

The strangled cry upstairs tore at his heart. Jack moved silently through the darkened house toward her room, picking up his coat as he passed. After all these nights together, he recognized the sound. She'd woken up again, disoriented and frightened.

"Hattie, it's me." He rested his forehead against the door. "Can I come in?"

She sobbed but wasn't awake enough to answer. Jack only hesitated a moment. He would have fought off a regiment of men to rescue her if needed. He wasn't going to let a door stand in his way. He turned the knob and pushed it open.

"What are you doing?" Hattie rubbed her eyes as she pulled the blanket up to her nose. "I told you to stay away."

"You were having a nightmare. I came to help."

"You don't have to. I can take care of myself."

Maybe it was the late hour. Maybe it was the eventfulness of the day. But Jack knew right then that he had to tell her.

He sat at the foot of her bed and dropped his coat to the side. Hattie pulled her feet up and tucked the blankets beneath her like there was a mouse trying to sneak under the covers.

"I have some bad news." He kept his eyes on the window as he gathered his courage. "Major Adams didn't request my transfer before he left."

She sniffed as she wiggled her toes. "And now you're stuck with me for longer than you thought."

"I didn't know exactly when he'd return, but I expected the paperwork to have been filed and approved by now. You're running out of time. If you miss your chance at this exhibition because of me, I won't know how to make it up to you." What it was costing her — that was what he had to remember. Not how much it was hurting him.

"How much longer do we have to wait?" she asked.

"A matter of days, if it's approved. If not . . . well, Major Adams will insist that they find me another post."

"Why are we doing this, Jack? Why don't we tell him no? Who cares if the Indians have their feelings hurt? It's your life. You can't ruin it because they made a mistake."

"I made the mistake." He turned to face her, and it was nearly his undoing. She looked so fragile, so trusting. And she deserved the truth. "I could've put you on a horse and headed back to the fort that day, but I wanted to impress you. I asked them for a ceremony."

She sat up straight in the bed. "You asked them to marry us?"

"No, absolutely not. I asked them to officially hand you, the captive, into my care. Transfer the responsibility, so to speak. They must have misunderstood."

"But why didn't you realize what was happening?" she asked. "You speak their language pretty well."

That was the embarrassing part — or at

least another embarrassing part. "You were the last person I expected to find in that camp. It'd been so long since I'd seen you that I couldn't concentrate on what they were saying. I was completely addled."

His confession seemed to surprise her. She tugged a lock of hair across her mouth.

"A tragic mistake," she murmured. "And we're both paying for it."

"But I can't let *them* pay for it. Hattie, I've seen what is happening out west. Some people think the Indians are inferior — that they can't learn like we do, can't function in society . . . or what we call society. As long as people can pretend that the Cheyenne and Arapaho are intrinsically different, they will justify their exploitation. I want those kids to have a fair shot at life, whether they decide to stay on the reservation or move somewhere else. But that's not why I'm mad." She was listening, but did she hear what he was trying to tell her? He turned toward her, the blanket wrinkling beneath him. "Hattie, I'm angry on your account. My fight with Major Adams wasn't because I'm in a hurry to be rid of you. It's because I know you, and I know that being stuck here is driving you batty."

"But why didn't Major Adams request the transfer before he left? You told him to, didn't you?"

Jack picked at a snag on the army blanket. "Daniel is a friend of mine, the kind who thinks they know you better than you know yourself. He got it in his head that we'd somehow find a way to make the marriage work. He thought that by the time he got back from his honeymoon, we'd . . ." He took a deep breath. Major Adams's hopes had been Jack's hopes, as well. He didn't have to admit that, but the words were still painful. "He thought that we would be in love, and the transfer would be unnecessary."

Jack stilled his hands as she took a moment to drink that in. Mercifully, she didn't laugh. "He doesn't know about the bargain we made, does he? Or is there a reason he'd think that we'd stay married?"

Good thing the light was dim. Otherwise she would have seen his stricken expression.

"Major Adams knows that we grew up together." One of Jack's flaws had always been his honesty. Usually his honesty caused other people pain, though. Not himself. "And then, maybe once or twice, I mentioned that I'd had an attachment to you when we were young. He knew that I wrote you on occasion. He probably remembered that and hoped the feeling was mutual."

Jack waited, feeling like he'd just set his heart out on a platter and offered it to a pack of wolves. Or one very becoming she-wolf, anyway.

"I know what a writer you are. You probably corresponded with dozens of ladies."

"No, just you." He picked at the snag again. "And my ma."

"What about this sweetheart that everyone tells me about? Didn't you write her?"

Had she really not figured it out yet? Keeping his word and delivering her to Denver was the only way he would keep his honor, and he needed his honor, because his pride was taking a beating.

"I only wrote you," he said, "because . . . because you're the only one I . . ."

Loved. Jack couldn't say it. It was ridiculous. Only now was he really learning who she was, but everything he learned only increased his regard. He tried to catch her gaze, looking for any sign of interest, but she sank her face farther into the sheets.

"You're going to the village tomorrow?" she asked.

That was it? That was all she had to say? Jack flexed the tension out of his fingers. By pretending she hadn't heard him, she was allowing him to save his dignity. Maybe that was the kindest response she could make.

"Yes. I'm talking to Chief Right Hand tomorrow about what's going on at the school." He cleared his throat. "Do you want to come?"

"I'd better stay here. I have some sketching I want to work on."

"Oh?" He nodded. "For your exhibition?"

"I can't turn in a pencil drawing, so it's probably futile."

"Major Adams's girls have paints."

"They have watercolors. I need oils, and by the time the mercantile gets them, it'll be too late."

Jack turned his face toward the window. "You'll be in Denver before then. Oil paint will be easy to come by in Denver." Everything would be easy to come by for her. He would be the one with all the regrets.

"Is that your coat?" she asked.

He handed it over to her.

She took it and drew it against her chest. "I wake with the roosters, or in this case with the bugles, so you'll get it back first thing," she said. "If I stay in this room tonight, can you hear me call?"

"I did, didn't I? And I'll be here in a heartbeat."

Her chest shuddered as she released her breath. Slowly, she lay down, pulling his coat over her. "Would you mind leaving my door open?" she asked. "It helps me feel not so alone."

Jack left the cold room, started down the hall, and wondered how two people could feel so alone together.

The next morning found Jack in the saddle, accompanied by a small unit of six men. While most of the Arapaho and Cheyenne chiefs had come to the table and were willing to work together, the memories of the Sand Creek Massacre and the Battle of Washita River were too fresh in the Cheyenne minds for peaceable relations. And if it wasn't the Indians aiming for them, there were plenty of ne'er-do-wells who would take their shot. There was a saying around these parts: "No Sunday west of St. Louis, no God west of Fort Smith." The missionaries were doing their best to bring Sunday to the land, and God had been on these prairies since He'd created them, but there were a good number of men who carried on like He didn't exist, and he didn't want to cross them alone.

Jack also didn't want Hattie to cross them alone. She wouldn't leave the fort without him, that had already been established. It was no wonder she felt like a prisoner, but he was responsible for her safety. While they had no reason to think the killer was in the area, Jack wasn't willing to risk her life on it.

The wind howled in straight from the north. That second layer of socks Jack had put on that morning would do him good. So would his overcoat, which Hattie had returned. Hopefully a storm wouldn't blow in before he got back.

"Let's go," he said, and they headed northwest toward the far-off horizon.

"The wind likes to bite clean through my leg," Private Morris said. "Hurts like the dickens."

"You should have thought of that before you got shot," Private Willis said, "although I can't think of a more advantageous location to take a bullet."

"If you're volunteering, we could try a few places and see how you like them," Sergeant O'Hare said.

Private Willis turned to Jack. "So is this the first time you've gone on patrol since being married? I don't mind taking out with a married lieutenant, because I figure he'll do everything in his power to get us back to the fort before nightfall."

"No one signs up for the cavalry to sit at the fort," Jack said.

"I don't want to sit," Willis said. "That'd

be boring. But I don't admire the cold."

"It's either the cold or the heat," Morris said. "And if the temperature's nice, the wind will knock you down. Nothing but misery."

"Aren't y'all a basket of cheer?" Jack said. "Just remember, if you desert with a horse, we'll hunt you down. If you desert without a horse, then you'll never make it across the reservation alive. Might as well see out your enlistment."

"The cavalry's the place for me," Willis said. "All the same, I can't wait until my next leave. I'm going down to Texas to see Miss Herald again. It's been too long."

"She's still putting up with your foolishness?" Jack asked.

"Yes, sir. I'm easier to stomach from a hundred miles away." Willis grinned. "But you're the one who needs to spill the beans. I thought I'd lucked out on my last assignment, but you went after some stagecoach robbers and came back hitched. How did you get her to marry you when you'd just met?"

Their formation tightened as the men rode closer to hear Jack's answer over the wind.

"We hadn't just met. I've known Miss Walker for years. We were schoolmates."

"You owe me a silver dollar," Private Morris yelled to Sergeant O'Hare. "I told you this was his sweetheart from back home."

"She wasn't my sweetheart," Jack said while patting the earring that rode in his breast pocket.

"She wasn't?" Morris rubbed his leg. "Then what did your sweetheart say about you getting married?"

"Whew," Willis said. "I wouldn't want to be the one to pen that letter."

"As if you write letters," said Morris, then to Jack, he asked, "If she ain't your sweetheart, then why did she agree to marry you?"

It was only a matter of time. Private Willis's sister, Louisa, undoubtedly already knew about the sham marriage. How long before everyone had reason to mock him?

"The only information you need to know," said Jack, "is that I don't have a sweetheart anywhere. My affections all belong to Mrs. Hennessey. As for the circumstances of our vows, the hand of God is a mysterious thing."

They hadn't gone far from the fort when they met two marshals and their top-heavy tumbleweed wagon. Jack's jaw tightened. It was good, he reminded himself. As a witness, Hattie needed to talk to them before she could leave. Things were falling into place.

"That wagon is riding awfully heavy," Willis said. "Reckon they caught someone?"

"We're fixing to find out," Morris replied.

One marshal rode ahead of the wagon to meet them and wasted no time in sharing the good news.

"We might have got the fella who shot up the stagecoach." Marshal Bass Reeves was a tall, imposing black man. He was respected by the Indians and hated by the outlaws, and you didn't want to cross him if you knew what was good for you. "We found him out and about the area."

Marshal Bud Ledbetter stared steely-eyed into the biting wind as he threw the brake on the wagon. "I have my doubts that this fella could take down three men alone, but I'd be glad to hang him for it if he did."

Even after the horses stopped, the wagon swayed in the cold wind. It couldn't be fun riding along the bumpy plains, but Jack had no pity for someone who waged war against innocent civilians. He rode to the side of the wagon to look through the bars at the man chained to the floor. The feckless-looking gentleman who returned his stare looked more likely to be hounded by a scolding wife than to be a murderer.

Reeves wrinkled his nose. "Then again, like Ledbetter said, he don't present as much threat."

But such things were hard to judge. A weakling was more likely to feel entitled to others' belongings. He might also have a motive, something personal, that they didn't know about.

"Not only that," Ledbetter said, "but we found the coach. It was burnt up, and the horses were gone."

"What about the last passenger?" Jack asked. "Did you find Mr. Sloane's body?"

"My guess is that he's been consumed by wolves," Ledbetter said. "We did find some luggage. Not the government's funds, but clothes and the like that we need to get back to the families of these men."

At this, Jack's ears perked up. "Goods from the stagecoach? Did you recover any women's items?"

"We sure did," Ledbetter said.

"Excellent. If you don't mind, I'll send Private Willis back with you, and he can see that the women's goods make it to my quarters."

"Now that you mention it" — Reeves's smile flashed wide — "I did hear that you got yourself wed to a mighty fine lady who happened to come across the territory. You don't waste an opportunity, do you?"

Not now. Not in front of his men. "Miss Walker and I are old acquaintances," Jack said.

"Oh? Is she the gal who broke your heart?" Reeves asked.

Jack's men leaned in.

"She lost a trunk," Jack said. "A bag, maybe. And some paints. She had paints with her."

"They're in the wagon," Reeves said. "We'll haul them to the fort while we go put this sorry animal in the guardhouse."

"That'd be dandy. Such things would just slow us down, and we need to move if we're going to make it back to our warm beds tonight."

Judging from the responses of Private Willis and Private Morris, the *warm beds* comment should have been left unsaid.

CHAPTER TWENTY-ONE

Hattie had sketched and re-sketched her picture of Tom Broken Arrow until she was pleased with the composition. A dozen times she'd thrown down her pencil and paced the room, asking God why, when she'd found the perfect subject for a career-starting portrait, did she have no paints? Then she'd return to her seat and further perfect what she already knew was her best work yet.

If only Jack were there to see it.

He had been besotted with her years ago. Not that Hattie was surprised, but what would cause him to talk about her here, as an adult? If she had realized that she was the only lady he was seeking correspondence from, she might have written back. After all, he wasn't the same lanky boy she'd known. And with that confession, was he letting her know that he no longer had feelings for her, or was it just the opposite?

The knock on the door set her heart racing. She pressed her hand against her chest. But Jack wouldn't knock on his own door, so she might as well simmer down. After a touch to her bare earlobe, she turned the knob.

It was only Private Willis with his usual confident grin. "Mrs. Hennessey, I have a delivery that you might be interested in."

A delivery? What was it? More books? She'd just cleaned out the office, and she didn't want to clutter it up again. But then she looked past the trooper and squealed in delight. "Bring it in. Bring it in." She threw open the door, then jumped out of the way.

Private Willis lifted her trunk with a grunt and followed her outstretched finger to drop it at the foot of the stairs. Hattie clapped her hands together and pressed them to her lips as he set a muddy carpetbag on the floor. It looked to be in terrible shape, but it was the most welcome sight she'd seen since Jack had appeared in his cavalry uniform at the village.

A high-pitched giggle formed somewhere in the roof of her mouth. "Is this all? Was there another box?"

Willis spun on his heel and bent just outside the door to retrieve the very thing Hattie had been waiting for. She was upon him before he could even turn around.

"That's it!" She ripped the box of paints from his hands, then stepped back. "I'm sorry. I didn't mean to . . ."

He laughed. "I reckon you've been anxious to get this back."

"You can't imagine." She ran her hands over the new scratches on the wooden box. It didn't matter, as long as the contents were the same. "Thank you for bringing this. Thank you so much."

With a tip of his hat, he was gone.

Hattie danced around the entryway, swaying with her box of paints like it was Jack on roller skates. Shaking herself out of the celebration, she ran back to her trunk and sat on the second step. She pried the lid open and pulled out handfuls of clothing.

Dried grass took to the air as she shook out her crumpled wardrobe. A few seams had ripped, and the cloth looked trampled. She shoved her hand through the heavy brocade skirts and warm blouses to sweep the bottom of the trunk with her fingers. When she hit a wooden box, she breathed a sigh of relief. Her funds. Had the robber missed it? But then something rough and uneven caught at her fingers. She tightened her hand on the box and felt the sharp sting of splinters. She pulled it up, snagging it on the fabric, and the wooden box fell apart before her eyes, empty.

It's only money, she told herself. *It can be replaced.* But it was her parents' money, and they wouldn't look favorably on her losing it. Even worse, when they heard how she'd lost it, they most likely would call an end to her experiment immediately. Dropping the broken box, she crushed her favorite Sunday dress against her face. The smell of home still lingered in the folds. She recognized the scents of baking day and of oil paints, a mixture that she hadn't even realized existed until she'd been gone from home long enough to miss it.

Until now, it was as if she'd been a different person. Living in a strange place, wearing strange clothing, and married to a . . . well, Jack wasn't a stranger exactly, but he was the last person she'd been thinking of when she packed this trunk.

Now she was getting her life back together, but just like the dingy dresses, she had to wonder if it would feel different. Accepting her parents' challenge had been a hasty decision, undertaken before she lost her courage. Somehow, the glory that she was trying to obtain in Denver had lost some of its shine, but the penalty for failure remained the same.

And that meant the paints could still be her salvation. The outlaw hadn't appreciated the treasure, and it had worked to her benefit.

With her gown still held tight, she began to plan her projects. Tom Broken Arrow's portrait would be first, but after that, she wanted to paint something for Jack, for all he'd done for her. Something that would complement his office and bring together the style she was aiming for.

Jack! Where was he? For the first time, Hattie wondered how her belongings had been recovered. Had they caught the man who'd robbed her? Had there been a shootout? Was Jack unharmed?

Hattie raced for the door. How callous she'd been. Jack was more important than her belongings, and she hadn't thought to ask about him. Wanting to remedy her mistake, she was poised to run to Major Adams's house when Private Willis stopped her.

"Is there something you need, Mrs. Hennessey?"

Hattie clutched her stomach. "Lieutenant Hennessey," she said. "Is he all right?"

"I'd imagine he is. When I left him, he was riding toward the settlement. He's the one who told me to deliver your duds to the house."

Her breath came easier. "He isn't in a shootout with the killer, then?"

"Naw." Private Willis smiled. "They got the killer locked up in the guardhouse over there." While he pointed across the parade grounds, Hattie retreated.

"The killer? He's here?"

"Don't you worry. There's no way out of that guardhouse. Believe me, I've tried. And even if he could pry off that one rusty bar, I'm posted right here at your door. He'd never get through me."

Small comfort. But at least Jack was safe. She thanked Private Willis and went back inside to see about getting her clothes cleaned.

By the time Hattie had carried armful after armful of her belongings to the kitchen to be washed, the early winter dusk had descended. After giving her clothes a good scrubbing, wringing, and hanging them all over the kitchen to dry, she grabbed a day-old biscuit and took a few bites before the drums of the Indians began.

Hattie hadn't lit the lamps yet, and the darkness had gathered. Her newly washed clothes dripped water like the ghosts of drowning victims. She shuddered. Her imagination was getting the better of her. No one was lurking in her house, but the thought made it impossible to look over her shoulder, and how could she sleep when the man who had killed Agent Gibson, Mr. Sloane, and the driver was near?

She hurried up the staircase to her room. Her shoes sat beneath her little bed. Her hats hung on the bedposts. She had her clothes, she had her paints, and she had her life. Someday, she'd recover everything that had been taken from her.

But it wasn't enough.

The drums got louder, and Hattie knew what was wrong. She had everything that Hattie Walker needed to get along, but Hattie Walker had changed. She'd had experiences that she couldn't reverse, and as much as she might want to go back, her life had transformed to encompass someone new.

Staying alone in her room was impossible without Jack home. Instead, she found herself carrying her pillow, dragging her blankets, and searching for a place where she could truly rest. She looked at the empty banister and sighed. No coat for her to hide behind tonight. Having it made all the difference. What it signified, she didn't want to fathom. And Jack had better not be speculating, either.

She turned toward his open bedroom door. Every other night, he lay there, eyes closed until she needed something, and then he would answer her. But he wasn't there now, and the hard floor didn't have the same allure.

Dropping the pillow and blankets, Hattie stepped inside his room. She had to stand on her tippy-toes to get a leg up on his bed. The mattress gave beneath her. After her lumpy straw mattress, it felt like a cloud. She dug at the top to find the edge of the blanket and sheets, then wormed her way between the covers. She wanted to know as soon as he got home; that was why she was here. Once she knew he was safe, she would go to her own room.

There was no coat to calm her, but these blankets, his linens, rested her heart. But where was Jack? Why hadn't he returned yet?

Lord, please take care of Jack. He's out there somewhere in the dark and cold. Be with him. Keep him in Your protection. He's a good man, God. Please don't let anything happen to him.

That was a lot of begging. Feeling like she shouldn't be so demanding, Hattie thought of a few other things she'd neglected to talk to God about.

And, God, I never told You thank You for saving me while I was out there in the prairie. You know how scared I was, but now that I look back, I know You never left me. You sent Chief Right Hand's nice people to find me, then You let Jack be the one who brought me in. I was in a lot of danger, and it could've turned out so much worse . . . but You had it planned all along. Her breathing was getting slow, and her mind was drifting, but she wasn't finished. *And if this marriage thing turns out to be binding, well, I guess it's better than being dead. Even if I'm trapped here forever, help me be thankful for Jack and for all You have done.*

She might not remember half of what she prayed by morning, but a sleep deep enough to erase her memory would be the best sleep she'd had yet. Her final prayers were mumbled into Jack's warm blanket. Something about him being cold.

The fort rested motionless. Taps had been played hours ago, and the only stirring was the twinkling of the icy stars above him. Jack's men followed him to his house on Officers' Row, where he dismounted, handed off his horse, then waved them on to the stable. He was used to coming home to a dark house, but it felt doubly lonely knowing that Hattie had already gone to sleep and he wouldn't see her until morning.

He'd spent the night ride from the village in prayer for Hattie. Praying that God would guide her to whatever success she was looking for. That she would be patient with him as he tried to get her back on track. That her fears would grow smaller as God grew bigger to her.

And that she had been able to go to sleep without him or his coat.

He held the door open to borrow the starlight before trying to make it across the room. Just as he'd hoped, the entry was littered with her empty traveling bags. Evidently she'd wasted no time reclaiming her belongings. He was only surprised she hadn't packed them up again, ready to leave Indian Territory.

He set the trunk aside so neither of them would trip over it in the morning, and then he went upstairs. The first thing he noticed was that the bundle of blankets in the hallway looked suspiciously flat. He knelt for a better look and flipped the blanket over. Nope, no Hattie. He wouldn't say he was worried. Not really. She was probably in her room . . . except her pillow and blanket were right here. Jack's gut tightened. Even in the dark shadows, he could tell her bed was bare.

He would raise the alarm. Scouts would be sent out. There was a murderer on the loose, and Hattie was the only eyewitness. Had the killer . . . ? The thought was too terrible to contemplate. Jack stomped down the hall, prepared to rouse the troops, but movement caught his eye.

He screeched to a stop, his foot against the softness of the blanket on the ground. Someone was in his room.

"Jack?"

His knees nearly gave way. He couldn't answer, his mind racing to understand what he was seeing. The bed creaked as Hattie reached a hand toward him.

"It's me." He dropped to his knees next to the bed and took her hand, not believing that she was there. "I couldn't find you. I thought you were gone."

She smiled up at him drowsily, with a sweetness too fragile for daylight hours. "I was worried about you. I thought you'd gotten hurt, or in a fight or something."

"No fights tonight, just some talking with our friends. But I was praying for you." He couldn't stop himself from brushing her hair back. "Praying that you weren't afraid here by yourself. Praying that you would be able to rest."

"And I was praying for you," she said. Her eyes closed. "Praying that you'd come back."

His throat caught. Her skin was so smooth. The darkness took away her courage, but it doubled his. "Don't worry about anything," he said. "Go to sleep, and we'll talk in the morning."

"Mm-hmm . . ." She smiled again. When she pulled his hand, he thought he was going to be reprimanded, but instead she lifted it to her lips and kissed him on the knuckle. Then she snuggled down under the covers and fell back asleep.

It was a long time before Jack could look away. Even longer before he could understand that Hattie Walker — no, Hattie Hennessey — had just kissed him. What had the world come to? But they were both safe, and God had answered both of their prayers that night. He couldn't ask for more.

Chapter Twenty-Two

It was still dark outside, but the bugle had blown at 5:30 that morning, and Jack was already with the troops doing their roll call. Hattie had waited until he'd left the house before slipping out of his room. If called upon to give an account for her shocking behavior, she had no answer, and yet she wasn't sorry. The discovery — the moments of answered prayer and reunion when Jack had knelt by her last night — left her with a sense of well-being that she hoped would carry her through the day. And she hoped that Jack was thinking of her, as well.

Hattie dressed quickly, sucking in her breath at the cold cloth against her skin. She scrubbed the morning warmth from her cheeks with icy water from the washbasin, then lugged her painting box downstairs.

She found the sketches she'd made of Tom Broken Arrow and then began to organize her supplies. The sun was up by the time she'd arranged the canvas and her paints and brushes in Jack's office — it had the best light. She settled on the edge of the chair, took her brush, looked once at the sketch, and then closed her eyes. Before catching him on paper, she had to feel her subject. She had to share in his emotion. This was a new practice for her. Landscapes didn't have the same procedure, but it was something she instinctively knew she had to do.

What had young Tom been feeling? Sadness at being separated from his people? Fear at what lay ahead? Surely some belief that the choice he was making would be good. That was what Hattie hoped, anyway.

Did she have a choice, or was she doing whatever Jack told her to do? In one breath, he told her that he was trying to get rid of her quickly. In the next, he was confessing that he'd always loved her. If he didn't know what he wanted from her, how was she supposed to respond?

By midmorning, she had the outline sketched on the canvas and was ready to start with the oils. Then she saw a figure pass in front of the window.

"Hattie, there's someone here to see you," Jack called as he stepped inside the house. As always, the sight of him in his uniform set her aback. "Marshal Ledbetter wants to talk to you."

Had any of the feelings Jack had confessed survived the years? Hattie saw a caring, honorable man, but she didn't see what she was looking for.

"I've already given a statement," she said, scrubbing her hands with a scrap of feed sack to get the charcoal off.

"We still need your help, though. If this man attacks another woman, I can't marry her, too."

"Very funny." She smiled a greeting at the grizzled marshal. Wrapped in buffalo robes and a beaver hat, he looked more animal than human.

The marshal tipped his hat. "Mrs. Hennessey, I won't waste your time. I caught a man trespassing in the Cheyenne and Arapaho Reservation near where we found the wrecked stagecoach and your luggage. I brought him in to see if you recognize him."

The hair on her neck tingled. "I thought you already knew he's the one."

"You have nothing to fear," Jack said. "They're going to bring him out of the guardhouse for you to identify. It'll only take a minute."

"I have to see him? Now?" She felt so fragile. Where had her strength gone? "I don't want to be anywhere near him." It wasn't logical, but Hattie feared that if she saw his face, it would be the last thing she ever saw. "I can't. Please."

Jack ducked his head. "We need you to do this," he said. "Take some time to prepare yourself."

She covered her neck with a trembling hand. How could she prepare to see the monster of her nightmares? Her eyes drifted past the marshal to where two young troopers were leading a short rumpled man across the green. He squinted up at the sun as the wind blew long brown wisps of hair over his balding head.

She blew out a shaky breath. "Is that the prisoner?"

Marshal Ledbetter looked over his shoulder. "That's him."

Hattie instinctively distrusted him, but her fear began to fade. Nothing about him reminded her of that fateful day.

Jack took her arm. "Are you ready?"

She nodded and left the house to confront the man being escorted to them.

"That's not her," the prisoner said as the troopers positioned him in front of Hattie.

"Shut up, you windbag." The marshal shoved his hands in his pockets to keep his coat from flapping in the wind. "I have to listen to him all the way to Fort Smith. Might as well hang him now."

"But that's not her." The prisoner's red nose dripped down his thick mustache. "You said we were coming here to get an identity, and I'm telling you, she's not the one I robbed."

If only someone this inept had attacked the stagecoach, Hattie's companions would have been safe. The way the prisoner's round head sat directly on his barrel chest was a distinguishing characteristic. His form would have been familiar to Hattie had she ever seen him before.

"He wasn't there," she said. "I'm sure of it. It wasn't him."

The outlaw bowed his head. "I'm partial to your help. Now, can we end our association, Marshal, and let me go?"

"Let you go? What about the woman you robbed?"

"Says who?"

"Says you. We have to find her and put you in jail."

"Pshaw, you ain't gonna find her. She lives all the way over in Okmulgee, and that's a long ways away."

The marshal's weathered face crinkled. "But I get paid by the mile." His hand rose toward his hat but paused midair as if struck broadsided by an unexpected thought. "Ma'am, your husband mentioned that you're a trained artist. Do you figure you could paint what you saw that day?"

Hattie closed her eyes. She'd avoided a confrontation with the murderer today, but he was still at large. What if she painted his likeness? But then, perhaps that would keep her from having to identify him later.

But could she do it? She'd peeked over the dirt ledge of the gully for only a moment, but she could recall the scene in startling color. While she might not have the words to describe the man, she could display him. Furthermore, with a canvas before her, more details would emerge. That was how it had always happened in the past, anyway.

"I don't like to think about what happened," she said. "I try not to think about it, but if I did . . ." If she did, she wouldn't be able to sleep at night again. She found herself looking to Jack. His face reflected her anguish.

"I'll be with you," he said.

"I thought we were leaving Fort Reno," she whispered. "You're being assigned somewhere else."

"But we're here together today. Shouldn't we do what we can to catch this murderer?"

A stiff gust of wind rustled her skirt and chilled her ankles through her wool stockings. Painting the scene would delay her work on Tom's portrait, but Jack was right. She couldn't refuse.

"I'll paint it," she said, "if it'll help."

"It just might," Ledbetter said. "When I make it back around, I'll check in and see if I recognize anyone in the painting."

Hattie was numb as he left. Prying open that horrifying memory would cost her. Her constitution would suffer, no doubt, but at least she had the comfort of knowing that Jack was with her.

But for how long?

Jack sat on the back porch as the sun came up, steam rising from his coffee cup. He could hear Mrs. Adams and the girls talking in the kitchen next door. Daisy sang "Joy to the World" as she walked out the back door to throw out a pan of cold dishwater. Seeing him, she waved, her strawberry-blond hair tied in curling rags.

Major Adams had found love twice, with his late wife and now with Louisa, but Jack couldn't imagine there being another woman in the world who could mean as much to him as Hattie. Surely God hadn't kept the love for her alive in his heart all this time only to have it remain unrequited.

Last night had been rough. Hattie had alternated between painting with deep, vigorous strokes and staring off into a bleak nothing. The look on her face scared Jack. He'd seen men with that look after a battle, and the scenes they were living and reliving were liable to return at any time. He didn't want that for Hattie. He didn't want her to relive the trauma she'd been through, but if she could show the world the man who had killed the three victims, then they might be able to find him. Then she would feel safe again.

As the night wore on, she painted slower and slower. The stagecoach appeared on the broad sheet of paper. The fighting driver could be identified. The outlaw's horse was visible, but not a trace of the man. It had seemed beyond her. Sensing that she had reached her limit, Jack had drawn her away, taking the paintbrush out of her hand and dropping it in a jar of mineral spirits as they went upstairs.

He'd brought his coat to her, and she'd taken it to her room without comment. For hours he'd kept an eye on his open bedroom door, but she'd chosen to face her fears alone.

Jack sighed and took another drink of his

coffee. He wished he could do more, but there were places he couldn't go with her, no matter how he loved her. All he could offer was to care for her needs while she let God look after her fears.

But caring for her needs left Jack in a quandary. There was just something that God had put into men that knit them to a woman under their care. The thought of separating from her — of taking her to Denver and watching her walk away — felt like part of his flesh would be ripped off. How could he stand it? How could he keep watch over her any longer, knowing that the day was coming when she would leave?

He had as many fears as she did.

When Hattie joined him at the buggy so they could attend church in Darlington, she looked every bit the pampered girl he'd known in Van Buren. Certainly there were changes. Her figure had thinned down and then filled out where it should. The roundness of her face had molded into shapely cheekbones and an elegant neck. Her newly recovered clothes showed that she still followed the latest Arkansas fashions, even if the dresses hadn't been cared for as they should have during their circuitous journey to her.

She kept her eyes down as she greeted

him, and yet he saw the shadows she was trying to hide. There was no reason for her to be embarrassed, but just mentioning the subject would mortify her. Instead he pretended not to remember her anguish from the night before. He'd spent his life hiding his feelings for her. This was nothing new.

"Are the Adamses coming to church with us?" Hattie asked as she spread the lap robe over herself. "I saw Caroline polishing her shoes on the porch, and she was dressed for Sunday."

"Most everyone here attends the chapel at the fort, as do I most of the time. But any excuse I can find to spend time in Darlington . . ."

There was no need to continue. She understood. Unbidden and unobserved by anyone besides a hawk flying over them, Hattie tucked her arm under his and pressed against his side. He switched the reins to his other hand and pulled the lap robe higher.

"Is that better?" he asked.

"Being married has its advantages," she said. "Otherwise this trip would be a lot colder."

His gut twisted. "And a lot lonelier."

Her forehead wrinkled. "How are you going to manage when I'm gone, Jack? You'll be leaving Major Adams and his family, the school, the Indians, and all your friends."

"Let's not worry about that right now."

"I have a confession. When I was organizing your office, I found something. It was a picture of your house and the valley in Van Buren. I think I drew it in school."

Was there no end to the embarrassment his sentimental nonsense was causing him? "You did draw it. Of all the artwork in the world, that's my favorite."

"You must miss home a lot," she said. "I worry how I'm going to feel when I'm all alone in Denver."

The reins tightened in Jack's hand, and the horses slowed. "Why are you going to Denver, again?"

Her chin dropped. "There was no reason to stay in Van Buren. You should understand. You left years ago."

"I guess I've always carried home in my heart. The people, at least." He wrapped his hand around hers. "The people I love."

Why couldn't she look up? Why couldn't she see the message in his eyes?

Hattie cleared her throat. "I just wanted to say that if it'll help, I'd be glad to sketch a picture of Darlington for you, or the fort. When we separate, I don't want you to forget the people who were here — the people you love."

She turned her hand and entwined her fingers with his. Jack's heart was in his throat, along with stanzas of suppressed love that he yearned to share. Would she be repulsed? Would she laugh?

And then she did. Hattie giggled as she slapped his arm. "A picture and my earring? Jack, you're a regular magpie hoarding shiny trinkets you find along the way. You really should reform your ways. Your house can't hold much more."

He swallowed down the declarations and tried to match her mood. "One earring doesn't take up any room. And it serves the same purpose as the picture. It's a memory I don't want to lose."

She squeezed his hand as they rode into town.

The Mennonite mission housed the Sunday services. One side of the meeting room bulged out with a rectangular addition to make room for the students who crowded the pews. Now many of their spaces would be empty.

Jack tied the reins to the hitching post before returning to help Hattie down. Peter Stauffer, a Mennonite missionary who'd been at the Cheyenne mission last week, greeted them at the door and seemed ecstatic to meet Jack's new wife. Had the whole world been this nervous about his marriage prospects? If he'd only known that tying the knot would mean so much to so many. And how would they feel when they crossed his path years from now and learned that Hattie was no longer part of his life? The thought of their disappointment sickened him.

They sat in Jack's usual place by the window on the north side. Through the pane, he watched as the Arapaho students were marched over from the school, boys and girls in separate lines with the smallest students in the front. A gust of wind pushed some students sideways, curving the lines. A few girls ducked their faces into their scarves and hunched their shoulders while the boys tried to pretend to be unaffected. Eyes squinting into the wind was all the quarter they'd give.

Perhaps next week Jack would visit the school and church at Cantonment, where the Cheyenne congregated. A few years back, the children of the two tribes had attended school together, but the constant fighting was deemed unsafe for everyone, and a separate school was built for the Cheyenne. Perhaps Cantonment would welcome the Arapaho children if the Darlington school closed.

Jack's eyes tightened. He wouldn't be in Indian Territory next week if Major Adams got the paperwork approved. Even while insisting that Daniel transfer him, it hadn't occurred to him that this could be his last Sunday to worship here. His last week in his big house crowded with books. His last week surrounded by the bare Cheyenne prairie.

His last week with Hattie.

Everyone waited patiently for the students to hang up their coats and file inside to their reserved seats in the front. When Tom Broken Arrow paused in the aisle, a stocky classmate shoved him in the back in good-natured fun. Superintendent Seger didn't appreciate the humor and cuffed the boy on the back of the head as they worked their way between the pews to their seats so the service could begin.

Reverend Voth had more gumption than Jack's preacher from back home. Then again, he reckoned anyone who volunteered to come to Indian Territory possessed a backbone of iron. Once the sermon started, the reverend's wild, curly hair bounced with his movements, which were plentiful. His plain words struck to the core of any matter he addressed, and his topic of the moment was idolatry.

Jack looked at Hattie, wondering how she viewed the sermon, the preacher, Jack's life in general. Could she have ever brought herself to appreciate military life? Or life with him? He had joined the cavalry to get away from his heartache, and God had shown him a love for the people who'd been entrusted to his care, but if she would have him, he'd give up all his work for her. He'd do anything for Hattie.

"Then the children of Israel turned from God," Reverend Voth said. "Forsaking their Lord and forgetting all that He had done for them, they took after idols, thinking that they would find happiness and blessing somewhere else. But they were deceived." He was getting wound up, and Jack was spellbound. "Friends, there are many temptations to lead you astray, but the price is too great. No substitute for God will ever bring you peace. No addition to God will ever make Him greater in your life."

Jack's heart sank. He rubbed his ear and then, thinking everyone was looking at him, quickly lowered his hand. While he knew that he loved Hattie, loved her purely and truly, somewhere along the way, he'd decided that his life would never be complete without her. Only she could satisfy him. And to his shame, he'd told God the same.

Jack had always viewed his life as it pertained to Hattie. He did well in school to impress her. He joined the cavalry to bury the pain of her disinterest. He wrote letters back home, hoping against hope that word of his success would travel from his family and eventually be repeated in Hattie's hearing. Everything he'd done or accomplished he judged by how she would view it. She was the invisible audience that he had performed for, the one whose approval he coveted.

And now she sat next to him. She had many imperfections, just as he did. She found it hard to concentrate on a book for long. While she could be thoughtful, she expected to get her own way. Not that she was mean or vengeful about it, but she took it for granted that if she asked for something, it would be provided. Jack had always been more than eager to cooperate, but what if he didn't? What if he had lived his life for the last decade for God's approval, instead of measuring everything he did by Hattie's standards?

She was only flesh and blood. She wasn't enough to build his life around.

Jack's sigh was audible. When Hattie

turned, he shrugged but held her gaze with new vision. Was this why God had brought her to him? So he could be free from her? So he could realize how frail his idol was? Her eyebrows wrinkled in confusion, and Jack took her hand and gave it a reassuring squeeze. It wasn't her fault. She hadn't asked to be his ideal. He was the one who'd wronged her. He'd put the responsibility for his happiness on her, and that was a burden no mortal should bear.

Things would be different, no matter how little time they had together, but before he could make things right with her, he had to do some confessing to God.

CHAPTER TWENTY-THREE

Something had happened in church, and Hattie wasn't happy about it. She couldn't quite put her finger on it, but Jack had changed. He was polite, he was considerate, but he'd turned into a stranger again. A different stranger than the one who had rescued her. One who was still dashing, determined, and delicious — okay, not delicious, but she'd wanted to stay on theme — and yet he was different in a different way. Or maybe she was different. That was it. It was like he'd forgotten who she was.

She shivered under the lap robe as she waited in the wagon for him to come out of the agent's office. Jack had asked if she'd mind waiting while he dropped off a report and had shown appropriate concern about her sitting in the cold, yet it wasn't the amount of concern that she had come to expect from Jack.

Canada geese glided overhead with the

strong north wind at their backs. Their honking faded as they disappeared behind the roof of the warehouse. People were leaving, too. There was a one-way exodus from the mission house as families split off toward their individual homes. The Arapaho children marched around the corner toward the school, where Hattie hoped a hot meal was waiting for them. Everyone was headed home. Everyone except for one man.

A horseman rounded the corner but hesitated at the flock of people headed his way. With his gun, bulging saddlebags, and bedroll, he was outfitted for travel, but he lacked a cowboy's gear, and he definitely wasn't a soldier. Not with that hand-tooled saddle and dusty Oxford shoes.

Hattie narrowed her eyes. She knew him, had seen him before, but he'd looked different then. Seeing him in Darlington wearing frontiersman's garb didn't fit. While she couldn't remember the specifics, her gut told her that she didn't like him. He had been rude and impatient with her. Was he from Van Buren? She couldn't place him there. Maybe he'd attended one of her exhibitions in Little Rock? He didn't look like a connoisseur of art, but . . .

He was disappearing back around the

corner he'd just come from, but he took one last look over his shoulder before guiding his horse into the alley, and with that look, he caught sight of Hattie. The recognition was immediate. She felt the connection, and with an unbelievable chill, she realized that he was supposed to be dead.

She shoved off the lap robe and stood, but at that moment Jack appeared in the doorway of the agency. His eyebrow rose in confusion as he approached the wagon.

"Sorry to take so long. Were you coming in to fetch me?"

Hattie watched the intersection ahead, but the man had turned and left the way he'd come. Was she losing her mind? The marshal had said that all three men had died. Or had he assumed the second passenger had met the same fate as the driver and Agent Gibson? She certainly had. Or did the rude man from Fort Smith have a twin brother?

"Hattie?" Jack followed her stare up the road. "What's wrong?"

"That man," she said. "I think I know him."

Jack climbed into the wagon. "You want to talk to him?"

Actually, she did. The ride through Indian Territory had changed her, and it was possible it had changed him, as well. Mr.

Sloane had undoubtedly witnessed worse than she. He'd fought for his life and endured a harrowing ride while she'd hidden in a gully. Surely surviving such a trial could cause one to reflect on his life and the various insults and indignities he'd inflicted on other good people.

"He was one of the men on the stagecoach," she said, "and not a very nice one."

Jack bounced the reins against the horse's back to pick up the pace. "Which leg of your journey?"

"The last one. The bad one."

"He was on that stage?" Now Jack looked worried, and he urged the horse down the street faster. "We didn't think there were any survivors."

"I'm almost sure that was Mr. Sloane from Fort Smith."

They'd turned the corner, but the street was deserted. Only an empty flour sack tumbled from one end to the other. Hattie's eyes darted from building to building. Where was he? Had she made a mistake? But he'd recognized her, too, and had disappeared immediately.

"I think it was him," she said, "but when I saw him last, he looked different."

Their horse flicked its tail as it waited in the middle of the road. Jack cocked his head as if listening for retreating hooves, but nothing could be heard besides the church members calling good-byes as they headed to their warm kitchens and Sunday dinners.

"As far as I've heard, they never recovered the last body, but everyone was fairly certain that all three men had been killed," Jack said.

Fairly certain was Jack's way of saying that she was making a mistake. He didn't want to contradict her and have her call him a know-it-all again, but he couldn't help himself.

Hattie sighed. He was probably right. Painting the picture had resurrected the memories. Besides, from such a distance, how did she think she could recognize someone?

The sun had peeked out from behind the clouds and was sharing some warmth with the flat land. Maybe it wasn't necessary to sit so close to Jack, but Hattie didn't mind. Hadn't he agreed it was one of the benefits of being married? Yet he didn't seem as keen to participate as he had been that morning. Hattie was nearly ready to wish the cold upon them again.

Once home, Jack didn't linger over their noonday meal. He complimented her chicken and dumplings, even though to

Hattie's taste they were too salty, and then he excused himself, saying that he had some studying he wanted to do. Instead of going to his office, he took his eyeglasses and set up camp in his chair by the parlor window — the one he declared to be his favored spot for meditation and Bible study.

It might be the Sabbath, but thinking about Mr. Sloane left Hattie anxious to work on her picture. The roll of paper crinkled beneath her arm as she picked up her paint box and carried it to his office. Jack shot her a sideways glance as she passed, but he kept his nose resolutely in his book. Just as well. Hattie had an image burning in her memory that needed to be put on paper before anyone could distort it.

With her brushes within reach, she arranged two candlesticks to hold down the corners of the curling paper. Another gaggle of geese passed overhead, their hoarse voices calling to each other as they sped through the air. Hattie closed her eyes and pulled on her bare earlobe. Slowly their honks were replaced by the angry shouts of the coach driver and the screaming of the frightened horses. Again she could hear the gunshots, could feel the cold red clay in her fingernails as she lifted herself up to peer over the edge of the gully.

There. That was the moment she needed to paint. A lone rider leaned forward with arm outstretched. He was aiming carefully, one eye closed and looking down the barrel. She didn't remember noticing his chipped tooth before, but there it was. The puff of smoke meant he'd already fired once when she first saw him. She flinched with every report, knowing that some would find a home in the warm bodies of her traveling companions.

Quickly, her brush dabbed the paper, staking out space atop the horse that she'd been unable to fill the night before. Now she saw the homemade wooden buttons on the shirt of the killer. She noticed the grim determination on the driver's face as he fought for his life and the lives of his passengers. Her brush moved lower, where the two men in the coach were fighting, as well. Hattie sketched the government man, Agent Gibson. His nostrils were flared, filling with the gun smoke scent that she'd never forget. To her surprise, she found herself darkening his coat. He'd already been hit once but was still firing.

And then there was Mr. Sloane in his dust-covered suit. He was behind Agent Gibson, as if trying to get out for an open shot at the outlaw. Now she knew for certain that the man she'd seen in Darlington was Mr. Sloane. The features she drew were identical to that man's, but she was having trouble getting his posture right. She watched as his face took form on the paper. Mr. Sloane's eyes weren't on the attacker. They were on Agent Gibson, which was understandable. The agent had already been shot. But again, Hattie paused when it came to positioning Sloane's gun. She closed her eyes and summoned the picture.

In slow motion, the brief moments played out: a puff of smoke, yelling, the awful choreographed dance as they shot, then ducked. Shot, then fell. That was when she'd yelled, but after that, she saw no more. On paper, she had to limit herself to one frozen moment, but that moment was horrifying enough.

The images on the page told the story, but were they accurate? Was she relying on her memories of the incident or on her recent encounter with a stranger?

A stool scooted in the parlor. Hattie flexed her tight fingers. Her chest filled with fear, and this time rage. Her hands itched to crush the paper into a wad and throw it into the fire. At the very least, she wanted to turn it over so the cold eyes of the robber couldn't see her, but instead she hammered her fist against the desk, then stood to pace until the paint dried.

When it was dry enough to carry, she stomped into the parlor with the paper in hand. Flopping onto the sofa, she propped it against a cushion, crossed her arms, and stared moodily into the fire. Jack lowered his book and pulled off his reading glasses. If she could only stay angry, then maybe she wouldn't give in to fear. She wouldn't start thinking how close she'd come to being in that coach when it had been attacked. Had she not drunk three cups of coffee that morning . . .

Even though the fireplace roared at full strength, Hattie shivered.

"How are you doing?" Jack asked.

Her heart was beating like a rabbit's.

He placed a bookmark between the pages of his book and smoothed the ribbon before closing the cover. His fingers lingered on the book as he stood, like he was loath to leave it. If Hattie hadn't already been numb, she would have taken offense. The cushions on the sofa folded as he sat next to her and reached for the roll of paper.

"I hadn't realized how vividly I remembered," she said.

"What you experienced will always be with you. In time —"

"I know, I know." She pressed her hand against the paper. She wasn't ready yet. "Maybe I'm wrong . . . but I know I'm not. This is exactly what I saw."

The paper crinkled beneath Jack's thumb. "If you're wrong, we'll figure it out, but this could help." He raised the roll of paper and held her gaze until, with a silent nod, she gave him permission to unroll it.

She'd seen enough of it, so instead she watched his face. His eyes darted over the painting, lingering on the criminal. His mouth hardened. "This is excellent," he said. "You are so good, I'd recognize this man if I ran into him on the street."

Her throat jogged. "I did. That man today, that's him." She pointed at Mr. Sloane.

"You're sure now?" He pulled the sketch closer to his face and studied Sloane's face. "Why hasn't he come forward to report the crime? How did he get away from the gunman?"

"I don't know. Afraid to be a witness?" Like she was. Then again, if Mr. Sloane wanted to find safety, he should have headed out of Indian Territory and never come back.

"Major Adams needs to see this," Jack said. "And it needs to be passed around to see if anyone recognizes the outlaw. You did superb work. I'll be right back."

"Right now? You're going right now?" She turned away from the picture. Even though their faces lived in her memory, she didn't like seeing them on paper. Her fear was too close to stay ahead of.

"Yes, right now. We want the marshals to get it before they leave the area."

She sat stunned as he rushed out the door with the painting. She might have captured the scene on paper, but the killer was still at large, and she was still terrified.

But where Jack failed, his commander made amends.

It was only seconds before she heard the door again and Jack stepped inside the parlor, hands dangling awkwardly at his sides.

"Major Adams said he'd take care of it, so I don't have to leave you." He sat next to her and shifted his feet beneath him. "He's the commander, after all, and with your picture, they can recognize the men without me." But his regret was obvious.

Her teeth started to chatter. The weather wasn't extreme, but with the killer's face fresh in her mind, she couldn't get warm. There was one thing she was willing to try, though.

"Do you remember when we were driving

to church this morning?" she said. "Do you remember me saying that one of the benefits of our marriage arrangement was that we didn't have to be cold if we didn't want to be?"

He sagged into the sofa. His voice was hoarse. "I remember."

"If I were cold here, now, don't you think the same rules should apply?"

She felt his arm lift to lay across the back of the sofa, but that wasn't good enough. Ducking her chin, Hattie turned, wrapped her arms around his waist, and buried her face against him. His hesitation surprised her, but when his arms wrapped around her, she didn't doubt him a lick. Whatever was holding him back wasn't as strong as his care for her.

"I could've died," she said. "I try not to think about it, but painting the picture brought it all back. Agent Gibson was just as alive as I am, and then he was just gone. I left him cold and alone in the dark."

Jack rested his chin on her head. "After an experience like that, you'll never be the same. Every trooper on this fort faces those same thoughts and realizes how fragile life is. Death will happen to all of us, but you know that's not the end."

Trust Jack to tell the truth and tell it

bluntly. Yet his practical words helped calm her heart. Instead of her fear, she had to focus on the blessings. She squeezed her eyes tight and considered all the good things that she'd gained since coming to the fort — the cozy parlor, the feisty sisters who lived next door, the row of neatly dressed children at the church service. All of those things made her happy, but it was the man holding her that she didn't want to leave.

She didn't want to leave? Hattie felt a stab of fear at the realization. What did it mean? She wasn't in love with Jack Hennessey, was she? The thought was ridiculous. Sure, she'd always thought him smart — a tad obnoxious, but generally nice — but love him? How did one know? Hattie had been in love with a lot of boys, but usually once she got to know them, she grew bored. Could Jack be the exception?

The lure of Denver was fading daily. Honestly, Hattie didn't have a clear picture of what awaited her there. She only wanted to avoid the future that her parents had planned for her back in Van Buren.

Here in Indian Territory, although geographically isolated, she was at a crossroads of cultures and peoples. She learned something new every day. It was no surprise that she would rather stay with Jack than go back home, but did that mean she was content to give up her other plans, as well?

He was good company, she gave him that. A gentleman, even before he was old enough to properly take the title. Considerate to a fault. And as far as the runtiness that had plagued him when he was younger, well, he'd whupped it like a champion. But as a beau, would he know how to give her the attention she craved? Could Jack set her heart racing, or had it only been the roller skates?

There was one way to find out.

Nestled against his chest, Hattie slid her hand to his stomach. She smoothed the fabric of his shirt with her palm, leaving her hand pressed against him until she learned the rhythm of his heart. Here she felt safe. Here she felt loved. Here she felt courage enough to explore these new feelings. Waiting for his reaction, she nuzzled her cheek against his chest. When he didn't resist, she raised until her face was fitted into the base of his neck. His hand dropped away from her back. His heart beat unevenly. She wanted to be closer. After all the time they'd spent together, wasn't it natural that she would care about him?

His clean woodsy scent reminded her of the overcoat she still slept with. She tilted her head against the bare skin right above his collar. Was he shocked? Was he annoyed? She couldn't tell. Only that his breathing had changed. Her fingers tightened on his shirt as she stretched up and laid her lips against his neck. His pulse throbbed beneath her mouth, making her heart race, too.

What would it take to shake him? How long could he ignore her?

"Hattie," he said.

She smiled, her lips moving against his skin. But then he stood suddenly, breaking her grasp and leaving her to fall against the sofa.

"I said that you don't need to pretend our marriage is real unless we're in public," he said. If she had thought Jack was fired up about the outlaw, he was downright twitchy now. "I'm not just a pair of shoes you can try on to see if you like the fit."

Hattie's face burned. "Goodness gracious," she cried. "I barely touch you, and you accuse me of claiming wifely privileges."

"Are you my wife, or aren't you?"

Any questions about him getting her blood flowing were pointless now. "You said that legally —"

He turned and stalked to the window, scanning the prairie beyond the fort, probably wishing he had left her alone here and taken out after armed killers instead. "I made a bargain with you that you'd be free to go when I get my reassignment, but there's a line, and if you cross that . . ." He shook his head. "Don't make this deal any harder to keep than it already is."

And with that, he walked out of the room and out of the house, leaving Hattie with more questions than she'd had before.

Was she mocking him? Tempting him? Testing him?

The cold air outside was welcome relief after the scorching events in the parlor. Gravel flew as Jack strode down Officers' Row toward the adjutant's office. He was angry. Angry that he didn't understand what had just happened. Angry that he'd hurt her feelings. And angry that he couldn't stay and see what she was going to do next.

If he'd stayed . . . Jack's pulse surged. He would march back home, throw open the door, and snatch Hattie off that sofa. He'd sweep her into his arms, and if she wanted to nibble on his neck, he'd allow it. Right after he kissed her senseless.

First, he'd kiss her for single-handedly beautifying the Van Buren secondary school. Her cheerful smile and ringing laugh brightened many a dismal study session. Then he'd kiss her for her kind soul and how she always listened to him, even though their interests were so different. But the deepest, most ardent kisses would be for the mature woman she was today — for helping him with his duties to the tribes, for playing with him and the kids, for fighting for justice while battling her fears, and mostly for keeping her end of their bargain.

If he didn't do it immediately, he'd explode. Jack spun on his heel to go back to his house and ran smack into Private Willis.

"Whoa there, Lieutenant Hennessey. Can't reverse course like that in formation. You'll cause an accident." Willis saluted. "Did you forget something?"

"What?" Jack asked. Then, following Willis's gaze, he reached up and tapped his own bare head. "Looks like I forgot my hat."

"You were in a powerful hurry, but if you have a minute . . ."

"Go on."

"I just came in from patrol. We didn't find any sign of the man the Cheyenne troubled. Looks like he survived long enough to get off the reservation." When not attempting breakneck stunts, Willis could be a valuable trooper.

"Thank you. Hopefully he made it somewhere safe and can get tended to."

"Speaking of safe, how's Mrs. Hennessey faring? She had a rough go of it."

His wife. How could Jack praise her for keeping their bargain when he was thinking of ways to sabotage it? He rubbed the back of his neck. "Have you ever made a promise that you regret?"

"Heaps of them," Willis offered. "And I'm not just talking about my enlistment."

"Watch your words, Private," Jack said, but only because it was expected. "Whether or not there's a court to enforce it, there's still a man's honor. A bargain is a bargain."

Willis's eyebrows shot up. "Are we talking about a promise or a bargain? A promise can't be broken, true, but a bargain can be renegotiated. There's always hope for better terms."

Jack looked again at his home on Officers' Row. One did not expect wisdom to come from Bradley Willis. As much as Jack wanted to embrace the young trooper's assertion, he couldn't help but consider the source. True, Jack could expose his cautious heart with hopes of winning Hattie, but what was the probable outcome? No matter what he did or didn't do, she had plans of her own, and those plans did not include him.

With a sigh and a salute for Willis, he continued bareheaded to his office.

CHAPTER TWENTY-FOUR

Snow swirled against the glass panes of the mission house's windows. Christmas was next week, and the students were having their first dress rehearsal for the pageant. Hattie removed her coat and hung it over the pew. Daisy Adams ran up the aisle, waving at one of the Indian students, a girl with sparkling brown eyes and a festive costume. Her big sister, Caroline, shrugged out of her coat.

"Too bad Daisy can't take classes here. It'd make my house more peaceful." Caroline pushed a lock of red hair behind her ear.

"You'd miss your sister," Hattie said. "From what Jack says, she keeps your father on his toes."

"And steps on mine." But she said it fondly. "On the other hand, with Daisy raising such a ruckus, it keeps the attention off me, so she does serve a purpose."

At this, Hattie's interest grew. "What are you up to, Miss Adams, that you need a diversion?"

Caroline's eyes narrowed as she smiled. "Why are you worried? You've already got Lieutenant Jack. There's no one else at the fort who's interesting to me."

Had the major's daughter set her cap for Jack, too?

But Caroline brushed away her confusion. "Jack could never see me as anything besides the daughter of his best friend. We wouldn't have suited, so I have to broaden my horizons if I want to find a man with whom to while away the hours."

Mrs. Lehrman clapped her hands, and the students took their places in three lines on the stage. Mary and Joseph knelt at either side of a manger in the center while Mrs. Lehrman hummed the opening note. Then the children chimed in, which nearly overpowered the very interesting conversation Hattie was enjoying.

"You shouldn't complain," Hattie said. "When I was your age, I would have given anything to live at a fort surrounded by eligible men. There were a few boys in my class at Van Buren who caught my attention, but none of those flirtations stood the test of time. After a picnic or two, their antics became so predictable that I would rather eat my fried chicken alone. Always showing off, boasting, trying to outdo each other."

"And you think they're any better now?" Caroline cast an eye toward the adults lined up in the doorway in preparation for the procession, but seeing that they were out of earshot, she continued. "Even my new uncle, Bradley Willis, is a hopeless roustabout. Perhaps individually they might have some admirable qualities, but in concentrated numbers they're more concerned with impressing each other." Her intelligent brow wrinkled. "And that's why I'm not settling for an enlisted man who is at the beck and call of others. I want a man who has a mission, a calling."

"A religious man?" Hattie asked.

"Not as a vocation, no. But with a dream that borders on religious zeal. That's what I find attractive." Caroline's cheeks colored, as if she feared she'd said too much. Her sharp eyes focused on Hattie. "But what about your classmates? You said there wasn't a single one you found interesting."

Still pondering Caroline's romantic ideals, Hattie answered, "Which is why I took this journey, so I could follow my dreams as a painter."

"But Jack was your classmate," Caroline said. "Did you forget about him?"

Caroline was watching her intently, waiting for a bride's account of the exemplary young man who'd won her heart. If only Hattie had such a story. Then again, maybe she did, now.

"What first attracted my notice was the way he looked after me. Whenever I needed him, he always showed up." That was true whether Hattie was being held by Indians or simply had to tote her easel from her house down to Lee Creek to catch the first light of morning. When she thought about it, it only made sense that Jack had been the one to help her. He usually was.

"I imagine Jack was probably a horrible bookworm when he was young." Caroline smiled as two students dressed as shepherds marched down the aisle to pay homage to the baby in the manger. "I'm surprised he ever got his nose out of a book long enough to notice you."

"Oh, he put the books down when I came along." That much was true, but what did he think now? Why had he scolded her that night when she'd tried to stir the embers a bit? Wasn't he curious? Didn't he want to see if this marriage might be something worth keeping?

"I saw your painting of the outlaws." Caroline tossed her red hair over her shoulder. "I'm not easily impressed, but you do have talent."

The mention of the picture turned her stomach, but Hattie forced a smile. "Thank you. I'd be happier painting a different subject."

"Maybe you'd do a better job of it. Something was wrong with the passengers. They were distorted so badly that it looked like one passenger was pointing his gun at the other instead of shooting at the outlaw."

Hattie should have been used to criticism of her art, but it still stung. "That picture represents a moment in time," she said. "In the melee, they were trying to get off any shot they could."

"Unless the man inside the stage was trying to harm his fellow passenger, that painting is misleading," Caroline said. "You should mention that before they take it as truth. Besides that, though, the image is remarkable."

Hattie closed her eyes to summon the scene, but in a chapel full of children and Christmas songs, it was impossible. What if Caroline was right? What if Mr. Sloane had accidentally injured Agent Gibson and inadvertently aided the outlaw?

As if her sour thoughts had tainted the air, the Christmas carol "Angels We Have Heard on High" changed its tenor. Something was amiss. The students had broken into chaos. The more active girls raced off the platform, while some were huddled, too stupefied to move. Word spread across the stage to the boys' side. The student playing Mary plucked the rag doll out of the manger and ran out of the room. The bottoms of her boots flashed their new soles.

"What's wrong?" Hattie turned to see two of the mission workers and the minister standing in the doorway, wearing jewel-colored robes. The Magi had come to worship the Christ Child, but the students were terrified. A few younger boys followed their fleeing sisters off the stage, while the older boys faced their foe with stern disapproval. The headmistress rapped her baton against the podium to restore order, but her efforts were futile. Tom Broken Arrow stood back, observing the chaos.

Hattie stepped around Caroline to intercept the fleeing girls. She caught Francine by the arm and dropped to her knees to look at the girl face to face.

"What's wrong, Francine? Why is everyone running?"

Francine tried to jerk her arm free, but

seeing that Hattie wasn't going to release her, she answered, "It's the man in blue. He's the one who steals our dreams."

Hattie looked over her shoulder. The minister? "No, Francine, that's Reverend Voth. Look again. Don't you recognize him? Has he been coming into your rooms at night?"

Francine paused. Her pert nose scrunched as she tried to get a better look. Hattie felt the tension leave her arm. "That's the reverend. It's not the spirit, but why is he wearing the robe?"

"You're saying the spirit that steals your dreams wears a robe like that?"

"It *is* that robe," Francine said. "It has the big sleeves and shiny material on it."

The minister had remained in the back of the room, his kind face crumpled at the distress he'd caused. The robe was made to represent an Eastern potentate, and it was very unlikely that there were two like it in the whole territory. And judging from the girls' reaction, Hattie had to believe that the connection was real.

"Where do they keep the costumes?" she asked.

Francine shrugged. The room had almost emptied, as the teachers had gone to round up the children. Regretfully, Hattie allowed

Francine to join the other students. Something about their terror convinced her that there was a real, human explanation.

Jack reached the school about the time Superintendent Seger and Reverend Voth stepped outside. With their heads bowed together and the superintendent's hands gesturing rapidly, their conversation felt urgent.

Jack had been busy that morning, so blessedly busy that he hadn't been able to squire Hattie around when she asked to go to town. *Better terms.* He couldn't get the phrase out of his mind. One more night of her sweet attention, and they would be irrevocably wed, whether they planned it that way or not.

When Major Adams mentioned that he was letting the girls take the buggy to town in the company of the quartermaster's detail, it seemed like a good way to entertain Hattie while keeping her safe. No outlaw would approach the girls as long as they were with the troopers. Plus, it kept Hattie out of his path for another day. But as luck would have it, a call had come over the lone telephone line from the agency to the fort with a request for him to meet the marshal at Agent Lee's office.

Jack tipped his hat at the two harried men as they passed. It was probably some issue with the missionary society. He had more important fish to fry.

He took the three steps up to the agency's porch in one long stride. The fire glowing through the window looked cheery. Entering, he found tinsel paper draped over a map that hung behind a cluttered desk, showing the Indian territories and nations. Agent Lee rose with an extended hand, and Marshal Ledbetter stepped back to give Jack room.

"Lieutenant Hennessey, thank you for coming," Ledbetter said.

"You've had time to look over Mrs. Hennessey's sketches?"

"Yes, sir." The marshal unrolled the paper on the desk. Jack could almost hear the horses blowing and smell the gunsmoke. The way Hattie had captured the moment of action was incredible.

"This picture is as good as a wanted poster," Marshal Ledbetter said, "but it raises an interesting theory. Look there." The paper crinkled beneath his glove as he tapped the figure of the passenger. "What's it look like Mr. Sloane is doing there?"

Jack pulled his spectacles out of his pocket and bent over the painting. "It looks like a fellow with no experience with a pistol is about to shoot his companion in the back." His mouth twisted. "She did the best she could, but she was under considerable anguish while painting this. It might not be her best work."

"Before you go questioning your wife's skill, would it make a difference if you knew that Samuel Sloane worked at the telegraph office in Fort Smith?" Marshal Ledbetter rested his hands on his belt, already heavy with cartridges. "Sloane bought a stage-coach ticket, boarded in Fort Smith, and walked away from his job without notice. He hasn't been heard from since."

A telegraph operator in Fort Smith. A missing telegram requesting an armed escort. No third body found with the stage-coach. Hattie's sighting of Sloane on Sunday.

"We wondered why we didn't get the telegram requesting an escort," Jack said.

"You can't get a telegram that wasn't sent," Marshall Ledbetter replied.

"And that would explain how they knew there was a gold shipment on the stage." Jack rubbed his brow. "Hattie — Mrs. Hennessey saw Sloane yesterday after church."

"Here? In Darlington?" Agent Lee cast a

nervous look out the window. "That doesn't bode well. Did he see her?"

"Yes, but he took off. I wanted to question him, but . . ." But he'd once again questioned Hattie's judgment and hadn't made a serious effort to detain the man. When was he going to learn?

"She's a witness, and with a memory like this, she's a good one. I'd keep your wife nearer home," Ledbetter said.

More time together would not be helpful. "She's here today under Major Adams's protection. But I'll keep her close."

Bud Ledbetter's weathered face spread into a wide smile. "Yes, sir, I reckon you will."

Agent Lee motioned to the picture. "Are you taking that with you?"

"Let's keep it here for evidence," Ledbetter said. "We don't want to lose it, just in case something should happen to our witness."

Jack's throat tightened. Shaken by the thought that Hattie had been unaccompanied when she saw Sloane, he spun on his boot heel and headed to the school. The doors opened to an intense conversation in progress in the headmistress's office. Much like the superintendent and the minister he'd passed a few moments ago, Headmistress Lehrman and Miss Richert had gathered close to discuss something in low, urgent tones. Jack didn't have to wait long before they acknowledged him.

"If you've come to watch the practice, I'm afraid it's been canceled." The headmistress dropped a pile of costumes on her desk. "The children can't make it through their songs without scattering in terror."

If there was no practice, then where was Hattie? "The last rehearsal I saw was going well," Jack said. "What's the matter?"

"It's these costumes," Miss Richert said. "The students took offense to something about the costumes and want nothing to do with the performance. I'm afraid we're going to have parents pulling their children out of the school over this."

Jack didn't know everything about Arapaho culture, but they were familiar with costuming in their own festivities. Surely nothing set in Bethlehem could be as exotic as their powwow gear.

"The trouble started with the wise men," the headmistress said. "We let adults fill those roles, since they don't do any singing, and it's always been fine before, but when they came in wearing the costumes, the girls were terrified."

"Did they give any reason?"

Miss Richert answered, "No. They were running away and chattering in their language. I couldn't make heads or tails of it."

"I heard one explanation," the headmistress said. "Evidently your wife has befriended one of our younger girls. Francine told her that the blue robe Reverend Voth was wearing is the same robe the ghost wears."

He gestured to the pile of costumes on the desk. "Is the robe here?"

Mrs. Lehrman dug through the pile and unfurled a satin men's smoking robe that had been requisitioned.

Jack held it up to the window to catch the light and then, spotting something, he drew it close. "Is that blood?" he asked.

Miss Richert stepped back as Mrs. Lehrman squinted toward the dark swipe nearly hidden in the print.

"Where's Hattie now?" His neck felt like it had spiders running up it.

"The last I saw, she was with Major Adams's daughters at the practice."

Then she should be safe for the time being, but Jack had a suspicion he wanted to follow. "Where are the costumes kept when they aren't being used?"

"In the basement," Mrs. Lehrman replied. "The stairway is in the west wing, at the end of the girls' dormitory."

"Would that be the dormitory where the ghost has been spotted?" Jack asked.

Mrs. Lehrman's pallor was his answer.

"Thank you, ladies." He pushed through the swinging door that led into the school, clomping down the quiet hall. Hattie would have to wait. If his suspicions were correct, the ghost hiding beneath the school could very well be the man Hattie had seen on the street on Sunday. Had he been wounded? Hattie hadn't mentioned it. Jack could only pray it was Sloane's blood and there weren't more victims.

Whatever the case, the ghost stories needed to cease. If the school lost even a dozen more students, it would have to close its doors.

Stepping inside an empty classroom, Jack found a lamp and lit it, then carried it into the dark, musty stairwell down to the basement. As expected, there were trunks, crates, and an old wardrobe down here, but no sign of a fugitive. Not yet, anyway. The walls were lined with sheet-covered shelves, so it was possible someone could hide beneath them. Jack lifted a sheet and found shelved books protected from dust. Despite the isolation, the room looked well cared for. He'd say it had been cleaned at least every semester or so, and the goods were tidy and neat, stacked against the wall for the most part.

But there was something hidden. Holding the lantern in front of him, Jack stepped cautiously around a support beam that shielded a pile of clothes. Further inspection revealed a messy pallet on the floor made of choir robes and curtains. Jack nudged a pile of crumbs and an empty bottle lying next to the pallet. No mouse had collected this stash. Someone had been bunking down here. Someone the teachers knew nothing about. He lifted a filthy winter coat, its bottom hem shredded. Sure enough, tossed to the side were strips of the same cloth stained with blood. A tourniquet or bandages? Either way, the fugitive was in need of medical help and warm clothing down in the unheated basement. No wonder the thick robe in the costume trunk had caught his eye.

A faint rustle alerted Jack that he was not alone. Switching the lamp to his left hand, he scanned the room. There was no space for anyone between the crates and the wall. He crept to the wardrobe. Taking the brass handle, he flung the door open but was greeted only by empty hangers. Another look at the wall of bookshelves revealed that one of them had a bulge in the sheet covering it. The person wasn't large, probably a student, but he had to be prepared just in case.

Setting the lamp down, Jack eased silently to the covering. If anything, he wasn't reckless. He didn't want to act until he'd decided the best course of action. He had nearly figured out what to say when the sheet moved. Whoever was under it had decided to come out and get him.

Wanting the element of surprise, Jack roared with all his strength as he wrapped both arms around the sheeted figure, lifted it off its feet, and dragged it into the open so he had room for a tussle. But the minute he had his arms around it — *her* — he knew with every bone in his body exactly whose kicks and punches he was enduring.

"Shhh." He held her arms to her side, then dodged as she made a strike at his kneecap. "Hattie, it's me. Be quiet."

He couldn't tell if she'd heard him or not, but when he released her, she turned her fight to the sheet that was still draped over her head. With a mad scramble, she wrestled it off, appearing gloriously tousled. With a hand at her hip, she blew a lock of hair out of her face. She might be nettled, but Jack's frustration at finding her in such a dangerous situation was too great for him to be sorry.

"You scared the dickens out of me," she said.

"What are you thinking, coming down here alone?"

"I was trying to find out who has been harassing the kids, which was exactly what you were thinking." She raised one finely shaped eyebrow. "In fact, this might be the first time in my life I had the same thought as Jack Hennessey. Your intelligence is rubbing off on me."

"I don't think it was very smart of you at all," he said. "Not if that pallet means what I think it means."

"I had to do it. He was in their room while they slept. Do you realize how vulnerable those girls are? Until we catch that man . . ." She shivered as she contemplated the left-over food and dirty linens.

"I'll catch that man, thank you." The longer Jack thought about her being down here alone, the more it irked him.

"But I can help. Caroline noticed something about my painting. Maybe Sloane isn't the victim we thought he was."

"You know about Sloane, and you came down here anyway?"

Hattie lifted her chin. "This was my

chance to be brave. My chance to beat the terrors that pester me at night. And besides, what if he hurt the kids? I couldn't let him do that."

No longer afraid of the Arapaho children, now she saw herself as their protector. Jack took a deep breath. He was proud of her. Terrified for her, but proud. And being stern was difficult when she looked at him like that. Her smile softened as her eyes traveled to his lips. She would be the death of him.

He forced himself back to the business at hand. "Did you see anyone down here?"

"No, thank goodness, but there's another exit." She picked up the sheet and replaced it over the bookcase before leading him to the back of the room and a ladder leaning against the wall. "I don't know where this leads."

"There's one way to find out." Jack climbed the wooden ladder until his head bumped against a tilted trap door. He climbed another step, then two, before forcing the door open with his shoulder. Light and cold flooded over him. Easing the door down behind him, he came out at ground level in an alley behind the school. He stepped outside, then turned to offer Hattie a hand.

"They need to keep this door locked," he

said. "It's not safe for strangers to have access to the school."

The massive commissary flanked most of the alley, and beyond that was a livery stable. Past those buildings, a man would be crossing Cheyenne and Arapaho territory, and, in general, they liked people to be invited instead of wandering across their land without explanation.

"Where did he run to?" Jack asked as he scanned the prairie past the alleyway.

"Now I have two villains to trouble me at night," Hattie said. "I thought I was making progress."

"We're closer to catching them now than before," he said. "And if I'd taken your hunches and gut feelings more seriously, I might have spent more effort hunting down Sloane when you saw him yesterday. Keep reminding me of how insufferable I was to you in school, Hattie. I can't seem to learn my lesson."

"I remember Jack Hennessey telling me something during our geology study in secondary school. He said, *'Some lessons are tougher than others, Hattie, just like the rocks. It's the student's job not to let their pickaxe go dull.'* " She fluttered her eyelashes and bared her man-killer smile. "Don't be dull, Jack."

CHAPTER TWENTY-FIVE

Hattie looked one last time at the portrait of Tom Broken Arrow. She couldn't say that she was completely satisfied with her work. There were so many emotions she'd wanted to explore — so many hopes and sorrows — that she had to accept it would never be done perfectly, and where it lacked pained her. And yet she'd attempted more than she had ever attempted before. Despite its failings, Hattie was confident that she had done as the gallery owners had recommended. She'd experienced more of life and found a deeper understanding of people.

If only she had a deeper understanding of Jack.

She had started on Jack's portrait while he was working in the adjutant's office, keeping up with all of Major Adams's correspondence. She wanted her picture to be accurate, but lately she had begun to wonder if Jack had ever been the boy she thought he was. Could it be that she had misjudged him from the beginning? Either way, whatever effect she used to have on him, he'd outgrown. Now it was she who craved his attention, while he found excuses to keep his distance.

She had painted him as he'd looked their first day back at school in their seventh year. His shaggy brown hair held a touch of blond from the summer sun, and he held his well-worn books beneath his arm as he stood in the doorway of the school, eager to show what he knew. In his eyes, even though she hadn't recognized it at the time, was joy at seeing her in the classroom. Maybe she was remembering it incorrectly, but as this wasn't a testimony to a crime, she should be allowed some license for creativity.

Hattie swirled her brush in the jar of mineral spirits to clean it. In the last few days, Jack had stopped looking at her like that. He'd stopped looking at her at all, if he could avoid it. Could it be his way of preparing for the separation? But Hattie wasn't sure she wanted to leave. Not yet. Maybe not ever. For now, she needed to be here. With Jack.

She heard the front door open. Time for dinner already? Her canvas wasn't dry yet, so she hooked her fingers on the wooden frame and rushed it into the pantry to hide until Jack left again and she could stow it in a spare bedroom. She had barely closed the door when he stepped into the kitchen behind her.

"I'm sorry I don't have anything prepared." She wiped her paint-covered fingers on her apron.

"It's too early for supper. I just came to take your painting of Tom to the post office before the post goes out for the night." He really was adorable. And thoughtful. And brave. "Are you still working on it?"

She looked at the swipes of paint now marring her apron. "No, I'm finished. The crate is already packed and addressed." She bustled into the dining room with Jack hot on her heels. "Here you go."

"If this is packed up, what are you working on now?" It was friendly interest. That was all. But she couldn't help but look for something more.

She caught his gaze and searched his eyes. What would he think of her painting him? She knew it would embarrass him, but would he secretly be pleased? With her heart in her throat, she ventured a parry. "It's going to be my masterpiece."

"Even better than Tom's portrait?"

She nodded. She should be batting her

eyes and flashing her teeth with a flirtatious smile, but she was too scared. Instead she just stood there, staring at him like a fool.

"Aren't you going to tell me what it is?" he asked.

How could he not know? "It's a picture of something very special to me," she answered. "Something that has become even more special recently."

Recognition flickered in his eyes. He looked at the ground. "Hattie, you don't need to say that. I promised that you would get your wish. I'll get you to Denver."

"Why would I say something I don't mean?"

"Because of our bargain. You've kept your end of it. Now I have to keep mine."

"What if my plans have changed? What if I don't want what I wanted before?"

"You don't know what you want," he said. He spoke with confidence, but the way he watched from the corner of his eye told Hattie that he wasn't all that sure. Was she finally getting through to him?

She didn't know how to act. She couldn't play with his emotions. She couldn't overstate her feelings when they were so new, but would he give her a chance if she told him about her doubts as well as her hopes?

She would take the risk.

"You're right," she said. "I'm not sure what I want for the rest of my life, but I know what I want tomorrow, and that is to stay here with you. And I want to stay here for the rest of this week, and maybe the next. Maybe even after this winter and on into summer."

He swallowed. "The longer you stay, the harder it will be when you walk away."

What if she couldn't commit yet? Would Jack want to call on her in Denver? Maybe their courtship would survive through letters and correspondence — she imagined Jack could write a love letter to keep a girl warm on a cold winter night. But she couldn't imagine saying good-bye. What did a boardinghouse in Denver have that compared with her days here with Jack?

He sighed. "Don't fear your decision," he said. "You have to find what God wants you to do, and He's got plans for me, as well. We can trust Him." He picked up the crate holding the portrait and carried it out of the room.

Hattie followed. "You'll be home for dinner in a bit?"

He stopped at the threshold. Only by looking over his shoulder could Hattie see Major Adams coming across the green.

"Jack, we've got trouble," the major said.

375

"Half the tribe is at the school, wanting to take their children home. Turns out the stories about the ghost, the costume, and the missing items have convinced the parents that there is a danger. You'd better get over there."

"Yes, sir," Jack replied, then held up the crate. "Do you mind if I take this along to post at Darlington?"

"Not at all. Take Mrs. Hennessey, if she's of a mind. It might do the mothers some good to see her." He turned his steps toward his own house, then spun around to them again. "One other thing. Your request for a transfer was approved. You'll both be relieved to know that this charade can come to an end. With the school closing, it's a good time to take up a station elsewhere, and Mrs. Hennessey — or Miss Walker, if you'd rather — will be free to continue her life as she sees fit." He tipped his hat. "The U.S. Army thanks you for your service, ma'am."

The buggy could haul the crate, and it was faster than a wagon. Since time was important, Jack had it prepared immediately, and he and Hattie were on their way.

Neither of them talked. So much had been said already, but nothing determined. He had steeled himself for her departure, but her uncertainty was chipping away at his resolve to honor their arrangement.

Major Adams's report had been correct. Horses and a few wagons crowded around the entrance to the school. Women with thick blankets wrapped over their long deerskin robes clamored on the steps, protesting any delay that left them out of their warm tepees on a day when the temperature was dropping. Chief Right Hand stood on the top step with Superintendent Seger and Agent Lee.

Jack hopped out. "Don't go farther than the post office," he said to Hattie, but his mind was already trying to form the words in Arapaho that might prevent the disaster in progress. "Chief, it's cold outside. Why come to town today?" he asked when he reached the top of the steps.

"No reason to wait." Chief Right Hand spoke clearly for the group of people who hung on his words. "These are my people in this building. I want them to come home, and I'm their chief. You must release them."

"You're correct," Jack said, "but can I ask why? What is the reason today? The Christmas celebration is later this week, and all the children will go back to their families after that."

"There's unrest," he said. "You promised to protect them, but they are not safe. Our daughters are in danger at night."

After what he saw in the basement, Jack had to agree. There had been danger, but the danger was past.

"Chief, I can show you what has frightened the girls. There is no spirit. It was a —" He paused, trying to come up with the right word. "A man who had taken refuge in the school. He was hiding and stealing food at night. I can show you where he was sleeping and the door he was using, but now the school knows about it. The door is locked. We could put a guard on it if you'd like."

"What man? Has he been punished? No man could creep into our tepees at night without punishment." The chief shook his head. "Until you protect our children as carefully as you would protect your own, they will stay with us. We know how to look after them."

CHAPTER TWENTY-SIX

Hattie paid the postage for the crate, then prayed silently as the postmaster carried the package out of her sight. Whether or not her work found favor in the eyes of the exhibition curators, she was pleased with the new direction it had taken. She hadn't needed the mountains to inspire her after all. If only Jack's plans had worked out, as well.

When Hattie returned to the school, the scene didn't look promising. Judging from Jack's open palms and pleading expression, he was making no progress with the chief. The doors of the school were open, and students were being marched out by teary-eyed teachers to their parents. Many of the students gave a last hug to a favorite teacher, but no one could miss their excitement at the thought of returning to their families. But did they know it was permanent?

Her little friend Francine walked slowly out of the school, holding on to Miss Richert's hand. Her dark eyes scanned the crowd, then her face lit up in a smile as a young woman darted through the others and knelt to hug her. Hattie made her way to them, anxious to meet the mother of the spunky little girl. Francine saw her coming and chattered quickly with her mother as Hattie approached. The mother replied something that made Francine cover her mouth and laugh.

In English, Francine told Hattie, "My mother said that your name is One Who Spills Stew in Anger."

Hattie ducked her head. "I think I've been given a lot of names. Now I'm known as Woman Who Can't Roller-Skate."

The girl shared the message and followed it with a lengthy description that included a hilarious pantomime of Hattie falling. Hattie could only be relieved that Francine hadn't seen her and Lieutenant Jack on their later attempts together.

"Francine, did you know that we found the place where the man was hiding under the ground? It's a room called the basement, and we have a lock on it now so he can't get back in."

"Did you catch him?" Francine asked.

"No, we didn't. But he can't get in your room again."

The girl shuddered. "If he was human, how could he walk with one leg broken? How could he come up the stairs?"

"One leg broken?" Hattie looked at the girl's mother before remembering that she didn't understand what her daughter was saying, either. "Honey, do you mean to say that the spirit had a broken leg?"

Francine nodded, but with her mother inspecting her school clothes, she had no time for more foolish questions from Hattie.

"I'm going home," she said. "When I come back to the school, we can talk again."

But Francine didn't realize that there might not be a school.

The families were dispersing, huddling together against the cold as they took their children home. Hattie watched as they filed down the path toward the settlements. Just like that, Jack's dream was scattering across the prairie.

Hattie wanted to fix it. In the beginning, she hadn't understood the importance or the selflessness of Jack's mission, but having met the children and seen their homes and the hopes of their people, she had more sympathy. She'd thought that she had helped him at the expense of her own dream, but she'd gotten so much more in return.

"I apologize for keeping you waiting in the cold." Jack climbed into the buggy and took the reins.

His transfer was approved. He was getting what he'd asked for, but not what he wanted. Yet if the school was closing, he'd failed already. Maybe his replacement would have more luck.

"You got the painting mailed off?" He shot a sideways glance at Hattie. At the very least, he hoped she would find success in Denver. Not only did he want her to be happy, he didn't want her to go home and marry the first fellow who asked.

"It's posted. It should make the deadline for the exhibition entries, but I don't know if I'm going to make Mother and Father's deadline. It still has to be accepted." A gust of wind threw a lock of hair across her dark eyes. She brushed it away. "What about the students? What did the parents decide?"

From one disaster straight to another. "Everyone is going home. A few might have been persuaded to stay, but not enough to justify staying open. The doors will be shuttered, and the teachers reassigned to other missions and agencies."

382

"I'm sorry, Jack. I know how disappointed you must be."

"I'll keep trying," he said. "We can get them back. It might take some time. . . ."

"But you won't be here," Hattie said. "Major Adams has your transfer, and you have to leave."

Jack tapped his foot against the floorboard. "That's the bargain we made. I wish it had worked out differently."

"Jack?" Her brow furrowed. "If Sloane was hiding in the basement, where did all the blood come from? I didn't notice any injury when I saw him in town, and Francine said the man from the cellar had a broken leg."

"Broken leg? A student told you that? Hattie, you amaze me. What else did you find out?"

His praise seemed to please her. "Nothing, really. I just talked to Francine while she was leaving, and she mentioned that he came all the way up the stairs with a broken leg. That's all she said."

"I keep thinking I can come back and search again tomorrow," Jack said, "but that's wrong. There's nothing to do now but go home and pack up our things. I'll go to the adjutant's office and pass on the information. There'll be a lot of things there to settle before we can leave."

Hattie was watching him. Jack turned to her, an eyebrow raised. She slid her arm through his. "Can the office work wait until morning? I'm sorry, but I don't want to be home alone."

Alone. The word had fit him for years. But not right now. Not yet. "I don't mind," he said. "I'll stay with you for as long as you need."

He'd promised himself that he wouldn't pressure her. He'd do everything he could to keep her from getting off track. But how could he abandon her when she needed him?

The evening passed quietly at home, while outside the wind was howling. After supper, Jack wandered through the house, picking books to discard and estimating how many crates he'd need to move the ones he was keeping. Hattie, who had very little to pack, was unusually pensive. After a spell upstairs, she came into the parlor and picked up a book he'd chosen to leave behind.

Perhaps they'd accomplished enough for one evening. He took his copy of Lewis and Clark's journal and sat in his favorite chair opposite the sofa. Hattie was silent. The chestnut curl she was twisting looked as ragged as a broom end. He missed her bubbly busyness, even though he was happy she'd elected to read. Unfortunately for him that evening, reading proved impossible, but he stayed and let the words blur before his eyes.

He looked up to find Hattie watching him, but instead of looking away in embarrassment, she held his gaze. "It's been a trying day," she said. "What can I do to ease your trouble?"

He felt his throat grow tight. He forced a swallow before he answered. "I'm in the middle of the greatest exploration of our continent. What else could I want? If you're tired, go on upstairs. No reason to wait for me."

She stood and walked to the window next to him. Sleet tapped against the glass with icy clicks. She was so lovely. He'd do anything for her, including letting her live her life without the weight of his age-old devotion. She turned to him, and if he hadn't known better, he'd have sworn that her eyes were full. Walking as stately as a queen, she bent over him. Lewis and Clark slid off his lap and onto the floor as she laid her hand on his shoulder and lowered her face to his.

"I don't know what I need to do to get your attention, Jack Hennessey." Her breath fogged a spot on his eyeglasses. "But when you think of it, please let me know."

He didn't move as she pressed her lips to his cheek. His eyes slid closed at their velvety softness and her sweet scent. She lingered long enough that his chest ached from his need to exhale. Then she trailed her hand down his arm as she straightened and walked away.

His eyes followed her across the room, her slow sashay hypnotizing. She caressed the post at the bottom of the banister as she spun around it and walked up the stairs.

Did she want him to follow her? He had studied zoology and how different species signaled to their mates. There hadn't been a chapter on Hattie, but if he were going to write one, he'd have to mention her current act as an effective summons.

No. He'd already told her he was going to stay up and read. He had no excuse for changing his mind and following her upstairs. No logical reason that he could defend.

It had been a trying day. That was what she'd said. He chewed the inside of his cheek. Could that mean that she was afraid to go upstairs alone? Could that mean that she wanted him to put his book away and stay with her? Yes. She was discouraged about the school, too, and he'd be a churl not to see if he could comfort her. When he stood, he barely noticed that he'd stepped on his book.

Lewis and Clark would have to continue their journey alone.

Hattie had made up her mind. She wasn't leaving. Her life was forever changed. She couldn't go on with her plans unaltered, and she didn't want to.

The fort, the tribes, the agency — they had all felt so foreign. The only comfort she'd found was Jack. Jack, who brought integrity to everything he did. His unselfishness, his service, his accomplishments. There was much to admire. And yet, he needed her. He needed someone who recognized the sensitive boy hiding within the capable man. Someone who would hold his hand through the discouragements and didn't feel slighted by the time he spent at his studies.

Hattie knew she could make him happy, and she wasn't going to waste any more time convincing him of it. No longer was she marking time, waiting for the next phase of her life. Instead, she had made her decision and was ready to stake her claim.

He'd said he was going to stay downstairs

and read for a spell, but his book must have disappointed him. Hattie barely had time to change into her nightgown and hop into bed before he came upstairs. His bed. From his pillow, she watched him pause in the hallway with the lamp and gaze at her bedroom door. His uniform jacket was unbuttoned and hanging open. He ran a hand through his hair as he listened, but then, dropping his head, he entered his room.

Safely under the thick winter blankets, she didn't make much of a bump. Not enough for him to notice, evidently, for he began to undress. Hattie's plan, which had seemed so brave and sure, suddenly felt reckless and embarrassing. With her face turned away and her eyes tightly closed, she cringed with every piece of clothing that hit the floor. She couldn't let this continue. What if she was wrong?

"Jack?" she said.

A deep cry, a thud, the smashing of glass, and the light went out. Hattie gritted her teeth.

"What are you doing here?" The lamp rattled as he set it upright on his bureau.

What *was* she doing here? "This is where I want to be," she said.

Even though her back was to him, she could tell he hadn't moved. His breathing slowed. "Well, you really should give a man some warning. I don't mind making a pallet for myself in the hallway, but —"

"I don't want you in the hallway," she said.

There was a long pause. Long enough for her to think through every time she'd taken him for granted.

"Then I'll go downstairs, but I have to be careful. I knocked the lamp chimney off, and if I step wrong, I'll cut my feet. Let me pull my boots back on —"

"Jack?" She rolled over and smoothed the blankets with her arm. The window outlined his profile, the bare shoulders and suspenders hanging down below his waist. A man. Not the boy she knew, but a man she wanted to know better. "Jack, I don't want you to leave. I want you to stay here. With me."

He might as well have been a statue. "In this room?"

She flipped back the blanket on the empty side of the bed, but she was losing her nerve. "If you could just stay with me. Hold me. That's all I'm asking."

"Oh, Hattie . . ." he whispered, then shook his head. "You've kept your end of our agreement, but this is too far."

"It's not far enough."

"No matter how we carry on in public,

how natural it feels when you take my arm, how much I love hearing people call you by my name . . . it's all make-believe. I didn't win your regard or your affection."

The ice ticked against the window. Hattie had come to love this cozy house on the prairie. She'd come to love the children and the school. And most of all, she'd come to love Jack. Love him fiercely and deeply.

"But somehow you have won my affection," she said. "At first I was angry. I was scared. I was frustrated. But this place has grown on me. I'm not so anxious to leave." She searched his eyes, looking for some encouragement to continue, but he remained shuttered. "In fact, Denver has no appeal for me."

"We're not talking about a choice between Denver and the fort," he said. "I already have orders to leave. If it's Indian Territory that you love, then you need to find some other way to stay."

"It's not the fort," she said, "it's you."

The furrows between his eyes betrayed his skepticism. "C'mon, Hattie. You know better than to taunt me. Words were said over us, holy words that I'm willing to honor, but if you truly want me, if you want this, there has to be a commitment. There's no going back."

It came to this. Hattie trusted Jack to take care of her. She found life on the fort exciting. Her dreams of painting had room to grow here, as did she. And with Jack's interest in scholarship, he made an ideal partner for her inquisitiveness. There was only one aspect that left her in doubt. Had he outgrown his devotion to her?

"You said not to pretend in this house." She wanted to hide, but instead she propped herself up on her elbow to look him in the eyes. "Away from here, you're affectionate and attentive. The way you look at me, even the slightest touch makes me feel desired. But when we're alone together, I have no effect on you. You're impervious to my smiles, my tears, my caresses. I know a lady shouldn't speak like this, but you've been so good to me, and you deserve the truth. I love you, Jack. I love your mind, your heart, and your goodness."

Had she gotten through to him? He sat at the foot of the bed, out of her reach. He leaned forward, his elbows resting on his legs, his hands clasped between his knees.

"You won't be my wife only here in Indian Territory. Everyone will know, even people back home. It'll be forever. And I'm not the easiest man to live with. When I get caught up in my work, I might forget you're here for hours. That's not to mention campaigns. Likely, there'll be months in the spring and summer when you'll never see me."

"I'm capable of entertaining myself." The life he described didn't scare her, but she was beginning to doubt her ability to convince him. "Jack, you don't owe me anything. If you need more time to think about this —"

"More time?" He laughed. "If you only knew how ridiculous that is. After all those years of thinking about you, you show up on the reservation, looking just as perfect as you always had." He bent, picked up a piece of glass, and set it on the bureau. "But it didn't take me long to realize that you weren't perfect. You get tired and cranky. You run towards bossy if left unchecked. You hog my overcoat and don't think twice about it —"

"Excuse me?" Hattie chuckled at his recital of grievances.

"I'm not finished," he said. "I realized that you weren't perfect, and that I'm more in love with you than ever. But hiding my feelings, that had become a habit. So you're right. I've been pretending here in this house, where we're supposed to be honest. If you want to know the truth, I'm ready. I'm asking plain. I'm asking for permission to love you with my mind, my heart, and my goodness, yes. But also with my body and soul. You will have all of me, Hattie. I'll give you everything."

She looked at the empty place on the bed. The old Hattie would have wanted a big to-do with all her friends and family to mark this passage, but that was all behind her. She'd belonged to Jack for weeks now. This decision was between the two of them, and it was overdue.

"Tonight, I'll just hold you," he said. "Nights are frightening for you, and I want that to go away first, but if I stay in this room tonight, the marriage is sealed. There'll be no undoing or parting. You understand?"

She wanted him next to her so badly that she ached. "Please," she said.

Picking both feet off the ground, he scooted backward across the bed and toward her. "Do you take me, John Hennessey, to be your lawful . . ."

A calm covered her. All the fears of how she was going to get out of this predicament dissolved. This path had been ordained since she was a young lady letting a studious boy correct her composition. "I do," she said before he could even finish. "What do we have to do to make it official?"

"Nothing, ma'am." The bed dipped next to her, and he pulled the blankets over himself. "By the power vested in me, by the United States government as commander of this post —"

"You aren't the commander anymore." She lifted her head as he slid his arm beneath her neck and pulled her against his side. "Major Adams is back." The length of him against her body affected her. She rested her hand against his chest to hold herself away, feeling like she needed to retain a little control, but he swooped her close, taking away the space between them and leaving her breathless.

"It doesn't matter," he said. "All that was missing was your consent. Nothing else stands between us."

The cold wind and the bad men somewhere outside didn't matter a jot to her. Not as long as she had Jack to help her face them.

It was late, and she was tired. But there was one part of the ceremony that couldn't wait until morning. With his heart and skin warm and alive beneath her fingers, she whispered, "Do you remember the fort's tradition?"

"The good-night kiss?"

"It's been neglected long enough."

His voice held a smile. "I'll remedy that immediately."

The arm beneath her head flexed as he sought her lips in the darkness. First she felt his palm on her cheek, but then his mouth found hers with such a sweet tenderness that she knew it was a kiss that he'd waited a decade to give. Such rich love took a lifetime to grow, but she could feel her love stretching to rival his.

After a while, he wrapped his hand around her waist, and with a few adjustments, they were both warm and happy. Hattie wouldn't be plagued by nightmares tonight. She was settled. And she couldn't believe she'd caught the eye of a man as wonderful as Jack. Maybe sometime before morning, she'd make him believe that she was his for good.

CHAPTER TWENTY-SEVEN

December 21, 1885
4:30 A.M.

Major Daniel Adams,

The events of Dec. 20th at the Darlington school have uncovered some potentially valuable information in regards to the disruption of classes. While in Darlington yesterday, a student whom my wife has reason to trust reported to Mrs. Hennessey that the specter that haunted them was a man with an injured leg. This is consistent with the blood stain discovered on the costume and bandages found in the basement of the school. I suggest that it is Sloane who has been hiding there, although I am not certain he has an injury. It's likely that he is somewhere nearby, and I would request a complete search of the area.

In other news to report, I regret to

inform you that I will not be available to lead those searches. Because of the unusual nature of my recent nuptials, I've hesitated to claim any leave time that would normally be granted to a bridegroom. In order to correct this oversight, I request a twenty-four-hour leave to better acquaint myself with my new wife. Because of the short duration of my leave, I have no plans to depart from the security of our quarters and would request no interruptions. If this is not permissible ~~you may accept my resignation I call you out to a duel~~ I beg you to grant me forgiveness.

All of my gratitude for the wisdom you have shared with me and your patient sufferance of my shortcomings.

Sincerely,
Lt. John Hennessey

P.S. Please cancel my reassignment from Fort Reno with all due haste.

Chapter Twenty-Eight

Lieutenant John Hennessey,

I received your dispatch of this morning and express my thanks for the timely report on your reconnaissance. I will personally scc to it that a thorough search is done of the area and will make you privy to the results.

As for the second matter, it seems only decent that your leave should last forty-eight hours. If the situation is as felicitous as I perceive it is, a mere day is not adequate. However, I fear that you are not outfitted properly for this campaign. Therefore I've commanded Colonel Nothem to deliver hot meals to your front porch in accordance with the mess hall schedule. Whether you open the door to receive them is wholly at your discretion. You will be expected to report for duty on December 23rd, when you will resume your duties at the fort.

The necessary dispatches have been sent to secure your future assistance here in Indian Territory.

Sincerely and with congratulations, your friend and commanding officer,
Major Daniel Adams

Chapter Twenty-Nine

December 22, 1885

Dear Father and Mother,

I'm married. To Jack Hennessey. Yes, Jack from Van Buren, the one who always wanted to help me with my schoolwork. It looks like I'll be staying in Indian Territory longer than planned, because he's an officer in the cavalry. He's the one who rescued me from the Indians, but they were nice. They rescued me from the stagecoach robber. I don't think I told you about that in my last letter, but everything is good now. Very good.

Isn't it funny? I was trying not to get married, and look at me now. I tried everything I could to get Jack's attention, and he ignored me for quite a while, but I finally won him over. This is better than painting the Rockies, although he tells me that he'll take me there someday. So now I'm an officer's wife. Isn't that a surprise? How everyone will laugh at me back home.

We both send our love and hope to make it home to visit our families on his next leave. Oh, and I did send in a portrait for that exhibition in Denver. I am waiting for news.

Love you both. Merry Christmas.

Your daughter,
Mrs. John Hennessey

P.S. Mr. and Mrs. Walker, I'm afraid your daughter is not being honest. I've been hopelessly in love with her for years and can't believe that she consented to honor me in this unfathomable manner. I am the most fortunate man alive.

I only regret that I wasn't able to ask permission to court her before we were wed, but the situation was quite unique. Be assured she will lack for nothing, most of all the knowledge that she is loved and respected. And I will prevail upon her to write you more often and to tell the truth in her letters.

Sincerely,
Lt. Jack Hennessey

CHAPTER THIRTY

At the first hint of dawn on the horizon, Jack was usually tuned tighter than a piano string. He woke with new thoughts, new ideas, and a burning desire to see what he could accomplish before the sun disappeared on the opposing side of the vast prairie.

This morning was different. Those rays coming through the window meant an interruption to the most joyful time of his life. An interruption, but not an end.

He'd made the coffee himself. The kitchen filled with the thick, rich aroma. It felt strange to be standing in his kitchen, fixing to go back to work, when so much had changed. The bugle sounded outside, calling reveille. Jack gulped hot coffee as he scratched a brief note to his bride, but then he heard her on the stairs and decided his love might be better expressed in person.

The green boughs of the Christmas decorations swayed as he whisked through the house to meet her before she reached the ground floor. He swept around the corner, snatched her off the steps, and swung her around.

Hattie squealed and wrapped her arms around his neck. She still carried the bed's warmth in her nightclothes, but he could also feel her own warmth through the soft fabric.

"Good morning," she murmured into his neck. "Is it time to leave already?"

His arms tightened around her. He grinned as he thought of thirteen-year-old Jack, who would never have believed this possible. "The world didn't stop turning, even for us," he said. Leaving her would be torture, but how sweet it would be to think about his return all day.

"I'll finish decorating for Christmas, now that we know we're staying here," she said.

"Should I send a guard to protect my books, or will you promise not to throw any out?"

"You'd better just watch me yourself," she said as she twisted a brass button on his uniform.

A shadow passed by the French doors of his office. It looked like Major Adams wasn't going to wait for him to make an appearance at roll call.

"Duty calls," he said. He kissed her ever-so-willing lips. "I'll carry this with me all day."

"As long as you need more by tonight," she said.

Major Adams knocked on the door. Had Jack not feared the major would kick it in, he would have followed Hattie back to their room and claimed temporary deafness. He waited until she'd disappeared upstairs before opening the door.

"Major Adams, sir!" Jack saluted as his commander stepped inside.

Major Adams sauntered by with his hands clasped behind his back and announced, "You are firmly in my debt. I expect it'll take the rest of your life to repay me for the good turn I gave you."

"What? How do you take the credit for this?"

"Because I'm the one who insisted that the wedding was binding. Your undying gratitude will be payment enough."

Jack leaned against the banister with his arms crossed. "Did you come over for a purpose besides gloating?"

"Ingrate. Yes. They found a man just like you said. Hiding upstairs in the commissary building on the third floor, and he wasn't just injured. His leg has more holes in it than a pepper box. Looks like the work of the Cheyenne."

"You think they shot up Sloane?"

"If they knew he stole their payment, they wouldn't have been so kind, but it's not Sloane. It's his partner," Major Adams said. "Olin Bixby's the name. The marshal thinks his likeness is similar to the one in Mrs. Hennessey's painting, but we haven't accused him yet. As far as he knows, he's at the Darlington infirmary for his own good. My guess is that he and Mr. Sloane split the money and took out in different directions. Then the Cheyenne caught Bixby alone and worked him over. Naturally he couldn't go to the doctor, so he holed up in the cellar of the school, waiting to heal and make his getaway."

"Or waiting for a chance to dispose of the witness," Jack said.

Major Adams placed a hand on Jack's shoulder. "She's secure here. She'll come to no harm."

"Where's the money?" Hattie came downstairs dressed, and for the first time in two days, her hair was pinned up and her shoes were on. "Wasn't that the whole purpose of the heist?"

Jack couldn't stop grinning. It took Major

Adams's obnoxious throat clearing to bring him around.

"Yes, the money. We have to recover it," Daniel said. "Things will get heated if the tribes have to wait on Congress to approve another payment. But before we can proceed, we need a positive identification."

Jack's smile faded. "I don't think she's ready for that."

"Are you talking about me?" Hattie asked.

"It's essential," Major Adams said. "Why haul him to Judge Parker when the witness is here? If he's not the one we're looking for, we're wasting time. She can go in with the doctor and pretend to assist him. Just for a moment, so she can get a look at him."

"Please, sir." Jack really hated contradicting his superior, but no one understood the nightly fears that tormented his wife. "Her constitution isn't strong enough. Not yet."

Hattie stepped between them. Her face was so pale it looked translucent. "I'll do it," she said. "I owe it to Agent Gibson and the driver."

Jack clasped his hands behind his back. He always hated giving his men difficult assignments, but never had he regretted one so much.

"When Dr. Graff asks for clean bandages,

you bring him this." Jack placed a bundle of white strips in Hattie's hand, but she could barely feel them with her cold fingers. "Take a look at the man on the cot and leave. That's all you need to do."

The smell of camphor would always remind Hattie of the nauseating feeling she was experiencing right now. She'd nearly died hiding from the outlaw, and now she was going to walk into a small room with him. The smell of gunpowder replaced the camphor in her memory. The driver motioning for her to hide. Her decision to face the killer, and then running for her life as he chased her from above and shot down at her. Darkness falling as she huddled in the cold.

"Hattie? Hattie?"

Her eyes cleared. Jack was stooping to catch her gaze.

"I'll be on the other side of the door," he said. "Even if Bixby is the killer, he probably won't recognize you. Just go in and take a peek. That's all."

Dr. Graff twisted his cravat pin nervously. "I never was much of a performer."

"You're changing his bandages," Jack said. "You've done it several times already. Nothing different."

"Except now I know he's a murderer.

That's a new piece of information. Why don't you pretend to be the doctor?"

Even through her distress, Hattie could hear Jack's frustration. "He's your patient. Now get in there." With an outstretched arm, Jack motioned to the hallway that led to the examination rooms.

The doctor straightened his spine and smoothed his cravat. "See," he mumbled to Hattie, "nothing to worry about." And then he disappeared down the hall.

She dreaded seeing Bixby with every ounce of her strength. Maybe it wouldn't be him. Maybe it was just a trespasser the Cheyenne had caught. But was that what she wanted? Wouldn't it be better for the killer to already be caught?

Jack placed his hand at the base of her neck. He squeezed, and only then did she realize how tight her shoulders were.

"It'll only take a second," Jack said. "You can do this. You've been so brave already."

Running away had taken no courage at all. Now she was supposed to go to him on purpose?

"Nurse. Bandages, please."

Hattie's stomach dropped. That was her cue.

Jack released her. She took a deep,

camphor-filled breath. "Go on," he whispered.

She took one step, and then her legs took over. They carried her so quickly that she was inside the room before she was prepared. She had to stay objective, but the injured man's presence repelled her. Instead she focused on the doctor, who was sawing through bloody bandages with a scalpel. The man's pant leg had been cut off, exposing a scarlet, infected leg. Hattie tried to look at his face, but she couldn't lift her eyes. Instead she placed the bandages in the hand of the doctor, bowed her head, and turned to leave.

The same panic that had propelled her through the frigid canyon drew her into the hallway. But she couldn't go. Not yet. Hattie grasped the doorframe of the examination room and held on for dear life. She wouldn't let Agent Gibson down, and she wouldn't let Jack down, but most of all, she wouldn't disappoint herself. If she didn't look this man in the eyes, she would always feel that she hadn't done her part.

Gritting her teeth, Hattie turned — just in time to see Olin Bixby reach for the scalpel.

Dr. Graff was holding Bixby's leg up as he wound the fresh bandage around it. Bixby never took his eyes off the doctor, but he was inching his hand toward the forgotten knife barely visible in the sheets. If she didn't do something . . .

Hattie rushed forward and grabbed Bixby by the wrist. He dropped the scalpel, and she snatched it up before he could recover.

"What do you think you're doing?" Bixby growled. He kicked his leg free from the doctor's grasp as he glared at her.

Hattie met his gaze — his black, furious gaze. The same narrow face. The same chipped tooth. Then his eyes tightened. He recognized her. He did. And that moment's hesitation showed what she thought she'd never see on him. Fear.

Hattie released his arm and stepped away, still clutching the scalpel. "Dr. Graff, you need to be careful where you leave your equipment. We don't want our patient to hurt himself." She was walking backward toward the door, not letting Bixby out of her sight. For the first time that day, she felt in control.

His brow was furrowed as he eased his leg down. His mouth curled into a smile, but it didn't reach his eyes. "Just trying to help out the doc," he said. "No reason to get jumpy."

He thought he still had a chance. Hattie saw the knowledge in his face. He imagined that she didn't recognize him.

She paused in the doorway. As badly as she wanted to scream for Jack's help and arrest him immediately, she couldn't predict how the villain would respond. She couldn't put Dr. Graff's life in danger.

"I apologize, Mr. Bixby. I didn't mean to startle you. Now, if you'll excuse me, I have more bandages to roll."

Her warm smile did the trick. Bixby laid back against the headboard. Dr. Graff stopped spinning his cravat pin and returned to the bandages, while Hattie made her way to the hall.

She'd faced the fiend, and he hadn't won. She could beat him. She'd wondered why she had survived the attack, and now she knew. Without her, there would have been no one to look at his face and convict him. It was because she'd survived that justice would be done, but she had to do her part.

But there was still one man free who could hurt her.

Sloane.

Chapter Thirty-One

With the evil spirit from the basement now identified and under guard, Jack had volunteered to take the happy news to the tribes that the school was safe and the Christmas program could recommence.

That left Hattie with time on her hands, and she was in the mood for some female companionship, so she gathered her paints and headed next door.

The Adams ladies were delighted that she'd braved the short, icy trip to visit, and when Daisy spotted her box of paints, she flung her arms around Hattie.

"I do love to paint. Grandmother brought me scads of shells from Galveston. Let's paint them."

"Painted shells? Who would want those?" Caroline asked, although her disdain for her sister's idea seemed manufactured.

"The Indians wear them as jewelry. They'll love them," Daisy said. "I'll be right back."

"Are you comfortable living next door?" Louisa asked. "When Major Adams and I were courting, he took me to dinner at Lieutenant Hennessey's a few times. After seeing his parlor, I've been worried about your safety. Bump into the wrong stack of books, and we might never find you again."

Hattie laughed. "I've got a hardy constitution," she assured her. "And I started setting things aright immediately. He needed my help."

"You never know, do you?" Louisa said. "Lieutenant Jack is the most articulate, disciplined man. One would expect his home to be as controlled as he is."

Hattie could feel her face warming. Jack wasn't as in control as he pretended. "Looks are deceiving," she said. Then, to draw the attention away from her suddenly pink cheeks, she pointed at the girl entering the room. "My, you have a lot of shells, Daisy."

Hattie reached into Daisy's basket and picked a white shell shaped like a fan. She flipped it over and rubbed her thumb on the smooth, flat underside of the shell. "There's room enough to paint here."

"Hurrah! Let's do them in the kitchen," Daisy cheered and ran off toward the back of the house.

"I'm sorry about her." Louisa ran a hand

413

over the curls that were gathered on her shoulder. "She's as jumpy as a frog sitting on a firecracker."

"Louisa," Caroline groaned, "where do you come up with these sayings?"

"This mule driver used to say that. He'd come through the Cat-Eye Saloon every spring on his way delivering supplies here in the nations. He had a temper, but when he was sober, he could tell stories like you wouldn't believe."

Hattie must have misunderstood. Louisa was as beautiful and refined as any lady she'd ever expected to meet in the big cities. What in the world was she talking about?

Seeing her confusion, Caroline said, "My new mother has a very interesting collection of skills. Don't ever challenge her to a singing competition . . . or a chess match."

"I wouldn't dare." But Hattie was glad to see that Caroline looked proud of her.

"Will you be giving painting lessons in Darlington?" Louisa asked. "Assuming the school continues, that is."

"I hadn't really considered that possibility. Perhaps if they'd allow it."

Louisa's smile was stunning. "I think you know the right people to make it happen." She started toward the kitchen, then turned to Caroline, who was watching listlessly out the window. "Don't you want to paint some?"

"Nah." Caroline flung her red hair over her shoulder. "Let Daisy play at it. My works are more suited to real canvases."

"Does Caroline paint?" Hattie asked as the young lady sauntered out of the room.

Louisa checked over her shoulder to make sure they were out of earshot. "Often and very poorly. Daisy is so much better, but we're conspiring together to make sure Caroline never realizes it."

"Would it crush her?"

"No." Louisa laughed. "She'd think we were lying and be furious."

They entered the kitchen, where Daisy had dumped the shells on the table. "This is a capital idea, Mrs. Hennessey. Do you think that together we could paint a shell for every student at the school?"

"What an excellent Christmas gift!" Hattie said. "I'd be honored if you'd let me help."

Louisa patted Daisy on the back as she hopped and clapped her hands together. Hattie was suddenly struck with the thought that she herself was a married woman. She had a husband, a house, and could soon start a family. It wasn't something she'd particularly planned for, but the thought of starting a family with Jack seemed intrinsically whole. She missed him. He'd only be gone for the afternoon, but already she missed him. What would he say about their prospects for the future? That would be a conversation she might find too sensitive to begin.

While Daisy and Louisa spread an oilcloth over the table, Hattie held a chalky shell in her hand and tried to think of what a student would want to see — or what a particular student would like. The first one she thought of was Tom. What could she give to help him not feel so far from home? What would he see as special?

Taking a fine brush, she started with his horse. The black pony he'd ridden from his village hadn't been stabled in town, and he undoubtedly missed it. When it came time to paint the boy, Hattie hesitated. Should she paint him as she'd first met him on the cold day he'd accompanied them to Fort Reno? That was the past. She'd rather give him a picture of the future. The boy she painted on the Indian pony was Tom, but it was Tom as he looked now. His hair was chopped, and he wore the school's uniform. Not that he couldn't do as he wished when he went back home, but she wanted him to remember that the outside appearance wouldn't change the things he loved.

Daisy stepped behind her. "Great Saturn's rings!" she gasped.

"Daisy," Louisa said, "didn't your father tell you not to say that?"

"But you do."

"Not anymore," she said. "Now what's the matter?"

"Look at what Mrs. Hennessey painted. It's Tom Broken Arrow."

Hattie turned the shell for Louisa to see.

"Great Saturn's rings," Louisa said. "That's amazing."

"Do you think he'll like it?" Hattie asked.

"He'll love it!" Daisy said. "Can you teach me how to do that? But I want to paint a tepee for Mirabel. She and I practice drawing them together when I visit."

"That sounds perfect." Just the thing Hattie needed to keep her mind off the slowly passing time until Jack returned.

The wind carried hard bits of ice that stung like someone was pelting Jack in the face with salt. But his trip had been worth it. The tidings of catching the thief hiding beneath the school both reassured the parents that the cavalry had taken their concerns seriously and proved that the problem had been dealt with. The fact that the outlaw had also been the one the Cheyenne had harassed gave them something to be proud of. It wasn't often that they were praised for their ill-treatment of guests, but in this case, they had slowed him down long enough for the authorities to catch up with him. Their only regret was that they wished they'd known Olin Bixby was the one responsible for their missing payment from the government. The Cheyenne and Arapaho were confident that Bixby would tell them where the gold was hidden once he'd experienced their arts of persuasion.

At any rate, the children were coming back to the school, and they'd be there in time for the Christmas celebration. Jack had at least accomplished that much.

The lights from the fort shone for miles on the black plains. The skies darkened early in the winter, so they had probably already missed the six-thirty roll call. Sure enough, when they reached the fort, Jack saw that the post flag had been retired for the day, but tattoo had yet to be played, so the men were on their own time.

"You want me to take your horse?" Icy slivers on the shoulders of Private Willis's coat sparkled beneath the light from the lanterns lining the thoroughfare.

"I appreciate it," Jack said. "Thanks."

"Thought you might be in a hurry to get

home. Just remember this when I get my next leave to go to Garber to see my lady." Private Willis winked before dismounting.

Jack took his gear and left the horse in Willis's capable, if often mischievous, hands. He stomped the thick, hard mud off his boots on his porch. Just as he'd hoped, Hattie's quick footsteps could be heard, then the door swung open. She was dressed in a simple gown, but her hair was arranged as expertly as if she were going to a show at the King Opera House in Van Buren. Her eyes sparkled as she caught him by the arm and dragged him inside.

"That was a quick trip. I'm so glad you weren't out late. I bet you're hungry. Let me help you with your coat."

Jack closed the door behind him. Her fussing over him was the best welcome he'd ever received. He waited patiently as she unbuttoned his coat and removed it. He allowed her to take his gear and drop it in his office. He handled the pistol and saber himself, then helped her with the boots. By the time she allowed him any farther into his own house, the stiffness had almost been worked out of his fingers.

"Come by the fire. I have some hot water on the stove. Would you like tea or coffee?" Hattie was always on a mission, and now his care fell under her domain.

"I'd rather sit with you," he said. "And we ate supper in the field. No need to make anything for me."

"Tea it is." She rolled up his scarf and strode into the kitchen.

Jack stretched his hands toward the fire and let the warmth seep in until the knees of his wool trousers were almost too hot to touch. Stepping back, he noticed dozens of seashells stacked on an end table along with scraps of twine and butcher paper. What was she up to now?

Picking up a shell, he turned it over to see a breathtaking portrait of a young Arapaho mother. Her cradleboard hid all but the top of the baby's head strapped to her back, and she was holding her hand down low, as if summoning another child.

Hattie handed him a mug of tea. "Do you like it?"

"Should I know her?" he asked. The fact that he could make out specific features on a miniature told much about Hattie's talent.

"It's Francine's mother. I met her the day they came to pick up the children at the school. I'm giving it to Francine for Christmas."

He turned the shell so it caught the light.

"Your work is exquisite. Either those men in Denver are going to be impressed, or they're dolts. Either way, I hope you don't regret not going there yourself."

Hattie took the shell out of his hand and laid it on the table. "I have space to work here, and I have someone to share it with. Besides, didn't you say that it's too late to change my mind?"

"Definitely too late." He moved her around to face him. "I was just thinking that something had to be wrong. My life can't possibly have turned out so well."

He couldn't wait to take her back home to Van Buren. He was proud of her. He'd spent so many years hiding his devotion to Hattie that it had become a habit. A bad habit. Now he could gaze at her with all the adoration he used to keep bottled up, and she seemed to enjoy it.

"You have to stop looking at me like that," she said. "Or everyone will know we were only faking earlier."

"I wasn't faking it, but I didn't realize how much more I could love you until now." A quick kiss, followed by a rather lengthy one, and then he thought to ask about her project again. "Are you painting a shell for each student?"

Horses, tepees, a woman at a cook fire,

men hunting — each picture was a tiny masterful glimpse of Arapaho life.

"Daisy and I are."

"The Christmas program is tomorrow. I could help wrap them if you need. Not that I will do a tidy job."

"I'll supervise," she said. "I'll tell you who I made them for, but I might need help with some of the names."

"Yes, ma'am." He picked up the shears and began cutting the butcher paper into squares for her. "You know, I'd be a fool to continue doing the illustrations in my studies when I have an artist as talented as you in the house. Look at these little pictures. You've already displayed the Arapaho better than my descriptions could."

Hattie beamed. "Me, helping Jack with his homework? My, how the scales have tilted. You used to intimidate me something awful."

"And you scared me something fierce," he said. "If you knew how much courage I had to gather every time I talked to you . . ."

"And then you wasted the opportunity by correcting my composition."

"Lesson learned. And while you're identifying my inadequacies . . ." He pointed down at the shells in front of him. She'd already wrapped two while he'd talked. "I'm no good at this, either. My fingers are numb."

"Don't give me any excuses." Her smile quirked at the side. "Especially when you're asking for my help."

"I'll try again." He lifted the paper, but he could only think of how much he wanted her attention for himself.

Hattie knotted the twine on another gift and asked, "Now that we have Bixby, what happens?"

"Once he's fit to travel, they'll haul him to Fort Smith in Arkansas, and he'll stand before Judge Parker. We'll go for the trial, of course." He held up the twine. "It tangled."

She leaned against the table to reach for it. Jack managed to brush his leg against hers as she caught the twine. Her eyes flickered, but they stayed on the string.

"What about Sloane?" She undid the knot he'd made and dropped the twine on the table in front of Jack, giving him no chance for another caress.

He folded the paper over a shell. "We haven't found him, but we will. It's just a matter of time. Could you put your finger here and hold this while I tie it?"

She leaned across his arm to pin the paper down.

"Bixby hasn't uttered a peep, but the

evidence suggests that Sloane was an accomplice. Which is why I won't let you wander around alone until this business is finished." He rested his hand on top of hers as he made the bow, but even after he pulled it tight, he didn't move away.

She remained focused on the gift, but her lips had parted. His wife didn't want to wrap presents right now. Jack was certain of it.

"There could be other, less noble reasons for keeping you close, as well," he said.

Hattie's eyes met his, and he saw the invitation he was hoping for.

"I can wrap these first thing tomorrow," she said as she took the gift out of his hand, her fingers trailing over his palm. "You weren't getting anything done anyway."

He winked. "If you insist."

CHAPTER THIRTY-TWO

Even though most of the Mennonite missionaries didn't display one in their homes, Darlington was lit up like a Christmas tree. Every light on the streets glittered. The government employees left candles burning in each window, throwing a festive atmosphere over the cold town. Although the temperature remained chilly, the evening would not be a beautiful snow-covered Christmas village like the ideal. Then again, nothing about the Christmas pageant would look like a traditional tableau.

Hattie adjusted the basket on her lap. She held half the presents for the children, while Daisy, riding in the buggy in front of them with Major Adams and Louisa, had the rest. In the two miles to Darlington, Daisy had craned her neck out of the buggy a dozen times to look back and check on Hattie.

"She's worried the shells aren't going to make it." Jack wore his dress uniform, as did the other officers who had come for the festivities. Hattie had brushed the lint off the coat for him when he pulled it out of the wardrobe. He'd been too busy sneaking something into the house that he didn't want her to see. It would take effort on her part not to snoop for whatever he had hidden in his desk drawer, but with Christmas coming in the morning, she should be able to wait that long.

They'd reached the school, and Daisy peeked out again even as her father pulled up to the hitching post.

"She's as excited as I am," Hattie said.

"Let's leave the gifts in the wagon for now. It'll be disruptive if we carry them in before the program."

"And we don't want Headmistress Lehrman cross with us."

He nodded as they went inside to join the Adamses and other families. The Arapaho families that had come from the reservation filed in as well, the women greeting each other in their own language, the younger children bundled up tight for the journey from their villages, and the men grouping together to question one of their own.

"What's going on over there?" Hattie asked.

Jack tilted his head as they passed, trying

to catch their words. "That's White Horse they're talking to. He's passing on the dispatch we received from Washington. Since the government lost their payment, they won't be getting it until next quarter. White Horse understands what happened. He knows it's not our fault, but the news isn't welcome. I hope it doesn't get in the way of what they see tonight."

Hattie had never seen the mission house so crowded. She clutched Jack's arm to keep from being separated from him. "What do they know about Christmas?" she asked.

"The missionaries, mostly Mennonites, have taught them the basic tenets of the faith if they wanted to learn. Some will know the story, but they've never seen it presented like this. Hopefully it'll bring them closer to understanding what a miracle it is that God would send His holy Son to live with us on Earth. It would do me some good to ponder that outrageous plan, as well. But I don't want to put undue expectations on the children. After the week they've had — closing the school and going home, only to get called back — I'll be relieved if they make it through the program."

Inside the meeting room of the mission house, anticipation made voices more melodic and the greetings merrier. Hattie was hugged by Mrs. Lehrman and Mrs. Voth, while Jack shook their hands. The teachers and agency workers had migrated toward the front, leaving the seats in the back open for their guests.

The situation didn't please Jack. His chin hardened as he stopped next to Major Adams's pew.

"Major Adams, must we all sit up front? Shouldn't we give the Arapaho the seats of honor? It's their children performing, after all."

"Simmer down, Jack." Major Adams flicked a pine needle off his shoulder. "I offered the same thing, but Right Hand was adamant. Their people don't feel safe being pinned in with all of us between them and the door."

Before, Hattie would have said that she didn't feel safe having a hundred Indians between her and the exit, but now that she knew them, it was the furthest thought from her mind.

"Then I withdraw my complaint," Jack said. He motioned to Hattie to take a seat. "As long as they're close enough to hear."

Superintendent Seger came to the stage. His mere presence was enough to silence the crowd as the few left standing found their seats. He welcomed them with halting words in Arapaho before gesturing to Jack. Hattie gaped as Jack stood and went to join him on the stage. The superintendent continued to line out the rest of the program, pausing every few phrases to give Jack a chance to translate to the rest of the audience. Hattie listened carefully, trying to pick out words that were repeated, but even as slowly as Jack was talking, it only made her head spin. How did he make heads or tails of it? By next year, he'd probably be speaking it as well as Coyote spoke English.

His gaze stole to hers. She lifted her chin. Yes, she saw him, and yes, she was proud. He walked a bit taller leaving the stage.

"You look just like you did when you beat Willie Porter at the spelling bee," she whispered.

"Learning that was a lot harder than besting Willie. He wasn't any competition." He took her gloved hand and squeezed it.

Mrs. Lehrman came to the front row and took a seat on the aisle. There was a rustling from the back of the room as the doors opened, revealing the children lined up, each one with a candle in hand. The procession down the aisle was met by appreciative murmurs of their parents. Most of the older students walked nobly to the front of the room, familiar with the importance of pageantry, but the younger ones waved as they spotted their parents in the audience. Only a speedy interference by a gray-haired grandmother decked in fringed buckskin kept a candle from toppling over. She righted it, then set the little boy back on his path.

Once they were in place, the students broke into the strains of "Joy to the World," but Hattie had never heard it sung like this before. Singing at twice the volume of any children's choir she'd ever participated in, they belted out the lyrics in their own tongue. But wasn't that how it should be? Why shouldn't the Savior's coming be expressed with enthusiasm? The angels' message may not have been delivered in this tongue, but it surely matched this fervor.

"I hope I translated that correctly," Jack whispered. "Coyote helped, but we had to take liberties with some of the phrasing to get it to fit."

"Sounds beautiful to me," she said.

From there, the program went through the basic Christmas story. Or at least Hattie assumed it did, but with the Arapaho narrator, she couldn't be sure. Arapaho Mary and Joseph arrived with quiet dignity and took their place on the stage. No longer did they have a rag doll Baby Jesus in the cradleboard. Now a bright-eyed little fellow was strapped to Mary's back. He'd managed to get a chubby arm out of the swaddling clothes. His beaded bracelet twinkled in the candlelight as he waved his arm. Two little girls on the front row of the choir hunched together, giggling over the baby's delight.

Hattie let the miracle of the season alight on her anew. God had come to Earth as a baby, entrusting His care to earthly, fallible parents — a mother maybe not much older than the girl playing Mary's part. And He didn't come to an elegant, civilized world, but landed Himself in a territory just as brutal and dangerous as Indian Territory had ever been.

And why had He come? For her. For Jack. For Tom Broken Arrow. For anyone who would call on Him. The supreme gift of Christmas gifts. The gift that often went forgotten and overlooked.

Three boys dressed in buckskin hunting clothes played the parts of the shepherds. Even with their hair cut short, they were still able to weave in beads and adornments for the occasion. They danced down the aisle with two spry youngsters bounding before them on all fours, baaing like sheep. The shepherds prodded their sheep more fiercely than they should, but that was the nature of boys. The girls who came as angels weren't in the traditional white gowns. Instead they wore finely worked buckskin. The dresses sparkled with smooth beads and polished elk-teeth buttons.

"Those gowns must weigh twenty pounds each," Hattie whispered to Jack.

"Each bauble was selected and sewn on with pride," he answered as the girls passed down the aisle, making their own music as the trinkets jangled against each other.

The Christmas program couldn't be any better, but Hattie felt some unease about what was coming. Would the children have any bad memories? She looked over her shoulder as the doors at the back of the room opened. The superintendent, Reverend Voth, and Agent Lee stepped inside, looking foreign and regal in their soft flowing robes. Hattie tensed as they made their way toward the stage. Francine's eyes widened. She'd stopped singing, but Cold Rain bumped her with her elbow. With a jutted jaw and lowered brow, she gave Francine a firm stare as if to warn her against disgracing them with cowardice. Francine bravely recommenced her singing, but her eyes never left the silky robe that Reverend Voth was wearing.

The Magi presented the gifts, which in

Indian Territory consisted of an eagle feather, a buffalo robe, and a piece of ledger art. The narrator finished his speech, and the children broke out into another rendition of "Joy to the World," but this time they sang it in English. Voices rumbled from the Arapaho side of the room. Were the parents unhappy? Jack seemed pleased.

"They're impressed that their own children are learning white men's words," Jack said. "They might not like what we say most of the time, but they understand the advantage it'll give their children."

The program had ended. The students streamed off the stage to join their families and make their way to the dining hall for the grand banquet.

"I hope we're doing what's best," Hattie said. "The school will change everything for them."

His eyes sparked with interest. "You made this possible. If you hadn't agreed to stay here and help me, many of these children would have had to go to Pennsylvania for school. Or had none at all." He searched her face in the dim light of the room. "Do you think it was worth the sacrifice?"

She wormed her hand between his arm and his side. "I can't rightly call it a sacrifice anymore, can I? This is so much better than

433

whatever I expected to find in Denver."

"Even if your painting doesn't succeed?"

It was a fair question. Had Hattie sacrificed her dreams of achievement for a more traditional role? While she intended to continue her quest, she would be naïve to think that putting Jack's career first wouldn't interfere with her own. On the other hand, there were always forks in the road. You could never guarantee what lay at the end of a journey. At this point, all she was sure of was who she wanted to be her companion along the way.

"The exhibit curator might not like the turn I've taken in my work, but I'm pleased. Those mountains will be there for generations of artists to paint, many of them more talented than I. But who is going to make a record of these people? Who is going to capture this part of their history?"

Everyone around them was getting up and filing out, but neither Jack nor Hattie felt any hurry to join them. "Thank you," he said. "Thank you for easing my guilt. I would always wonder if I could've avoided this mess. I'd always be afraid that someday you'll regret your decision."

"But it was my decision, and I decided to stay."

"Just because you could never find your

own bedroom."

"Shush," she whispered. "People will hear you. And don't you start correcting me again."

"It's my favorite mistake of yours. Now, let's go see about this fancy supper they've worked up."

The line for food stretched out the dining room door. Hattie felt out of place, since all the agency women and schoolteachers were serving. Caroline was entertaining a dapper-looking frontiersman, much to Daisy's amusement. Spotting Hattie, Daisy waved and left her place in line. Her father joined them, as well.

"Splendid performance tonight," Major Adams said. "I only wish we had as much success at the Cheyenne school in Cantonment."

"Give me time," Jack replied. "With the similarities in their languages . . ."

"Mrs. Hennessey," Daisy said, "don't you think we should get our presents now? Once they finish eating, everyone will go home, and we won't see the kids again until after break is over."

Jack and Major Adams weren't likely to resolve their discussion before their plates were filled with food. Hattie took Daisy's hand. "Let's go," she said.

Forgoing their coats, they dodged through the crowd and into the chilly air outside. The stars blistered through the cold dark sky, but Daisy was in too much of a hurry to appreciate their strength.

"I can carry my own," she said. "How heavy is yours?"

"Don't worry about me," Hattie replied. "It's just one basket."

The two buggies were parked next to each other on the hitching post. The horses nickered in greeting, blowing warm steam from their nostrils. "We won't be much longer," Hattie said to them, but they didn't seem to care one way or the other.

She'd climbed up on the side of the buggy to reach her basket when she heard Daisy behind her. "Got mine, Mrs. Hennessey."

Seeing that Hattie had her own basket in hand and was on her way down, Daisy skipped ahead and ran back into the building. With both feet on the ground, Hattie adjusted her skirt, but before she could take after the impulsive child, a man stepped in her way.

"Mrs. Hennessey? That's an interesting development."

The blood in Hattie's veins chilled. Sloane stood in front of her. Her throat tightened. Everything inside her urged her to run, but she couldn't move her feet.

"Don't tell me you've gone and married one of these soldiers." His debonair appearance was ruined by the stains on his wrinkled clothing. She gripped the spoke of the wheel behind her, wishing it would break off into a club. "How very conventional of you. I thought you were seeking a grander future."

"I thought you were dead," she said. What if he didn't know they'd figured it out? What if he thought he wasn't a suspect? She cleared her throat. "Good news," she managed to say. "They caught the man who attacked us. Lieutenant Hennessey says we should be safe now."

"Lieutenant Hennessey, your husband?" His eyes darted to the school building. "How quaint. Did they find him in the commissary? I heard something about the third floor."

This man had planned to kill her. He'd lain in wait, patient with his jibes and faux pleasantries until he had his chance. And he was doing it again.

Hattie looked at the mission house. Daisy had already made it back inside. Knowing Daisy, she'd slipped past the adults and was handing out presents to the students. Would Jack realize that Hattie was missing, or was he still talking to Major Adams?

"I don't remember exactly," she said. "Let's go inside where it's warm and ask someone." Her fingers ached as she released the spoke. Hooking her arm through her basket, she slid her shaking hands into her pockets and turned toward the mission house.

One step. Two steps. Was he following her? Hattie was about to look over her shoulder when the fire bell sounded. She drew in a long breath. No smoke. Could it be a Cheyenne attack? But the troopers had their own procedures. Major Adams would be alerted personally, not through the fire bell.

Mr. Sloane grabbed her by the arm. "We're going to the commissary," he said.

"No. I'm not going with you." She dug her heels into the dirt road, but it was little help. He pulled her away from the mission and toward the alley across the street.

Two troopers ran from the hospital toward the mission, but they weren't looking her direction. The doors of the mission burst open, and people spilled out. Hattie could make out Jack and Major Adams's blue cavalry uniforms amid the dark suits of the agency men and the Indians' buckskins. They were all talking, fast and urgently.

"Jack," she yelled, but her air was cut off

as she was thrown against the wall. Her head bounced against the brick, causing white flashes of light beneath her eyelids. She dropped the basket as she put her hands against the wall and tried to push away, but Sloane was stronger. The bells covered any weak noise she could produce.

"They can't hear you," he growled against the back of her head. A thick point pressed against her corset into her ribs, and Hattie knew it was a gun. "You're going to show me where they found Bixby, do you understand?"

Her nightmare had returned. She managed to nod, but the cold bricks against her face felt much like the hard wall of sandstone she'd hidden against that night. All the warmth, the lights, the music of the mission house had faded, and she was alone again in the cold. And she was scared.

Sloane took a handful of her hair while keeping the gun shoved against her, forcing her deeper into the shadows between the massive commissary and the livery stables. With its splintered doorframe and dented brass doorknob, it was evident that Sloane had been to the commissary before. He swung open the door and pulled Hattie inside.

The cavernous room only had a few

windows, but through their light, Hattie could make out a door on the opposite side. Voices outside were raised. The commissary's thick walls drowned out all but a sharp occasional word.

"What do you need me for?" she asked. She tried to curve her rib cage away from the gun digging into it, but he jerked her hair and pulled her closer.

"We're running out of time. I have to find the bag and get out of here before they catch Bixby."

"Bixby? Bixby is in the hospital." More noises outside. Hattie looked up at a high window. Bixby had escaped. That was why the alarm had been raised. They were searching for him. With the chaotic search, would anyone realize she was gone?

Sloane dragged her across the warehouse toward the staircase. She stiffened her legs. Her shoes slid across the floor. The vastness of the commissary felt as cold and deadly as her night on the plains, but this time the enemy already had her. Despite her feet dragging, he was drawing her closer and closer to the stairwell and farther from the searching people outside. Wherever he was taking her, she didn't want to go.

"No use in being stubborn." Sloane yanked her arm. She struggled to keep her feet. "If you help me find what I'm looking for, I'll let you go."

But he wouldn't. He knew she was a witness against Bixby and him, and he couldn't let her survive.

They'd reached the staircase. Hattie tried to drop to the floor, but pain shot down her neck as he wrenched her to her feet by the hair. She hoped she was buying time. Hoped that Jack would realize she was missing. Maybe he'd even connect her disappearance with Bixby's. But he didn't know where to find her. With a gun against her side, she had little choice but to stumble up the stairs.

The vacant third floor looked nothing like it had when they'd skated here. Boxes, crates, and barrels made ominous black voids in the room. Instead of laughing children, she was alone with a killer. Instead of Jack rescuing her, she was going to have to save herself.

Sloane's fingers bruised the inside of her arm as he holstered his pistol. "This is the room Bixby was in. Where are the hiding places?"

The hiding places? How was she supposed to know? No one was coming to her rescue. She had to act on her own. How could she outsmart this man? "What? What are you looking for?" she asked as she scanned the room, looking for anything to give her an advantage.

He forced air out through his nose. "You're even dumber than I thought."

Then she saw the thin sliver of light coming through the double doors at the end of the room — the ones that had worried Jack when the children were skating.

They were dangerous, Jack had said. Well, today, so was she.

"They found his cot over there, by the door to that closet." She pointed ahead, but the way was obstructed by stacks of the weekly rations handed out on distribution day.

Sloane's face hardened with determination. He hesitated as if deciding whether to take her along or not. She had to convince him that he needed her, because once she was useless to him, she'd suffer the same fate as Agent Gibson.

"If it's locked, there's a key somewhere along the wall," she said.

"Let's go."

Now she could count the steps to her fate. Would her gamble pay off? She'd know soon enough. Could this be her salvation, or would Jack find her body discarded and cold?

The same God who had stayed with her when she was frightened on the prairie was with her now. She might be seeing Him face to face in a moment, but a peace passed over her. She'd faced terror before and suffered from the repercussions for weeks, but during that, she'd learned that God had provided for her. And now, even if He didn't provide her a way out of her fate, He was going to see her through it.

But she still had a chance.

By stepping ahead of Sloane, she steered him to the door she wanted him to find.

"The handle is here somewhere," she said.

Keeping a constricting hand wrapped around her neck, he swept his other hand over the wood until he clutched the handle. Being as careful as she could, Hattie hooked her foot beneath the bolt in the floor that held the second door securely closed. Did he notice the breeze coming through the crack? Did he suspect that this door didn't lead to a closet? Rocking her weight back on her heel, she forced the bolt upward. Now, with just a touch, both of the doors would swing wide over nothingness.

In his anxiousness to find where his partner had hidden the loot, Sloane forced the door open, momentum carrying him forward. He teetered on the threshold with nothing but air before him and tried to pull against Hattie, but she yanked out of his grasp. The cold wind rushed at them — standing at the highest point for miles around. Sloane clawed the air, looking for something solid to brace against, but his death grip only landed on the twin door — the one that had been unbolted and now also swung free. He rocked on his heels, and Hattie couldn't hesitate. She planted her boot on his backside and shoved with all her might.

A shout from outside. Someone saw him. But then he disappeared from Hattie's view. She ducked to the floor and covered her ears. Sloane had been given more time to prepare for his death than he'd given Agent Gibson. That was what she had to remember.

She crawled away from the drop without looking down. Her breath came in painful jerks. She'd beat him. For weeks, she'd been terrified of the wicked men in the robbery finding her, but she had faced them, and she'd defeated them both. Good didn't prevail over wicked men every time, but she thanked God that twice He'd spared her.

Tired to the bone and sore from the fight, Hattie got to her feet and shuffled across the room, but instead of heading to the stairs, she made her way to the barrel she'd stood behind while she watched Jack skate.

The room was filled with bags of flour, sugar, and coffee, each marked with their contents in black stenciled letters. There were also crates and barrels, but she'd seen a sack the day they'd gone skating, and as far as she could tell, it was unique. With her artist's memory, she could picture it perfectly, and there were no others like this one. Her knees nearly gave way when she knelt behind the barrel and pulled the sack away from the wall where it had been stuffed. Someday she would wonder why she didn't rush downstairs to freedom, but in her numbness, she felt like knowing whether she was right or not was more important. Her fingers felt clumsy with the drawstring, but the knot finally pulled free.

There were people coming up the staircase. Several people. She started laughing before Jack even reached her. From the confused look on his face, she realized that she wasn't acting naturally, but he should be used to that by now. After all, no sane woman insisted on sleeping with an overcoat every night.

He knelt and held up a lantern, nearly blinding eyes that had become accustomed to the darkness. He motioned for the townsmen with him to search the rest of the building, but they were drawn to the open doors at the end of the room.

"That man who fell," Jack said, "what happened? What are you doing in here?"

Hattie's head spun with all she had to tell him, but she chose to start with the obvious. She turned the sack upside down and let the heavy gold coins drop into her lap. "I found the Cheyenne and Arapaho's money," she said and then collapsed into his arms.

CHAPTER THIRTY-THREE

He'd told Hattie that she had to stay with the doctor until she recovered, but really it was Jack who needed the recovery time. He'd been filling his plate with wild turkey and hot rolls when the alarm sounded. Jack still didn't remember what happened to his plate of food. Surely someone caught it as he ran out the door with Major Adams.

"We were all looking for you." He offered Hattie a mug of stout coffee. "Once we realized that someone had sprung Bixby from his guards, we knew you were in danger. Everyone — troopers, agents, missionaries, and the Indians — was looking for you."

Hattie waved away the coffee. Her foot tapped against the floor as she sat on a low cot. "If the dinner has resumed, that's where I want to be. I don't want this to be the only memory of our first Christmas together. Even if I could just watch the children and their excitement, it would help me not think about what could've happened today."

"Is that healthy?" Jack asked the doctor, who was taking her pulse. "Won't she be susceptible to overexcitement right now? Shouldn't she go home and rest?"

"Why are you asking him?" Hattie said. "I've been through enough trauma in the last month to know what to expect. I think I'll carry on just fine through the dinner. I won't have any infuriating attacks of feminine weakness until bedtime."

She sat up straight. Jack recognized the look. She was trying to convince him that she was strong and able. And she was, but her drawn face evidenced the toll the night had taken on her.

"I don't want to overtax you," he said.

"This party is only once a year. And I have the shells I painted for the children. Daisy will be so disappointed if I don't get them to the party."

Those painted shells were the least of Jack's concerns, but since they were here already . . .

"It's my pleasure to escort you to the Christmas Eve supper," he said. "I only hope there's still some food left for us. No running away from me this time."

The doctor stepped out of the way as Jack

helped Hattie into his coat. She must have forgotten to grab hers when she'd gone for the gifts with Daisy, but it was fitting that she had his on now. Jack pulled a trooper aside and, with Hattie's help, instructed him on where to find her basket.

"Jack?" Hattie shivered once they'd stepped into the brisk night air. "What happened to Sloane? Did he die?"

"Either that fall or the gallows was going to break his neck. It doesn't matter much which one got him first."

"To think, I was riding with him all along, and he was just waiting for his time."

"And if the Cheyenne hadn't slowed Bixby down, the partners would've met up and gotten away with the money. With Bixby injured, Sloane had to come back for him."

"Does everyone at supper know?" she asked. "I hate for this to ruin their celebration."

"They won't shed any tears for him. Especially on a night like tonight."

She hoped Major and Mrs. Adams wouldn't act overly concerned. Hattie didn't like being a victim. She wanted respect, not pity. With Bixby back in custody and his partner no longer a threat, she was free to move on.

The party was in full swing. A quartet was harmonizing Christmas carols while two Indian men slapped a beat on an upturned bucket and added their rhythmic voices to the song. The children, awed by the tinsel and greenery, remained in their places even though their plates had been cleaned long ago. But being well-behaved didn't stop them from laughing and calling to each other across the room. Although separated by language, culture, and seating arrangements, all the adults seemed to be having a good time, even if they were having it separately.

Jack motioned to the table by the window where the Adamses sat. Daisy waved excitedly. The tension in Hattie's chest loosened. She'd get back to her seashells, and all would go on as planned. She lost sight of Daisy when a couple of Arapaho came to their feet. She tried to slip through the gap between the tables, but then more stood. Hattie stopped and looked at Jack. Was everyone leaving now? Was she too late?

But they weren't leaving. They were looking at her. One ancient woman with long silver braids pounded on her table. Two young mothers with soft eyes and strong hands joined in. Others joined in until the quartet was overtaken. The standing Indians

450

parted as Chief Right Hand made his way toward them.

The room quieted at his upraised hand. He pointed at Jack. The fringe on his sleeve swayed with every one of his deep, bass syllables. Jack ducked his head as the chief continued. He was talking about Hattie. All eyes, mostly brown, but a few blue and green, were turned her way. Hattie's heart beat painfully and unevenly. Was she in trouble for Sloane? Did they understand what had happened? Or did they think that once again she was a victim in need of rescuing? She looked at the brave mothers who had made the hard choice to send their children to school. Hattie didn't want to be a victim in their eyes.

The chief ended his speech. Major Adams and Superintendent Seger watched Jack expectantly.

"Well," said Major Adams, "what did he say?"

Jack shot her an apologetic look. Hattie's eyes dropped to the ground as she waited for whatever uncomfortable pronouncement Jack was forced to translate.

"It's been made known to Chief Right Hand and the rest of the tribe that the gold shipment meant for the Cheyenne and Arapaho tribes has been recovered by Mrs.

Hennessey. They also understand that by her quick thinking, she was able to bring the second bandit to justice."

Hattie's hands clenched. That wasn't the announcement she was expecting. She looked up at Jack, surprised to see him smiling.

"Furthermore," he said, "since we were married in an Arapaho ceremony, they feel they have the right to claim her as one of their tribe as a daughter, and they want it known that the gold was recovered by one of their own."

Hattie watched Chief Right Hand through tear-filled eyes as he walked forward and took her by the shoulders. Placing her in front of him, he pulled a feather out of his braid and threaded it through her coif.

Next, Spotted Hawk stepped forward. With a toothy grin, she said something that Jack quickly translated. "They won't call you One Who Spills Stew in Anger anymore. She will tell the chief that you have a new name. From now on, they will call you Found Treasure."

Hattie had to laugh. She wished she had something to give them back. It didn't seem like the money should count, since all she'd done was remember where it was.

But she *did* have something. Clapping her

hands together, she spun to Daisy. Daisy read her smile and snatched her basket off the table. It felt heavenly to greet the students and hand them their gifts.

Daisy skipped as she wove through the tables, finding every last child she knew and handing the unnamed packages to those she didn't know. At first the children held the paper-wrapped bundles curiously, turning them over and over. But Tom Broken Arrow snapped the string on his, and then there was an avalanche of rustling paper.

Hattie watched as Francine's shell fell out of the paper and into the girl's hand. Francine turned it over, and her eyes widened. Her face glowed as she touched the smooth interior that held the painting of her mother and younger sister. Her mother was bending to get a better look. Her brow wrinkled in disbelief as she leaned in. With a quick word, a young man who had to be Francine's father leaned in to see. He grunted with pride, his eyes traveling from the shell to his family and back again.

Francine ran across the room to Hattie with her parents following. She could barely take her eyes off the shell.

"Father wants to know if you painted this," she said.

"I did," Hattie replied. "I'm sorry he's not

in it, as well. I didn't see him that day at the school."

Francine translated, then waited for his response. "He's asking if you could make another one. Except this time he wants it to be a picture of me." She smiled up at her father before continuing. "He wants to keep it with him while I'm away at school. Then he can see me even when I'm not there."

Both parents looked eager for her answer. Hattie nodded. "If I can find enough shells, I'd be glad to do a portrait for each child."

"We will provide the gift," her father said, according to Francine. "It is little compared to the beauty you add to them."

Hattie wanted to tell them that the beauty was provided by God and shown through them, but she didn't want to tax little Francine's vocabulary. Either way, she was honored to create keepsakes for the family, especially if it made their separation easier to bear.

Painting was what Hattie did. It was her gift to share with others. And if it gave her an excuse to spend more time with these children, then she was amply rewarded already.

CHAPTER THIRTY-FOUR

They didn't have a Christmas tree. To even get firewood on the prairie, the army traveled east all the way to Council Grove, so making a special trip for a tree was out of the question. And it didn't matter much. After all, they'd gone to Major Adams and Louisa's for Christmas Eve after the dinner in Darlington, and one Christmas tree was enough in Jack's book.

But one could never have enough mistletoe.

Jack waited just inside the dining room as he heard Hattie coming. After church, she'd baked while he looked after his correspondence in the adjutant's office. Now the house was filled with the scents of cinnamon and nutmeg, his work was complete, and the rest of Christmas Day was all his. His to share with her.

She was humming to herself as she came down the stairs. "Hark! The Herald Angels

Sing," it sounded like. Her footsteps faded as she crossed the parlor rug, then returned as she neared the passage into the dining room. He knew better than to jump out at her. She'd had enough scares to last a lifetime.

Instead, he stepped into the doorway just as she reached it. Her humming halted. She drew up, pulling a large flat bundle against her chest, then broke into a laugh. He wrapped both arms around her waist and drew her against him despite the awkward package between them.

"How surprising," she said. "It appears you've caught me under the mistletoe again."

"What a coincidence."

"I'm not so sure. It seems like there's a sprig of mistletoe over every doorway, support beam, or lamp."

"Which is exactly why I haven't allowed Major Adams or anyone else to visit. Not until I take it all down. In the meantime, you're my only victim."

Hattie moved the package out of the way as she smiled up at him. "A willing victim." She tilted her head back, allowing her husband to gleefully prove his love for Christmas traditions.

Kissing his wife was enough to make Jack

forget about any Christmas gifts. Well, almost enough.

"Is that a present?" he whispered as he strayed from her lips.

"Of course." She still held it in one hand, although its safety seemed precarious.

"Is it a painting?"

Her eyes narrowed, and she pushed him away. "You aren't supposed to guess."

"Is it a painting of me?"

Her jaw dropped. "You are wicked, Jack Hennessey. Have you been snooping?"

He couldn't help his devious chuckle. "It's just deduction, dear wife. Look at the shape of the package. Of course you painted a picture. Why would it be wrapped up? Well, it is Christmas, after all. And of all the fascinating subjects you could choose from, what would you find most endearing?" He shrugged. "The answer is obvious."

Hattie twisted, trying to pull out of his embrace while swatting at his hands, but he kept a hold of her and stumbled into the parlor as she dragged him along. She was feisty, twisting and spinning in ways that only encouraged him in his advances. When they landed on the sofa, they barely took up half the length of it. Her skirt splashed across his lap. His feet tangled with hers. With a quick adjustment, he bounced her into a cozier position and took the package from her.

"I could deduce that it's a picture of me, but I doubt it's flattering."

"Why should it be flattering? My aim is honesty."

Jack winced. "Honesty in words is admirable, but if you looked like me, you'd be more appreciative of flattery when it came to portraits."

"Misplaced humility." She laid her head on his shoulder. "Are you going to unwrap it or not?"

The paper crumpled beneath his hand as he reminded himself that Hattie was an excellent artist. No matter how painful the portrait looked, it would be accurate. And he had to act thrilled, even if it hurt his vanity.

But instead of a portrait of Lieutenant Jack Hennessey, it was a picture of a puny youngster standing in the doorway of the Van Buren secondary school.

Jack was captivated.

"Is this how I really looked?" Throughout his life, he hadn't spent much time in front of mirrors. He did have a good recollection of a family photograph around that time, but his whole family looked starched and stiff in it, so he hadn't taken it for truth.

"Exactly how you looked," Hattie said. "Remember how your arm was white when your splint came off in the autumn? See right there, where your sleeve is rolled up. And you're carrying the book on horses. I always thought it was funny that you read books on horses instead of riding them, but look at you now. You're a regular . . . what is it?"

"Centaur?"

"No . . . horseman. That's it. And the second book you're carrying. It was poetry, right?"

Jack squinted at the spine. "That's *Sonnets from the Portuguese.* That's right. I read them when I was recovering from the broken arm. How do you remember this?"

"It's just a picture of you I'd carried with me."

Jack groaned. "It's a wonder you ever talked to me at all if this is how I looked. Such a defenseless bookworm."

"Look again," Hattie said. "I'm learning about myself and how I paint. When I painted that picture of the outlaws, I hadn't understood the significance of what was right before my eyes, but I was able to paint it, even so. That's what happened here. Look at this boy. No, he's not the strongest boy in the schoolyard, but look at that determined jaw. Look how straight and proud he walks, even past the boastful bullies. Look at the sensitivity in those brown eyes. When you see all that, it's no surprise the boy will grow into a man like you."

It was all there in the painting, just like she said. Jack didn't believe her memory was accurate, not this far removed, but if he had to decide between a love who remembered everything perfectly and a love who colored the past in his favor, he knew which he'd choose.

"I love it," he said. "Mostly because it reminds me how lucky I am to have adored you for so long. Found Treasure is an apt name."

She purred as she snuggled into his side. "I'm glad you like it. I'm sure I'll like my gift just as much."

The minx. "What makes you think you're getting anything?" But Jack had never learned how to bluff. He pulled an envelope out of his coat pocket. Hattie snatched it out of his hand and moved to the edge of the sofa, suddenly as alert as a hawk.

"There's a bump in it," she said as she felt along the length. "You tried to hide it by putting paper in there, but I can feel the bead. Next time you should consider wrapping it. A simple box —"

"Just open it," he said.

She pried her finger beneath the flap and then paused. "Maybe you should keep it. It was part of the bargain."

"I am keeping it. It was my wedding ring, and I'm never letting it go. This is just a replica. But that's only part of the present. You didn't even look at the papers."

She was too busy putting on the earring, although her habit of wearing only one had grown on him. "The papers?" She nearly ripped the two sheets pulling them out of the envelope. "Tickets?" Her eyes sparkled. "Tickets to Colorado? Oh, Jack, it's wonderful. And you're coming with me?"

"I've already arranged it with Major Adams. I wouldn't miss your first exhibition for anything."

"My first — ?" Her face went pale and her eyes filled with terror. "What are you talking about? What have you done?"

"I received a telegram from the Denver Exhibition saying that they accepted your painting of Tom Broken Arrow as part of their show. They also said that one of the board members owns a gallery, and he is interested in any other paintings you might have."

Her hands squeezed his like a vice. "My painting was accepted? It was accepted?"

She darted forward and kissed him on the mouth. "You are the most wonderful — wait! Did you say they want more paintings to display?" She pressed her hand against her heart. "More paintings? And we're leaving in a month? Oh, my dear, what did you do to me? I've got to get to work. I have some sketches that are coming along nicely. A couple of them might be worthy of the canvas, but I hadn't considered . . ."

And just like that, she was up and gone.

Jack hummed to himself as he eyed the portrait she'd left behind. Propping the picture up against the window, he smiled at the ambitious little fellow. "Don't worry if she flits around," he said, now that it was just the two of them. "Once she comes to her senses, she'll see you. And when she does, she's worth all the waiting you've done."

Then, with a wink, he went upstairs to see what he could do to remind his wife that they were sharing the most wonderful Christmas ever.

A NOTE FROM THE AUTHOR

Dear Reader,

You've reached the back of the book. I sure hope you've finished reading the story and aren't skipping ahead to see what happens. If so, you won't find out here, because this is where I tell you about the real history of Fort Reno and the Darlington Agency.

The first thing you should know is that the Arapaho school in Darlington did exist (you can still walk its foundation today), as did the larger, more well-known Carlisle Indian School in Pennsylvania. If you're curious about the philosophy of Indian education in the nineteenth century and what many of the Indian students went through, I encourage you to search out the extensive resources about the Carlisle school online. It's all there — the good, the bad, and the ugly.

As for the main plot of *The Lieutenant's*

Bargain, the enforcement of an Arapaho wedding ceremony, it was also inspired by research. White settlers were not allowed on the vast lands of Indian Territory without a connection to the tribe. Unscrupulous men often courted and married Native American women just for access to the tribal funds and land. All too often, these speculators would decide to seek easy money elsewhere and leave behind a wife and children, claiming that the Indian wedding ceremony wasn't binding on them. Over time, the government enacted different policies trying to prevent the exploitation of the tribe, but it remained a problem for decades. For that reason, I thought it plausible that a cavalry officer might be pressured to honor a ceremony that he misunderstood. (If you don't think it's plausible, I hope you at least thought it was entertaining.)

Many of the characters who make an appearance in *The Lieutenant's Bargain* were real people, including the Marshals Bud Ledbetter and Bass Reeves, Agent Lee, scout Ben Clark, Reverend Voth, and Superintendent John Seger. When possible, I borrow the last names of people or towns in the region to create new characters. Most of the school's teachers were named in honor of those first Mennonite missionaries that settled in Darlington to educate and evangelize.

Even our hero, Lieutenant Jack, has a name inspired by true but less uplifting events. Locals will recognize the name of Hennessey as being a town north of Darlington and the fort. They might not know that the town was named after Pat Hennessey, a freighter who was killed by a band of Cheyenne (with possibly some Kiowa, Osage, and Comanche participants) in 1874. In fact, it was the murder of Hennessey and the four other members of his team that brought about the establishment of Fort Reno to protect the workers at the Darlington Indian Agency. Our fictional Lieutenant Jack is blissfully unbothered by his connection with the tragic tale and intent on leaving his own happier story for posterity.

Speaking of happy stories, I'm so glad you're the kind of reader who appreciates both history and fiction. If you're looking for more fiction, you can find me and news about my books at www.reginajennings.com or on Facebook. If you're looking for more history about Fort Reno, just head on west of Oklahoma City and drop in to visit the folks at the fort. They'll love to see you!

God bless, and thanks for reading!

Sincerely,
Regina

ABOUT THE AUTHOR

Regina Jennings is a graduate of Oklahoma Baptist University with a degree in English and a minor in history. She has worked at the *Mustang News* and at First Baptist Church of Mustang, along with time at the Oklahoma National Stockyards and various livestock shows. She lives outside of Oklahoma City with her husband and four children.